P9-DGM-238

PLOT SUMMARY

Joe is a bold and crass surgeon, who scoffs at anything above or beyond himself and freely indulges his passionate appetites. Adam is a painfully shy and anxious medical researcher, who seeks security in devout religious practice, but finds little relief from his discomfort. These most unlikely of associates come together with four other individuals under the watchful eye of David Web, their group therapist. In order to find healing, the patients must tell their stories, and in so doing, Adam and Joe find a common bond in war-torn Europe and its soul-numbing Holocaust sixty years before. Both Adam and Joe must confront ghosts from that time, ghosts that now live in them. Adam and Joe struggle together until both are forever changed, hope is renewed and a new spirituality is forged.

Michael Culligan

ENDORSEMENTS

Dr. Milgraum is a gifted story teller. Like a fine symphony, themes present at the beginning are developed as the work evolves. There are moments of crescendo and of fortissimo, unexpected turns, but a confident direction... Never Forget My Soul is a brave work that touches the soul and invites us to remember a way that can nourish and not destroy the soul.

—Michael Berenbaum, former Director of the United States Holocaust Research Institute at the U.S. Holocaust Memorial Museum

Dr. Milgraum's novel is one of those "can't put it down" books that takes you on an exciting journey, all the way to the end. This highly readable story will appeal to a wide range of readers. I enjoyed the insight into the dynamics of group therapy. This author is very skilled at weaving the past histories of the characters into their present stories. The story clearly illuminates the multigenerational effects of such a devastating trauma as the Holocaust, for all to understand. But it goes beyond that: it reaches into the very soul of the reader and causes one to examine one's own life. And it all happens as one is enjoying reading this wonderful book. Truly an uplifting experience!

— Ellen R. Price, M.Ed., Manor College, Jenkintown, PA

Dr. Milgraum's compelling new book is very much for our times, yet goes far beyond our times. His narrative takes on a history of destruction and the shattered parts of ourselves with the profound conviction that there must be a better way to live. His story demonstrates gently and with compassion that hope is renewed the moment a human being opens his heart to the plight of another. And much more than a mere story, *Never Forget My Soul* is a journey toward the discovery of ripened, abiding spirituality.

—Dr. Yael Danieli, Distinguished Professor of International Psychology at the Chicago School of Professional Psychology

Michael Milgraum's first novel is a refreshing approach to the issue of Holocaust survivors and in this case, appropriately, the children of survivors. The novel uses as a catalyst the setting of a group therapy session, where all the attendants, including Adam, the son of survivors, work through different issues. The reader can empathize with the problems exposed in very detailed discussions among the patients and experience catharsis along with some of them. Even those who know nothing of the Holocaust can relate to Adam and Joe, another character who comes to understand the reasons behind growing up in a dysfunctional family.

— Deborah Adiv, English Professor, IDC University, Herzylia, Israel

WHAT OTHERS ARE
SAYING ABOUT THIS BOOK

*This book might very well start a movement for
a different kind of book club and therapy groups
everywhere. It takes away the taboo and the fear of a
group encounter. So many are trapped in loneliness and
pain, but do not have the courage or the encouragement
to finally have an encounter with themselves. This book
totally relieves them of their encumbrances. Such a
hopeful, helpful, and downright interesting book to read!*

*Long after the end of the book, you will find yourself
thinking of the themes and the characters – they stay
with you and impart a personal courage to look into
one's own soul, along with a desire to face one's own
existence and purpose.
In the looking, one finds understanding of self, of
others, of the missing parts of life. It is here that healing
happens.
This book heals...if you only let it!*

— Anne Maloy, University of Maryland

Dr. Milgraum's book is a true gift to any reader who is interested in an exciting, suspenseful plot with an added depth that is uncharacteristic of many fiction novels. The author masterfully portrays the excitement of a psychological odyssey as he weaves together history, interpersonal struggle, and self-confrontation. The reader is taken along on this adventure and is challenged to reassess him- or herself. This book is thought-provoking and stays with you, really stays with you. Now that I have finished it, I want to read it again!

— Alicia J. Odum, M.D.

ACKNOWLEDGEMENTS

Notwithstanding the stereotype of the isolated, struggling novelist, the production of a novel is a group endeavor. I want to first and foremost thank Dr. Yael Danieli for the attentive ear and trained clinical eye she has turned towards Holocaust survivors and their progeny over many decades. Without her inspiration and insights, this book would likely have never come to be. Her research revealed the presence of distinctive types of survivor families, and I have used two of these types in creating the story herein. Not only did Dr. Danieli's work serve as inspiration and guide for this book, she also extended to me the kindness of reviewing my manuscript and making detailed comments and suggestions for improvements. I am particularly gratified that our collaboration on this book led to further work together, as I assisted her in refining a questionnaire assessing the mutigenerational effects of the Holocaust.

I want to also acknowledge the many other sources of wisdom and inspiration that have played their role in the formation of this novel. My teachers—psychological and spiritual— have, over the years, helped me to refine my vision and deepen my understanding. Although they are far too many to name, I would like to at least acknowledge three—my father and mother, Leonard and Sylvia Milgraum, whose devotion, intelligence, wit and wisdom I have taken as models for the man I want to be; and the recently departed Rabbi Noah Weinberg, may his memory be for a blessing, whose infectious love and warmth led a new generation back to its spiritual heritage. In addition, no acknowledgment would be complete without mentioning my patients, who, over the years, have inspired and truly astounded me with their courage, honesty and strength.

In terms of the technical aspects of this novel, I am grateful for the fine editing and stylistic input from Erica Thompson, copy editing by Lynn C. O'Connell, superb cover design and text layout by Kit Oliynyk, and my other readers—my additional sets of eyes—for giving further input, including Naomi Singer and Lea Milgraum, my wife and soul mate. Further, I want to particularly thank Lea for tolerating the great time expense involved in creating a novel and bringing it to fruition.

Finally, there are two more to thank. The first is Michaela Lyons, who all those years ago handed me a notebook and suggested that I make regular notes of my thoughts and observations, so I remember them for all those books I planned to write. The second, and most important, is God, who has made this and all our blessings possible.

FOREWORD

To confront the Holocaust some struggle with God, some with humanity and some with memory. In this moving novel, *Never Forget My Soul*, Michael Milgraum struggles with all three..

The two central characters, Adam and Joe, are both descendants of Holocaust survivors. Adam is the child of survivors, the son of a family where memory haunted his childhood home. His world was divided between those who could be trusted and those who could not. The content of his Jewishness was fear and anguish. Adam's mother was barely functional; she internalized her pain. His father's aspirations were seemingly modest—safety, security, survival. Yet only after seeing what he had seen and entering into the world of the *Shoah*, could one appreciate how significant an achievement that was.

Over the vehement objections of his parents, who wanted him to avoid danger and stay close to home, Adam journeyed to Israel in the post-1967 euphoria, a pilgrimage that brought him into the presence of a Rabbi, a man of faith and learning, who despite his prior internment in the concentration camps and his life under Nazi persecution, did not lose his belief in God or in life. He taught Adam that faith, and he modeled an alternate Jewish path as to how to grapple with memory. Adam desperately embraced that path, but could not overcome the legacy of his past. His religious praxis was perfect; his spiritual development arrested. His prayers were by rote and yet he was both comforted and tormented not by his inner spiritual attainment, but by the idea that there could be one, should be one, one that was not his.

Joe is the grandchild of a Holocaust survivor, a hero, one of the few who escape Treblinka, where some 900,000 Jews were murdered and there were less than 100 known survivors. Scott Cohen had participated in the Treblinka Uprising and escaped the death camp in its aftermath. In response to his youth, he was living, what Primo Levi described in his magisterial work *If This Be a Man*, falsely re-titled to give it an upbeat feel for an American audience *Survival in Auschwitz*, "the cold life of a joyless dominator."

Joe's grandmother was submissive, and Joe's mother sought to escape her father's domination by marrying a non-Jew who seemingly was everything her father was not, yet who, as often happens in marriage, shared much in common with her father. He was a determined dominator, yet, unlike her mother, she escaped, neglecting her children, by burying herself in a successful career.

Brilliant and impulsive, selfish and hedonistic, Joe rebelled, seeking refuge in drugs and sex and acts of daring, then, at least externally, finding his own way through life as a successful physician, an indifferent husband, and an occasional father, drowning himself in sex and work. The fact of his grandfather's survival seemed of no importance, and he last made contact with his own Jewishness when he stormed out of his own Bar Mitzvah sermon, having spoken defiantly, confronting God and Abraham and mocking those who revere sacred scripture.

Both Adam and Joe are driven to therapy and find themselves in group sessions with diverse characters led by David, a wise and caring therapist who seems to know precisely when to intervene and when to remain silent. The skill of a good therapist is not only in knowing what to say, but also when to say it. As one who has done some significant counseling as a chaplain and rabbi, I always marvel at the patience required. A scholar, writer or preacher must tell the truth that he knows; a wise counselor must guide the person being counseled to discover their own truth. Milgraum is a therapist, and one can tell from this novel that he has grappled with these issues himself.

Milgraum is a gifted story teller. Like a fine symphony, themes present at the beginning are developed as the work evolves. There are moments of crescendo and of fortissimo, unexpected turns, but a confident direction.

I suspect that I have been asked to write this foreword not for my understanding of literature – I am but an appreciative reader but not a literary scholar – but for my efforts to grapple with the Holocaust, God, humanity and memory and also, perhaps unknown to the author, for my appreciation of literature as an important form of theology, especially to Jews.

The Torah, as any student of Rabbinic commentary knows, is not only a work of law. Rashi, the great French commentator (1040-1105) wrote in his commentary on the first words of the Torah, that had it been just a book of laws, the Torah would have began with the first commandment in the 12th chapter of Exodus and not with the Genesis and Exodus narratives. If Greeks might say: "in unity there is strength," Jews would be more inclined to tell a story of "two dogs that killed a lion."

So what does this story tell of the Holocaust?

Viktor Frankl, the eminent Viennese psychoanalyst who was an inmate of the camps, wrote of liberation: "only later-- and for some it was much later or never – was liberation actually liberating."

Milgraum does not choose the easy path. He portrays the painful truth of survival, which tends to be obscured in our feel-good society. Adam's parents and Joe's grandfather and mother, paid for their experience of trauma. The Holocaust did not end for them, not in the conventional sense. They did not overcome; they endured, paying an ongoing price for all that they went through, for childhoods interrupted, witnessing the death of parents and siblings, the murder of their entire community, the demise of a whole world. The anguish does not end with the generation of survivors, it is transmitted directly and indirectly, knowingly and unknowingly, in ways that are acknowledged and in a manner that cannot be, to the generation after, and even beyond.

Theologically, he offers no cheap grace, no feel-good story and no way out of the abyss, without confronting the darkness. One must respect the integrity of the writer and of the therapist who resists the all-too-prevalent temptation in our world to retell only the good, to describe strength and not probe weakness and to offer easy triumphs. The impact of the Holocaust is lasting, and even though survivors demonstrated manifest, dare one say awesome strengths, in the very fact of their survival, they paid a price for that survival, an ongoing price.

Twice during the work Milgraum insists that there is only one way to confront the Holocaust and that is to go into the darkness.

This endears him to my heart. Permit me a personal story. When I was writing my Ph.D. dissertation on post-Holocaust theology and the work of Elie Wiesel, I found myself drawn to the image of the void, absence where presence had been. I considered three Jewish theologians — Emil Fackenheim, Richard L. Rubenstein and Eliezer Berkovits, who were among the earliest of the American Jewish theologians to confront the twin revolutions of American Jewish life, the Holocaust and the rise of the State of Israel. Fackenheim had achieved fame by speaking of the 614th Commandment:

The Commanding Voice of Auschwitz says:
Jews are forbidden to hand Hitler posthumous victories.
They are commanded to survive as Jews, lest the Jewish people
perish. They are commanded to remember the victims of
Auschwitz, lest their memory perish. They are forbidden to
despair of man and his world, and to escape into either cynicism
or otherworldliness, lest they cooperate in delivering the world
over to the forces of Auschwitz. Finally, they are forbidden to
despair of the God of Israel, lest Judaism perish. A secularist
Jew cannot make himself believe by a mere act of will, nor can he
be commanded to do so . . . And a religious Jew who has stayed
with his God may be forced into new, possibly revolutionary
relationships with Him. One possibility, however, is wholly
unthinkable. A Jew may not respond to Hitler's attempt to
destroy Judaism by himself cooperating in its destruction. In

ancient times, the unthinkable Jewish sin was idolatry. Today, it is to respond to Hitler by doing his work.

Richard L. Rubenstein had also achieved fame by speaking of the "death of God", not in the sense of the Christian theologians celebrating humanity coming of age, but of living in a world without a Judge and without Justice, a world in which the fear of God is no longer real and unrestrained human power had been and can be absolutely lethal.

Fackenheim had to back away from the abyss, fearing the consequences of confronting the darkness. See his use of the word "lest." He would not allow us to go there. Rubenstein had gone beyond the abyss, living in a godless world where humanity is the ultimate arbiter of all things. After "the death of God", everything is permitted – everything. Berkovits had postponed the conflict, believing God answerable in the end of days for the anguish of the created world in which humans alone are responsible for history. Only Wiesel, the early Wiesel, the writer before he had achieved prominence and internationally celebrity– grappled with the darkness and worked through the abyss. He became my model, asking challenging questions, refusing falsely comforting answers, neither backing away nor resolving the issue but living in the tension. I found in Milgraum a kindred soul.

The denouement of the novel comes in two parts. The first is when David finally intervenes and says to the two men:

You are both fighting against the same thing, hopelessness, or perhaps I should say that you are both trying to protect yourself from the pain of hopeless. The only difference is that, Adam, you protect yourself against hopelessness by denying it, while Joe, you protect yourself from hopelessness by embracing it, by becoming its chief protagonist.

Had one spoken such words of Fackenheim and Rubenstein, they might have concurred.

The second part is the confrontation between Joe and the Rabbi, whose synagogue he stormed out of a quarter century before. Now aging and more frail, the Rabbi too has known loss, the death of his wife and the loneliness of being a widower, but he also knows where to find consolation.

There is an intriguing, ritualistic phrase that pious Jews recite to the mourner." *Hamakom yenachem*, May the Place [a name for God] console you." I have often interpreted this phrase more literally: "May there be a place where you will find consolation. That place for the Rabbi is the book of Job.

What makes a holy text timeless is its potential to speak of each generation and each reader at each stage of his or her life as if it was written for them, here and now. Joe barges in on the Rabbi in anguish and in despair. The Rabbi cannot answer his anguish, but he can, like Elihu (a key figure in the book of Job), acknowledge the despair and listen to the anguish. By listening, and by acknowledging, there is the possibility of alleviating.

And finally, Joe and the Rabbi return to the two basic texts of Genesis, Abraham's confrontation with God over the fate of Sodom and his non-confrontation with God over the command to sacrifice his own son, his beloved son, his Isaac. For the Rabbi, God's gift to Abraham at Sodom was the opportunity to demonstrate love of others in action. "The root of all human goodness," the Rabbi says " is the awareness that we are not alone in the world."

Joe responds: "I see no gifts, only a cold world where the strong survive and the weak are crushed."

The Rabbi remembers the rules of counseling: "To treat the darkness you have to bear your own entry into the darkness." That is the inescapable beginning.

But one need not end up in that darkness. Some in that darkness can discover God. God did not answer Job in the whirlwind, God addressed him. With presence there is the possibility of meaning, without it, there may just be despair.

And some in that darkness can discover another person and find that loneliness can be bridged with another, anguish can be shared with another. To protest the cold cruel world, one can reach out toward the other and share the warm embrace and with that comes healing. There may be some light out of the tunnel.

Never Forget My Soul is a brave work that touches the soul and invites us to remember a way that can nourish and not destroy the soul.

Michael Berenbaum
Los Angeles, California
July 20, 2012

To Lea, for loving me and my dreams,
To Yael Danieli, for having the courage to listen when others didn't,
To M., my gentle teacher and guide,
And to Hirsh, Shayna, Rena and Hannah... our future.

© Michael M. Milgraum December 2011

All rights reserved. No part of this book may be reproduced or transmitted in any form or by any means, electronic or mechanical, including photocopying, recording or by any other information storage and retrieval system, without the written permission of the copyright holder.

All characters appearing in this work are fictitious. Any resemblance to real persons, living or dead, is purely coincidental.

Published by Guidelight Books
9525 Georgia Avenue, Suite 203
Silver Spring, MD 20910
guidelightbooks@gmail.com

NEVER FORGET MY SOUL

A NOVEL BY MICHAEL M. MILGRAUM

PART ONE

Were I to keep silent now, I would expire.

—Job 13:19

CHAPTER ONE

G race was eight years old today. As her party wound down, she played tag with two friends in the front yard, awaiting their parents. The afternoon sun sent slantwise golden rays across the lawn, causing the girls' shadows to lengthen. It had been a glorious, blue-skied, autumn day, during which Grace had immersed herself in the pleasure of being celebrated and having her friends near. At times, she would think of her father and wonder why he had not kept his promise to attend. But her feelings about his presence were mixed, so she would push the thoughts out of her mind quickly. Now, as the sun lowered in the sky, the day faded, and a chill entered the air, her dark thoughts began to intrude on her consciousness again. She wondered when her father would return and what state he would be in when he did.

Two cars pulled up, and each of the friends recognized her respective ride. The first friend to leave was Tracy, a bubbly girl who had a quick smile and a giddy laugh. Tracy waved and blew Grace a kiss and went sprinting across the yard towards her mother's car.

Laura, the other remaining guest, was Grace's best friend. The girls hugged each other. Laura attempted to pull back from the hug, but Grace kept a firm hold. Grace felt that she was safe only as long as she held on to Laura. Laura, who was tolerant of Grace, half spoke and half whined, "Grace, I have to go!" Still, Grace's grip did not loosen.

Grace said quietly, "Please stay."

"Can't. Love you, but can't. Mom says no sleepovers on Sunday nights," said Laura, pulling back from Grace and tugging at her arms, so that Grace finally let go.

Laura began to walk away, looking back with a reassuring smile and a "thank you" directed at Grace.

Grace's eyes followed Laura as she approached the car. Laura's long brown hair bobbed behind her as she ran. Laura opened the car door, stepped in, seated herself, and reached out for the door. Grace got a last glimpse of Laura's face as she closed the door, and then Laura's form rolled away in shadows of tinted glass.

Grace went inside and saw the mess her guests had left behind. Grace's two younger brothers had each taken a large piece of cake for themselves and were playing marbles on the dining room floor. Their paper plates, with cake on them, were at their sides on the floor, and crumbs were strewn about the plates. A plastic cup of orange soda was spilled on the wood floor, next to her youngest brother. Grace entered the kitchen and saw her mother feverishly preparing dinner. She had placed pans, mixing bowls and utensils in precariously-stacked high piles and was attempting to rapidly complete dinner preparation in the small counter space that had been liberated. This sight caused Grace to spring into action. She dashed to the kitchen table and began to clear and clean it. Remnants of breakfast and lunch were on the table — a bowl, half-filled with milk and a few Cheerios, which were engorged from ten hours of soaking; a half-eaten tuna sandwich; a plate with watermelon rinds surrounded by a cloud of fruit flies;

plastic cups, filled with small amounts of milk, juice or water; a few toys and children's books; and an assortment of eating utensils. In ten minutes, Grace had managed to clear the table, stack the dishes and wipe off the crumbs and food scraps.

She paused for a moment, with a look of relief on her face. Suddenly, her face dropped as she remembered her brothers, the cake and the state of the dining room. She grabbed a towel and knelt down to wipe up the orange soda. Just then, she heard the door open and close. There was no voice, but she could hear the footfall, and she knew it was her father. She stopped, as a small animal might freeze when it expects it is being watched, and she wondered: Which way, the bedroom or the dining room, which way? Her unstated question was answered immediately as she heard him approach the dinning room. Grace's stomach clenched. He appeared, a tall and muscular man wearing a brown T-shirt and blue jeans, covered with grease and grime. He had a hard expression on his face. His face was always the same when he was sober – not angry, annoyed, or worried, just hard. He walked past the boys and Grace, not acknowledging them, and grabbed a glass and a bottle out of the liquor cabinet. He disappeared into the living room. Grace resumed her work of cleaning up the dining room. Fifteen minutes later, she heard her father's steps again, as he entered the kitchen and said, "Where the hell is dinner?!"

Grace heard the mollifying voice of her mother, "It's ready. You can come sit down."

Grace's mother then entered the dining room, quietly telling Grace and her brothers to come to dinner.

The family gathered at the table. Grace's father sat silently, looking at his plate and drinking a beer. The boys were in and out of their seats. Occasionally, their father would growl at them to sit down, and each time he did so, their mother would look up nervously. Grace kept her eyes on her plate, like her father. When dinner finished, her father rose without a word and returned to the living room. Grace's mother asked her to clear the table. Grace picked up a plate to scrape its contents into the garbage, when she heard her father's heavy, rapid footsteps enter the kitchen.

His face was no longer frozen into its "hard" position. It was red, with a furrowed brow, tight lips and fierce eyes. "Who made that mess!?" he shouted, pointing to the dining room.

Grace's mother answered quietly, "It was Grace's party today, dear, I'm just a little behind — "

"A little behind!" he yelled, nostrils flaring and eyes widening. "This whole place is a mess!" His gaze turned to Grace, "And you, you ungrateful sh**! You get a party and leave it for everyone else to clean up! I bet you were playing games all afternoon and didn't even think about the others that have to live in this sh**hole!!"

Grace did not know why she answered. She knew it was stupid. She knew nothing good could come of it. But she remembered how she had jumped to action when she saw her mother's distress and how hard she had tried to clean up quickly. She answered quietly, "I didn't get to the party mess yet, I was clearing the kitchen table for din — ." In a blur, her father approached her, and she smelled the hot stench of his alcohol-laden breath. In a blur, he raised his hand and brought it down hard against her face, so hard that she stepped back and almost fell. For a few moments, she did not see and only heard — her father's voice, "**YOU WILL LEARN TO RESPECT ME!**"; his footfall, heavy and angry; her brothers' tears; her mother trying to comfort the boys and Grace. When Grace could see again, she immediately ran out of the kitchen and into her room, burying her sobs in her pillow. She did not know how much time passed before she fell asleep.

Grace awoke with a start, feeling a weight on the mattress beside her. In the darkness, she heard her father's voice and she again smelled the alcohol as he spoke.

"Princess, please forgive me, I beg you." Her father's words were accompanied by sobs and rapid breathing. "Sometimes I get like a little boy. I just want everything done when I want it. Can you ever forgive me? Daddy never wants to hurt you."

She felt his hot hands begin to stroke her hair. Then his hands were on her shoulders and her chest, as he began to undress her. She felt panic in her stomach. She was frozen — helpless and frozen. Not again, please God, not again.

⟹◦◦◦⟸

"I've come here because I don't want to throw away ten years of marriage and I don't want to lose my kids. And, truth is, my wife deserves better than this. She's been good to me, and she didn't ask a thing from me in the home, took my mind off everything, while I developed the practice. I'd be an idiot if I just let my family slip away, because of my anger."

Grace observed the dark-skinned African-American man sit silently after he had finished speaking. The man's name was Tyrone. He was a large, imposing man wearing a blue three-piece suit and a blue and red tie. His shoes were black and shined with a perfect polish. She noticed his big hands and feet. He must have weighed two hundred pounds, but he did not look fat. He spoke with a natural sense of authority and a deep, sonorous voice. It was the kind of voice you deferred to, the kind of voice that you would immediately assume knew what it was talking about.

Grace did not know how much of Tyrone's comments she had missed. She knew that the images had flooded her mind shortly after Tyrone had started speaking, and that he was still speaking when she was again aware of the present. But she could not say how much time had passed while she was "there," as she referred to it.

In order to more fully pull herself out of "there," she reminded herself what "here and now" meant. She spoke in her mind, "I'm thirty-two years old and I'm safe. He's dead, he's gone, and mom's suffering is over, too. I'm in this room to get help. And I think that man over there can help me." She looked across the room at a face that was very different from Tyrone's. A face with blue eyes, staring fixedly ahead, seeing the surface and beneath, reflecting the devotion with which he was listening. The eyes were kind and warm, and when she saw them, she was reminded of the way they could twinkle from time to time. The twinkle conveyed a gentle humor that was there to ease a burden or to teach. She saw the man's full head of hair — brown, but streaked with lines of grey. His beard had the same coloring. His face and general form were round but not fat, the roundness, she assumed, of a man who liked to eat. He had a large nose, full lips and heavy eyebrows. He was David Web, her therapist and the therapist for the group of clients in this room.

Grace looked back at Tyrone. She recalled how he had started speaking. Before Tyrone had spoken, David had explained the ground rules for the group therapy, which were surprisingly few: Not revealing information shared in the group, referring to group members by first name to help ensure confidentiality, and revealing to the group any outside contacts between group members. Then, David had fallen silent. The group had sat uncomfortably, until Tyrone said, "Well, I guess I'll start. My name is Tyrone and I'm here because I have an anger problem. I get angry too easily and I yell. I guess some people today would call it verbal abuse. My wife says she has had enough of it and that I need to be in therapy and change it, or else she's leaving." Now that Grace had returned to the present, she hoped she would be better able to follow what was being said.

———————◦◦◦———————

As Tyrone started to speak, Adam wondered why he was here. How was this black guy's anger control problem of any relevance to Adam? Adam was feeling tense and uncomfortable, as he usually did in social settings. He felt that all eyes were on him, judging him, thinking he was such a spineless, scared wimp. In his mind he knew this was not true, that he was of no particular interest to the others in that room, but his mind was of little help for his problems. He felt a different reality in his flesh, in the tension of his shoulders, in the beating of his heart, which would sometimes accelerate for no apparent reason, and in the sweating of the palms of his hands. He *was* being watched in this room. There was nothing he could do to shake that feeling. And, as far back as Adam could remember, it had always been crucial that others not see his fear.

Adam surveyed the room with furtive glances. He noted that there were six other people sitting in the room. As he looked around the room, his eyes settled on Grace. She looked like she was in her mid-thirties. She had a pleasant face and shoulder-length blond hair. The form of her body was hidden under a gray, loose-fitting dress; however, her double chin suggested that she was substantially overweight. Her eyes were lowered and the expression on her face suggested that her thoughts were far away. This expression made her look remote to him … and very fragile.

———◦◦◦———

"Quiet!" hissed Adam's father. "You mustn't upset your mother. She has a very bad migraine. She suffered enough in her life. Do not disturb her with this!" Adam's father never needed to yell. Somehow his father was able to convey the most intense range in a whisper, a hoarse whisper that particularly frightened Adam. The intensity of his father's whisper and the flash in his eyes could silence Adam and his sister in an instant.

Adam was nine years old. He had been bullied and beaten up by a boy in school today. The incident had occurred when Sammy, a fat kid who was a head taller than Adam, had approached him on the playground. Adam regularly sat or played by himself on the playground. He would often read, and some kids would taunt him as an "egghead." Today, Adam had been reading and Sammy had walked up and knocked off Adam's hat. Adam had responded by doing what his father taught him to do in such situations. "Just ignore bullies," his father would always tell him. "They want to see you cry. They pick on you because you break down and cry. Pretend they aren't there and they will go away." So in response to Sammy, Adam silently picked up his hat, not looking at Sammy, and continued reading. As is always the case on playgrounds, the other assorted children instantly sensed the possibility of entertainment in Adam's vicinity and thus clustered around Adam and Sammy. "Ignore, ignore, ignore," Adam thought to himself, the tears beginning to well in his eyes. "Don't let them see you cry." He tried to continue reading.

"What's wrong, egghead?" sneered Sammy. "Did you forget how to talk? I guess all that reading made you forget how to use your mouth."

He knocked off the hat again.

"That's the way Jews are," said Sammy to the audience, drawing out the word "Jews" for dramatic effect. "They don't talk to us. They think they're better than us. Or maybe they just like to be beat up." Sammy knew his audience well, which consisted of no other Jews. There were numerous chuckles among the assembled in response to Sammy's witticisms. Sammy moved his face two inches away from Adam's and blew on it. Adam tried to hold back the tears, but the print in his book become blurry. Sammy knocked off the hat again. Adam did not respond and just looked at his book.

"See?" announced Sammy. "Jews don't fight back. They — never — have." Sammy said the last three words very slowly and then pushed Adam on the shoulder. Sammy laughed heartily, and numerous chuckles echoed in the audience.

NEVER FORGET MY SOUL

In an instant, Adam rose to his feet and swung at Sammy. But Sammy was an experienced fighter. He easily sidestepped Adam's fist and responded with a solid blow on Adam's cheek, which almost knocked him over. Adam jumped back at Sammy, lunging at his chest. Adam made contact, but this appeared to have little effect on Sammy. Sammy stepped back, and, before Adam could think, there were blows falling on his chest and his face.

Just then, Mr. Summers had bounded into the center of the circle, shouting at the boys to stop fighting and grabbing Sammy. After a little inquiry, Sammy was led to the principal and Adam was sent to the nurse's office. As Sammy was being led away, he looked back at Adam, smirked and mouthed the word "Jew" to Adam, with a look of disgust and hatred.

When Adam's father picked him up, Adam was holding an ice pack to a black eye. The bleeding in his nose had stopped, but he still felt the crusty flakes of dried blood around his nostril. His father's face was sad. "Why couldn't you just ignore him?" he said, shaking his head. "Haven't we suffered enough?"

Adam's father was silent throughout the car ride home. As his father parked the car near their apartment building, his father turned to him and said, "There's no winning with them, Adam. You can't fight them. I can't lose time from work like this anymore. I need to work so we can live. This *is* going to stop, Adam!"

Adam opened his mouth, but nothing came out. In his mind he replayed his efforts to avoid the conflict, Sammy's insistence, and Sammy's stinky breath blowing in his face. "Jews don't fight back. They — never — have." The words replayed and seared his brain. Adam began to sob.

"Come on, come on," said his father impatiently. "Stop crying. Let's go inside."

Adam followed his father into the apartment building, still crying quietly to himself.

It was when they approached the elevator that his father

hissed at him that he must be quiet, so he would not upset his mother.

Adam was used to being hushed. His parents did not tolerate loud noises or any vigorous physical activity in the apartment. "Shhhh!" they would say. "Don't disturb the neighbors." But Adam knew it was not only the neighbors his parents were considering. His parents disapproved of any extremes in sound, in movement, in emotional expression. "We just want peace and quiet," they would say. Well, quiet there was, but there was rarely peace, not the sort of peace that makes your stomach relax, not the sort of peace that makes you smile. There was always a sense of tension at home.

The main rationale for the imperative of quiet was the health of Adam's mother. There was always a pain somewhere, always a problem — headache, stomachache, backache. The condition varied, but there was always a condition, always a reason to be quiet and "not disturb your mother." Today it was a migraine, which she had about once a week. At the beginning of a migraine she would retire to her room, and Adam would not see her for the rest of the day.

Adam went into his room, closed the door, and began crying quietly into his pillow. After a while, he was calm enough to hear muffled sounds in his parents' room, which was next to his. He heard his father open the door to his mother's room and say something to her. She moaned a response to him. Looking up at the window to his room, Adam noticed that the sky was getting dark. He sat in the gray half-light of his room, wishing that, as the light faded, so would the gnawing pain in his chest.

<hr/>

When Tyrone finished speaking, the other group members again waited nervously, wondering who would speak next.

"Well, if no one is going to talk, I guess I will," said Marcia. Marcia was blond and blue-eyed. She had a pretty face and an attractive, thin, form. She was fifty years old, but took good care of her health and looked younger.

"I'm Marcia. I'm here because I want to get married," she said. "Well, not necessarily to any of you," she added giggling, and a couple of group members chuckled. "But ... well, you see, I was married a long time ago and it didn't work out so well. Mind you, I was very much in love and he treated me well, for a while. And we did have three wonderful children. But he cheated on me. I caught him, and he promised never to do it again, and I suppose he only kept that promise until his next date with whoever he was fooling around with. So I sent him packing. Well, anyway, long story short — God was good to me. It was a struggle, but I got on my feet financially. Not only that, I found out that I could make money better than my cheating ex could. And I raised those three kids — every one a gem. Now the last one is out of the house and I'm, frankly, lonely. Not that I haven't had my share of boyfriends, but I'm just getting tired of that. I'm together with a guy for three or four months, then he wants to move on or I want to move on, and so I have to go out looking for a new one. I guess, it was fun once, now it's a drag. I've thought of remarriage before, I've even been close, really close, like break-it-off-on-the-day-of-the-wedding close. I guess I just couldn't bring myself to trust another man like that again." She was silent for a few moments and looked thoughtful. "But now, there is no one left at home. I'm lonely and I really want to try. But enough about me. I'll let someone else have a turn at bat."

"I guess I'll go next," said Terry. Terry was a petite woman, in her mid-thirties, who created a social impression that was somehow bigger than her actual size. Perhaps it was the intensity of her dark brown eyes, or the keen intelligence that her face projected. Or perhaps it was the enthusiasm in her manner. But whatever the reason was, Terry was used to the attention of others and naturally drew that attention to herself.

"My name's Terry," she said. "I'm here because David thought it would be a good idea," she said, motioning with her hand to David. "I'm not really sure why. I don't have a problem with people. I like people and I make friends easily. But although I am loath to admit it, David often sees things that I miss, so I'll give him the benefit of the doubt and try this thing. I guess the most important thing to know about me is that my life went through a fundamental change seven months ago, when I became sick. I don't know what the illness is. The doctors are also still trying to figure it out. I have frequent stomach cramps and chronic muscle pain. Then I started to pass out without warning. I tried for a month to continue working, but eventually the pain and fatigue were too much. So I left my research position in Maine, moved down here with my mother, and I'm bored out of my skull. So I go to David for individual sessions and talk about how bored I am, and he tells me how angry I am with my father. And I say, sure I am, but that's not my problem. My problem is that I've lost what I have been working for all my life, and I don't know what I'm going to do with myself now."

"What have you been working for all your life?" asked Marcia.

"To be a university professor, a full professor, and I got it," responded Terry.

"You, a full professor," said Marcia, her voice pitch rising in disbelief. "But you're so young."

"Yeah," responded Terry, "but I did it. This was my first year as full professor. You think *you're* surprised. I couldn't believe it when my department chair told me last year. I almost fainted, and that was before I was sick." She smiled in recollection of this honor she had received. Then, in what seemed to be an effort to provide some explanation for this achievement, she said, "I've always been a workaholic, since grade school. Always A's. Finished undergrad at age 20, Ph.D. at 25. I got an associate faculty position six years ago. I worked hard, published a lot. They like me there. I guess they wanted to make sure I would stay. Lots of people said I was lucky. But that always bothered me. I wasn't lucky. I worked, and I had to work double because I'm a woman. Male chauvinism is alive and well in the ivory tower. But when you work hard and long enough, it pays off — people can't ignore it any more."

"My goodness, you sound like me," said Marcia. "And Lord knows, I've dealt with my share of male chauvinism in my professional life. You're right, Terry, it's a war. We women just have to perform well enough and long enough, until the males have to admit that they can't do without us....I think you and I are going to be friends."

"I think you're right," responded Terry. "You remind me of my mother. She was divorced when I was ten. She didn't have higher education, but she made a decent living as a paralegal. Life could just never push her down. She always told me that people fail not because of the cards that they are dealt, but because they give up on the game halfway through." Terry paused, thinking of how she could apply her mother's lesson to her present condition. "Only problem is," she continued, "I have no idea what to do with the hand I'm holding now." She was silent, and it was clear that she had finished speaking for now.

The group sat in silence. The silence became uncomfortable, as if all were waiting for something. Three group members had not yet spoken. One was an athletic-looking man with curly brown hair, a mustache and dark brown eyes. He appeared to be about forty years of age. He wore a green T-shirt and jeans, and his muscular biceps could be seen protruding from short sleeves. He wore a blank expression on his face, and his eyes appeared to be looking beyond the room. As the group members had spoken, he appeared to be somewhat interested in what was being said, but he also appeared distracted and somehow detached. He slumped in his chair, as if his shoulders carried a great weight and he needed the chair to assist him with his burden. This man finally broke the silence: "I guess I'll go next. My name is Joe. My life is really OK. I'm a surgeon, and I make good money, way beyond what my parents could have ever dreamed of. What does a man need? Money, food, sex — I've got those things, so I have no reason to complain. Yeah, I've got some problems with my wife, but doesn't everybody — especially after being married for fifteen years. She's not so interested in sex. I mean she's willing to do it, but she just goes through the motions. And for me, if sex isn't alive, it's like being with a corpse. Since she's not interested in sex, I've found someone who is and we're good together. I've got my wife, I've got my kids, and I get the sex I need, so everything is covered. The only problem is this feeling of depression that I get. It keeps coming and going. And lately it's been coming more often. It's like a weight on everything and I don't know where it comes from. So I met with David a few times and he suggested that I do this group thing as well, and here I am."

"Does your wife know about your mistress?" asked Marcia.

"No," answered Joe.

"Don't you think it's wrong to deceive her?" she asked.

"What do you mean by wrong?" he responded.

"Not the right thing…immoral," she said, with a note of impatience in her voice.

"I've got my morality, you've got yours," he replied nonchalantly. "What, am I supposed to live by your morality? I get the sex I need, she gets the children she wanted, and she gets a better standard of living than she would ever get without me. So who is hurt? I don't understand what people mean when they say 'morality.' Some African tribes think it's moral to eat other people. When I hear someone say 'morality,' all I hear is that they want to make the rules to govern my life. I don't need other people's rules."

Adam felt increasing discomfort as Joe spoke. In fact, it was

NEVER FORGET MY SOUL

more than discomfort, it was dislike, a dislike that expanded as Joe continued to speak. There was a confidence, glibness and abrasiveness in Joe's style that made Adam recoil. Adam knew this kind of man — successful, thinks the world belongs to him and that others are there either to defer to or serve his needs. Adam sensed that Joe engaged neither in self-scrutiny nor in second-guessing himself. If Joe wanted something, Adam presumed, Joe would simply grab it. Adam had been raised with stories of people who grabbed things and used other people as implements to serve their ends — confident Nazi soldiers shouting orders to shivering naked prisoners. These soldiers were untouched by any of the suffering. On the contrary, they exploited it, by stealing whatever they could from the prisoners, indulging their passion to beat others, making rape into a sport. And at the top of it all was Hitler, the ultimate example of using others — capturing, torturing and killing — in order to maintain his power. His parents had repeated these stories to Adam — about the crowding of the ghetto, the final evacuation and the hell of the camps. These experiences had twisted and contorted the souls of his parents. His mother had emerged broken, lifeless and depressed. His father carried a quenchless anger and hatred for all those who were in power. Adam realized that he inherited this hatred and it was part of him. Politically, Adam always voted for the guy who supported the underdog. And Adam intensely disliked people like Joe, who think that the purpose of life is feeding their appetites, regardless of who gets hurt.

Adam turned to Joe and said, "But you're married. Marriage is a promise. You're breaking that promise."

Joe looked at Adam, who was sitting two seats away from him, in the circle of chairs that David had arranged for the group. It was the first time Joe noticed Adam. Adam was thin and tall and appeared to be in his thirties. His hair was red and his eyes blue. He had an intense, self-controlled look about him. The tension in his neck muscles and the anxious furrowing of his brow revealed his general discomfort. For a few moments, Joe was confused, wondering how such an anxious and shy-looking person could say something challenging. Joe looked for someone else in the room who could have made the statement, but it had come from Adam's direction and it was a man's voice. The only other people sitting on that side of the room were Marcia and Terry. When Joe looked more closely at Adam, he noticed that Adam was wearing a yarmulke. Then Joe understood. He thought, "This guy has no backbone, just like he looks. He's just a religious fanatic loyally mouthing his doctrine. That's all I need. Thanks, David."

Joe finally smiled and said, "And who do I have the pleasure of addressing?" his voice dripping with sarcasm.

"I'm sorry," Adam responded, nervously. "I'm Adam."

"I don't recall you being present when I met my wife, when I had sex with her for the first time or when we married. How do you know what promise we made?"

There was much Adam could have responded. He did not want to let this rationalizing, slimy creep off the hook. It was obvious that the man did not want to face himself, and he was simply spinning flimsy arguments to avoid accountability. Adam wanted to say this. He did not want to let another person suffer from such self-serving callousness. But the words did not come. Adam's eyes met the angry gaze of Joe, and Adam shriveled. He was simply too afraid of the confrontation. Adam shrugged and looked away.

The group sat in a nervous silence for what seemed like a very long time. Then David spoke. "Well, I am impressed. I have never seen a group get into things this early. Remember what I said at the beginning of this session. The key to progress here is being as honest and authentic as possible. I see the group members diving right into that. But maybe you all are a little too eager to dive in and we've missed some introductions. Perhaps the group members are still wondering why Adam ... and Grace decided to join this group."

When he finished speaking, David turned his gaze to Adam, as if David were inviting him to say more.

"Well," replied Adam, "I — I'm here because of social anxiety. I'm just very uncomfortable with other people. And the bigger the group of people I'm with, the more anxious I get. I'm especially uncomfortable in conflict situations." Adam kept his eyes on the floor as he spoke. After speaking, his eyes darted around the room, as he tried to avoid the gaze of others.

"Nice to have you," said Marcia with a warm smile. In a maternal attempt to draw him out, she asked, "Are you married?"

He appeared to respond to her warmth, relaxing his posture slightly.

"Yes," he replied, "and I have four children."

"I see that you have a yarmulke on your head," she said. "Are you an Orthodox Jew?"

"Well, yes," he said. "My parents were not observant. In fact, they did not even believe in God. But I've been Orthodox for about twenty years."

"How old are you?" she inquired.

"I just turned forty," he replied.

As the group became silent once again, David took the opportunity to shift the attention to Grace. He knew that Grace would not speak at all without assistance. She had said as much to him. While he had offered her no promises, because he knew that such gestures of salvation undermined the therapeutic process, he felt that her avoidance of speaking was not a choice, but a deeply ingrained instinct. He did not feel that her request for assistance was an attempt to control him or deny her power. It was simply an accurate reflection of the response of those who have been victimized, degraded and burdened with dark secrets for too long.

"Grace," he said softly. "Perhaps you could take a turn."

Grace's response was even softer, so soft that the group

members leaned forward to hear what she was saying. "I'm Grace. I'm here because I'm fat and depressed and scared all the time. I'm by myself and I always have been. David thinks there's hope, but I don't see it. All I see is more unhappy or less unhappy, but no actual happiness. That's all there is."

"What are you depressed about?" asked Terry.

"That's a long story," answered Grace. "I don't think I can tell it now without crying, and I'm tired of crying. I don't want to cry today. It's hard enough for me to sit in this room as it is. I don't feel safe here. I feel anger between people. And from what I have seen, when there is anger, people get hurt…But I said I would not talk about that today. There's just so much that is not in my control."

Grace seemed very young and lost, as she spoke. Many of the group members reacted with a desire to take care of her and make her feel welcome.

"I don't know what you've been through," said Terry, "but I certainly can relate to the last part. My life is in shambles because of a disease that I can't control."

"I grew up on the streets of New York," said Tyrone. "There was plenty I couldn't control as well — the poverty, the violence, the corruption…and a lot more."

"And I couldn't control the fact that men can be selfish pricks, sometimes," said Marcia. "I would have had a radically different life, if I had chosen a man who was loyal to his vows, to his promises." She glanced towards Joe.

Grace responded to these acknowledgements with the faint trace of a smile. It was a smile like weak rays of sunshine briefly showing though a gray sky, but rapidly swallowed again by the clouds. Such is a light that does not warm or truly illuminate, but merely emphasizes the absence of the sun.

The group took up the rest of the time discussing what group therapy was actually supposed to be. David had given all of them little guidance in this respect. He had just told each of them that

NEVER FORGET MY SOUL

he believed group therapy would be helpful treatment for them. The conversation was mostly carried by Marcia, Terry and Tyrone. Tyrone expressed the opinion that the group was there for the other group members to give suggestions on how to improve things. Marcia thought that they were supposed to discuss painful experiences so they could "get over" them. Terry wondered out loud if there was any structure. For example, should they each take turns around the circle to talk about what was going on for them, or would each person just call out when they had something to say? David contributed little to this discussion, allowing the group members to figure things out for themselves. Adam and Grace returned to their silent shells and Joe just stared into space, making occasional comments.

CHAPTER TWO

A dam's father, Reuben Schwartz, was twenty years old when he was released from Auschwitz. While many people called this event "liberation," Reuben never used this word, for it was *not* liberation. The possibility of any future liberation had been violently wrenched from him. If one had asked him when this loss had occurred, he would have had a difficult time answering, because it was the cumulative effect of countless acts of violence and degradation.

Perhaps it began when his family stood shivering from cold and squeezed by the crowd at the train platform. He huddled with his two younger sisters, his father and his mother, who was holding his third sister, a three-month-old baby. As German guards shouted out orders for each group to enter the train, Reuben found himself praying that the rumor he had heard was true — that the relocation was a good thing. He had heard that they would be sent to a better and more hygienic place. The ghetto had been filled with sickness, starvation, crowding and hopelessness. He had heard that they were being sent to the country, where they would have to work, but at least they would be fed properly and the sick would receive proper treatment. He prayed because he had heard other rumors. These were the sort of rumors people only spoke in whispers, as if speaking them out loud would make them come true. And these rumors were always short and cryptic. Someone would remark that perhaps things would be improved after the relocation. Then another person would respond, "Better for the Germans — fewer mouths to feed," or, "They're just impatient that they can't kill us fast enough in the ghetto."

Reuben desperately hoped that the first type of rumors was true, that things would finally change for the better. The ghetto had already taken a terrible toll on his family. His eleven-year-old brother, Dov, had taken ill four months before. Dov's hacking cough and wheezing had become progressively worse. His parents had sat by his bedside, trying to comfort him. His mother would put a cool towel on his forehead and stroke his hand. His father would force a smile and talk to Dov about how things would be so much better in the summer, when he would take the family to the beach, as they had loved to do in the past. For seven days, Dov's weakening body had struggled for air. When he died, there was such a peace that came across his face, as if to say, "Finally, I can rest." One month later, Reuben's grandfather died in a similar manner. His grandfather had been a large man, with big warm hands, an equally big smile, and blue eyes. His grandfather had been an Orthodox Jew, who shared his love of God through song. He would compose *niggunim*, chants, that he would share with his family. As his grandfather sang, with eyes closed, swaying to the music, Reuben had always felt God near. With the passing of his grandfather, Reuben sensed a sustained chill and loss of direction descending on his family. Although Reuben's father was a pleasant man, he was shy and inward and often it seemed as if he did not know how to communicate with his family. Reuben's mother was a bossy and chronically irritated woman. Reuben sensed that her demeanor was partially because she wanted leadership to come forth from her husband, but he never delivered it. Without his grandfather, an essential glue had been lost from the family. The children were left with their father's silence and their mother's temper and did not know where to turn for reassurance. The coming of the new baby had delivered a small ray of hope to the family. The beauty of a new life, even under such oppressive conditions, took up the family's attention and distracted them from their unhappiness. The baby, who was named Sarah, had a dark complexion and lively blue eyes that seemed to hunger for connection with others. She smiled easily, and Reuben entertained the crazy notion that his grandfather, who had died two weeks before the baby's birth, had returned within this little body, to help the family maintain hope.

Reuben stood on the platform praying that the worst was over, but the worst was just beginning. German guards came close and started shouting and pushing the crowd around Reuben and his family onto the train. As the crowd surged forward, his mother fell. Reuben turned around and tried to help her. He tried to reach out to her, but the press of the crowd was too strong. The last he saw of his mother, she was trying to rise, while holding the baby, and screaming for her family. Reuben lost his mother, Sarah and grandfather in that one horrible moment. Even after all of the torture of Auschwitz, he never felt more helpless than he felt at that moment.

Reuben entered the railroad car with his sisters and father, as the crowd pushed around them. When there was no room to squeeze more people into the car, the door was sealed and darkness descended. The only source of light was the cracks between the planks of wood that comprised the carriage. Reuben tried to talk reassuringly to his sisters. He told them that they would see mother and Sarah again when the train arrived at its destination and things would be much better there. He could not see his sisters' faces, but he heard their cries and the cries of many other children that filled the carriage. He huddled with his sisters in an attempt to soothe them. His father was there, but he would not speak, beyond the simple acknowledgment of his presence. Father's spirit died on that day. It took only a few more days for his body to follow.

Life in Auschwitz was a series of thefts. There was the theft of his family, which occurred concurrently with the theft of understanding. Reuben emerged from the train after days in darkness. Guards, some leading dogs, marched about, herding the new arrivals. One tall guard with hateful eyes and a menacing expression strode up to Reuben, who was still trying to huddle with and protect his sisters. He shouted something at Reuben. For a moment, all Reuben was aware of was the guard's large mouth moving vigorously. Reuben could not make sense of the words. Then Reuben understood that he was being ordered to get in line with a group of many other young men. Reuben tried to keep his sisters with him, but another guard approached and pulled them in a different direction, while the first guard pointed his rifle at Reuben and shouted the command that Reuben join his designated line. Reuben watched his sisters and father being herded away, as a guard's voice boomed that they were being led to the decontamination facility. Ruben never saw his sisters and father again. Within one hour, they would be murdered. But it took time for Reuben to realize that this had happened. He needed to understand the connection between the dark clouds that emerged from the smoke stacks, the deliberate sorting of the "useful" from the weak, and the sense of death that pervaded every corner of the camp. For a while, the Germans had stolen his awareness that his remaining family were not being washed, but were being murdered. He had been robbed of the chance to cry, to say goodbye, and to know the otherworldly inhumanity of his surroundings.

Next, they stole his individuality. He stood, naked, in the showers, surrounded by other naked men, all scrubbing themselves with tiny slivers of soap. The nakedness, the shaven heads, the prisoners' uniforms, the serial numbers tattooed into their flesh — all designed to erase individuality, will, or any perspective beyond day-to-day survival. In fact, lacking individuality became a way of life, because anyone who stood out was more likely to be beaten, or worse.

Following the theft of individuality was the theft of a normal emotional life. The only way to survive in the camp was to not feel. As the beating, exhausting labor and hunger continued, Reuben felt himself drifting away from his body. When he slipped in the mud, while marching to another day of labor, a guard beat him with the butt of a rifle (the guards were usually close at hand, ready for such an occasion). Reuben knew that he was being beaten, and he reacted appropriately, by rapidly rising to resume his march, but Reuben did not experience the beating directly. Rather, he was watching another young man, lying on the ground, receiving blows to the back and shoulders, and struggling out of the mud. It was all happening to another person and there was no sensation connected to it. Apathy pervaded his existence. Perhaps he would live today or perhaps not. It really did not matter. After he left the camp, the apathy faded away, but he continued to have the sensation that he was watching himself from the outside. He regained the ability to feel anxiety and anger, which he felt in abundance, but these were the only emotions he could feel for the rest of his life.

There were many more thefts — the theft of his strength, the theft of his dreams, the theft of a home — many thefts, and each one irreversible. That is why he hated the word "liberation" — there was no liberation, only survival.

By the age of twenty-one, Reuben found himself living in a one-room apartment in New York City. He was only dimly aware of the chain of events that had brought him to the United States. If he had thought hard about it, he could have told you the essentials, but he had no interest in thinking hard about it. In fact, he had no interest in thinking about anything but his prior suffering, his hatred for the selfishness and cruelty of humanity and his anger towards God for causing him to be born into such a world. He obtained a job as a bus driver and held the same job until he was fifty-seven, when he died of a heart attack. He saw thousands of faces pass before him over those years, and countless times the image would go through his mind of lines of prisoners assembling for the final judgment — live or die — each face doomed to either an immediate death or a lifetime of remembering and suffering. When he was thirty-five years old, an acquaintance of his who was also a bus driver encouraged him to attend a dance. "You never get out, that's why you're always in such a sour mood," the man had said.

Reuben attended the dance. He entered the room, heard the band blasting upbeat music. He looked at couples swirling on the floor. He laughed cynically to himself about them. They see cause for celebration. But it's all illusion. Soon enough, each one of them would find out the truth — hell is not reserved for the afterlife, hell is here, a gift to every living person. His eyes wandered aimlessly across the room until they came across a pair of eyes that appeared to share his thought. They were brown, deep, sad-looking eyes that belonged to a young woman, a few years younger than he. She was standing inconspicuously in the corner of the room. Her face had a drawn, serious expression, the seriousness of someone who has seen too much and can never forget. He felt an irrational urge to take her in his arms and take care of her, to soothe her pain. He walked up to her, and they began to talk. They never stepped onto the dance floor, but one month later they were married.

Adam was born one year later, and his sister, Rachel, followed one year after that. Adam's mother, Tamar, had a similar background to Reuben. She too had lost all of her family in the war and had been interred in a concentration camp for a year and a half. When she was released, she was within a hairsbreadth of death due to illness, starvation and exhaustion. It took her months of recuperation to regain any level of normal physical function.

From the standpoint of Reuben and Tamar, only two things were real in the world, which set the tone for the Schwartz household. One was the war era, which Adam's parents repeated and rehashed to the eventual disgust of both Adam and Rachel. Adam and Rachel's young minds were filled with images of emaciated figures — starving, shivering and falling beneath the butts of German's rifles, or being marched off to be gassed and burned. The other thing that was real was the world within their two-bedroom apartment. The world outside was a dangerous blur, conspiring to cause the family harm. Selfish, prejudiced, violent people were believed to be lurking right outside the door to attack anyone who emerged. And if the family somehow evaded the malice of others, additional calamities awaited — they could be hit by a car or catch a disease or fall on the steps or fall in the river. In the world outside, everyone and everything was dangerous.

Since Reuben and Tamar lived and breathed loss, they clutched ever so tightly onto what they had — each other and their children. It was an embrace that the children came to feel as a stranglehold. To the same extent that the doors to the outside world felt locked and barricaded, it was as if no doors, no privacy, no separate identity existed within the Schwartz household. Every time the children would frown, one of their parents (usually Tamar, who was their caretaker) would worriedly ask, "What's wrong?" She would ask this question with such a degree of intensity that the children quickly learned not to frown, but to maintain a blank uninterpretable expression, so as not to cause their parents pain.

There were so many things that Adam and Rachel wished they did not have to hear. Reuben and Tamar would bicker endlessly, usually about the children. Tamar was very lenient with them. Even when she said the children should be punished, she always relented on it. Reuben, on the other hand, felt the children were not learning how to show their parents and each other proper respect. He regularly exploded at the children, yelling at them with such intensity that they felt themselves physically shrink before his glaring eyes and searing voice. The children fought frequently, likely a response to the oppressive unhappiness that surrounded them at home. They both wished they could stop, but reasons for anger and reprisal seemed unremitting. Reuben insulted the children in an attempt at discipline — "Stupid little sh**," "Ungrateful bitch" — he had many epithets. He hurled similar epithets at his wife. He would yell, and she would respond in a hoarse, intense voice, as if she were struggling to speak, to force air through her throat while someone was holding it. As their parents fought, the children would huddle together in their room. When the fight was over, their father would storm into his bedroom and their mother would come to the children. She would hold them in her arms and tell them again everything that had just happened, everything they had already heard so clearly.

She generally said something along these lines: "Your father is a very angry man. He is too strict. He wants to spank you two for fighting. My dears," she would cry, "I won't let him hurt you. He can yell at me, he can insult me, but not you, not my dears, I will keep you safe. He says I never loved him, that I do not listen to him, that I think him a fool…Well, he is, to carry on such and…I do not love him, if he will treat you this way…" Her words would be cut off by sobs, as she buried her face in her hands.

Adam and Rachel became very adept at sensing the mood in the home, even before any words had been said. They would feel a certain tightness in their stomachs when they sensed an argument was brewing or that one had occurred while they were out of the apartment. Adam sensed that what his mother wanted and needed most was for him to be physically close to her and to

NEVER FORGET MY SOUL

listen to her. His parents did not seem to have much of a physical relationship — the children never saw them hold hands, hug or kiss. Adam became clingy, not out of any conscious attempt to serve his mother's need, but because he was responding to the need of something that was so close to him that it was part of him. Just as one's hand may instinctively rub one's bumped head, so Adam responded to his mother, even as a toddler. He would incessantly want to be by her side. He feared the dark and even at the age of eight would crawl into his parents' bed to cuddle with his mother. In bed, she would stroke his head and tell him, "Yes, my dear, there is much to fear, but at least we are here together." As Adam developed, the physical closeness grew into the closeness of listening. It was a listening that was devoid of self, that made oneself a vessel for the communication of the other. She would talk of her family before the war, how much she had loved her mother, how her mother was beaten by German youths because "her nose was too long," how Tamar and her mother huddled together in the cold of the concentration camp, and how one day her mother took ill and was taken to the "infirmary" and Tamar never saw her again. And as a refrain, she would often repeat this thought, "I do not understand why I was chosen to live, while so many others, who were so much better than me, were murdered. I do not see why a selfish and ignorant woman, such as I, deserves to be here to tell these stories." She would talk about what a bad child she had been, about how much suffering her mischief had caused her parents. Her father had been a university professor, a philosopher who was highly regarded in his time. She looked back on the stature of her father with a sense of awe. "But I did not understand at that time," she would say, "the greatness of the man, how much he contributed, how much more he could have contributed. All I wanted to do was run around with my friends and do pranks and get in trouble and distract him from his work. He should be alive today, not me." Her stories were repeated endlessly, and Adam listened, opening himself to her experience and living the deaths, despair and hopelessness with her.

From an early age, Adam started giving his mother advice on how to handle conflict with his father. Even at the age of eight, he was telling her that she needed to calm down, that everything would be OK, that father screams, but the anger won't last, he just needed time to calm down. Adam would tell her that she should not start by immediately disagreeing with his father, that she should first listen and show respect for his opinion and only then meekly suggest a different way of looking at things. He was her marriage counselor, and would have been his father's counselor as well, if his father had the ability to let anyone close to him.

Adam faced his first day of kindergarten with a sense of trepidation. Attending kindergarten meant leaving his mother's side. She prepared for the big day for weeks — labeling his clothes, making sure he had the right bag, lunch box, school supplies. But most of all, she prepared him by earnestly instructing him on the way to behave "out there." She told him that teachers were not lenient like his mother, and that he had to follow the rules, like not calling out and staying in his seat and always being polite and respectful. She warned him to stay away from bullies, to not stand out too much, to walk away from conflict with peers, to let others have a toy if they wanted it — there was no reason to fight over things. Adam absorbed her agitation about the event. He screamed at the top of his lungs, as the teacher held him, shooed his mother away and his mother rushed out of the classroom. He cried, whimpered and moped for the first week of school. After that he learned to contain his tears, but the tears remained in him and never really left. He lived with those tears inside, and they became a barrier to him having any normal friendships. Instead, he turned to his schoolwork and reading, the latter of which he especially loved.

Adam's first day of school had a similar effect on his mother.

NEVER FORGET MY SOUL

He remembered seeing her after that first day. She was waiting outside of the school to pick him up. She had obviously been crying. She kneeled down and grasped him tightly. "It killed me to have to leave you there, my darling. I'm so sorry. But you have to learn, that is what school is for." There was a strange tone in her voice, as she said the words "that's what school is for" — it sounded like hatred. After Adam started school, his mother became more depressed and the frequency of her aches and pains increased. There was a look of such emptiness and despair in his mother's eyes when she dropped him off at school, that it scared Adam.

As Adam grew into adolescence, he obtained a part-time job as a checkout clerk in a department store and spent less time at home. With his growing independence, the barrage of questions and warnings began: Don't stay out too late; button your coat; don't buy trashy food on the street corner, it will only make you sick; don't spend time with bad kids, they will only get you into trouble. His parents would interrogate him about every step he had taken since he left the apartment, every word he had spoken. It felt as if they demanded that every choice be presented to them for their approval, for there were no minor choices. When Adam wanted to go to a rock concert, his parents took hours discussing, agonizing and fighting about it. Who would be there? How loud would the music be (maybe it could hurt his ears)? Did people get violent there? Would there be drugs? Would Adam smoke something and lose his mind and jump in front of a train? The agonizing even took place over the choice of an elective in high school. Adam wanted to take music. His father angrily responded to this suggestion that his high school transcript was a springboard to college and that such artsy courses would brand him as not a serious student. He would consequently only be admitted to a second-rate college, if he was admitted to one at all and end up having to "shovel sh**" as a job, for the rest of his life.

When Adam was sixteen years old, he dated for the first time.

The girl's name was Mae, and he remembered shivering with anticipation and fear shortly before he asked her out. He was nearly astounded when she shyly responded yes to his request that they go out to a nearby hamburger joint. He did not walk home on that day that she said "yes," he floated. But as he approached the apartment, the familiar tension settled into his stomach. She was not Jewish. While being Jewish did not mean a great deal to his parents, there was one imperative about this identity; one must *never* marry out. Jews belonged with Jews. No one else could be trusted. So Adam quickly drew himself down to the ground and transformed his smile into his usual blank expression that he wore at home. As he entered the apartment, his mother asked him what had happened today. As Adam knew was required, he gave her a detailed account of his activities, but he carefully circumvented mention of Mae. Adam became aware, on that day, that there were some ways that his world and that of his parents could never meet.

For Adam, socialization was always a struggle. For his parents, it was an impossibility. Adam wanted to interact with others and to learn from them so they could help him learn a different way of living. His socialization was hampered not by hostility towards others but by focus on his own limitations — fear of inadequacy, feeling judged, being tongue-tied, feeling he had nothing interesting to say. For Adam's parents, socialization was never an end, it was always a means. Adam's parents cultivated a "friendship" with a young couple in their apartment building, so that the parents would know someone to watch the children in an emergency or when Tamar was ill. Reuben invited coworkers home occasionally so he would have someone to cover for him at work, if needed. Every contact with the outside was utilitarian and took a great deal of emotional energy out of Adam's parents. Whenever someone was invited into the apartment, everything had to be perfectly clean, organized and prepared. Reuben would shout at the children for making a mess shortly before a guest was to arrive, as he nervously paced around the living room area in anticipation. Adam's parents were so isolated that their view of the world became increasingly distorted. Adam came to realize that his parents simply did not understand the changes in social trends and lifestyles that were happening around them. His parents relied on him and Rachel to give them information on what life was like in the 1970s, what people expected of each other, what people's goals were. Adam and Rachel provided some of this information and withheld other information that would lead to too much concern and questioning from their parents. However, the basic truth could not be changed that Adam's parents were like inhabitants of a different planet, who could indirectly hear about life in another planet, but never live in it.

After graduating from high school, Adam attended the University of Maryland. Adam had other choices that were closer to home, in New York, but deliberately chose to attend a school that placed him at a fair distance from his parents. When he hugged his mother on the day that he set off to college, he had the impression that she was collapsing within his arms. Guilty thoughts gnawed at his mind — he was killing her by leaving, he was a bad son. But he fought back his tears, shook his father's hand and then turned and left, knowing that if he did not leave on that day, he might stay inextricably frozen in his parents' world.

In the summer of his freshman year, Adam joined a tour of Israel. His parents were very opposed to the trip, because of the *Intifata*, the violent Palestinian uprising within Israel. They cried, begged, and pleaded that he not go. It was the first time he had seen his father cry, when he begged Adam "to not put your mother through this." His tears quickly turned to anger as he said, "She's suffered enough in her life! If you don't care about yourself, at least think about her! You're everything to her. You placing yourself in so much danger — it's like sending her back to the camps!"

Adam was surprised by his calm in the face of his father's

rage. He simply responded, "Mom's family and your family died because they were Jews. And I have no idea what being Jewish means. If I don't find out, then your families have died in vain and Mother has suffered for nothing. I'm going to find out what I belong to, to give some meaning to this terrible history we share."

His father did not appear to understand a word Adam was saying. His father merely began to shake his head, and between sobs, repeated, "You selfish, selfish boy."

Adam had begun wondering about his Jewish heritage after meeting some young Jewish men and women at his university. The first revelation these young people provided Adam was that they did not see being Jewish as a heavy, sorrowful burden. They varied in their involvement in and understanding of Judaism, but the ones who were not indifferent actually associated being Jewish with positive feelings. They would talk of love for learning and/or debate, pride about their heritage, and a mission to improve the world. Some of them had visited Israel and spoke about what a meaningful experience they had had.

One night, before deciding to go to Israel, Adam had a dream that he was in Germany, with his parents and Rachel, hiding from the Nazis. They had all crouched and huddled together in a bombed-out building, while soldiers marched outside, shouting that everyone had to come out of the building, which was going to be burned. In the dream, Adam reached into his pocket to reassure himself that he still had his airplane ticket to Israel. A German soldier banged loudly on the door, commanding them to come out. His parents rose sadly to march to their doom. But Adam and Rachel refused to follow. "There is nothing left for you here!" their father shouted, and Rachel reluctantly followed her parents, but Adam continued to crouch on the floor. The soldier kicked the door open and pushed Adam's parents and Rachel out of the room. Then he turned to Adam, telling him to follow or die. At that point, Adam looked up at the guard and said, "This place is not my home." He held up the ticket to Israel, and pointing to it, said, "Here is my home." The soldier nodded and let Adam remain. He woke up from the dream sweating with fear and knowing that he had to go to Israel.

Adam had arranged for a three-week tour of Israel. If he had been asked, he could not have actually specified what he hoped to find in Israel or where he would find it. He hiked, took pictures, listened to the historical presentations of the tour guides, and enjoyed the sunshine and beaches. He kept on having the gnawing feeling that this was not what he had come to find. Then finally, in Jerusalem, what he had come to find found him. He stood in front of the Western Wall, the only remaining outer wall of the ancient Jewish temple. All around him, he saw Jews of various backgrounds and nationalities. There were the very religious-looking men with full beards, black hats and black suits; soldiers in their green uniforms, carrying rifles by their side; tourists wearing sneakers, T-shirts and jeans, avidly taking photographs. But what most captivated Adam was the prayer of those in prayer shawls, leaning on the ancient wall. He watched men standing beside him, whispering prayers with such sincerity and solemnity. He had been told that they prayed for a time when the holy temple would be rebuilt. One elderly man leaned forward and kissed the wall and let out a moan of sadness and longing. Adam had been raised in a world where sadness was about the past, not about a longed-for future. It suddenly became to clear to Adam, that although these mourners for a destroyed temple also suffered loss, their life was not meaningless, for they hoped and prayed for a better time.

Adam became jealous. These people were this way only because their parents had taught them how to hope, that there is something to hope for and there is someone to whom one can supplicate. Adam only had a void and he did not know how to fill it. He could not pray. It was just too foreign, too strange to him.

Even if there was a God, why would He concern himself with something as puny and meaningless as us? Adam was lost in these musings when a man in his fifties, with a long beard, caught his eye. The man was dressed all in black, in the garb of a religious Jew. He looked like a rabbi to Adam.

"Where you from?" the man asked, smiling.

"Maryland," answered Adam, "originally from New York City."

"What you doing in Israel?" the man asked.

"Just touring," responded Adam.

"Touring," said the man. "There's so much to see here. You like it?"

"Yes," said Adam, "I'm enjoying it."

"You know," said the man, "no one's tour of Israel is complete unless they see a yeshiva." The man was referring to a Jewish religious school. "Would you like to see one?"

"OK," said Adam, who was relieved to have a distraction from his frustrated musings and loneliness.

The man walked Adam to a nearby yeshiva and introduced him to one of the rabbis, Rabbi Goldberg. Rabbi Goldberg had a broad, wrinkled face, a long white beard, thick glasses and a large smile. He shook Adam's hand warmly and invited him to attend a class that he would be giving in twenty minutes.

Five minutes before the class, Adam entered the classroom and found approximately twenty other young men and woman about his age. Adam took his seat and soon Rabbi Goldberg entered. He stood in the front of the room and for a moment looked at the faces in front of him, smiling. Then he introduced himself.

"Hello," he said, "I'm Rabbi Goldberg. The topic of today's class is: What is the purpose of life? How many of you are in university?" Almost all of the hands went up. "Good." he said nodding. "Inquiring minds — the kind I like best. You know at university they teach you how to make a living, but they do not teach you how to live. Here, we teach you how to live. You see, whenever you set out to accomplish something, you have to know what you goal is. Who here does not want to live a good life? I see no hands raised, which does not surprise me. But here is the question, how can you live a good life if you don't know what the *purpose* of life is? Every corporation has a mission statement and the CEO of the corporation has to state specific ways for the company to meet its goals and be a success. If the CEO did not set those goals or chose bad ones, the board of directors would get fed up with him and throw him out. But when it comes to life, many people do not have a mission statement. If I press them about the purpose of life, the best they tell me is that the purpose of life is to live. What does that mean? It's like saying the purpose of a car is to drive.

"In Judaism, we have a *mesorah,* which means the teaching of the wise ones who came before us. And that *mesorah* clearly tells us what the purpose of life is. What it tells us is that the whole universe is just like a corporation. The mission statement of the corporation is formed upon its founding. Well, God, when he created the world, had a mission statement in mind. You see, the rabbis tell us that God is all good and has no needs. Since he has no needs, all he ever wants to do is to give to others, to bring them happiness. But before the world was created, there was no one to *give to.* Thus, he created us so that we could experience happiness and he created the world to give that happiness to us. The purpose of life, then, is to receive all the goodness that God has created for us and to enjoy that goodness.

"Now, Judaism teaches that there are different levels of goodness that God gives us and that each higher level brings higher levels of enjoyment. The lowest level is the body. Undeniably, that level can bring great enjoyment. Every time I have my wife's cooking, and she is some *great cook,* I experience that enjoyment. But there are higher levels of enjoyment. For example, there is enjoyment of the mind. When you have been working for hours on a difficult intellectual project, such as a paper for school, and you have finally expressed clearly what you wanted to say, and you get positive feedback from your professor, you can have a degree of happiness, a 'high,' that stays with you much longer than the enjoyment of a good meal. At a yet higher level is the enjoyment of doing the right thing. Let's say you know a single mother, who works till very late and constantly worries about her son getting into trouble, hanging out with the wrong type of kids. You could ignore her plight. Or you could take the young fellow under your wing, show him some guidance, teach him how to stay out of trouble. Let's say you see him years later, a respectable young man, helping others that are less fortunate than he. What a sense of satisfaction you would experience.

"Every level of enjoyment is important and God wants us to have it. There is, however, a highest level of enjoyment that can only come from the highest source, God himself. The highest enjoyment for man is when we learn how to bring ourselves close to God. How do you do that?" he raised his eyebrows, anticipating his audience's curiosity as to the answer, and pausing for dramatic effect. "Well, the answer to that question takes time. More time than we have today. But we can teach you. Stick with us for a while, and we'll get you on the right track.

"I can only give you a glimpse of an answer today. There is a story about a man who was riding his motorcycle on a mountain road. Suddenly the motorcycle skids and flies off the road. Down he falls to his certain death. By a miracle, his shirt gets snared on a protruding branch and he survives, with hardly a scratch. That night the man has a dream that he is standing before God himself. The man humbly bows and thanks God for sparing his life. God responds, 'I spared your life so you would bow to me with gratitude … and by the way, I also pushed you off the mountain.'

"What is the meaning of this story? You see, the first step of becoming close to God is to realize that all things come from him and all things are designed for our good. Every experience, good

NEVER FORGET MY SOUL

or 'bad' is given to us to make us spiritually stronger, wiser, more charitable or more aware. This world may look like a random chain of events, but that is only to the untrained eye. This world is actually a school, where every experience comes to us to help us find our potential for greatness — for abundance of spirit and care and commitment and love.

"But these ideals by themselves are just pretty words. So in Judaism, we have a system of self-improvement. This system helps maintain a daily, weekly, monthly and yearly routine whereby we can gradually develop these traits ..."

After the class, Adam walked through the streets of Jerusalem, deep in thought. He wandered by buildings built with yellowish-brown stone, which had earned Jerusalem the name "City of Gold." Rabbi Goldberg's presentation had been both fascinating and troubling. His position was refreshingly different from the worldview of Adam's parents. In his parents' eyes, no enjoyment in this world was possible and the only thing one can hope for is the minimization of suffering. In addition, Rabbi Goldberg's ideas were profoundly different from many of Adam's peers, who also believed the purpose of life to be enjoyment, but knew of no greater enjoyment than the pursuit of physical pleasure. Even his more industrious peers at school believed that the school week was something to be "gotten through" and that "real living" occurred on the weekend, when they could party. (There were exceptions — peers with different values, but they were few and far between.) To party was to become drunk or high, dance wildly and, if one got lucky, engage in various sexual pleasures. While at college, Adam had turned to alcohol and marijuana himself, in an attempt to become less self conscious and more sociable. But the alcohol just made him feel depressed, and the marijuana made him feel paranoid. And worst of all, it always felt like pretending, like frantically running away from an ache within him that never went away. The alcohol and drugs always felt like a mask to him, a mask that he could put on to momentarily mislead others about the pain, but that never actually removed the pain.

Adam realized, at that moment, how very similar were the worlds of his parents and the worlds of the partying youths, because both lived lives devoid of *meaning*. Rabbi Goldberg spoke of a universal plan, goals and a structure to attain those goals. This was a life *infused* with meaning.

And yet there was the troubling part. God was the one who pushed that man off the cliff. No one knew better than Adam the implications of that thought. So God pushed the Jews into the death camps? God murdered the innocent children? God wrenched his grandparents away, marched them into the gas chambers and reduced their bodies to smoke and ash? Better not to believe than to believe in such a God.

These last thoughts were enough to make Adam put Rabbi Goldberg and the yeshiva behind him, and never think of them again. But something gnawed at him. What if he did not understand? His parents were trapped in their world because they thought they understood everything so well — that the world was cruel, that no one outside was to be trusted. Perhaps, Adam was making the same mistake. Somehow, the warmth and depth of Rabbi Goldberg's sparkling eyes made Adam suspect that the old rabbi could help him with these thoughts and hope that the rabbi's answers would not be shallow.

The next day, Adam called the yeshiva to request a meeting with Rabbi Goldberg, who told him he could meet with him that afternoon. As Adam entered the Rabbi's office, Rabbi Goldberg was leaning over a large book filled with Hebrew letters. As he read, he muttered something to himself and stroked his beard. Adam cleared his throat, and Rabbi Goldberg noticed him.

"Hello, Adam!" he said enthusiastically, his facing lighting up in genuine warmth.

Adam proceeded to tell the Rabbi his story — his family

history, his upbringing, the despair that pervaded the world of his youth. He told the Rabbi about his troubling theological thoughts, how the very thing that Rabbi Goldberg had introduced to make him appreciate God's involvement in our lives had almost pushed Adam away from Judaism forever. Adam felt tears well up in his eyes as he spoke, but they were not tears for his past. They were tears of longing, longing for the life of hope and purpose that Rabbi Goldberg promised and fear that the chance for such a life was rapidly slipping through his fingers.

When Adam stopped talking, the rabbi sat silently for a long time. He looked into the distance, far beyond Adam. Finally, he looked at Adam and with a gentle expression on his face and said, "Adam, there are two types of events that God creates in this world. One type is the events that are within the normal range of human experience. Although we never can truly know God's purpose, I believe it is still our duty to try to understand the deeper meaning of these events, so we can learn the lessons that God is trying to teach us. Then there are extraordinary events. These events have three characteristics: They are enormous in scope, they are unprecedented, and they are pivotal turning points in history. These extraordinary events cannot be understood in the same way that we understand other events. Their nature is too vast, their ramifications too far-reaching. The only response to such events is to stand in awe at God's power, and humbly submit our will to His. I would never say God marched us into the gas chambers. Although this seems like a logical conclusion, it is a lie, because it will make me believe a lie — that God is bad. Instead I say this: God created a world where suffering is possible. He has His designs for doing so, and when I see all the good in His world, and all of His blessings, I have faith that His designs are for our good. Adam, my life's work is to talk with people like you — yearning, searching souls, hungry for the truth. There is such good, such decency, such courage in the people who come here, who are willing to make a new life for themselves and see the world in a different way. I consider people like you *my* blessing, and I feel so fortunate that God gave me the opportunity to help cultivate such bright minds.

"You know, Adam, our relationship with God is really like the relationship between a baby and its mother. The baby derives complete security and soothing from its mother. If it could talk, it would say it trusts its mother without questions or doubts. Now, the time will have to come when the mother has to take the baby to the doctor for shots. What must the baby think, when its trusted mother not only brings the baby to this strange person with a big needle, but then actually restrains the child while the strange person causes the baby pain? What understanding does the baby have of the inoculation? If the mother explained the purpose of the inoculation to the baby, would that help? Of course not. The inoculation is administered for the baby's good, but the baby has no way of understanding that. Now consider this: After the inoculation, does the baby decide that the mother is bad and hate the mother forever after? No. Why? Because there is a relationship of trust between the baby and mother. The baby cannot deny the pain or that the mother took part in administering the pain to the baby. But there is so much good that the mother has done for the baby previously and that she continues to do for the baby, that the baby sees the pain as an unexplainable deviation from the normal state of affairs — that is, nurturing and soothing from the mother.

"Our relationship with God is the same. If you build up your awareness of his blessings and establish a sense of trust in him, then it becomes bearable that the purpose of some suffering is beyond comprehension. It actually helps us let go of the suffering. Some suffering is too vast for our shoulders to carry; it can only be borne by God."

Adam felt himself struggling inside as he listened to Rabbi Goldberg. His words were so beautiful. So much of what he said made sense. But another voice screamed inside of Adam, and he felt his parents scream along with him: "What can he know?! Here he sits in security spouting his pearls of wisdom! Those who saw the evil — face to face — they know different."

The rabbi paused and looked fixedly at Adam. He seemed to sense exactly what Adam was thinking.

"Adam, I know what I'm talking about. Here, I have something to show you."

Rabbi Goldberg lifted his shirt sleeve, and on his forearm were tattooed five bluish-black digits, a memorial of his interment in a concentration camp forty years before.

Adam made the decision on that day to stay in Israel for a year to study Judaism, and to try to understand how a man with Rabbi Goldberg's background could maintain such a positive approach to life and maintain his faith. Adam learned many things during his stay, and they did indeed transform how he thought about life. He returned to the United States as an Orthodox Jew, committed to the structure taught to him in yeshiva. He prayed at a synagogue three times a day, observed Jewish dietary laws, refrained from work on Saturday and regularly went to *Shuirim*, classes on the Jewish sacred texts. He reenrolled in the University of Maryland, and eventually obtained a Ph.D. in molecular biology. He met and married a warm, understanding and supportive woman named Devorah, and proceeded to have children and raise a family with her.

Externally, his life was good. He liked his job working as a research scientist. He found it interesting and stimulating. His children were smart and beautiful, and Devorah was his anchor. But Adam experienced a continuing sense of anxiety and unrest. He never felt he could relax, let go and be himself, even with his wife and children. He was especially uncomfortable and awkward in social settings, which interfered with his ability to form friendships, as well as his professional advancement. He had found answers for his mind, but within his heart there still gnawed the darkness and despair of the past. He often felt that all his religiosity was a pretense and that his core contained the same hopelessness that his parents had lived and died with. In hopes to change things for the better, he entered psychotherapy with David. After two sessions, David recommended that Adam join one of David's therapy groups that was about to begin. Adam said he could not afford group and individual therapy. David thought carefully about this and said, "Then I recommend you do the group. You need to find your place amongst others. Then you'll be able to address your anxiety."

It was raining when Adam drove to the second group session. He watched the drops of rain glimmer with the rays of the passing street and car lights. The night was cold, and Adam wondered why he was dragging himself out to talk with a group of strangers, when there were much better things that he could be doing with his time. He thought about the different worlds he had lived in during his life — the world of his parents, his secular life at the university, his life as an Orthodox Jew. He sensed that in therapy he was entering a different world, a world he did not understand, with new rules and expectations. He was tired of having to adjust to new worlds. He wanted to just settle down into what he had and learn how to appreciate it. Ironically, for all its newness, this therapy group had hidden within it much that would be familiar to Adam.

CHAPTER THREE

"My wife took the kids and left," said Tyrone. In contrast to his polished professional appearance in the prior session, he was wearing grey sweatpants, a faded sweatshirt, and old, dirty sneakers. "I found this note on the nightstand this morning." He showed a folded piece of paper to the group, then unfolded the paper and began to read:

Dear Tyrone:

I married a man I admired — a man who had lived through hell, who had struggled with the devil and had prevailed. I married a man who was strong of heart and mind and will. And I married a gentle man — a man who was gentle because he knew what the world was like without gentleness. I trusted that man — I trusted that his dance with the devil was over, that he had put those ways behind him, and that he was a better man because of the struggle he had faced. Tyrone, my darling — the devil is not gone. He still walks within our house, and I am afraid. It's not that you yell at me, it's how you yell at me *when you do. There is hate and rage in your eyes. I see it, the children see it. I have to leave to protect them. Darling, I pray for you. I am not sure that I can return, but I pray that some day I will have the courage to. And I pray that if that time comes, you will have ordered the devil to leave once and for all, and that we have a home where we are all safe to love each other.*

> *In dreams,*
> *Doris*

Tyrone folded up the letter and put it in his pocket. "We fought last night," he continued. "It was something stupid. It's always something stupid. But it always seems so important at the time. Anyway, I exploded at her. I knocked a vase off the table. Glass went flying everywhere. The kids were crying. I told her I was sorry. She just kept repeating, 'Too many times, too many times.' I couldn't get anything else out of her. And then I woke up to find this note. I must have sat there in bed for an hour, deciding whether I should pull out the gun and kill myself. Well, here I am. I decided to stick around. But I didn't go to work today. I went for a long walk. I must have been out for hours. I really don't know how long it was. All I know was that by the time I came back, it was time to come here."

Tyrone was quiet, and a heavy silence hung in the air. Finally, Marcia spoke, "Tyrone, I'm glad you came here and didn't just suffer through this alone. I've had terrible down times in my life, and I really don't know if I would have survived, if I had to go through it alone. Could you tell me what that *devil* is that your wife talks about?"

"Well, that's a long story, and I don't think I'm up to long stories." Tyrone had a look of resignation and deep weariness on his face.

"Marcia is right," said David, in his quiet, penetrating voice. "It's not a good time to be alone. If you don't tell your story now,

Tyrone, you will be alone again. Why don't you try?"

Tyrone's brow furrowed as he considered David's words, and then he began. "My mother was seventeen when she became pregnant with me. My father was some teenage, hormone juiced-up kid, who was just interested in a hot night and a pretty girl. And nine months later, there I was, with one confused mother and no father. My mother stayed with her mother, 'til I was three, and it was really my grandma who raised me during that time. Then Mama and Grandma had a fight, it was something about Mama sleeping around too much, and Grandma threw her out. I went with my Mama. At the age of twenty, Mama really knew nothing about how to survive alone. So she married my step-dad, the laziest liar and son-of-a-bitch you could ever meet. He was a drunk, who was always 'looking' for a job, but could never find one. He would rage against me and my mother, and we both ended up with plenty of bruises and welts. Mama grew hard, all her warmth was smacked out of her. There was nothing for me in that home. As soon I was old enough to say, 'see you later,' I was out of that door, spending most of my time on the streets.

"Now those were the streets of New York City. The streets were better than my home, because at least there were kids there who you knew you could count on, who were on your side and could watch your back. But the streets were dangerous, too. You had to be hard and quick and smart. The worse thing of all was if others sensed weakness in you. They fed on weakness and they would eat you up. You had to learn how to look just mean enough so that no one would dare pull a gun on you, but not so mean that they felt you were about to pull one on them. There were plenty of dead kids, lying in the streets, who did not figure out how to play this game right or who were just in the wrong place at the wrong time. Luckily I grew fast. I was already bigger than most at thirteen. I carried a gun, and let others know I would not hesitate to use it. Everyone knew not to mess with me — kids, neighborhood adults, teachers. I would look at them and they would look the other way. And that was just fine with me, because it was my way to stay safe.

"Everything was about power for me. As long as I had power, I was safe. I started to hate all those who were in power — police, adults in general, teachers. I really gave my teachers a hard time. I used all my intelligence to annoy, frustrate and intimidate them. But back then I didn't know that I was smart. I mean, I didn't know that I could be *book* smart.

"Then I met Eva. I was fourteen. I didn't think much of her when I first met her. Just another annoying white teacher, trying to get me to be a compliant student. But then one day, after I had been a real cut-up in class, she asked me to stay after. I stayed, not because I was afraid of her; I just wanted to let her know who was boss, freak her out after everyone else had left. Or maybe I was just amazed that she had told me to stay. No other teacher had ever dared do that. Anyway, so after the other students left, she said to me, 'You're really angry.' I told her she should shut up and stop trying to read my mind. She ignored that and just continued, 'And you think you're angry because the world is filled with jerks. But that's not it. You're angry because you're an intelligent young man, but everyone looks at you and can only see a thug.' I told her that plenty of formerly intelligent young men are lying dead in the street, and I would stick to being a thug. But that Eva, she never gave up, she had a will greater than mine. I think it was because she knew how to love, while, at that time, I had no idea what love was. She looked at me with her gentle but determined blue eyes and said, 'But you don't want to be a thug. What you want is power. I can show you power.'

"'Yeah,' I said. 'I keep my power loaded in my pocket. Do you have a power greater than that?'

"'Yes,' she answered, and held out a book to me. It was a biography of Martin Luther King. 'Your gun can only protect you from the world. It cannot change the world. If you want power, use your intelligence. Learn. Then you will find out how to change the world, so those kids can *stop* dying in the streets. It's not bullets that kill them. It's ignorance, the ignorance that keeps them trapped here.'

"I took that book home and read it. And I came back to her for more books. I started to have questions about what I read. And we discussed my questions and my thoughts and she helped me to see that I was smart. I was hungry for knowledge ... I loved Eva, more than I loved my own mother ..."

A strange look of pain washed across Tyrone's face.

"She died, two years later. Shot by a stray bullet. Warring gangs. They probably didn't even see her fall; they were so wrapped up in their little war. I saw her at the hospital before she died. I promised her that I would get out of the city, use my mind, make something out of myself. It's because of her that I went to law school, and started my own law practice. I made a million dollars last year. I'm living a life I never could have dreamed of on the streets."

Tyrone turned to Marcia. "The devil Doris was talking about is the violence of those streets. It's still in me. They killed Eva. They have to pay. But I don't know who they are. So I just end up making everyone pay."

"Tyrone," asked David, "will you tell the group the meaning of what Doris said in the note — 'In Dreams?'"

"That's our little code for each other. I met Doris when I was sixteen. She was kind of like me, the new me after I met Eva. We both dreamed about a life together, where we could start anew, raise kids who were free from all this hell. Whenever we would part, we'd say 'in dreams' to each other, to remind ourselves of that dream." Tyrone hesitated, as if he were not sure if he wanted to go on, and then said, "I wrote a poem, when I was eighteen, when I was about to leave home for university. It tells all about the world I was leaving and the new life I dreamed about — the change I wanted to make." Tyrone began to recite the poem, from memory:

From men to boys,
From boys to men
The generations go again.
Who's an enemy?
Who's a friend?
From men to boys,
From boys to men.

The sun comes up.
The sun goes down.
Do things change as years go 'round?
Can you make a different sound
From those who lie beneath the ground.
The sun comes up.
The sun goes down.

You threaten me.
I threaten you.
And one will fall before we're through.
But fallen ones will strike back too.
You threaten me.
I threaten you.

From hate to hurt,
From hurt to hate.
The strong survive; the weak ones wait,
That some will care about their fate.
From hate to hurt,
From hurt to hate.

As fathers do,
So children see
Or do not see, but hear, maybe

Of lives lost behind the jailer's key.
As fathers do
So children see.

They can't relax.
They can't let go.
A puff of smoke is all they know
To ease the pain they will not show.
They can't relax.
They can't let go.

The future children
Understand
That their lives lay
In these young men's hands
To choose each day
To hope or hate,
To work or shirk,
To jump or wait,
To respect or to reject,
To undo their father's neglect.
The future children understand
And they watch questioning each young man.
From men to boys,
From boys to men.

After a few moments of silence, Tyrone said, "Look, that's enough. I've told my story. I don't think I can take any more of this tonight."

An awkward silence followed.

Finally David spoke. "While you were speaking, Tyrone, the thing that kept coming into my mind was what a difference one person can make in another person's life, and I am curious how the other group members might respond to that thought."

"Oh," said Terry, "I couldn't agree more. Eva meant so much to Tyrone. She was the difference between life and death to him — she gave him his ticket away from the streets. And as for me, David, to answer your question, more directly, my mother is my life preserver. Things would be so bleak without her. I've lost so much, but I still have her — her love, her support, her understanding. She makes a tremendous difference in my life."

"Well, David," said Joe, "I just don't see things that way. When I think back about who made a big difference in my life, there's no one. I guess I have my intolerant, aggressive father to thank for me becoming a coke addict when I was a teenager. But I don't think that's the sort of gratitude you were hinting at. My parents marched me through a long line of psychologists and social workers, but those therapists sure as hell didn't make a difference in my life. Each one was more false, hypocritical and self-righteous than the next. No one changed my life. I just decided I got tired of living from fix to fix. I decided I needed some structure. So I went to medical school. That gave me structure, and I stopped the drugs. I worked hard and that's why I became successful."

There was something about Joe's flippant attitude that was so enraging to Adam, and for a moment, he once again forgot his shyness.

"Maybe there was no one who made any difference in your life," said Adam, "but you have got to admit that Eva made all the difference for Tyrone."

Joe looked at Adam as if he were an annoying flea. "No, I don't. Tyrone made the choice to change and learn. Eva didn't read those books. Eva didn't study for him. And she was dead by the time he was in law school. How could she help him if she was dead? He decided to get through law school and take the bar."

"What makes you think that the dead can't help?" asked Adam.

"Because the dead are dead; they don't do anything. Anyway,

NEVER FORGET MY SOUL

I'm not interested in death. I'm just interested in living my life. I don't have time to think about those who are rotting in the earth."

"Well, as for me," responded Adam, "there *are* people who have made all the difference in my life. Some of them were alive, some were dead. But all of them were my teachers. I learned from their wisdom and it made me a better person."

"Great for you," said Joe. "Go learn from the dead. I've learned from the dead, too. It was when I cut up my first corpse in medical school. I learned that there is nothing in that corpse but used-up parts, so you better use them while they still work. I learn from the dead every day, or from people who are nearly dead — hopeless cancer patients — yeah, I'll cut out their tumor, try to fix their machine, but for many of them it's too late. And lots of them find themselves wishing they had spent less time waiting for someone to 'make a difference in their life' and more time living. I know people who look for others to 'improve their soul.' I've sliced the human body every which way. There is no soul there. The body just works for a while and then it rots. I'm interested in using it while it works."

"Why are we spending all this time talking about the dead?" Terry broke into the discussion, leaving Adam relieved that this callous and empty man had stopped talking. "Look, who cares if the dead make a difference, Joe? Are you telling me there is no person who makes a difference in your life now? Is there any relationship that matters to you?"

Joe looked thoughtful for a moment and answered, "No, I don't think so."

"You mean you're completely indifferent to other people?" asked Terry.

"Not at all, there are lots of people I really enjoy."

"So, how can you say that no one makes a difference to you?"

"Fair question," answered Joe. "Let me explain. I truly am not interested in any relationship, but I enjoy *relating*. I like the stimulation. I get into it when there is a lively discussion. I like the heat of the moment, me challenging people, seeing how they will respond. I like playing with people, especially women, flirting with them, the rush of wondering how they will respond to me and what excites them. The *relating* is great, but not the relationship. Take Tyrone, for example. It was a great story. I was really into it. Man, Tyrone, you've overcome so much. You're a warrior, who threw your passion and your fight into everything you do. It's inspiring, to rise from the streets of New York and become a successful lawyer. But I *know* that the moment I leave this room, you will be of no significance to me, because you will be in the past, and I'm not interested in the past. The only thing that matters to me is the moment, the excitement of the moment. I can take you or leave you; all I need is the stimulation."

"So we're all irrelevant to you?" asked Marcia. "Does that mean that you'll be in this group as long as it amuses you and then you'll be gone? I need to know if I want to invest any energy into you. If you've got one foot out of the door, then I think it's best to ignore you."

"That's your choice," answered Joe, "but women usually find it hard to ignore me." He smiled at this last statement. "Yeah, I have no commitment written in stone about this group. I'll stick around for a while. If I like it, I'll stay. If it's a pain in the ass, or you all turn out to be pains in the ass, I'll leave. And I'd advise you all to do the same. Don't waste your life doing something that you feel you're supposed to do. Just do what feels good, what makes you happy."

"Well, there certainly is going to be a problem," said David, "because therapy is not designed make you happy. It's designed to help you suffer in a different way."

"Well, maybe therapy's a crock of sh**," responded Joe, "and maybe I won't be here next week."

"So why do you take up our time?" said Marcia with anger in her voice. "Playing with us, making us matter to you and then you

NEVER FORGET MY SOUL

can just disappear, because you get challenged. You don't have a good answer for David, so you just have to take your toys and go home! You are so like my ex-husband; neither of you can feel anything for anybody. I can't believe such selfishness."

"People stay in bad relationships," said Joe, "because of some twisted idea of duty, and they try to pretend that they don't hate the other person's guts. I'm not selfish, I'm just honest. I let you know up front. I'll stay here as long as I'm enjoying it. You won't have to wonder if I'm staying here to uphold my *duty,* but that secretly you repulse me. When I don't like this place, I'll leave. And maybe leaving would even be wrong. But we all have to make choices and live with them. If I start second-guessing myself, I'll end up like all those frightened, frozen people who can't make a decision. Now *that's* death. When you cannot move, you might as well be a corpse."

"You don't seem so happy in your marriage," said Terry. "Why do you stay there?"

"Good point," said Joe. "Truth is, I don't always live up to my principles. In some areas, I'm still a coward. I'm afraid of fighting over the house and the money and especially the kids. But still it's a good question, why I stay there. I hope that some day I have enough guts to do something about it. Maybe if I — "

"This is ridiculous," interrupted Marcia. "All this time wasted on this selfish man, who could be gone next week, when Tyrone has poured his guts out for us and needs some help. *He's* not using others for pleasure. He's just haunted by the past, by all that was violently taken from him. Tyrone, is there anything more you need out of the group tonight?"

"I need to let go of the anger," Tyrone answered. "I need to fundamentally change, so Doris can trust me again. Thanks for the offer, Marcia. I need to give some thought to how the group can help me with this. But actually, the discussion has helped me some already. It's reminding me how important it is for me to do whatever is necessary to get Doris back. Even Joe is helping to clarify things for me. He is helping me remember who I was when I was a teenager – a self-centered, pleasure-seeking youth. To some degree, I grew out of that, and I never want to be that again. But when I become enraged, it comes back — all I see is my point of view, my need, my demand that I am obeyed. I see that this selfish part of me is what I have to change. I have to be willing to empathize, to see things from others' point of view. I also feel like I matter to this group — well, most of the group," he looked at Joe as he said this, "and it makes me feel less desperate."

CHAPTER FOUR

David Web jogged along the road in the afternoon sun. His sneakers hit the soft grass beneath him, giving a springy sensation to his stride. To his left, across the road, trees, vines and thick underbrush intermingled to form a web of green. To his right was a wooden fence, lining the green fields of his neighbor's farm. He was about to reach a path in the woods, across the road. He had jogged this route countless times and no longer thought about when he had to turn — his legs just took him there.

He recalled how it was ten years ago, when he and his wife, Margaret, and his three children had first moved out here to the country, that Margaret had returned to the house one day, saying, "Dave, I found the most amazing path in the woods. It's only about half a mile away from the house." The kids were away, visiting their grandparents. So with the spontaneity that such moments engender, he took Margaret by the hand and asked if she would show it to him immediately. Off they went, on a warm spring day, similar to this day. Margaret led him into the darkness of the forest, on an ascending path, which followed a winding brook, to the top of a tall hill. The forest, with its dense trees and thick greenery, made him feel cut off from the rest of the world, both protected and removed from every source of distraction, irritation and strife. It was so silent in there. Yes, there was the sound of the brook, and of the occasional passing car, but these sounds faded into the background of his awareness. (It was on this path that David encountered a silence that, over the years, became precious to him. There, he could think in a deeper and more focused way than he could anywhere else.)

David and Margaret did not talk as they climbed the path. They merely held hands, sharing an unspoken awareness that there was something very tender and precious in their exploration, a tenderness that they did not want to spoil with any spoken sound. Eventually, the path veered away from the brook, and as it did, the silence of that place became even more pronounced. David instinctively reached out to put his arm around Margaret's waist, perhaps to reassure himself that the mystery of this place was positive and not sinister. The surrounding forest became darker and more overgrown, but the path was clear and wound further up the hill. Finally, when it seemed that the darkness and the silence were becoming oppressive, the trees and greenery parted and he and Margaret found themselves taking the final steps to the top of the hill, where they could see the other side of the hill sloping away from them and then continuing to slope into a lush valley. The valley was spotted with the occasional barn and farmhouse. They could see small groups of cattle in the distance. Far away, the valley sloped up again into green mountains, with occasional patches of grayish-brown rocks. The sky above the mountains shimmered with the brilliance of bright blue. Here everything was clear; all the dark mystery of the forest had faded. He and Margaret sat together on a rock outcropping to enjoy the view and the gentle breeze that blew across the top of the hill, providing a welcome cooling sensation in the intensity of the afternoon sun. He kissed her, and they hugged, a long, unhurried hug that only a couple that has been married for many years can share. He thanked her for "pushing" him to leave his comfortable suburbia and live in the country.

David's thoughts emerged from these memories and returned to the present. He realized that he had entered the forest path without even noticing it. He thought about how many therapy cases he had pondered and analyzed while running along this path. For David, as for most therapists, it was very hard to lay down his work at the office. In fact, some of the most important aspects of his work involved his musings and wonderings away from the office, where new questions and insights could lead to a completely novel interpretation of a case. It was very clear to David why this path was such an ideal place to ponder his work. This forest path, much like his work, dealt with the hidden, twisted and tangled. Every therapy client in David's office presented him with text and subtext. The text was the story of their lives that they would tell, or the conversations they would have with the therapist or, in the case of group therapy, with the other group members. But this text was often as much a distraction as it was communication. There was another reality contained within the subtext — old wounds, present fears, rage, primal impulses, which were simply too threatening for the clients to reveal to others or even to themselves. This forest path was his symbol for the psyche, a place where eyes could deceive and one had to use a mix of experience and intuition to discern the client's true needs and actual struggle. During some of David's darkest moments of his therapeutic work, times when he was lost and confused and feared that he could be making a terrible mistake with his client, he thought of this path and the clearing above. And with that thought, he would remind himself that if he was afraid, his client was probably twice as afraid, because the client did not know what David knew and had seen often — eventually there is a clearing. Eventually, so many of his confused, conflicted and even self-destructive clients had dared to speak the subtext and in so doing, and in having David witness this process, were able to enter the light of day. In this light of day, where their psychic resources were no longer invested in pretending to be something they were not, both the client and his or her relationships were transformed into a more genuine, open, and peaceful way of being.

"Yes," thought David, "but there were many who were 'lost in the woods,' and I was never able to get them out." David felt he always had to remind himself of this, so he would not become too cocky, because overconfidence is the undoing of many a therapist. David had seen clients who appeared worse when the therapy was terminated than when they had first come. In addition, over his twenty-year career, two clients had committed suicide. Even to this day, he would sometimes wake up in a cold sweat, having dreamed about one or both of those clients about to jump off a cliff, or run into a moving car, or blow their brains out, and, in the dream, David would just be paralyzed. He would neither be able to speak nor act, and would watch helplessly as the clients plunged themselves into their own deaths.

So he had had his share of successes and disasters, and here he was, jogging up the same hill, thinking about his work once again. He thought of the group: Adam, Grace, Joe, Terry, Marcia, and Tyrone. He repeated their names in his mind, in order to invoke their imagined presence. He had seen many varieties of groups in his work. Some were very tentative and would spend weeks or months talking about irrelevant matters before they would get into anything substantial. Some were "over-therapized" and would attempt to use up the group time by interpreting each other's behavior, according to each group member's favorite psychological theory. They would spend so much time analyzing feelings that they would not have any time to feel them. Some groups knew what they wanted from the outset and would launch into an honest exploration of their issues much earlier. The present group was unlike any of these. They were very stimulating to each other. The members were somehow touching wounds, remembrances and longings in each other, so that mere avoidance or intellectualization had become impossible. However, the group did not fully realize this yet. They squabbled, challenged, criticized and defended, but it was in a blind, groping way, not fully understanding what they were looking for or what they hoped to accomplish. While David had a tentative understanding of the subconscious needs that were operating in this struggle, his understanding of the group was still forming in his own mind. Thus, he tried to keep his mind open as the process unfolded.

The twisted vines, bushes and trees were becoming denser around David. This dense foliage, David had often thought, was a wonderful symbol for the complicated web of interrelationships that occur within the group setting. When David would teach courses about groups, he would tell his students, "The group session is always very crowded. You may find parents, siblings, old friends, lovers, spouses and children appearing without any prior notice and demanding attention." What he *meant* by this was that the relationships that develop in a group often stimulated memories of important relationships in the patients' present and past. These stimulated memories were so strong that patients often responded to certain group members as if they actually *were* spouse, mother, father, sister, etc. It was through these reactions that power was allocated within a group. Some group members simply had more power — *meant* more — to a particular group member. And power was what group work was all about. The members fought for power, which usually took the form of power to be noticed and power to direct the course of the group discussions. Often intense jealousies would occur in a group, as a group member or members would feel excluded from a special level of significance to another group member. The ultimate power in the group was to attain the status of "group leader," the group member who is generally acknowledged as the one who sets the tone for the group or directs its flow.

David sensed that a leader might arise in this group, and he wondered who that leader would be. Tyrone had potential. He had the confident bearing and the life experience of one who had had to either dominate or die. But there was also something soft about Tyrone, something his wife had alluded to in her parting note, and something David had seen in individual therapy with Tyrone. Tyrone had dominated on the street because of necessity, and he could dominate when he needed to as a lawyer, but all things being equal, he would prefer not to. He had a generous heart and was sincerely interested in other people. He studied other people, as he had studied books with such interest, and his greatest satisfaction came from understanding what was going on within another person. Sure, he had his angry, explosive side, but that only arose when he felt directly criticized and attacked. Without such a challenge, he had no interest in domination. The question was how much he would be challenged in the group, especially after he had warned everybody about his capabilities, when he told about his past and his explosive rage.

Marcia was another possibility. She had the hunger for others' attention. She clearly enjoyed the sense of power and confidence she had developed after the divorce. And she had certainly jumped right into the group process and made some very challenging statements to Joe. Yes, maybe it would be Marcia. On the other hand, Joe's confidence and unworried bluntness might allow him to overtake Marcia. Group members either admire or hate those who appear to lack any anxiety. The way things were going, Joe had certainly inspired more dislike than admiration, but David had seen too many of his assumptions overturned too many times to place that much stock in his own predictions. So the race was

NEVER FORGET MY SOUL

presently between Tyrone, Marcia and Joe. The others had too little a sense of their own power to vie for leadership at this point.

As David continued to jog, he thought of some of the special relationships that were arising in the group. David was convinced that Tyrone's potential for explosive rage was very frightening to Grace and reminded her of the abusive outbursts she had received from her father. David was actually worried about Grace. She had been so quiet and withdrawn in the past two groups. Her eyes would glaze over and David suspected she was reliving the abuse, during the group, in such an intense manner that she was unable to interact with the others. She would need more assistance from him in the future to stay engaged in the present, so that the group did not forget her entirely.

He thought of other developing group relationships: Marcia had become Terry's "mother" and Terry her "daughter." Joe had become the cheating husband/father that had been featured in each of their lives. Adam had told David in individual therapy that Grace, in her pitiful helplessness, reminded him of his mother, who had been chronically ill with psychosomatic ailments.

And what about Joe? Who was significant to him? Of course, according to Joe, no one was significant to him, because he claimed to be oblivious to relationships. But something very interesting was happening in the group. Joe was somehow unsettled by the person David would have thought would be the most unlikely of challengers — Adam. The sense of dislike and opposition was mutual there. There was a dry, hot, crackling tension between Joe and Adam, and David did not understand its origin. Sure, there were the obvious differences. On the one side there was Adam — serious, religious, and moralistic: a family man, who valued his place in his community and in society. On the other side was Joe — a flippant, irreverent, selfish, sensation seeker who was out for himself and could not care less about society. One of David's students might propose these differences as the cause for the acrimony, but David was too experienced to be fooled by such surface characteristics. He had known many extremely different people who could develop at least the ability to tolerate each other. In David's experience, when an interaction crackled with this level of animosity, the two group members were not fighting over their differences, they were fighting over a similarity. This similarity invariably involved a parallel life experience or relationship that both had encountered and to which both had to adjust. *But what was that similarity?*

Joe had spoken to David in individual therapy about his overbearing, autocratic father, and his mother who worried about him too much. The angry outbursts of Joe's father had parallels with those of Adam's father, but there was an important difference. Adam's father was intensely involved with his children, while Joe's father treated his children as an inconvenience, who merely interfered with his own enjoyment. Surely, the difference between these two fathers was so great that Joe and Adam did not sense that their fathers had had a similar emotional tone. And as for the mothers, Adam's mother was terrified of the world and hid from it, while Joe's mother was a successful lawyer, who was quite functional and respected by many. The powerful link between Joe and Adam was not explained by their parents. Now, Joe's mother was Jewish and Adam was a committed observant Jew, but how significant could those factors be? Joe had told David that religion meant nothing to him, because he was only interested in things he could touch. In addition, Joe's father was Christian, and his mother was ambivalent about what Judaism meant to her. No, the Jewish connection did not explain anything.

David was approaching the darkest portion of the path. The incline of the path increased, and David felt himself exert more effort in the back of his legs, as he tried to maintain the same pace. He enjoyed working against the resistance of the hill. He listened to the rhythm of his footfalls against the ground beneath him. His

NEVER FORGET MY SOUL

thoughts turned back to Joe and Adam, and he considered some other possible explanations, but nothing was satisfying. Then David entered the clearing, ran to the top of the hill and saw the valley sloping away beneath him. The sun was becoming golden orange as it lowered itself towards the horizon, making the surrounding scenery glow with the same light. David sensed the approach of evening, followed by night and then sleep beside his beautiful Margaret. David had learned that when his mind was stuck on a problem for a long time, it was best to let go of the problem and sleep on it. Perhaps the new day would bring new insight. He looked out at the reddening sky once more and breathed in the fresh air deeply, extending his arms in a wide circle. He then returned once more to the dark wood, towards the peace and security of home.

CHAPTER FIVE

dam sat in the waiting room of David's office at 6:55 on the next Wednesday evening. He had chosen a chair in the corner of the room, in order to create some physical distance between himself and the other group members who were waiting. On the other side of the waiting room, Tyrone, Terry and Marcia sat on adjoining chairs, discussing who they thought would be the ultimate winner of the latest reality TV show competition. At precisely seven o'clock, the door to David's office opened, and David appeared with a warm smile, inviting the group members to enter. The four group members chose their positions in the circle of chairs. Adam always chose the same chair — the one closest to the door. Grace appeared just as David was beginning to close the door and Joe entered a few moments later.

Adam still felt uncomfortable in the group. He knew that his thinking was irrational, but he always felt like all eyes were on him, and that his every movement and every word were being evaluated and criticized. Adam had learned strategies to create an emotional buffer between himself and other people, so that the emotional intensity of their impact on him would be lessened. He began utilizing one of those strategies — instead of focusing on the other people in the room, he focused on the room itself, letting the people in the room fade into the background. Across the room from Adam was David's large desk, with a pile of files on the left front of the desk and two neat piles of papers on the back right. A thick book lay open on the middle-front workspace of the desk, where Adam could get a glimpse of dense lines of text. David sat in a high-backed swivel chair with his back to the desk, facing the group. Above the desk was a painting of a forest. Most of the image was shrouded in the darkness of the forest, where one could make out the black vertical lines of tree trunks, dark foliage and a forest floor covered with dry brown leaves and a couple of fallen tree trunks. A small section in the background of the painting stood in stark contrast to the dark, dismal mood of the foreground. This background revealed a clearing in the forest, a clearing that seemed very distant and yet strangely close at the same time. In that clearing, one could get glimpses of blue sky, lush green grass, rich orange autumn leaves and golden sunlight. Adam felt strangely reassured by this painting. On each side of the painting were windows, which, during the day, showed a view of surrounding shops and houses, but at this time only showed the dark of night and small areas of illumination from street lights and windows below. The wall to the right of Adam was lined with a large bookcase, covering most of the wall and nearly touching the ceiling. Adam wondered how many books were there — perhaps a thousand. Had David really read all of those books? On the left wall was a clock and a painting of a mother bathing a child who appeared to be six months old. The child looked healthy, happy and well-fed, with fat legs and a big round stomach. The mother was holding the child up in a free-standing circular tub and was engrossed in rubbing the child's back with soap. The baby appeared to feel completely safe in its mother's care, and the mother had a serene and loving look on her face. "So what's on the wall behind me?" Adam asked himself, then he remembered - diplomas and certificates, that was it, David had his share of them. Adam had been able to study them briefly in the past — Ph.D. in Psychology from Harvard, Master's from the University of Virginia, Licenses in Pennsylvania and New York, and various certificates and awards.

While Adam studied the walls, David studied the group. David knew that the first few moments spoke volumes. How the clients entered the room, when they entered the room (late or early), their posture, what their eyes were doing, superficial comments made to each other — all these elements were hints to the patients' concerns, fears, worries and struggles. David noticed how Adam's eyes avoided his gaze and the gaze of everyone else. To Adam's right sat Grace, who had her hair tied back in a ponytail. She wore a gray dress, black stockings and an oversized gray matching sweater. Her hands were folded in her lap and she sat relatively motionless, but her eyes moved from face to face within the circle. Marcia was to Grace's right and immediately to David's left. Marcia wore a colorful pants suit, in which swirls of pastel pink, turquoise and yellow played against each other. She looked comfortable, confident and ... hungry, yes, hungry to be noticed and appreciated. Terry was next in the circle, on David's right. She slumped in her seat, with a far-away look in her eyes. She looked as if she carried a great weight and was growing wearier by the minute. To her right sat Tyrone. He was dressed in his normal professional attire. He looked much less broken than he did last week. His face still seemed troubled and his demeanor seemed burdened, but he appeared to have regained some of his previous aura of strength and authority. Finally, there was Joe, dressed in a blue tracksuit. He jiggled his foot and appeared to be staring at one spot on the wall opposite him.

To David's surprise, Grace was the first to speak.

"I went out on a date last night," she began. "I get so fed up with dates — they are always the same. As long as the man is talking, I'm relatively OK. I nod, try to appear as interested as I can. I ask the occasional question. But then the man says something like, 'And what about you' or, 'What do you think,' and then I panic. I mean, my mind goes blank, completely blank. I cannot, for the life of me, tell him anything interesting about myself, and I have no idea what I think about anything. And then I start thinking, well, he must think I'm a complete idiot, like I can't even talk. I go through the evening with these thoughts and just pray to God that the whole thing will end. Finally, it does and I rush away as soon as I can, convinced that the man is happy to get rid of me. I feel like I've wasted his time and my time, and I get mad at the people who rope me into these things. That's why I usually avoid dates. They never lead to anything. They just make me feel worse. The man never calls again. Who am I — "

"Grace," interrupted Joe, "you know what your problem is?"

"What?" asked Grace, with a tone of voice indicating that she would rather avoid his notice and commentary entirely.

"You can't think, because you're so afraid," Joe continued. "It makes your mind shut down. Why do you care whether he thinks you're smart or dumb or the Queen of Sheba? It doesn't matter what he thinks. What matters is how you feel. Do you enjoy being with him? Is he interesting? Do you like listening to him? Does he turn you on? When I'm with a woman, these are the things I think about. Look, Grace, let's say that a guy thinks you're dumb, real dumb, what's the worst that will happen?"

Grace responded in a somewhat warmer manner, perhaps because she sensed that Joe cared and wanted to help. "The worst that will happen, I guess, is that he might think I'm an imbecile and not call again. It might sound mundane, but it hurts every time it happens."

"But why should it hurt?" responded Joe. "Why do you weigh your value based on whether some jerk liked you or not? I think you get hurt because you do not even try. You were so afraid of him not liking you, that you forsake what's most important — what you feel, what you want. These things could go totally different for you. You could think: there's a lot of idiots out there and some guys I enjoy. Let me meet a few people, just be myself, see who I like to be with. If it doesn't work out, meet a few more people. Look, Grace, I try to speak my mind with other people. If I offend, so be it. At least people know what they're getting. I don't try to please and I don't try to pretend, and I tell whoever I am with that I want the same from them. In the end, it turns out to be a lot more fun, with no guilt, worry or blame."

Grace responded, "That all seems to come so easy when you say it, Joe. Still, when you talk, the first thing that comes to mind is that those things work for you, probably because you were raised in a different kind of home. I was repeatedly abused by my father — sexual and physical abuse. He also beat up my mother and brothers countless times. But you know, of all the things that he did, the thing that I carry with me most heavily is his constant, terrible condemnation — 'You're fat, you're ugly, you stupid bitch.' The bastard, on the same night that he would call me a lazy fat cow, he would crawl into my bed, a few hours later, and start fondling me. And you know what was the worst of it?! As much as those night-time visits repulsed me … I also … treasured them! It was the only time he spoke nicely to me. He would call me his queen, say that I was beautiful, that there was no one in the world so precious to him, that he hated himself for the mean things that he did to me!"

She buried her face in her hands and began to cry. No one spoke. It was moments like this that were most difficult for David. He intensely wanted to speak, to reassure her, to soothe her wounds, but he knew that what she needed the most was for him *not* to speak. And she needed to reveal this wound to the others without his help, to fear the attack and condemnation of others and then to respond to the actual reactions of others. The group stayed silent. It seemed as if the whole group had become a reflection of the anxious Grace on a date, paralyzed in the intensity of this encounter with another person. Joe looked particularly lost. His brow furrowed, he frowned, and his eyes darted back and forth, as if he were intensely thinking of something to say. He appeared tense and uncomfortable and shook his leg vigorously.

Finally, Grace spoke again, "For many years I avoided any dates because I knew that my father screwed up my head so much that there was no way I could tolerate them. But I'm lonely. So I go out. But the fear of the judgment, anger, and condemnation is just so strong. It's hopeless, I'm a hopeless case."

"The past *was* hopeless," said Joe. His demeanor appeared to have changed — he was no longer troubled. He had the same intensity, but he no longer appeared lost. His body leaned forward, and his dark eyes seemed very engaged with Grace. "But that was the past. Grace, you seem like a nice enough woman to me and you're pretty, too. You just tell yourself that maybe your bastard of a father robbed your youth, but he is not going to rob your happiness now. I'm sure there were plenty of times you wanted to hurt him back. Well, this is your way to fight back. Don't give in to him. Don't let him win. If you give up on yourself, you let him win. But, I don't think you will let him win. That's why you're talking about him now — so you can solve this problem, and move on, so you can be yourself and start living."

Grace smiled, "Thanks, Joe," she responded. "I'll think about it." She paused, as if uncertain to go on, and then said, "Actually, I'll take a risk right now and say something I'm not sure how you'll take. When I first met you, I thought you were pretty much a self-centered jerk. But you're being very helpful tonight. You're giving good advice and I really get the feeling that you care."

"Look," said Joe, "if I'm saying things that are helpful to you, fine. But I'm not saying them for *you*. I'm here in this group to help myself. When I hear people talk about mistreatment in their youth and how hopeless it makes them feel, I begin to think about those things in my own life. Those thoughts make me uncomfortable, so I start to talk about things that I do for myself to overcome those feelings. It makes *me* feel better. It changes my focus from helplessness to… well, not so helpless. I'm not ashamed that I'm in this group for myself. I think everyone should be. Let's not delude ourselves that this is a social group or that we're good friends. We are in here to maybe learn something and then feel better or make things better… then we'll move on."

Grace looked thoughtful and then said, "You know Joe, right now it really doesn't matter to me why you said what you said. I felt you listening and responding to me and what you said was helpful. I'm still grateful."

Joe shrugged, glanced at Grace and then stared at the wall.

Terry spoke next, "Grace, you have a lot of guts to be so open about the way your father treated you. It must not be easy to talk about. I wanted to tell you that when you were talking about dating, it struck a chord with me. I also have a problem with dating, not the same problem, but it's related. As I've described, I've got this chronic illness that no one can explain. Whenever I get asked out, I try to avoid the topic. I mean, I have no problem talking to anyone. I enjoy conversation with people, especially men who think I'm attractive. But the problem is that whenever the conversation gets steered around to my professional past or present, then I start to feel worried and embarrassed. I don't want them to ask why I'm not working any more. I don't want them to know that I'm sick. Because who wants to date a sick girl? They'll just think, maybe there is something very wrong with her, maybe she'll die or at least won't be able to have children, better not get involved. So I hide it, as long as I can. And then, when they find out, which they eventually do, I think they resent my secretiveness. So I haven't dated for a while, so I can avoid this whole struggle."

"It's the same thing that I said to Grace," said Joe. "Why do people worry so much about what others think about them? If I were you, I would tell men about your illness as early as possible. If they run, it just shows they are more interested in getting a perfect woman than enjoying a real one. Look at it, Terry. You're attractive, you're really smart, you enjoy good conversation. Why hide things? Let the fainthearted run after some dream of a secure and perfectly planned life, and the ones that remain are the ones for you anyway."

"Well, it does make sense, Joe," responded Terry. "It may not be easy, but it seems like it is the way to go."

"I have to agree with Grace," said Marcia. "I really didn't like you when I first met you, Joe. And until tonight, I had seen nothing to change my impression. But tonight, you're making a lot of sense, even giving me something to think about. Yeah, I might look confident, but lots of times I worry about the impression that I'm making on a date. It gets tiresome after a while, takes all of the magic out of it. I know you say you're just interested in helping yourself in this group, but the way you are acting *is* helping others. Maybe you care more than you realize. I just wish you weren't cheating on your wife. It makes it so much harder to completely like you."

"Look, I'm not a priest," said Joe. "I'm a man, and I need to have sex with someone who feels alive to me. My wife is not that, so I had to find a way to deal with it. I didn't want things to be this way. When I married her, we were very turned on by each other — the sex was great at first, really great. Then the first kid came and things took a nosedive. She just wasn't interested in sex anymore. What am I supposed to do? Get divorced, end up giving all our money to lawyers and tearing our kids into pieces? I love my kids too much and I'm not doing that to them, so what option do I have left? I'm not the first man who has chosen such a solution to things."

"I want to like you, Joe, I *really* want to like you," answered Marcia. "Well, let's just say that my husband wandered when our relationship was good, really good. So I'll say you and he are different. Then, maybe I can let myself like you."

"That's between you and you," said Joe with an unconcerned tone in his voice. "It won't make or break me either way."

"Well, it *does* matter to me," said Marcia. "I wanted to cry for Grace earlier. She's been so hurt. I wanted to say something to her, but I did not know what to say. And right away, you instinctively knew what to say. She felt supported by you, and that was beautiful. It somehow seems very important to me right now that I can let myself like you."

Joe shrugged and made no response.

The group was silent for half a minute. Finally, Tyrone spoke, "I'd like to say a few things. First, I think Joe's point of view is refreshing. He says he's here to help himself. There's nothing bad about that. It's the truth. Isn't that why we're all here? Second, he's right, absolutely right. It is terribly hard to enjoy anything with anyone if we feel we constantly have to wear a mask. I'm like Joe. What you see is what you get. It's a strategy that's always worked for me, because it helped me identify who my true friends were. If they were willing to put up with me as I am, I wouldn't have to worry if they found out something about me and wanted to drop me. So I try to tell them as much about me as possible. Anyway, I wanted to catch the group up on the saga of me and my wife. I spoke with her on the phone yesterday. I told her I missed her. I promised I would do my best to work hard in therapy and examine what's eating at me. I told her that I told you all my story last week, and that it felt good to share it. She said that she will come back. She just wants another week away. She wants me to know that she means business this time and that things have to change. She never just left like this before. I feel very lucky that she's willing to come back. I don't know what I would do without her."

"So what is it going to take for things to be different in the future?" asked David.

"Well, we've spoken about that, David. I have to learn how to trust a relationship, right?"

David gave the barest trace of a nod, as if to indicate not agreement, but only that he had heard Tyrone's statement. David often used this technique, when a group member was looking for answers from him, and David felt that it was not productive to help the client avoid the struggle of figuring out the answer for himself.

"So how do you trust a relationship?" asked Marcia.

"Well, I'm not sure," answered Tyrone. "I did not grow up with healthy relationships. My father was only a source of pain, and Ma was cold. I couldn't rely on either of them. So who was there? My peers on the street? Some were the most devious, manipulative, violent and selfish kids you could ever meet. Some were more solid, they stuck with you, but there was a distance at the core of even those relationships. We did not let ourselves care too much, because we knew we could lose each other at any time. So, then there was Eva. She gave love without reservation, and for a while I began to feel safe with her. But then what happened? She couldn't be there either. It doesn't matter that leaving wasn't her choice. The conclusion for me is the same. I just can't rely on anyone."

"Seems to me," said Marcia, "that perhaps the purpose of this group is to learn how to do that. *We* can be those relationships that are solid and honest and supportive, and when we are together long enough and begin to trust each other enough, we'll start to let down our guard. We can need each other and respond to each other in a caring way, just as Joe did tonight. Maybe we can learn here that we can be soft and not be hurt again."

"But that can only happen over time," said Grace. "I know I have a lot more crying to do. I want to see if you all can't take it and disappear before I'm finished. I'm not sure how far I'm willing to go with opening up in here, if I don't feel you all are in it for the long haul."

NEVER FORGET MY SOUL

"Well," answered Marcia, "David suggested that I make a year commitment to the group, not an official thing, but I intend to stay at least that long, before I conclude that I won't get anything out of it any more. That sounds like a good idea to me."

"I'm not good at such exact time lines," answered Grace, "but at least if I know that no one will be leaving abruptly, I'll be more willing to keep my guard down in here. Are there any rules about that?"

Everyone expected David to answer, but he remained silent. He felt it very important that the group pursue this present discussion without his assistance.

"Well, that sounds like a reasonable request," said Terry. "I'm certainly willing to say that I will give the group two months' notice before I leave."

"I'll do the same," said Grace.

"Well, I'll be here for a year," said Marcia, "and I'm willing to promise two months' notice after that."

"I'll give two months' notice, too," said Tyrone, "and I'm with Marcia — I'll be here for at least a year. David suggested that to me as well."

"Two months' notice is fine with me," Adam added. Although he had had difficulty entering into the discussion this evening, he felt that everyone was expected to provide some response at this point.

"Sorry to break up the party," Joe remarked, "but I don't agree with any of this. I'm in this thing as long as I'm getting something out of it. I don't stand on ceremony and I don't do things out of duty. I come here, I'll talk, I'll listen. I'm still skeptical about getting anything out of any of this, but this seems the best option for now. I've tried medication, and that did nothing for me. It just made me feel like I was floating, like I couldn't feel myself. It was a messed up feeling. So I'll come here and maybe it will help me. But I don't *owe* anything to David or any of you. So I'm not making any promises about when I'll come or when I'll leave."

"But that doesn't make me feel safe," complained Grace. "How can I trust you, how can I open up, when you might just be gone next week?"

Joe's face turned very serious. "Grace, I could be hit by a car tomorrow or have a massive coronary, or maybe I'll be shot in the streets by one of Tyrone's old compatriots. What are you trying to rely on? All we have is now. We're here to be ourselves and be honest, not fabricate more rules to weigh us down and further complicate our lives. If I start making promises to you, then I can't be in this group for me. And you'll screw up the group for yourself, if you feel you have to start making promises. No, you'll see me here as long as it makes sense for me to come. I'm not going to be your tower of strength or your shoulder to cry on."

"But Joe," responded David, "I sense that today you were both of those things for Grace, both powerful and a support, and she is hoping that those things will not disappear."

Joe responded with an angry tone in his voice, "David, I've gotten into this with you before. I live my life now and for me. I don't believe in anything else. You are not going to make me into an image of you."

David smiled, "Joe, you are such an exceptionally good liar."

"I really don't care what you or anyone else in this group thinks about my truthfulness or reliability or anything else," answered Joe. "I'm here to use what I can and then I'll leave."

"Joe, if you live your life just for you, then why do you stay in your marriage because of your children?" asked David.

"That's different, they're just an extension of me. Caring about them is the same thing as caring about myself," Joe responded.

David paused. Mentally, he took a step back and surveyed the psychological territory that they had entered. Joe had taken a leading role in the group today. The group had then coalesced around a commitment to be available for each other and Joe had, predictably, and quite forcefully, resisted this pull. David was now challenging Joe's stance of untouchability and unconcern. Joe certainly could use such a challenge, but David felt himself getting too drawn into a struggle that would be better handled by other group members. David thought of eliciting responses from the group. But then he remembered Adam. Adam — who appeared to have almost disappeared today. Whenever David had glanced at Adam, he looked tense and disengaged. The session time was drawing to a close and David wanted to somehow bring Adam into it. But he did not want to blatantly invite Adam to enter into another fight with Joe. It was up to Adam to decide if he wanted that. David turned to Adam and said "Adam, you've been very quiet today. I wonder how you've been reacting to the discussion."

Adam did not look at David. He continued staring at the wall and responded, "No children should be an extension of their parents. When children are an extension of their parents, they are sacrificial animals, nothing more, sacrificed to the whims and needs of their parents. You can't love someone who is just an extension of you. You can only use them."

"Whatever," responded Joe, rolling his eyes. "Thank you, Mister Philosopher. I am not guilty as charged. I've got a good relationship with my kids. They would be a lot more messed up if they were just stuck with their mother. She yells at them, but never follows through on anything. They know that when I say they have to do something I mean business. But I can also talk *with* them, reason with them, so they stay out of trouble in the first place. Maybe you just have a guilty conscience about something, Mister Philosopher. Or is it just your fine religion that teaches you to look for the worst in people?"

There was so much that Adam wanted to say. *His fine religion!* Yes, his fine religion! It was only when he had learned about an observant Jewish way of life that he had learned that it was possible to look for the best in others. He had been raised to see the worst in others — that was all his parents could see in their self-imposed isolation from a world that was entirely too frightening to trust. But the comment about Adam's religion was not what truly angered Adam. It was the stupidity of this selfish bastard who was persisting in the same blindness that Adam's parents had — thinking that love meant that there is no boundary between the lover and the object of one's love. Such a "love" is not love, it's suffocation, thought Adam, and Adam wanted to shed tears for Joe's children, even though Adam had never met them. Adam's parents had had no existence separate from their children, who were their whole meaning in life. For his parents, the past was only shrieking death and destruction. The only hope for life was through the children. The moment his parents contemplated any separation from their children, it was like all of his parents' life would be snatched away from them. That is why his parents had taught Adam that the world is a dangerous place and that he was ill-equipped to cope with it. The only protection from this danger was the family — a protection that was really designed for the parents themselves, not for the yearning spirits of youth, who desire to explore, discover and risk. How many times and in how many ways had Adam and his sister felt the heavy burden of guilt, as they tentatively ventured out of their parents' world and felt they were mortally wounding them by doing so? There was so much Adam wanted to say, so much he wanted to yell — just like he had wanted to yell at his father, countless times, but had never done so.

Adam was beginning to formulate a response when he glanced at Joe. The combination of scorn and rage in Joe's eyes snatched all words out of Adam's mind. Adam was suddenly with his father, who was grabbing Adam by the collar to pull Adam away from a scuffle with his sister. Adam's father violently pulled him into the children's room and threw him upon his bed.

"**YOU LITTLE SH**!**" his father bellowed. "Is it not enough that I had to see all of my family murdered!? Is it not enough that your mother was beaten up and laughed at and dragged through the death camp, just like me!? Now we have to watch you torture us, fighting endlessly with your sister over nothing! You're ungrateful! Both of you! You want to drag your mother into the grave!"

His father's face was a few inches away from his. Adam lay immobilized on the bed. His father's face was red with fury, his eyes wide, his breath hot.

Adam wanted to speak, to explain, to talk about his sister's part in the fight. But he knew that if he said a word, he would be smacked in the face. It had happened before. His father glared at him for a few more moments and stormed out of the room.

Adam could see Joe again. His father's image had faded, but the mood from that interchange with his father long ago was still present. Adam was frozen in that moment, immobilized by the rage. As much as Adam saw hatred projected towards him, Adam felt hatred — hatred for men who ask too much from their children, hatred for men who are so lost in a merciless world that they look to their children to soothe their way, hatred for his father, hatred for Joe. Adam felt he had to speak — for the sake of all the children — and as he had done so many times before, Adam betrayed himself, and all those children. He could not face the slap.

"I'm just talking about myself and my life," he said. "This is the way it was in my family. Maybe it doesn't apply to you." Adam knew the last part was a lie. He knew what he had said applied to Joe. Adam felt it in his gut, but he could not face the slap.

CHAPTER SIX

When Joe awoke the next Sunday morning, his wife, Lisa, was already downstairs making breakfast for their three children. Lisa liked to make Sunday mornings special for them. She had little time to cater to them on the weekdays, with her holding down a full-time job. So Sunday morning breakfast was made to order — pancakes, eggs, bacon, toast with butter and jam — whatever pleased each of them on that day. Joe could hear the three boys arguing about something downstairs, with Lisa intermittently yelling that the boys should "Stop it!"

"Joe swore to himself, thinking that he was the one bringing the real income into this family, and he deserved some rest. Couldn't she control them enough to let him sleep a little later on a Sunday morning? Joe yawned, stretched, put on his bathrobe and quickly went downstairs to see what the problem was. As he descended the stairs, he saw his eldest, Rick, who was eleven years old, straddling nine-year-old Timmy, who was lying with his back on the floor. Rick had Timmy's hands pinned to the floor and Timmy was flailing his legs and yelling something unintelligible at the top of his lungs. Robert, the six-year-old, was trying to pull Rick off of Timmy, but the size disparity was too great for him to shift Rick.

"RICK, TIMMY, ROBERT, STOP IT! STOP IT NOW!!" boomed Joe.

The three boys looked up and were frozen, like animals caught in the glare of headlights.

"GET UP! ALL OF YOU!" Joe yelled, and they immediately complied. "Now I don't know who did what to whom, and I don't care. You are each to go up to your rooms and stay there until breakfast is ready. Any questions?" The boys did not respond. "Good — **SO GO!!!**"

All three ran upstairs without a word. Joe entered the kitchen. Lisa's back was to him as she was preparing an omelet on the stove. The sizzling sound of the eggs in the pan and the aroma in the air was making Joe hungry. Lisa was wearing jeans, which emphasized the slimness of her waist. Her silky dark brown hair hung in a tumble of curls against her back. For a moment he thought to himself, "What an attractive woman she is." Then she turned around, and his amorous feelings disappeared. For a number of years now, she only looked attractive to him when she was not looking at him. There was nothing really unpleasant in her expression now, and she had a pretty face. It just always happened that when they were looking at each other, he suddenly found her to be decidedly unappealing.

Lisa smiled at Joe and said, "I'm so glad you're here. I was having the worst time with them. Ricky has to be the boss of everyone. Timmy has really had it with him. Ricky told Timmy that Ricky wants to watch *his* shows. Timmy said it wasn't fair because there was something he wanted to watch on a different channel. So I told them we would compromise, fifteen minutes for Ricky, fifteen for Timmy. But then when they're in the living room, Ricky

NEVER FORGET MY SOUL

starts threatening Timmy and telling him to turn the TV to Ricky's channel and keep it there. So they started fighting about that. I had to pull them apart three or four times. After the shows were over, they started fighting about something else. I don't know what the last fight was about. You spared me that."

Joe's tone was dry and cold. "Who cares what it was about? You should just let them know that you won't take that sh** from them and they'll cut it out. Lisa, you plead with them, yell at them, pull them apart, but you don't really do anything to them. They know that — that's why they won't listen to you."

"Look, Joe," Lisa said with a note of conciliation in her voice. "I know they listen to you better and you're right; I have a hard time putting my foot down with them. I'm working on it. Let's not argue."

"I'm not arguing, and I'm not looking to argue. I just don't want to hear everyone's stories — their stories, your stories. I want to sit down, read the paper and have breakfast in peace!" He grabbed the newspaper off the kitchen counter and buried his face behind it. Lisa sighed and returned to her omelet. She had been hoping, an unreasonable hope, that perhaps if she were truly pleasant to Joe, the tone of their communication could change today. She had read in a woman's magazine that the woman sets the emotional tone of the house and that a pleasant smile and positive comment in the morning will create an improved relationship with one's spouse. So she had tried it today. Unfortunately, Joe appeared to have no interest in her tone. Still, she would not retaliate; maybe his mood would improve after breakfast.

As Lisa continued to prepare breakfast, her thoughts drifted to the day, twelve years ago, that she first met Joe. She and a female friend had attended a "mixer" for singles. At the time, Lisa had been enrolled in nursing school, and Joe was two years out of medical school. The gathering had been a rather dull one, as mostly awkward graduate students clumped together in small groups and either joked in an inane and childish way or pontificated, transparently trying to impress members of the opposite sex. In her memory, Lisa was standing opposite a twenty-year-old "genius" who was bragging about his enrollment in a Ph.D. program at his young age, and explaining his abstruse theories of astrophysics to her. "Strange," she thought to herself, deliberately tuning out the boring drone of the young man, "he's only two years younger than me, but he seems like such a boy." She glanced around the room, in hopes of finding someone who did not look like a boy to her. Her eyes came to rest upon two dark brown eyes. The eyes belonged to a man who Lisa felt had been looking at her for quite a while. "Looking at her" were not quite the right words to describe what he was doing. He was "studying" her. No, that was not right either... Then the words "drinking me in" came to her mind, and she felt a tingle of excitement, mingled with the slightest hint of fear. The intensity of his stare caused her to look away and refocus her attention on the boy in front of her, who continued to drone and appeared to have had no awareness of the wandering of her eyes and her restless boredom with him. She *knew* that the brown-eyed man was looking at her, but she resisted looking back, starting to resent the brazenness of his stare. In the end, he won — she glanced back again, and his eyes were unchanged, staring fixedly at her. She briefly took note of his handsome face and broad, athletic build. It seemed as if he took her second glance as a signal, because, after she glanced at him a second time, he approached her. When she saw this, she quickly looked down. She muttered an expletive and thought "he's coming, what do I do now? ... Just listen to Junior here, maybe Mr. Brown-eyes will go away." Lisa suddenly feigned an overwhelming interest in astrophysics and began to give animated nods to the boy's "lecture." When she saw Mr. Brown-eyes in her peripheral vision, she thought to herself, "just ignore him... just ignore." But his form remained, and she felt as if little magnets were drawing her eyes towards him. She glanced at him. He was making no attempt to join the conversation. He simply stood at arms length from her and continued to stare at her. She became angry. She was about to say, in as irritated a voice as she could muster, "I don't know who you are, but please stop staring at me. It's bothering me."

"Excuse me for a moment," she told the boy, as she turned to Joe, getting ready to give him the brush off.

When she turned to him, he smiled, in a warm and disarming manner, and said, "Allow me to introduce myself — I'm Joe Barns. Please excuse me for staring. It's just that I rarely have opportunity to gaze upon such beauty."

To this day, she did not know how he did it — how with that smile he could immediately melt her discomfort, calm her fears and entice her interest. But somehow he pulled it off, and half an hour later, they were sitting on the moonlit beach together, smoking a joint and laughing at the absurdity of life.

The romance that developed between Joe and Lisa brought all the excitement and chagrin that she had intuited on the day of their meeting. They would stay up all night dancing in nightclubs or dive naked into the ocean at midnight, followed by passionate sex on a blanket, amidst the sand dunes. In contrast to these joyous experiences were the many times that Joe would just disappear — not show up for dates, or be unreachable for days on end. He would apologize for missing their dates, with some lame excuse about being too absentminded. He did not provide an explanation for his "incommunicado" times, only saying that their relationship would only work if they could respect each other's privacy, and he did not want to discuss these extended absences further.

Then the day came when she told Joe that she had been to the doctor, who had told her that she was pregnant. Neither Joe nor Lisa had anticipated this and the news had come as a shock to Lisa, who was scrupulous about using birth control. When she told Joe, his face became serious. "Pregnant," he said, as if he were trying to comprehend the meaning of the word. He turned to her and asked, with a note of tentativeness, "So, what are you going to do?"

She paused, inhaled deeply, exhaled through pursed lips, and finally said, "I want to keep it, Joe. But I don't know. I'm still young. I'm not married. I haven't even graduated yet. How am I going to take care of a child myself?"

Joe's eyes became distant, impenetrable. He stared across the room for such an extended period of time that Lisa became concerned that something was wrong with him.

"Joe?" she said, seeking his response.

He turned to her and said, without further hesitation, "I'll marry you. We can have this child together."

She smiled, a grateful smile, feeling truly surprised that he would offer this.

"Thank you, Joe," she responded. "It's so nice of you to offer. I need to think about it. Let me get back to you. OK?"

He looked at her with earnest, almost pleading eyes, "I want to raise this baby with you and I want you to be my wife," he said. "It will be hard waiting for your answer, but I will. Let me know as soon as you can." He kissed her on the lips, turned and left the building.

The next day, Lisa talked Joe's proposal over with her best friend, Nancy.

"I don't know what to do, Nancy," Lisa said. "Joe's not like any man I've ever met. I wonder, perhaps I just haven't dated enough men to have a good sense of these things. You know, I've only really been involved with three guys in my life, including Joe. But Joe — he seems like he's been out with almost every girl in town, and that bothers me. Maybe he'll just get bored with me after a while — he's so into variety. I always thought that Joe was great for a good time, but that I'd better be careful about getting too emotionally involved. I never thought of Joe in terms of marriage, until he asked me yesterday. There was something so touching about it

— his seriousness and the way he asked me. He said he wanted to 'raise the child with me.' I think he's fascinated with the prospect of having children. And that made me realize something about Joe — he's not all fun and games, there's another side to him. He doesn't like other people to see it. He wants people to see him as confident, doing his own thing his own way. But sometimes I see something different in him — something soft and sincere peeking out. Sometimes he looks like a lost and unloved boy, a boy who believes there must be love somewhere in this world but does not know where to find it. When he has that look, all I want to do is take him in my arms, soothe him, help him find his way."

"You can't marry a boy," said Nancy, with a note of irritation about Lisa's swell of romanticism. "You need a man to raise that baby with you."

"But he *is* a man, Nancy," Lisa insisted. "He's strong, brilliant, successful. He has a reputation around the hospital as being a rising star among the young physicians. I think he *can be responsible.*" Her emphasis on these words seemed to be as much a reassurance to herself as to Nancy. "And look what he did yesterday. He *immediately* did the honorable thing. He did not ask me to get rid of the baby. He proposed to me."

Lisa turned to the window. The snow was falling, and she could see two young children playing with a man on the front lawn, building a snowman. A young woman, apparently their mother, came outside with some large buttons and a carrot and gave it to the man to add to the creation. The young woman gave each of the children a kiss and then gave the man a longer kiss, stroking him on the cheek, before going inside.

"I always wanted my own family, Nancy," she said, not turning around. "Look at those kids. Isn't it sweet? I want that for myself, and I want a man like that on my front lawn. I've always been so afraid of risk. I don't want to be forty-five someday, wondering why I never lived my life. God tricked me, gave me a child before

I thought I was ready. Now I'm going to hold onto that child... and to the man that makes me happy." A tear welled up in her eye and she turned to Nancy. "You'll see. We'll make it work...we'll make it work."

Nancy took Lisa in her arms and they stood there in front of the window, holding each other for a long time, as the snow continued to fall, the children continued to play and Joe restlessly awaited Lisa's answer.

<hr>

Lisa was aroused from her reverie by the crackling of the omelet, which had started to burn. She turned it over to inspect the damage, found it irreparable, threw it out and started from scratch.

A half hour later, the three boys, Joe and Lisa were all sitting at the kitchen table. Lisa and the boys were finishing their breakfast, while Joe read the paper. Joe looked up from his paper and saw the three boys hungrily and happily clearing their plates. Joe felt a tingle of energy rise from his stomach to his chest. He loved to see their hunger, their activity, even their rambunctiousness, as long as it was not disturbing his life.

"How about a game of football?" he said, smiling broadly.

"Yeah!" all three of the boys yelled, responding to their father's enthusiasm.

"Joe," said Lisa, "remember we agreed that Rick and Timmy would do their homework first thing today, so we don't have the same problem of leaving it to the last minute like last week?"

Joe glanced at his wife. She had a serious expression on her face, with a note of irritation. Then he looked at the children. Their eyes were pleading.

"Awww," said Rick, "Dad, please? Look outside. It's such a great day for football. Let's do it before it rains."

"It's not going to rain today," responded Lisa sternly. She

looked to Joe for support, for him to keep his promise that he would make them do their homework earlier in the day. Usually, weekend homework got pushed off and pushed off, until it was late, the kids were overtired, and homework either become a terrible showdown or it just didn't get done. Lisa had had enough of this.

Robert got up from his chair and climbed into Joe's lap. Joe wrapped his arms around his son and enjoyed the warmth of his son's body against his. "Daddy, please? It's not fair. You said it alweady."

Joe recalled when he was six and how he had yearned for his own father to throw a ball with him, play a game with him, even talk to him. But all that his father had given him was a scowl and an order to stop disturbing his work. No — it did not matter what Lisa said or if Joe had promised something to her or not. These kids deserved a childhood.

"Homework can wait," Joe announced decisively as he led the boys outside into the spring morning. Lisa threw her fork to the floor and ran up the stairs to her bedroom to weep.

As Joe and the children exited the house, the air was slightly cool and exhilarating. The sun warmed their heads and backs as they set up their goalposts — a soccer ball, a toy car, and two sand buckets. The grass still had little droplets of water on it, which glistened in the sun. This was Joe's favorite part of the day, in his favorite part of the year. The electricity of spring — he felt it deep within him — the hunger of the animals to come out of their hiding places and find a mate, the hunger of the trees to blossom again, the pollen — that driving force of life — that he could smell in the air. Joe announced the teams — he and Robert against the two other boys. Joe was a strong man who easily could have overpowered all three boys at once, but he played his part in this morning contest, as the perfect father. He was challenging enough to Rick and Timmy, so that they would enjoy the competition, but not so much so as to frustrate them. At the same time, he did not exclude Robert, even though he was so much smaller than the others. Joe would plan his play in the huddle with Robert. Robert would go to his designated position. The two boys then had to choose between both of them trying to cover their father or one of them covering Robert. Double-teaming was clearly necessary to have any impact on Joe's maneuvering through the yard. But when Rick and Timmy double-teamed Joe, he would sometimes deftly dodge them, give a quick sideways pass to Robert, just as quickly receive Robert's return pass and run for a touchdown, with Robert cheering. But Rick and Timmy would always have their revenge, and so the competition continued, moment after glorious moment.

After about an hour of play, the boys were so winded and tired that they were sure they could not take anymore. Then Joe announced what was always his favorite part of their play together.

"Wrestling time!" he announced to his sons, who lie panting on the grass. He was sitting beside them. The boys knew exactly what this meant and Joe's announcement appeared to give them a second wind. Robert grabbed onto Joe's shirt, Timmy wrapped himself around Joe's leg, and Rick grabbed Joe's waist. The object was for all three of them to pin their father to the ground. Joe could have stood and freed himself from the burden, but he never did, for the best part was when they pulled him to the ground and he felt them climbing all over him, trying to pin his arms, legs and back to the ground. He never felt closer to his children than during these wrestling times. He loved the sound of their quickened breath, the sight of their determined faces, the feeling of their muscles straining against his and the warmth of their bodies piled on him. It was in moments like these that Joe could be alive with them and feel their aliveness. Joe drank in the adrenalin, the rapid beats of their hearts. He was a bear in a playful tumble with his cubs, unburdened, untroubled and free. For Joe, this and *only this* was life.

When Joe and the boys returned to the house, Lisa had

composed herself enough to calmly ask Joe if he would speak with her in private.

"There's nothing we have to hide from the boys. Let's just talk reasonably and we can talk here," said Joe.

"Fine, whatever," responded Lisa, although she sensed that she was making a mistake. She was just so tired of all this. "Are all *four* boys finished playing?" she asked, her voice thick with sarcasm.

"What is that supposed to mean!?" demanded Joe.

"It *means* that you went out there because *you* wanted to play, and little things like responsibility and promises just shouldn't get in the way, should they?"

Lisa's eyebrows were raised, and her face was twisted into a superior expression that Joe hated. "What's your problem!" he said. "You need them to do homework? Fine, they'll do homework! You're just afraid of them! You feel you have to drag them to do homework before they even get a chance to breathe, so you get it over with and don't have to dread it. The kids have to play, too. They're just kids…Look, I'll get Rick to do homework. I'll do it right now!"

Joe went to the family room where he found Rick playing a computer game.

"Rick, off now," Joe said, his voiced filled with irritation. "It's time to do your homework."

"Awww, Dad, I was just getting into the good part of the game. Look! I got to level two. I never did that before."

Joe strode up to his son and grabbed him by the ear. "**NOW, I SAID,**" Joe yelled and pulled his son to his room. When they entered the room, Joe pushed his son into a chair. "You have no idea how lucky you are!" Joe yelled in his face. "You're spoiled! You have anything money can buy, while I break my ass making it for you! I play games with you, I take you places, I listen to you. When I was your age, my father hardly knew I was alive! When I tell you to do something, you do it. That's it. No discussion. There are fun times and work times. We did the fun time already. Now get to work!"

Rick looked at his father with an odd type of defiance, which Joe had not seen before.

"**NO!**" said Rick.

"*What!?*" his father asked.

"No." repeated Rick. "I'm sick of your all-you-do-for-us and how your father ignored you. To hell with you! I've had it with this place — your craziness, Mom's craziness. You two need babysitters!"

Joe was temporarily stunned. Then, suddenly, he found his hand acting of its own volition and slapping his son across the face.

Rick did not cry. He hardly reacted at all to the slap. He merely turned around calmly and picked up a backpack from the floor. He then proceeded to grab clothes from his drawers and stuff them into the bag.

"What are you doing?" Joe asked.

"I'm leaving," responded his son. "I'm just leaving. I gotta get out of here."

Joe gently but firmly took hold of his son's shoulders and forced him to sit on his bed. Rick did not resist.

Joe spoke to him quietly, "Ricky, you have nowhere to go. You're only eleven years old. You don't have to like it here, but this is your place until you're eighteen. Look, just stay here and calm down and after you've calmed down ... just do your homework."

Rick did not respond to his father, nor did he look at him. He just sat motionless on the bed. Joe turned around, left the bedroom and closed the door.

———◦◦◦———

It was now the evening of the same day, and Joe drove along the dark streets, in excited anticipation of a liaison with his mistress.

NEVER FORGET MY SOUL

He felt a thrilling tingle in his body, which had been refreshed and reinvigorated by his afternoon activities. He was in the process of training for a local triathlon competition. That afternoon, he had worked on the swimming and biking portion. He had biked twenty miles to a lake. He remembered the delicious wind rushing past his face, whistling in his ears, as he relished pushing himself and his bike to higher and higher speeds. He was in "the zone" — that unification of mind and body, when the lungs rapidly take in air and the heart greedily laps up oxygen, when "will" and "doing" are one. Occasionally, he would feel fatigue in his leg muscles. He especially enjoyed the challenge of such moments — the pull down of body and emotions, the drive to do more, the willful push forward, and the adrenalin rush, as he discovered newfound energy. When he arrived at the lake, he lay down his bike, quickly removed his shoes, socks and T-shirt and dived into the cool water. It was about half a mile to the other side of the lake. He churned through the water, with powerful overhand strokes and rhythmic sideways breaths. He rarely paused as he single-mindedly pulled himself across the lake. When he tired, he would create an image in his mind of Ann, his mistress, on the other side. In his imagination, she was waiting there for him, reclined in her bathing suit, relaxing and soaking in the sun. He imagined the redness of her lips, her soft blue eyes, her smile indicating that she knew what he wanted. He imagined her watching him there, out in the water, her excitement as she saw the strength with which he stroked through the water to her. His muscles swelled with pride, and he picked up his pace. Finally he emerged from the water, panting, spent, ready to fall in a contented heap on the ground, to rest, and to recover, until he was ready for his next adventure.

Activity, challenge, movement, stimulation — these things were essential to Joe. It was the only way to live. Sitting around, talking, passively whiling one's life away — that was for the almost dead, like his mother-in-law playing bingo in the old-age home, her memory slowly slipping away from her, looking more like a corpse every day. He hated old people's homes. In fact, he hated the old. He supposed he should have pity for them, but he only had scorn — scorn for their uselessness, scorn for their endless needs and helplessness and the way that they produce nothing. But most of all he scorned their passivity, as he scorned the passivity of any person, young or old. That was perhaps the thing that estranged him most from Lisa. She wanted to "talk," to "relate," to "share," she used all these puffy female words, but what did they all really mean? Joe didn't want to relate, not in the way she meant it. He wanted to feel her, to rub himself against her silky skin, to listen to her panting breath, as she was overwhelmed in animal desire for him. But Lisa wanted to talk, so Joe found someone who understood what he needed, and Ann certainly fulfilled that need. Joe smiled to himself as he thought about it.

There were many boring and tedious aspects to Joe's work as a surgeon, but one of the things he liked was when the pressure was on — racing against the clock in an emergency surgery, nurses clustering around him, hurriedly handing him whatever he requested, feeling time and the patient's life draining away, and the satisfaction of having pulled this poor creature from the greedy arms of death. Unfortunately, too many of his operations were routine, but as a physician, he knew the potential hazard of any operation, and as such, there was always the thrill of holding life and death in his hands. Over the years, he had developed an efficient, focused skill and the ability to make rapid decisions. To act otherwise could mean the death of the patient, and it was the power that Joe held in his hands that allowed him to maintain an interest in his work.

On the other hand, there were many times that he thought of walking out of the hospital and never returning — the tedium of insurance paperwork, arguing with insurance company employees who sounded like they were fresh out of high school, hospital politics, annoying residents who wanted to look up to you and learn something from you — all these things were torture to Joe. There were times that Joe had printed his letter of resignation and was walking to his department head's office to deliver it, just to reconsider at the last moment. What would he do instead? Every job had its tedium. Perhaps this job was the least of all the other possible "evils." Well, then, forget jobs, he would tell himself. Just take some cash and his motorcycle and drive. It didn't matter where, just drive to see new places, drive until the money ran out. And then work for a while, until he had enough money to go on his next adventure. He hated to be tied down. He hated people to have expectations of him. Two things stopped him from delivering that letter — his children and Ann.

Joe pulled into Ann's driveway. He felt his breath deepen in hungry anticipation as he walked to her door. He inserted the key in her door and opened it. He walked through the dark entry hall, and turned left into a dimly lit living room with three candles burning on the mantle piece. There she was, lounging on the couch, in a similar position to how he had imagined her in his fantasy earlier that day. Her long black hair cascaded around her shoulders. She gave him a little smile, raised her eyebrows and extended a hand, saying softly and gently, "Hi, Joe." He knelt down beside her and kissed her on the lips long and deeply, and she met his kiss, greedily pulling herself towards him, running her fingers through his hair. Joe gave himself to his desire without restraint. This was the wrestling with his children, the churning of the water, the feverish rush to save a patient's life, all wrapped up into one…and more. It was the animal triumph of life over death… and, finally, it was the peaceful quiet that surrounded him, as she lay with her head on his chest, and he succumbed to sleep, his passions finally spent.

<hr />

Adam attended a scientific conference on that same Sunday. He dreaded conferences, because it usually meant at least one presentation on Adam's part, detailing his latest research findings. Such presentations were essential, because they gained one recognition among one's peers, and, without professional recognition, there was no funding. Adam was always terribly nervous at such presentations. He would fumble with the computer, invariably pushing the wrong button, causing the PowerPoint presentation to display the wrong thing, while he anxiously endeavored to correct the problem. He would stand before the audience and desperately try to keep his hands from shaking and his voice from quivering. Adam was an intelligent man, he knew that, but he always felt like an idiot at these things, and he was sure the audience agreed with him. Giving the presentation was bad enough, but answering questions was even worse. At least when he gave the presentation, he could have a prepared script, but during the question session, anything could come up, and Adam was forced to nervously think of an answer that would be satisfying to the questioner or at least convince him that Adam was not a homeless man who had wandered into the conference and was just pretending to be a scientist. Adam always left such presentations with a sense of defeat and exhaustion.

As Adam drove home, the afternoon sun sank towards the horizon and shined into the eyes of Adam and the others driving around him. He quickly folded down his visor and tried to see through the glare. He didn't need this now, he was tired enough. The bright glow of the sun and the slowing traffic were very irritating to him. His shoulders ached and his mind raced over the events of the day. He reviewed his answers to audience questions. Had he said the right thing? Had he made a laughingstock of himself? Would he get his research funding renewed? He was so lost in his thoughts that he did not notice how tightly he gripped the steering wheel or how constricted his breathing was. After five minutes, he was relieved to turn off the highway and away from the glare of the sun. He turned down a couple of side streets and into his synagogue, to attend the afternoon prayer service.

Adam entered the synagogue a few minutes before the prayer service began. A few clusters of men stood around talking. Most of them were dressed casually. Adam took a volume of the Talmud off a bookshelf at the back of the sanctuary, found a seat close by and began to read. He did not look up until he heard the voice of the prayer leader beginning the service. Adam closed the Talmud and picked up a prayer book. He quickly recited an introductory Psalm and then took three steps backward and three forward, in preparation for the recitation of the *Amidah*, a whispered prayer containing praises of God, supplications for needs and acknowledgement of blessings. *"Baruch Atah ... "* Adam began in Hebrew, meaning, "Blessed are you ..." He continued to rapidly mouth the words in the prayer book, but his mind just as quickly raced away to other thoughts. "I'm hopeless," he thought. "It's all in my mind. If I could just forget what the audience may be thinking of me, just say what I have to say. That was important stuff that I was presenting on. It could lead to a cure for breast cancer. Separate myself from my work, that's what I have to do. The work is important, even if I think I'm not. Just say what I've found, the work will speak for itself. How can I make things better next time? I'll practice more. No, that's never helped. Maybe I should take a tranquilizer. But I'm afraid that could make me fuzzy, make me unable to defend my position. I can't do this anymore. Maybe I can get out of this line of work, and do something where I don't have to defend what I'm doing, where I don't have to convince them that I'm not wasting grant money. But what could I do? What could I do? ..."

On the thoughts went and on the prayer went, Adam mouthing the Hebrew words from the prayer book, but paying no attention to them. He was already three quarters through the prayer when he realized what he was doing. "Now, I'm really being an idiot," he thought. "Here I am worrying about everything, pretending to pray, when it's God and only God who can give me the power to make things better." He felt a sinking feeling in his stomach, as he realized he had wasted most of the prayer on useless worries, and he knew that this pattern repeated day after day. He resolved to do better right then and there. He started reading again, pointing to every word, as he read in Hebrew. The words spoke of thankfulness for daily miracles, kindnesses and blessings showered on us from God. He thought of his Devorah and his four children, how much they meant to him, how empty life would be without them. Then he thought of the pressures of parochial school tuition, of his oldest son who needed dental work, the next oldest son in occupational therapy and of the rising costs of living. How could he keep up with all the financial demands? Devorah was working part-time, but that was all she could do. The kids needed time, love and attention. There were so many needs to take care of. Suddenly, Adam realized he had finished the prayer — his mind had wandered off again. In the past, he had tried every method he could think of to remain focused on his prayers. He had read slower, faster, pointed to each word, looked at the English translation on the facing page (while reciting the prayer in Hebrew), even read the whole prayer in English. But it was not a language problem. Although he had learned Hebrew later in life, he had spent considerable time studying it and knew it well enough. It was a problem of focus. He just had so much on his mind, so many worries, that he felt like he had to constantly be thinking of solutions. He knew this was foolish, that much of the thinking was circular and unproductive, but he could not break the habit, could not "let go and let God," as Rabbi Goldberg used to say. He could not stay focused on the prayer.

Adam thought of the way Rabbi Goldberg used to pray, when Adam observed him during prayer services in Israel. There was something timeless about the way he stood to say the *Amidah* prayer. Rabbi Goldberg had told him the reason why the Jewish people take three steps forward when saying this prayer. "It is because they are entering the palace of the heavenly King, to praise him and to supplicate before him," the rabbi had said. Adam had no doubt that when Rabbi Goldberg took his three steps forward that the Rabbi felt himself entering a palace of light and was gratefully stepping forward to greet his Father. Rabbi Goldberg had told him that people think that they earn money at their job, but that was an illusion. The real place where they earn money is in the King's palace, when they enter and acknowledge that all good comes from Him. "God wants only the sincerity of our prayers and that we be devoted to Him, His wisdom and His commandments," he would tell Adam. "If you give Him that, He will find a way for you to make a living." Watching Rabbi Goldberg pray filled Adam with a sense of love, as Adam witnessed the rabbi's gentle, rhythmic swaying forwards and backwards and the serene repose in his face. This man was a walking exemplar of the peace that Adam yearned for so much in his own life. Why, after all these years, was Adam still distracted by worries and unable to focus on the "palace of the King?"

Adam wondered if it was because he had been raised in an environment where God was absent. Adam's parents had no interest in religion and only scorn for those who were religious. Religious Jews, his parents had believed, lived within the strictures of meaningless rules and rituals and would not take a step without consulting with their rabbi. Adam had found the reality of Jewish life to be much different and in many ways he had outgrown his parent's cynical views of Judaism. However, something from his parents' world did stick with him — the feeling of the absence of God. For his parents, it was not just a feeling, it was a conviction — Adam might even venture to say, an article of faith. Adam's life course had led him to a different type of faith, which Adam experienced as a yearning hope that there was something more in the universe than the struggle of life for a short period of time, followed by an eternity of nothingness. Adam yearned for a Spirit that filled the vast reaches of space and the anguished depths of his soul. This hope was always with him, but also with him was the despair of his parents, the feeling of being ultimately alone and irrelevant in the world — a world shepherded not by God, but by a random, cold and empty reality. So he was left with a hope, a feeling of distance and a pervasive sense of doubt: Is there really anyone out there? Am I praying to nothing?

After the prayer service, some men stayed behind to chat about their activities that day or to engage in some joint religious studies. However, Adam hurried away, not wanting to talk with anyone in the synagogue. He was too tired.

Ten minutes later, he entered his home and found his three- and five-year-old girls playing in the living room. They ran up to greet him. The elder hugged him around his waist and the younger, around his leg. He knelt down and gave them both a kiss. The five-year-old, Shoshi, grabbed his face and put a warm, wet kiss on his cheek. Adam then rose and entered the kitchen, where he found his ten- and twelve-year-old sons helping Devorah set up for dinner. He greeted both of his sons and Devorah, but he did not smile. Devorah realized that it had been a hard day for him, just as she had expected; these conferences always had this effect on him.

After dinner, Shoshi asked him if he would play Barbies with her. He wanted to say no. He wanted to just lie down in his room, turn off the light and forget the world. But he had said "no" to her too often, so he consented. She delightedly took him by the hand and led him to the playroom. She was indeed a beautiful girl, with dark brown eyes and hair, and a cherubic round face. But the real beauty was from within, the sparkle of excitement that played across her face, the joy of being with her father and sharing her game — her manner so untroubled, unburdened, and free.

Shoshi showed him three Barbies, with their legs outstretched in front of them sitting on the floor. They wore elegant evening gowns. Facing them, Shoshi had leaned three other Barbies against a toy spaceship. The standing Barbies were wearing flippers, pants, shirts and snorkeling equipment.

Shoshi knelt down on the floor, motioning for her father to join her. Adam sat beside her.

"These," said Shoshi, indicating the sitting Barbies, "are the three fairy queens. And the other ones have just traveled from 'the star of wishes' to greet them and make peace between their two planets. The fairy queens speak charm language. It goes like this: Ula Inta Ukha Feluha!...Now you try it, Daddy, you speak charm language."

"Well, I don't know charm language, dear," Adam answered.

"Come on, Daddy. Pleeease, I know you can do it."

"Oh, OK, umm….Lu Lu Lu Lu."

"*Nooo*, Daddy, that's not charm language. Charm language always ends in an 'ah' sound."

"You speak charm language, dear. I'm not so good at it."

"OK, well then you speak wish language, that's what the other ones speak."

"How do I do that?"

"You just say: wish wash wish wash wish wash, like that, you understand."

"Yes, dear, wish wash wish wash wish wash."

"No, Daddy, that's all wrong, the Wish people never speak before the fairies speak. That makes the fairies mad. They have to wait for the fairies to ask them questions."

Throughout this interaction, Adam was watching both Shoshi and himself. The contrast was painful to him. There she was — so creative, alive, hungry for his attention, understanding and affirmation. And here he was — tense, tentative, distant — just wanting this silly game to be over, wanting to withdraw and be by himself. He tried to force himself to listen to her better, to show more enthusiasm. But he couldn't relax and there were too many criticisms in his head: "I'm an awful father — I know it, she knows it. She'll bore of me soon enough, run to her mother, who has so much more life to give her. What do I have to give her — only despair, hopelessness. I can't be who she wants me to be."

CHAPTER SEVEN

Grace opened up the group discussion again in the next session. She had a pained look on her face. Her body movements and speech were slow, as if every action on her part required great effort.

"I had a terrible week," she started. "I'm staying up too late and having the hardest time waking up in the morning. And I don't know what I stay up so late for. I just feel so nervous, when I'm home by myself. I try to soothe the nerves with eating, but even if that does work for a while, then I start feeling guilty for eating like a pig. Then I turn on the TV to turn off my mind. I sit there and stare, like a zombie, for hours. I don't want to go to sleep. When I lie there in the darkness, so many thoughts and memories go through my mind. I want to make myself exhausted first, so I'll fall asleep right away. But I make myself so exhausted that I can't get out of bed the next day. I was late to work three times this week. My boss told me that I'm skating on thin ice. And the weekend was even worse. I must have slept for fourteen hours on Saturday, maybe more on Sunday. I didn't get out of the apartment at all. I felt like I was burying myself, deliberately burying myself, and I hated myself for doing it."

"What's your job?" asked Joe.

"I'm a bank teller."

"What do you do when you aren't working?"

"Nothing," she responded. "I mean, I shop, cook, watch TV, sleep. Occasionally a nagging friend gets me to go out on a date, but most of the time, well, I just don't do that much."

"Do you exercise?" he asked.

"No," she answered. "I've paid out too much money to health clubs that I just attended two or three times and then never went to again."

"Grace, I think that's part of your problem," said Joe. "You don't do enough. If you were more active, you wouldn't feel so agitated in the evenings, because you would have used your energy during the day. I really wonder whether I would feel that different from you, if I were not active. I got plenty to be depressed about. My wife is insane. She gets angry about the most ridiculous things. Take last Sunday, for example. I get up; it's a beautiful sunny day. I want to go out and run around with the kids, get them to enjoy the day. And she says they have to do homework first thing in the morning. They got a whole day ahead of them! They can do homework anytime. Why did they have to do it then? There I am with my kids. I get the chance to spend some time with them outside and she has a fit, because she says they should get to work first thing in the morning. She's negative, she's cold, to them and to me. Whenever I try to hug her, it's like holding wood. I can't stand the woman, but divorce means losing the kids, so I have to put up with this, but it's depressing... So I find things to keep me occupied, things that give me pleasure. I exercise – I'm presently training for a triathlon – I have my girlfriend, and I also take a weekly shift with my volunteer fire department. These things keep me from falling in the dark hole that you're describing. I've got

NEVER FORGET MY SOUL

pleasure in my life — so, I keep myself happy."

David could not let Joe get away with this. True, he had some coping strategies that Grace did not have, but the misstatement that he was keeping himself happy was a lie that was in service of neither Joe nor Grace. Sure, Grace needed to do more, to get out more, but in truth, both Joe and Grace were in a self-imposed prison. In a way, Joe's prison was worse, because he did not even realize that it was a prison. His isolation was at least as great as Grace's, and he could never overcome it through such lies.

"Joe," said David, "why did you come to this group?"

"You suggested it," answered Joe. "I supposed that with all those diplomas and stuff hanging on the wall, that you probably know something."

"Fine, I suggested it," said David, "but now that you have come to a few sessions, do you have any more of an answer?"

"No," responded Joe. "Frankly, now that I have come to the group, I have even less of an answer. I'm not finding people's comments helpful, I'm not learning anything and I'm bored a lot of the time."

"I'm so surprised," said David. "In last session and again today, you appear quite engaged. And both times the person whom you're responding to so strongly is Grace. Any idea why that might be?"

"She just looks so hopeless," said Joe. "I can't stand hopelessness. It makes me want to do something, anything, rather than sitting around and feeling hopeless, so I try to get her out of her funk, so I don't have to see that depression. I've seen it in my wife...I just can't stand it."

"So why did you come to this group?" asked David, using a technique that he had often found to be useful — simply repeating the core question that the patient was avoiding.

"I told you the answer," said Joe, who sounded like he was starting to become irritated.

"Does anyone remember what Joe said about why he came to the group?" David asked, glancing around the circle of chairs. "He said something about it in the first session."

"He said he had recurrent feelings of depression," said Adam, who was staring at the floor, and did not look up as he spoke.

"Yeah, I said I was depressed — so what?" challenged Joe.

David was tempted to let Adam take it from there, but, seeing that Adam was not attempting to respond, David decided to offer his thought: "You said you're keeping yourself happy, which seems to be a direct contradiction to your statement that you're depressed. Which one is it, Joe?"

"*David, don't twist my words.*" Joe was clearly angry now. "Yes, I get depressed, life is depressing, there's so much crap to put up with. But I try not to dwell on that. I seek out pleasures and that keeps me happy."

Adam had been thinking about many things as Joe and David were talking. Adam thought about his father's anger and how memories of it had silenced Adam during the last session. He thought of his own anger towards Joe, who had been repeatedly insulting towards Adam, and who lived life as if the whole world were created to serve his needs. He thought of Rabbi Goldberg, who had always lectured that there is a profound difference between pleasure and true happiness. "In fact," Rabbi Goldberg would say, "it's often a choice between one and the other, because true happiness requires the willingness to tolerate pain, while still keeping your heart open." As Adam thought about these words, he felt a sense of shame, because he had not lived up to them. Adam had succumbed to fear, he had hidden from others, avoided contact with them, because he could not face the anxiety of being with them. Adam felt he had to say something. Joe was preaching that pleasure was the point of life. How many lives had been ruined by such an empty philosophy? If Adam had not found Rabbi Goldberg, he would still have been drifting in a world devoted to pleasure-seeking and feeling inadequate because he could not throw himself with abandon into that orgy. Adam felt his heart begin to race, pounding powerfully in his chest as he thought of speaking. He felt a sense of panic, but he would not succumb to it. He had been silenced too many times. He *did* have something to say.

"Happiness and pleasure are different things," said Adam defiantly.

At first it was unclear whether Joe would even respond to Adam's comment. He finally slowly turned his head to Adam and said, with an air of unconcern, "I don't know what you're talking about."

"Animals feel pleasure," Adam pressed on. "Only *humans* experience happiness."

"Thank you, Dr. Dolittle," responded Joe sarcastically. "I suppose you've interviewed the animals on this matter."

"No," said Adam, "but I belong to a four-thousand-year-old tradition which has studied what it means to be a human."

"Yeah?" inquired Joe. "And what does your *doctrine* tell you?" He drew out the word "doctrine" in contempt.

"The Bible tells us," answered Adam, ignoring the contempt in Joe's voice, "that God breathed the breath of life into the first man, and man became a 'living spirit.' Now, we have a tradition in our Biblical interpretation that says that things are not always as they appear on the surface level. Thus, we rely heavily on our traditional interpreters and commentators. There is a famous translation of the Bible into the ancient language of Aramaic that takes that term 'living spirit' and translates it as 'speaking spirit.' You see, God's gift to us is the gift of speech. No other animals have it. It is the ability to use speech, to think, that is the *true* gift of life that God gave us. It enables us to see above and beyond ourselves, to have meaning in our lives, even to see beyond death. Animals experience pleasure by having their needs fulfilled. To experience happiness, you have to rise above being an animal, to see that there is more in life than fulfilling your needs."

Joe responded with less contempt in his voice than he usually showed to Adam. On the other hand, he did not act like he was particularly impressed with Adam's insights. "That's just where you and I differ, Adam," said Joe. "I'm not interested in denying the animal in me. In fact, I regard the animal as the best part of me. Everything else is phony, a mask I put on to play the role that society requires. When I am the animal without pretending to be anything else — me in bed with my girlfriend, swimming across a lake, or tumbling with my kids — those things are what I live for and make life worthwhile. I need to be in the moment, feel the excitement, and I need to feel it in my body. Without that pleasure, I might as well not be alive."

Adam felt stuck. He did not know how to communicate with or have an impact on this man who so proudly and unapologetically preached the virtues of his animal instinct. Adam was filled with a deep discomfort for a life devoted to animal desires, but he was not sure how to communicate his feeling to Joe. Adam was not even sure why it mattered so much to him. Why did he care so much about what Joe believed or did?

David was more than a little surprised by the interchange between Adam and Joe, and David was also quite pleased with it. Adam had actually spoken up for himself. For a few minutes, he had refused to be cowed by Joe's anger. Further, the subjects that Joe and Adam had brought up were fascinating to David, and seemed very relevant for the other group members. Seeing that Adam had fallen silent, David decided to ask a question that would hopefully keep the discussion going.

"I have been listening closely to the discussion in the group so far," said David, "and, as I did, a phrase kept coming through my mind. The phrase was 'Animal suffering is very different from human suffering.' I wonder if the group has any responses to this thought or anything else they have heard."

"Well, I'm not quite sure what to make of that phrase, David," said Terry, "but I did have a thought about what Adam said. Adam, I don't see how you feel you can be so sure that animals don't experience happiness. I have a dog, and when I come home, he's happy. I can see it. Not just because I feed him and have the ability to fill his stomach. He's happy to be with me, even after he's fed. He wants to play with me, to cuddle with me, just to be with me, and that makes him happy. You also say that animals don't use language. Dolphins do. They have a quite sophisticated language system. I don't understand why people feel compelled to say that we are fundamentally different from animals. We *are* animals. For anything that humans do, you can find a parallel with other animals. But somehow that's too disturbing to us, so we have to invent ways that we are different from animals."

"But wait a second," Tyrone broke in. "I've seen people who live like animals. I was once one of them. It seems to me that it's always the people who haven't seen that side of life who romanticize acting on their animal instinct. Let me paint a picture for you. I was out there on the streets with only one purpose: to survive. There was no yesterday, there was no tomorrow. I did not know if I would be alive tomorrow, so I just didn't think about it. I actually thought very little; I just acted on my instinct, and I was always on the alert. It became a way of life. I became so attuned to my environment that I would just feel something on the back of my neck, and I knew that someone was looking at me. I never ignored such stares, because ignoring could be misinterpreted as fear and fear meant that you could be their prey. So I would stare back and it would be no different from two dogs baring their teeth and growling, seeing which would back down. And it could go different ways. Sometimes we would sense that we had met an equal, who was not interested in fighting and then we could just look away and let it go. But other times I saw not just the meanness in those eyes, I also saw hunger — hunger for power, hunger to dominate, and willingness to kill, if need be, to obtain that power. You know, there's always a few dogs in the pack who want to control. Those hungry eyes were always the most dangerous. You dare not walk away from them, but to fight them could mean death, because they would not back down. I always chose to fight in such situations, and I lost count of how many times I came within an inch of death. I have the scars to prove it — bullet holes, knife wounds … These are my trophies from living in the world of an animal.

"But that's only part of it. Imagine living in such a world day after day. How do you keep yourself from going crazy? Remember, there is no hope and there is no tomorrow. So instinct keeps you alive and it also keeps you sane. What I mean is you keep yourself occupied with the most immediate pleasures — money, drugs and sex. Money, because it is the most direct way to obtain the other two. There was a time that I was smoking a joint every night, trying to drown out the tension of the day — that endless scanning of my environment for threats. Then there was sex — the meaningless succession of girls — groping them in the utility closet of the apartment building, behind the bushes in the park, touching them everywhere, but never letting any of them touch me, having no idea what it meant to be loved, to be cared for, to be understood. Tyrone the Tiger, they called me. I'd use them and lose them, especially if one of them started getting emotional on me. I couldn't stand that. If one of them started getting attached, I would tell them, 'This is not about love. You got something that I want, I get it, then we're done.'

"When I look back, that's the saddest thing about it — that there was no emotion to anything, just instinct and reaction. I remember when the school sent me to a few sessions with a counselor. Man, did I have an attitude with that poor guy, but that's another story. He would ask me how this or that makes me feel, like, 'How does it make you feel when so and so insults you?" And

NEVER FORGET MY SOUL

I would answer, 'I hit him.' So he would then tell me that hitting him is what I *do*, not how I *feel*. So I answered, 'I hit him, I don't need to feel, I'll just make him feel something that will make him stop.' That was feeling to me, the infliction of pain. Feelings were not to be discussed or understood. They were just to be protected in oneself and exploited in others to make them weak, to keep them off their balance, to keep myself safe. That's why we told Momma jokes. You know, like 'Your Momma is so fat she has her own zip code.' We were testing each other, seeing if we could be strong in the face of these jokes about the one person who we probably still had some tender feelings for. The ones who laughed and came right back with a Momma joke against you — they were strong, maybe you would hang with them, because they could take it. But the ones who lost it, who took a swing after the first joke, they were the weak ones, and you knew you would always win in a conflict against them. They would just fall apart. We used laughter a lot to protect ourselves from feeling. Everything was funny, especially the most gruesome topics — the violence on the streets, rape, OD'ing on drugs — we laughed so we did not have to feel, and we had sex and did drugs for the same reason. 'Cause feeling made you soft. We did not have the language for it back then, but it is very clear to me today that what feeling did was make you too human, it made you think about the suffering of yesterday, the hopelessness of tomorrow, and that made things unbearable.

"If I had continued to devote my life to pursuing immediate pleasures, I would still be there, prowling the same streets, looking for the next girl or high to take away the boredom…No, I would probably be dead, I would have lived like an animal and died like an animal. Without Eva, I would have never known that I was human. Of all the things that Eva taught me, the most wonderful thing was this: who I am inside matters, I have something to say and someone wants to listen to me. It was as if I had found a new man inside of me, when Eva showed that she was truly interested in how I *thought* about things. When we talked about things, it gave me a strange new pleasure that I had never felt before. It made me feel more real, like before I had been living in a dream world that I had no control over, but that now my life was in my hands and I could *choose* what direction I wanted to go in. Most of all, I realized how terribly alone I had been before I met Eva, but I had never known how alone I was until she opened up the door to the man in me."

Tyrone's story had come out in a flow of words. When he finished, he had a wistful look in his eyes, as he thought about Eva, his gratitude for her and his astonishment that this white woman could have so much love that she reached out to him in the way that she did. The group had listened to Tyrone with rapt attention. The group members did not notice it, but a single tear rolled down Adam's face as Tyrone spoke, which Adam quickly wiped away. But David noticed. He had been trained to not just look at the speaker, but at the audience as well. David decided to not call anyone's attention to Adam's tear at this point.

"Look, Tyrone," said Joe, "I admire what you've done with your life, but I don't see how it has anything to do with me. You lived in a terrible place. You studied hard because you wanted to get out of it. Now you have a better life. More power to you. But I'm not talking about entering gang warfare or becoming a pothead. I'm just talking about the things that make me feel alive and are important to me. You wanted to be a lawyer and have a family — that's what makes you happy. I've got different things that make me feel happy. And for the record, I'm not constantly just pursuing my personal pleasure. Take my work with the volunteer fire department. I've saved lives doing that. Sure, I like the thrill of it, but people are acting like all I do is help myself and no one else. Have any of you stepped into a burning building that could collapse any moment to save a two-year-old girl in her crib? Do you know what the heat feels like, how the flames and smoke blind you, how the next step could send you crashing through the floor, how one malfunction in your equipment and you're dead — you become fuel for the fire? And what about the people you don't save in time, the people with limbs burnt off or bodies that are so burnt up they hardly look human any more? It takes a lot of guts to do that work. I'm really starting to resent everybody saying that I'm some selfish bastard only out for myself."

"I have the hardest time figuring out if I like you, Joe." said Marcia. "One moment you say you're only interested in pleasure and yourself, and the next moment you're reaching out to other group members or telling us about your work as a firefighter. My brother was saved by a firefighter when I was six years old. I remember my mother screaming for him as we stood on the front lawn of the house and her tears of joy and relief as the firefighter climbed out of the bedroom window, holding my brother in his arms. I have always had the warmest feelings for firefighters, since that day. Maybe, Joe, you're just one of those guys who are good at heart, but can't bear letting anyone know."

Joe paused for a moment, as if he were surprised about such praise coming from another group member. His face seemed to relax briefly, and there was the faint glimmer of a smile. But the warmth in his face disappeared quickly and he replied, "I'm no hero, I'm just a guy who likes excitement. Look to someone else if you're looking for someone who wants to make the world a better place."

"But if you're not looking to make the world a better place," asked Marcia, "why do you risk your life as a firefighter?"

"I told everyone before. Activity keeps me happy. I like excitement. In fact, what I would most prefer to do is be a soldier, but I'm not into taking orders and I like the money too much to give up on being a surgeon. So I do part-time firefighting instead."

"Why would you like to be a soldier?" asked Terry.

"It's the excitement of the moment. It's live or die. It's making quick decisions and living on the edge. Kill or be killed. I love that stuff."

"*Kill or be killed?*" repeated David. "It sounds like you actually might enjoy joining a street gang."

"You misunderstand me, David," answered Joe. "It's not really the destruction that I'm interested in, it's the thrill. As a soldier you can take that raw instinct — self-preservation — and do something productive with it. It's the same thing as being a firefighter, a productive way to have that thrill."

Adam, who had been listening intently to the discussion, turned to Joe, and, with a note of challenge in his voice, said, "You just said the word 'productive' two times. Why is it so important that you do something that is thrilling *and* productive? Why not skydive, bungee jump or go shark hunting?"

"Well," responded Joe, who was pensive because he had not considered this question before, "it just seems important that there be a *reason* for the thrill. I mean, I have plenty of thrills in my life that I just do because they feel good. But I don't want to do just that, I also want to be involved in things that *mean* something."

"But why?" persisted Adam.

"I can't tell you," answered Joe. "It just makes me happy."

"I think it's because, when you do something meaningful, you get a chance to see that you're *not* just an animal," responded Adam. "In fact, I don't believe the danger you face is always pleasurable. You described it as the complete opposite of pleasure. It makes you happy, even though it *does not* give you pleasure. *That* is the difference between a man and an animal. Only a human can experience happiness, because happiness is the ability to appreciate the goodness of life even in the face of terrible pain. When animals are in the face of pain, all they can do is feel it or try to escape it. When humans are in pain, we can seek understanding, and that understanding may tell us to not avoid the pain, but rather to bear it, so we can uphold something that is precious to us. It's just like

David said: 'Animal suffering is very different from human suffering.' You choose a thrill that involves suffering and meaning, so you can experience that you are not just an animal."

Joe smiled and said, "I guess you're right, Adam. But don't go thinking that I'm going to become an Orthodox Jew. My grandfather gave me the blessing of realizing that Judaism is filled with empty superstitions, and he liberated our family from it. He was an asshole in a lot of ways, but I'm grateful to him for that. I don't need some myth about a man in the sky to help me cope with my life. I don't need a Daddy, metaphysical or otherwise. I can manage my own life, thank you."

"That grandfather, was he your mother's father?" asked Adam, intrigued that by Jewish law, Joe might actually be Jewish, since membership in the religion follows the maternal blood line.

"Yea, my mother was Jewish and her mother was Jewish. That's right, Adam, the Jewish cult would regard me as Jewish. Don't think that it's any revelation to me. But all that has no significance to me anyway, it's really useless crap to me. I live by what I can feel and touch, not ghosts, spirits, gods or goblins."

David had been paying special attention to Grace for a while now. She was being subjected to something that often happens in groups. She initially brought up a subject that was emotionally evocative for the rest of the group members. (David knew that many of the group members struggled with considerable depression.) Her comments then became a springboard for the group discussion, but the original person who brought up the feelings was forgotten. David sensed that the group actually preferred to talk about the causes of depression, rather than exploring their own depressive feelings. Grace had become the vessel for depression, and the group, dreading the prospect of being drawn into that darkness, had conveniently forgotten about her.

"I'm wondering, Grace, about you," said David. "You opened up the group and then became silent throughout the discussion that followed. What has your experience of being in the group been like today?"

Grace paused for a long time before responding, so long that it was unclear whether she would respond at all. She finally said, "Pretty lousy. I've been forgotten. Everybody has their own interests to talk about. I said what I said to seek help from the group. Joe tells me some stuff about how I have to become more active, get out more. I'm not looking for people's advice. I want to see if there is anyone out there who actually cares, when I say that I'm depressed. I'm... I'm so angry. I don't matter to anyone, I never have."

"Grace," asked David, "where is your father?"

"What do you mean, David?" asked Grace, her voice rising in pitch and volume, indicating that this question was only serving to agitate her more. "He's dead. Dead, buried, gone. You know that."

"Dead and buried," answered David, "not gone. Where is your father?"

"What do you mean!?" asked Grace, tears welling in her eyes.

David tried to say the next words as gently as he could, so Grace could stay focused on the work and not get distracted by complaints against him. "Grace, no one hurts us that deeply and just disappears, if you could point to a place that your father is right now, where would that be?"

"He's sitting over there in Joe's seat," said Grace, keeping her eyes steadily on David and not looking at Joe.

"Say more about it, Grace," encouraged David.

"Just like my father — sometimes he was the warmest, most loving man with me. He would speak softly to me, assure me of his love. Then, all the love would disappear, just disappear. All that was left was coldness and hatred and anger." Grace trailed off, as if she dared not say more.

"Keep going, Grace," said David. "This is the place where you can leave your father behind, but first you have to be willing to

NEVER FORGET MY SOUL

talk about him."

"Well, it's just, Joe," she said, turning her face, an angry, hurt face, to Joe, "...you were so kind to me last session. I really felt like you cared, like I mattered to you. It made me feel good, so much less lonely. When you started up again today, it brought those old feelings back. I'm just so hungry for attention, and it is flattering to have the attention of a handsome man, such as you. But then it was like you forgot me. You just started talking about what gives you pleasure and defending yourself to everybody. I felt some of the same feelings towards Tyrone as well." She turned to Tyrone. "Tyrone, you had your hard time a couple of weeks ago, now things seem to have calmed down for you. And now it's my turn. What is it about men that they can only see another person for about two seconds and then everything becomes about them!" She glared at Tyrone, as she said these last words.

"Now hold it, Grace," said Tyrone, who seemed surprised at the intensity of Grace's reactions. "I didn't mean to ignore you. I figure if anyone in here has something to say, they will just speak up. Joe and Adam's discussion brought up some pretty strong memories in me. I just needed to talk about them."

"How many times have I heard that!?" responded Grace. "Men saying to me, 'I assume you'll just speak up.' Not everybody just speaks up, Tyrone! Some of us can't speak up unless we actually get the feeling that there is someone out there who is interested in listening. And I don't get that feeling with someone, if he is constantly talking and won't shut up for a second."

"He?" asked David. "Who do you mean by 'he?'"

"Who is he?" she repeated, as if she were having difficulty understanding the meaning of these words. "*He* is Tyrone, *he* is Joe, *he* is my father who could only think of two things — his mouth and his dick, his mouth to get drunk and then shout at everyone and his dick, when he got tired of using his mouth... But I'm sorry, Tyrone, it's not really you. Yeah, it scares me when I hear about your angry outbursts, but you are not the one that makes me shiver. It's you, Joe, and it's what you said last time. You're not interested in any relationship. You will milk people for stimulation until it bores you, but you make no commitments, you'll disappear when it suits you. The world and everything in it are there for you to use. Don't get the kind of sex you want with your wife? Fine, there's plenty of that to go around, you'll find it with someone else. My father did the same thing. He told me the reason he molested me was because my mother would not put out. I'm nothing to you, right, Joe!? I guess once a man marks you, like my filthy father did, others can read the sign and assume they can treat you the same way!"

"Whoa, hold on, Grace," said Joe. "Look, I'm sorry you were abused. I'm sorry you had a hard life. I'm sorry you're depressed. But I'm not your father. I didn't do those things to you. I'm getting tired of being this group's punching bag. Looks like you all need someone to hate. Well, I don't recall volunteering for the job. I'm just here to — to — well, I don't know why the hell I'm here. I guess I want to unload something from my life, have some guts to change things. That's what I'm trying to do. I hope you are trying to do the same. I didn't come here to help you or anyone else. I just want to do this little psychotherapy thing and then move on with my life. I can't be to you what you want me to be."

"I don't want you to be anything," answered Grace. "I think I'd be happier if you weren't here."

"Fine," said Joe, "I can leave. Do people want me to leave? I'll just be on my way if I'm interfering with everyone's *treatment*." There was a sense of irony, as he said the last word and glanced toward David. Joe did not seem upset and the truth was, as long as David had known Joe, he had hardly ever seen him upset — yes, irritated, sometimes somewhat angry — but never actually losing his temper. Joe always seemed to be in control — in control of the situation and of himself. The phrase ran through David's mind, as a random thought, "To let go is to die." David had learned to pay close attention to such random thoughts. They were usually the wisdom of his subconscious, which had reached a conclusion about a patient long before his conscious mind could catch up. What this message told David was that Joe's air of indifference was a façade, and that he was feeling terribly threatened in that room. Joe was looking like he was ready to walk out. David sensed that if Joe did, David might never see Joe again, and that months of psychotherapy and this man's life would go down the drain. David had to say something quickly, to calm Joe down and keep him in the room.

"You say you're seeking courage, Joe," said David. "The greater courage would be for you to stay."

"David," responded Joe, "I don't see the courage in staying in a bad situation. People are not enjoying my presence here. I can't say I'm enjoying it either. It's not courage to stay. It's stupidity."

"But I told you before, Joe," said David. "This group is *not* about enjoying yourself. It's about courage and suffering and change. Why do you keep on thinking that we all have to be having fun in here?"

"I do things that are fun for me," Joe replied. "When the fun stops, I move on — "

"No, Joe," said David, shaking his head. "You do *not* move on. Remember, you feel stuck, you want to make a change in your life, you're tired of carrying the burden of a bad marriage. You do not move on. You merely distract yourself. You can leave this group if you want. That would be yet another distraction. But if you want to make changes, I suggest that you stay." David would normally have employed a stronger word, like "urge," rather than "suggest." But he knew that Joe's response to authority was to do the opposite, so David used mild language, so as not to invoke Joe's usual defenses. David had learned to be very selective when challenging other's defenses, and would only do so when they appeared to be in a suitable state to benefit from the challenge. That is why he had been deliberately vague when talking about Joe's marriage. The truth was that he hoped that Joe could see the value of trying to salvage his relationship with his wife. But Joe was looking for a way out, so David gave words to that feeling — "tired of carrying the burden of a bad marriage" — which David anticipated Joe would interpret as possibly freeing himself from the burden. "I don't mind if he thinks that," David told himself, "if it helps him to stay in the group. He'll discover other possibilities over the course of time." And then, as a reminder of the limits of his own power, he thought, "Hopefully."

Joe looked serious as David was talking. Then he smiled, shrugged and said, "I'll stay if people don't object to me being here — I mean, I'll stay as long as it makes sense to stay, and, if no one objects, I won't walk out right now. Let's put it to a vote. Does anyone want me to leave?"

No one spoke. David held his breath. Everything depended on whether the other members sensed that they needed Joe here more than they needed him gone. Joe waited silently… Still, no one spoke.

"You see, Joe," said David, "just because some group members may not enjoy you does not mean that they don't want you here. Sometimes we may not enjoy people, even those who are very important to us."

"I'm not looking to be important to anyone. But I'll stick around…for now."

The group was silent for what appeared to be a very long time. David patiently tolerated the silence, knowing that not he, but one of his patients should be the first one to break it. There was an intensity and rawness of emotion in the room. Anything David said, even something innocuous, would put his own interpretation, his own spin, on the recent discussion. He watched, waited and did his best to remain physically calm and mentally poised. He remembered very distinctly what his internship director and supervisor, Dr. Matthew Owens, had said to him when David had discussed his experience of leading an intense group therapy session, so many years ago. "You're smart, David, very smart," Dr. Owens had said to him, furrowing his bushy white eyebrows, "but to be a good group therapist you have to be so much more than smart. You have to be present. Keep yourself as relaxed as possible; accept yourself. You are going to have reactions, just like everyone else in the group. Some of those reactions are going to be very intense. But the worst thing that you can do is to clench down and try to fight those reactions. Don't try to be perfectly objective, fair and perceptive all of the time; just be yourself. It's a meditation — a meditation of experiencing, letting go, experiencing some more, and letting more go. You cannot expect to contact another's point of view unless you are willing to relinquish your tight hold on your own. Your patients will take their cue from you — not just from what you say. They will be observing how you hold your body, how you breathe, how much silence you can tolerate. They are facing hell. To them, it feels like no less than the fires of hell. They will want to shut down, to do anything they can do in order to not feel. And if you don't watch out, you will be subconsciously taking your cue from them — to tighten, to close down, to try to take control, to do anything, so you can avoid feeling. Let the group process flow through you, but do not grasp it. Then, it will carry you to where the group needs to go." He often thought of Dr. Owens during group sessions, but just as Dr. Owens had implied, the main thing that David remembered was not Dr. Owens' words, but his face — a wise, warm and caring face, a face where there was no ego, only concern for the other, desire to help, desire to understand. David envisioned this face to remind himself of the type of therapist and the type of man he wanted to be.

The first person to speak was Adam. Years later, David

thought back to this moment in the group, because it represented such a difficult and positive step forward for Adam. In addition, Adam's next comments opened up a discussion that finally helped David understand the battle between Adam and Joe, its true cause, and what they both were struggling with. And when David thought back to this moment, he would muse that it was the silence and openness that David had projected that helped Adam take the next step.

"I want to talk about something," started Adam tentatively, "but I don't know where to start." He paused as if he was unsure if he should proceed.

"Don't say a thing," David cautioned himself in his thoughts. "Just listen. Adam has to find his way for himself."

"Well," Adam finally said, "Grace, I think the group has forgotten you again. You got mad just now because you wanted some recognition and some help from us, and we kept getting distracted with our own concerns. So, you let Joe have it. He gets all huffy, says he's going to walk out. Everybody gets excited about that, and once again we forget you. I want to let you know I have not forgotten you, Grace. I want to listen to whatever you need to say."

Grace smiled a gentle smile and raised her eyes to Adam. "Adam, that's so sweet. I think it's all too much for me now. But can I take a rain check? I need a rest from all this for a while. I'll just listen."

"Oh," said Adam hesitantly, "well, do you mind if I talk about some of my reactions to you? I have just begun to realize how strong my reactions are to you."

"If it helps, Adam, sure," she answered. "I don't mind, especially after you made such a nice offer to me."

"Well, Grace," Adam began, "up until today, you reminded me of my mother. She was a very depressed and passive woman. She only went out of our apartment when she had to and avoided socializing with anyone. The constant refrain of my childhood was, "Don't upset your mother." My father spoke about her as if she was so frail and could not survive any excitement. She had frequent migraines and other unexplainable aches and pains. So my sister and I would tiptoe around the apartment, well, as long as kids can tiptoe, fearing that our noise would bring torment to our mother and the wrath of our father. But the tension of living under those conditions was too great, so my sister and I would frequently fight, and then we would really get it from our father. Anyway, up until today, I saw my mother in you. I saw your sadness and despair, and I saw how you carry the burden of your former abuse with you everywhere. I must tell you, it made it hard to look at you, because when I looked at you, I saw her. But today I saw something different. I saw your anger, and strangely enough, when your anger came out, I did not see my mother any more, I saw my father. And then I realized something — my mother and father had suffered a similar trauma in their lives. They behaved differently — my father with anger, my mother with depression — but inside, I think their feelings were very much the same. My father was probably as depressed as my mother and my mother was probably as angry as my father, they just expressed things in different ways. I've spent my life fearing others' anger and criticism and hating my own depression. But what I've lost sight of is the anger that's hidden behind my depression and the depression that lies behind any criticism that I anticipate in the world. I expect the whole world to see the negative in me, because that was the world of my youth — always seeing the negative in everything. I've read that seeing the negative in everything is a symptom of depression. But I'm starting to realize that I can't see other people at all. They simply get obscured by my own fears and depression. There might be people who like me out there and I can't even see it."

"You said your parents suffered a similar trauma in their lives, Adam," said Grace. "What was it?"

"They were survivors of Auschwitz, lost all of their families to the German killing machines. They talked about their experiences of the war all of the time. It was like the milk that I was raised on, as a baby. And I was thinking. Maybe people like Joe just can't understand my values because they have a completely different background, a completely different history. Tyrone suffered his own losses, his own trauma; he understood. He knows what it is to live like an animal, just like I know that when Europe was given the 'permission' to indulge their blood lust, hell was unleashed upon the world, so that the world would never be the same. In fact, it was Hitler himself who very eloquently said that the reason he hated the Jews was that we had the temerity to preach to the world that there is a greater law than the laws of nature. He criticized us for caring for the weak and helpless, for insisting that not only the 'strong' survive. In his view, morality was just an excuse to protect the weak, when all the laws of reason and nature dictated that the weak should die, so that the human race could advance itself. You see, Joe, that is why I hate any 'animal instinct' philosophy. It is always preached by the strong, and it does something horrid to people. A human who really pursues the life of an animal is not an animal, he's a monster."

"Hold it, time out," interrupted Joe, "I'll ignore the monster remark and assume you mean present company excluded."

"I don't think you are a monster, Joe," said Adam.

"That's OK, I don't need your reassurance, and even if you want to think I'm a monster, go ahead, that really does not matter to me. But there is something that you don't understand. My grandfather was in a concentration camp. Your past is not so unique, Adam. The difference between you and me is not that there is trauma in your history but not in mine. I think the difference is in my grandfather. Crazy bastard to be sure, but there was something sane in him that spared me this burden of the war that you carry. He didn't talk about it. He got on with his life, made a fortune in the United States. He put his past behind him. So my

NEVER FORGET MY SOUL

mother didn't have to get a dose of it, and I was spared all that crap from her, which is fine with me, because my parents had a lot of other crap to give me when I was growing up. But I'm not interested in that — their complexes, their mistakes, their problems. I'll just take the cue from my grandfather — move on, don't dwell on things that can't be changed. He was a workaholic, so I'm a playaholic, I like to play. That's why I can live in the world, Adam — I found something I want to do with my life. And you're afraid of living in the world because you don't live in the world; you're just stuck in the past."

PART TWO

Under the influence of a world which no longer recognized the value of human life and dignity, which had robbed man of his will and had made him an object to be exterminated... — under this influence the personal ego finally suffered a loss of values. If the man in the concentration camp did not struggle against this in a last effort to save his self-respect, he lost the feeling of being an individual, a being with a mind, with inner freedom and personal value. He thought of himself then as only a part of an enormous mass of people; his existence descended to the level of animal life. The men were herded — sometimes to one place then to another; sometimes driven together, then apart — like a flock of sheep without a thought or a will of their own. A small but dangerous pack watched them from all sides, well versed in methods of torture and sadism. They drove the herd incessantly, backwards and forwards, with shouts, kicks and blows. And we, the sheep, thought of two things only — how to evade the bad dogs and how to get a little food.
— Victor Frankl, *Man's Search for Meaning*

CHAPTER EIGHT

J oe's maternal grandfather, Yitzchak Cohen, was placed in the concentration camp of Treblinka in February of 1942, when he was eighteen years old. The night before the deportations, rumors had furiously circulated through his small Polish town about Germans who were coming to send them away. Yitzchak had heard these rumors, as he had heard countless others, and there had been no way to know about the validity of such reports. There were so many rumors that circulated at that time, many of them contradictory. But this time, this particular rumor was true. Early in the morning, when the gray of the cloudy daylight had just begun to overtake the darkness, the Germans had come marching with rifles raised.

Yitzchak looked through the window to see a tall blond man with a loudspeaker in his hand. "We are evacuating all Jews!" he announced in German. "You will report to the village square in one hour! Only one bag per person. Anyone disobeying this order will be shot!"

One hour — how many emotions can be experienced in

one hour, shock, rage, bewilderment — all of these and actually all of these but none of them fully, because there was not enough time to feel, just time to make decisions. The first decision was whether he should comply with the order or not. Yitzchak lived in a small two-room house with his parents. There was no option to simply hide in the house, they all knew that the Germans, always thorough, would search every house and that those who disobeyed the order would face immediate death. So the choice was to either go to the village square or to flee to another location. The feasibility of flight depended on how well guarded their area of the town now was. This would take time to assess, time that Yitzchak and his parents did not have. If it had just been Yitzchak by himself, he might have tried to make a run for it. But this was not an option for him. His parents were no longer young — his mother was fifty-eight, his father sixty-five. Living conditions in their town had been difficult and his parents' health was poor. Thus, running away into the woods was not an option. Even if, by some miracle, they eluded the scrutiny of the soldiers who occupied the town, his parents would probably not survive for a week, hiding in the forest, while trying to find other quarters in which to stay. Thus, there was no choice but to obey the orders.

While Yitzchak's first reaction was to think, his mother's first reaction was to pack. She quickly lay out three small suitcases and hurriedly threw in the essentials — clothes, undergarments, food for the journey, a prayer book and Bible, shoes, needles and thread. She made sure to include extra sweaters, which she had knitted herself, to protect them from the bitter cold. She put in the silver candlesticks that her grandmother had given her and eight candles for the Sabbath, all of the candles that she had in the house. The way a woman made the Sabbath holy was by lighting two candles on Friday evening (to mark the coming of the Sabbath) and by saying a special heartfelt blessing for her family. Although the candlesticks would add extra weight, she felt that they would protect her little family. Her father, a rabbi, had always taught that if the Jewish people protected the Sabbath, then God would protect them. Yitzchak's father assisted his wife with the packing. While Yitzchak was still thinking, his mother looked up at him and noticed his inaction.

"Pack, my dear," she implored. "There is no option, there is nothing to be done. To resist is to die. Please, we will obey and put our trust in God."

Yitzchak's mother had given birth to him when she was forty years of age. Yitzchak's parents had been married for twenty years before his mother gave birth to Yitzchak, and they had given up hope of having children long before that time. They had named him Yitzchak in commemoration of the biblical story of Abraham and Sarah who were blessed with a child when Abraham was one hundred years of age and Sarah was ninety. In the story, Abraham and Sarah believed that Sarah had long passed her child-bearing years. When God announced to Abraham that a son would be born to him, he laughed, out of joy, at the miracles that God could perform. Sarah later laughed, when she overheard Abraham talking with angles about the upcoming birth, but Sarah, who appeared to have taken a more practical, down-to-earth view of this announcement, laughed at the absurdity of such a promise. Abraham and Sarah named their son Yitzchak in commemoration of the laughter that surrounded the circumstances of his birth. Mrs. Cohen had often told her son that she named him Yitzchak for the same reason — that her new baby and growing child had brought laughter into the lives of two people, who were "sometimes too serious about things."

When Mrs. Cohen begged Yitzchak to obey, she was responding to a sense of dread within herself, a dread that her precious gift from God, Yitzchak, would do something rash and end up brutally murdered by the Germans. Yitzchak was a strong boy, with a quick temper. He had been in fights before with Polish residents of the town. She feared he would listen to his fighting instinct.

To her relief, Yitzchak complied with her pleas and the family finished packing fifteen minutes before the designated assembly time — enough time to make it to the village square, which was a short walk away. As they walked through the snow-covered ground, they huddled closely together to avoid the cold breeze. Yitzchak heard his father, who recited a chapter of Psalms every day "for protection," begin to mutter verses from memory. Yitzchak joined in with his father, in order to give him a feeling of solidarity.

As the family walked, they encountered other villagers, trudging forwards to comply with the German orders. Yitzchak gave a quick nod as he met the eyes of other villagers. Everyone, including Yitzchak, looked grim. The sound of the German loudspeaker grew louder as they approached the village square.

"You will go to your designated places and line up as ordered!" boomed the voice. "The line on the right will be taken by foot to trains which will transport you to new settlements. The line on the left will be taken for questioning." Yitzchak's stomach tightened at the last word, "questioning." Two lines — that meant separation, and "questioning", that meant something sinister; Yitzchak did not know what, but it sounded bad.

Yitzchak and his parents approached the crowd in the village square. German soldiers were striding about, their heavy boots stomping on the ground. They would roughly grab and push people, ordering them to go to one of the two lines. Some soldiers merely stood by and pointed their rifles menacingly. Yitzchak caught a close-up view of a soldier's face, which was twisted into a sadistic grin as he watched another soldier kick an elderly lady and shout at her to stay in line. When he saw this, Yitzchak's hand clenched into a fist. His mother seemed to intuitively sense his reaction. She held his arm tightly and said to him quietly, "There is nothing to be done now. We must obey. Just do what they say. My darling boy, that is the only way to survive."

Just then, Yitzchak felt a rough hand grab his arm and wrench it out of the grasp of his mother. The hand belonged to a young soldier, likely close to Yitzchak's age.

"You," he commanded Yitzchak, "get over to the line on the left." He pushed Yitzchak in the direction of that line, and then spoke to Yitzchak's parents, while pushing them in the other direction, "You will go to the line on the right."

There are moments, in the course of one's life, when time stands still, forever burned into one's memory, while simultaneously, time seems to speed forward so quickly that, try as one might, one cannot grasp hold of it at all, to make any sense of it. This was such a time for Yitzchak. Suddenly there was no thought, no meaning, only unconnected sensations. He saw his parents' faces — his father's shock, his mother's wild-eyed panic. He heard her call his name. Then he heard the soldier shouting orders, roughly pushing his parents away. He saw his mother's face suddenly change from wild to blank, absolutely blank, and he heard her emotionless, but insistent voice, "Go. *Do what they say.*" He felt rough arms grab him, push him forward. He felt his body moving through space, hitting the ground, a heavy boot kick him. Again, there was an ordering voice, "**GET UP NOW! LINE TO THE LEFT!!**" Then there were faces — faces of young men, dismayed, afraid or emotionless, some in ragged coats, some better dressed, but all hopeless, men who lined up behind and in front of Yitzchak.

The bitter cold wind crept into Yitzchak's clothes, as he stood there in an unthinking blur. He heard a scream and thought it was his mother. He looked around to see a soldier kicking a woman who lay in the snow, while he commanded her to get up and go to the right. Yitzchak heard a few shots in the distance, more commands over a loudspeaker far away, more shots. Time slowed to a standstill as he stood, shifting from one foot to the other, trying to maintain feeling in his toes. Finally came the shouted command: "March!!" At first there was no change, but slowly the line in front of Yitzchak began to move and he marched forward.

Yitzchak did not know how long they marched. It could have been two days; it could have been a week. Time stopped from the moment that he was torn away from his parents. As he marched forward, the cold in his hands and feet turned to numbness, as did the pain and fatigue in his legs. Occasionally, sensation in his legs would return, giving him a powerful urge to simply drop to the ground and lay motionless. Sometimes a fellow-marcher in front, or behind, of Yitzchak would succumb to this urge, and a soldier would kick him and shout at him to get up. Some complied, some did not. The ones who did not were shot. Yitzchak reacted little to this brutality. It was as if his self had suddenly shrunk deep within him and he was untouched by anything that was happening around him. The march was timeless, but finally came to an end at a "community" of buildings surrounded by barbed-wire fences.

Yitzchak had arrived at Treblinka. This was Treblinka I, a labor camp for those accused of crimes by the invading Germans. In Yitzchak's case, the Germans had encountered some resistance by the Polish residents of his village, when the Germans had come. The German response was to round up all the young men in the village, Jew and Gentile, and to march them off to Treblinka.

After arriving at the camp, Yitzchak was so weary from the march that he complied with all orders unthinkingly. He undressed, showered, put on the prisoner uniforms that were issued to him, ate a bowl of thin soup with some foul-tasting vegetable floating in it. He drank greedily any water that was given to him. The prisoners were then commanded to assemble, and their work duties were explained to them. They were all to work in the gravel pits. They would be awakened at 5:30 in the morning and would be expected to assemble to march to the pits at 6:00. Yitzchak and a large group of men were then led to their sleeping quarters — long rooms, crowded with bunks composed of boards of wood. Yitzchak then collapsed in his bunk and instantly entered a fitful sleep.

Days, weeks, months, passed. Yitzchak did not know how many. Time hardly seemed to matter there. Life was merely an endless succession of early risings, a body that almost refused to move out of the bunk, trudging to the gravel pits, the backbreaking labor, the blows and shouts of guards to work faster and harder, to keep marching. There was the unsatisfying soup, a small piece of stale bread, insults, laughter of the guards, and the saliva running down Yitzchak's face, after a guard would spit at him and command him not to wipe it off.

On many occasions, Yitzchak simply wanted to end it all, to run out towards the barbed-wire fence at the perimeter of the camp and meet welcoming bullets from the guard towers above and a blessed end, blessed rest. Then he would hear his mother's voice, which had been burned in his memory: "Go. *Do what they say*," and he would comply. It was somehow an act of homage to his mother that he would comply with her advice, stay alive, if not for himself, at least for her. By focusing on his love for her and his desire to live for her, he kept his self, which had been buried deep within him, from being annihilated. He felt that if he let go of his mother, he would become something completely non-human. He already felt that much of his humanity had been stripped away. He was herded mercilessly to and from the gravel pits while the guards reacted without sympathy to weakness, suffering or pain. He saw himself as a donkey whipped by an impatient owner who pushed him to work harder. Both the guards' commands and his mother's former plea were pushing him in the same direction — to not question, to not think, to simply march and follow the cruel orders.

His body weakened, and he became increasingly thinner on the meager rations that were provided to him. He tried not to look at his own or others' bodies while they were undressed, because of the death-like impression their skeleton forms created in his mind. After working in the gravel pits for about half a year, he was transported to Treblinka II. "You will be going to a sister camp for a new work assignment" –this was the only explanation given to him and to the fellow prisoners who were reassigned to that location. Treblinka II was the killing center. At first, Yitzchak tried to hide this fact from his conscious mind. German attempts at secrecy and deception conspired with his mind's attempts to repress the truth. Incoming prisoners were sorted, then they were told that they needed to be sanitized to guard against disease. All heads were shorn, and then the prisoners were forced to undress and run down a fenced-in path to the "bathhouse." These measures were all presented as reasonable precautions to avoid outbreaks of disease in the camp. But Yitzchak had seen enough of the German practices, and had heard enough of the mutterings of his fellow prisoners, to know what was occurring. Although he was not responsible for the removal of the gassed bodies, it was impossible to ignore that thousands entered the "bathhouse" but no one was ever seen emerging from it. And then there was the terrible black smoke that started to emerge from the camp smokestacks, day after day, indicating that the German machine of destruction was now firmly in place.

Yitzchak's job, along with a number of other prisoners, was to sort through prisoners' belongings. He would put the belongings in different boxes and crates — for jewelry, clothes, shoes, glasses, children's toys, money — lines of boxes and crates. And when one was filled, he would carry it to the outgoing area (from which another prisoner would carry it to the storage building), and he would put another container in its place to fill it with more "treasures." Occasionally, a German soldier with sandy blond hair and a mustache would come into the sorting area. He would fish around the jewelry box for a few minutes and pull out a particularly attractive piece of jewelry. He would smile to himself and say something like, "So easy to buy a girl these days." He would then frown at the prisoners and command them to sort faster. After that, he would stride out of the room.

Although Yitzchak was not directly involved in the killing machine, he hated the work and he hated himself for participating in it. Still, he would hear his mother's voice, and dream that some day they could be reunited and that he could take care of her and his father. So he continued to comply with the orders, and tried to push into the dark shadows of his mind the horrors that were occurring a few hundred yards away.

One night, after he had been in the Treblinka camp complex for about a year, he climbed into his bunk and saw one his coworkers from the sorting room lying beside him. The man's name was David. He was balding, in his forties, with a gray rim of stubble around the perimeter of his shaved head.

"It's coming to an end," said David.

"What is?" asked Yitzchak.

"This camp is," replied David, "this whole killing machine. They're going to take it down. Then they'll force us to clean it up, to hide the evidence. Then they'll kill us, the witnesses. It's all coming to an end. Don't you notice, fewer and fewer people are coming in these days? I've been talking with a group of prisoners who talk with those who know. Our only hope is to fight back and get the hell out of here."

Words filled Yitzchak's mouth that were not his own. He said, "To resist is to die," faithfully repeating his mother's warning.

Suddenly, Yitzchak felt a sharp pain on his cheek. It was David smacking him.

"You stupid idiot! I shouldn't even be talking to you. Maybe I'm the idiot, for some reason I like you, so I wanted to give you a chance to survive. If that's your attitude, you can just stay here and rot with the other cowards." David covered his face with his hands and whimpered. Prisoners generally did not cry, but sometimes they would whimper. Strong displays of emotions were dangerous. It called the guards' attention to prisoners, and marked the prisoner as someone worthy of torment. In addition, strong displays of emotion wasted precious energy that was needed for survival.

"How many mothers and children have been marched to their deaths," David finally said, "while we have stood idly by, helping the Germans loot their belongings? They kill, we steal. I've had it with being their partners in crime. I'm going to get out of here and kill some Germans."

David's words had smacked Yitzchak much more than David's hand had. When David had mentioned mothers being marched to their death, a few impressions were aroused in Yitzchak's mind, almost simultaneously. First, he had the image of his own mother, shivering in the snow, roughly pushed by a guard to her extermination. Then a hatred arose in his breast, a ferocious hatred the likes of which he had never known before. And suddenly the fog lifted, a fog that had surrounded him for over a year, the fog that had descended on him when the German soldiers had roughly separated him from his parents. In this moment, lying beside David, Yitzchak felt the self that he had buried deep within start to expand. He had been a willful youth, not taking bullying from others, always ready to fight when challenged. He had turned into a frightened, herded animal, with no individuality or will of his own. All that Yitzchak had tried to hide from himself suddenly emerged. The Germans were systematically exterminating Europe's Jews. He was nothing to them. The time would come when Yitzchak himself would go marching into the "bathhouse," never to return, or he would be simply shot and thrown into a trench. To resist might be *likely* death. But *not* to resist was certain death; it was only a matter of time.

Yitzchak turned to David. "Do you have a plan?" Yitzchak asked.

NEVER FORGET MY SOUL

"Do *I* have a plan?" David asked, turning earnest eyes toward Yitzchak. "Yes, *we* have a plan." He looked around suspiciously, lowered his voice to a barely audible whisper and continued, "We've been talking about it for months. There's a group of us, at least sixty solidly with us. We are going to sneak into the armory, grab every weapon we can get our hands on, kill some Germans, torch this place and get out."

"When?" asked Yitzchak.

David leaned forward and whispered into Yitzchak's ear, "Tomorrow."

The Treblinka camp rebellion on the second of August, 1943 was mostly a failure. Before the resistance leaders could gain full control of the camp's arms, a shot was fired, which killed a suspicious SS guard. This shot did two things. It alerted the camp guards and it prematurely signaled the beginning of the revolt to the other inmates. In the ensuing pandemonium, some gunfire was exchanged between the inmates and guards, and some camp buildings were set on fire. Hundreds of prisoners tried to storm the fence and escape. Most of these prisoners were gunned down by watchtower guards. About 300 prisoners actually made it past the camp's gates, but most of these were captured and killed by forces patrolling the area around the camp. Some did survive, however. Yitzchak was one of them.

Yitzchak rushed out of the camp, over the fence that had been flattened by the mass of prisoners surrounding him. Bullets whizzed overhead. Shouts, screams, and smoke filled the air. He ran as fast as he could. The inmates turned from the road, seeking to get to the cover of the woods as quickly as possible. He heard more shots as men fell around him. He did not look back. He finally entered the woods with a small group of men. They sat to rest for a few minutes and planned what to do next. One man next to Yitzchak was badly wounded — his shirt was soaked with blood. Yitzchak opened the man's shirt and saw a rough gash in his left side.

"It's no good," the man said to him, weakly. "I'm finished. At least I think I got a few of those bastards. Take my rifle. Maybe you'll have the chance to kill a few of your own."

Yitzchak hesitated.

"Take it," the man insisted.

Yitzchak reached out and gingerly lifted the rifle strap over the man's head.

The man lay quietly for a few minutes. He then groaned, and made a gurgling sound in his throat. He started gasping for air. A few minutes later, he was dead.

The group of men continued to discuss their options. Suddenly they heard shouts, and gunfire. They could see more soldiers in the clearing approaching their hiding place. The inmates got up again and began to run. In all the confusion, Yitzchak was separated from the rest of the group. He ran on through the woods, for as long as he had strength to run, and then he collapsed on the ground, unable to keep his eyes open, as sleep overtook him.

When he awoke, it was night. He thought it best to keep moving, since the cover of night was the safest time for him to travel. Luckily, a full moon assisted him in navigating his way through the forest. Nonetheless, he would sometimes trip over a tree root or some unseen branch. After two hours of walking, he came to a clearing in the woods. In the clearing, he could see a small house and a barn, about fifty yards away, in a valley below. Yitzchak was terribly hungry and even more thirsty. Perhaps, there was some nourishment to be had at this place. He carefully approached the barn.

When he reached the barn, he gently pushed open a creaky door, just wide enough for him to enter. In the moonlight, he could make out the form of a horse, which appeared to be sleeping. Beside the horse was a water trough. Yitzchak put his lips into the trough and greedily sucked in the water. He began to explore the barn for any signs of food. He found a crate of old potatoes, of which he ate his fill. They tasted disgusting, but they filled his stomach. As he was eating, it began to rain heavily. He decided to try to wait out the rain. As he crouched in the darkness, a feeling of warmth settled in his filled stomach and eventually traveled to his head. Before he knew it, he was asleep.

After a long blackness and silence, he dreamed. In his dream, he was blind. He was running with a man holding his arm. He could tell from the man's voice that it was David from the camp. Gunfire sounded all around him. David said to him, through panting breaths, "Germans, everywhere. We can only hold out a little longer. Let's just kill as many Germans as we can."

"But I can't see," responded Yitzchak.

"Just shoot, they're everywhere," answered David. "You're sure to get some of them."

"Kill Germans! Kill Germans!" shouted Yitzchak, as he opened fire.

Yitzchak was still muttering "kill Germans" when he awoke to the feeling of a sharp pain in his side. He groggily looked up to see a human form standing above him. He then came to shocked awareness and saw that it was a man, holding a rifle pointed at Yitzchak. The gun looked just like the one Yitzchak had taken, and Yitzchak glanced around him to discover that his own gun was gone.

The man was about six feet tall, although he looked much taller with Yitzchak sitting on the ground beneath him. He had dark hair and a big mustache beneath a large nose. His face was broad and fat. He looked like he was in his mid-forties. His boots were covered with dried mud and his pants had splotches of mud on them as well. The man grinned at Yitzchak and said, in Polish,

"So you want to kill Germans. From the looks of your costume, you've come from the camp. Get up!" Yitzchak did not move. Both his mind and body seemed to be moving in slow motion, and he had to go through deliberate laborious steps to first conclude that he was in great danger and then override the fatigue throughout his body.

"Get up!" the man repeated, his face serious and threatening. This time, Yitzchak complied.

"Drop your pants," said the man.

Yitzchak was surprised with the way he complied with so little emotion. Under other circumstances, Yitzchak might have been frantically wondering what this man was after, with such an order. But Yitzchak had been subjected to so much demoralization, so many forced undressings, work beyond endurance and heartbreak beyond emotion, that what was one more demeaning command?

The man gasped when he saw Yitzchak's emaciated hips and legs. "My Lord! Do they starve you there? You're nothing but a skeleton." And then he added, making note of Yitzchak's circumcision, "a Jewish skeleton." He cocked his head to the side for a moment and thought. Then he said, "What's your name, Jew?"

"Yitzchak."

"Ok," the man said, "you can put your pants on again. And, for goodness sake, sit down. You need to take it easy. You look like you're about to fall down." The man lowered the rifle and held it loosely in one hand. He squatted in front of Yitzchak who had lowered himself to the floor. The man extended his hand.

"I'm Roman, a pleasure to meet you," Yitzchak reluctantly took his hand and gave it a limp shake. The man continued, "You and I have something in common, Yitzchak the Jew. We both want to kill Germans. In fact, I would be far from here doing it right now if it wasn't for my cursed mother. It's all her fault and God's fault. You Jews read the Bible, right?" Yitzchak gave a small nod.

NEVER FORGET MY SOUL

"All that stuff about honor your father and mother. Well, Dad's dead, that one's off my neck. But Mom, well, she just won't die. Eighty years old, this December. I can't leave her here by herself, and all of my siblings had the good sense to get married and run off to... God knows where. So here I am stuck with her. I hate Germans, I know what they are doing to this country. They've just come here to rape, kill and steal, and it's really pissing me off. But what am I to do? I know the way God works these things. He's got a special room in hell for people who abandon their parents. I don't know exactly what they do there, but I've heard it's horrible. They probably force you to stay there for eternity and listen to your mother tell you that you're a lousy, good-for-nothing... Hmm, maybe I'm in hell now. That's what it's like living with her. I wait on her hand and foot and everything is — 'the soup is too hot... the tea is too cold.' Then she spends half the day telling me that if I had not been such a lazy good-for-nothing, I could have made some money and got a good house and not subjected her to live in this dump. But look, that's my problem, not yours. Your problem is that you want to kill Germans. And it looks to me like you have good reason to. But you're in no condition to fight anyone now. You need to get some food and some strength into you. I'll make you a deal. Since you find my barn so comfortable, it can be your home for a month. But remember, if anyone comes around snooping, and finds you, then I'll say I don't know who the hell you are. It's up to you to hide in the hay or in the cellar or behind the horse, wherever you want to. But no coming out of the barn. I insist on that. I don't want anyone accusing me of knowing about you, 'cause then they'll shoot me and leave my poor mother to die and then God will force me to have to listen to her groaning that the soup is too cold for eternity. You stay here, rest. You'll need exercise too, to get stronger, but leave the exercise for the night, when you are less likely to be noticed. Then, in a month, when you are ready to go, you'll get your gun back. I'll just hold onto it for now. A person has to be careful these days. Is it a deal?"

Yitzchak was more at ease now. Roman seemed to be sincere. Yitzchak's face formed into a weak smile and he shook Roman's hand. "Thank you," said Yitzchak quietly.

"The way you thank me," said Roman, with a serious look on your face, "is you kill some of those Germans for me. OK, let me get you some breakfast. And I'll get you a change of clothes, too. Wouldn't be good for someone to see you in your prisoner's uniform." Roman paused, looking pensive for a moment. He then grabbed a bucket that lay close by and handed it to Yitzchak. "Poop in the bucket," said Roman, "and cover it with something. I guess I'll have to dump it for you, since you can't go out."

———⊃०ॖ०⊂———

Roman kept his word. He faithfully fed Yitzchak well and removed Yitzchak's excrement once a day, after dark. One month later, in the middle of the night, Roman awoke Yitzchak and handed him his gun.

"It's time," said Roman. "The German patrols are getting too close to here now. You have to go. Go into the woods and start looking. If you look for long enough, you will find groups of partisans, who will help you with your war against the Germans. Good luck, Yitzchak, the Jew. And a word of advice: Don't call yourself Yitzchak. Call yourself Stephan. There are too many partisans who are less then kind to Jews, and for heaven's sake, don't let them see you with your pants down. Good luck. Kill some Germans for me."

Yitzchak nodded, smiled and said, "Thank you, Roman." He offered a firm handshake and departed.

Yitzchak disappeared into the dark of night. It did not take Yitzchak long to find the partisans. In fact, they found him. The next day, he was walking through the woods, when he was suddenly surrounded by a group of men, all with their guns pointed at

NEVER FORGET MY SOUL

Yitzchak. None of them wore soldiers' uniforms. Yitzchak kept his cool, introduced himself as Stephan, and said he was glad that he had found them, for he wanted to fight with the partisans. A short, stout man, who appeared to be their leader stepped forward and began to interrogate Yitzchak. Yitzchak stated that he was Polish, that he had escaped from Treblinka, that he had been living in the woods and was looking to join a partisan group. Yitzchak managed to pull it off, and he was accepted into the group.

Yitzchak fought with the partisans for the remainder of the war. He managed to maintain his assumed non-Jewish identity throughout that time. Life with the partisans was one of constant struggle — struggle to obtain food, adequate clothing and shelter from the harsh Polish winter. When they could, Yitzchak and his companions would build dugout shelters from the ground, sometimes sealing them with stolen barn doors. However, in order to avoid detection, the partisans had to frequently be on the move, and thus leave the relative shelter of these crude dwellings. Often Yitzchak had to sleep on the forest ground, in the freezing rain and snow. The partisans would huddle together to share body warmth, as the winter steadily stole heat from their bodies through their drenched clothes. On some particularly cold nights, Yitzchak simply ran for miles, to keep his blood circulating and to avoid freezing to death. When they could, his companions would steal boots and shoes or take them off dead bodies. Some partisans were shoeless and had only strips of cloth to wrap around their feet. In winter, some of these shoeless individuals soaked their cloth-wrapped feet in water, and walked in boots made of ice. Yitzchak had an old pair of boots given to him by Roman. They were uncomfortable and too big, but he stuffed them with rags, so he could wear them. When they started to leak and disintegrate, he wrapped rags around them, to hold them together and try to keep out the snow. Whenever possible, the partisans would sneak into small towns and steal food, clothing or needed medical supplies. Sometimes they would force Polish doctors to remove bullets from the wounded at gunpoint. At other times, the wounded had to extract their own bullets with crude instruments sterilized with vodka. At one point, Yitzchak had to resort to this procedure.

The main work of Yitzchak and his small group of twenty partisans was to mine train tracks, thus disrupting German supply and transportation channels. They were also involved in destroying communication lines. Yitzchak rarely saw actual arm-to-arm combat with Germans, but he was satisfied with the knowledge that his work had led to the death of many Germans operating the train lines and was having a larger impact on the course of the war.

Notwithstanding the hardship of his time with the partisans, Yitzchak never felt the sense of hopelessness that he felt in Treblinka. For much of the war he was cold or hungry or in pain, but he was free and he could fight. He rested as little as possible and preferred to be always on the move, stealing more supplies for himself and his fellow fighters, scouting around their encampment to check for enemy activity, communicating with sister partisan groups. He detested sitting still or waiting. The moment he did, he started to feel an oppressive sense of being trapped, an irrational feeling that by sitting still the Germans were getting control of him again, and that soon he would be back behind barbed wire. His fellow fighters came to respect him for his tireless devotion to "the cause." But they did not realize that Yitzchak believed he had no choice. It was much better to keep moving than to stop, feel and allow his mind to re-experience those sneering, merciless German faces from the camp, the naked, freezing, emaciated prisoners, and Yitzchak's own previous zombie-like state.

When the war was over, Yitzchak maintained his tireless activity. As soon as he could, he obtained a visa to go the United

States. The immigration official on Ellis Island had no idea how to spell "Yitzchak", and was unable to communicate in the three languages that Yitzchak knew — Yiddish, Polish and Hebrew. "Screw it," said the official as he wrote down "Scott Cohen." Thus Yitzchak became "Scott". He did not mind. "Yitzchak" was a biblical name and reminded him that before the war, he had been a religious Jew. While the camp had not murdered his body, it had murdered his faith. He had concluded that God, if He existed, had abandoned the world during the war. He was not interested in having a relationship with such a God. He was of the belief that only his own effort, cunning and grit had brought him through the war, and the less he thought of a loving heavenly father, the better. The very thought disgusted him. He also disliked the name "Yitzchak" because it made him think of his parents. "Yitzchak" would always be the boy who brought pleasure to his mother, who had thought herself barren. There was no mother to please; there was no father's hand to hold. The only way to avoid the enveloping pit of despair was to act, and he threw himself into his activity with a superhuman passion.

His work became the venue through which he chose to channel his passion for activity. He started selling food on the street corner, working twelve hours a day. He managed to save and borrow enough money to open a small hat store. He read about fashion tirelessly and developed an uncanny skill at predicting upcoming trends in women's headwear. That little store became quite successful. Ten years after disembarking in America, he had managed to invest, build capital and buy a clothing factory. His schedule changed very little from the time that he worked on the street corner — twelve-hour days. The only change was that, when he bought the factory, he allowed himself an eight-hour day on Sundays.

About a year after coming to America, he married Miriam Sachs, an American-born Jew. Even with all of his work, he never had problems getting a girl. They were attracted to his dynamism and intensity. But he had become tired of serial relationships. In truth, his main reason for disliking such relationships was that each new woman had new needs and demands, and he had very little interest in figuring all that out. He hoped that marriage would provide more predictability to satisfy his sexual needs, without all the drama of the girl needing to be courted. He was upfront with Miriam about his work habits.

"I work hard and long hours," he told her. "If you want to get anywhere in this world, that's what you have to do. Most people are lazy pigs and that's why they spend their lives wallowing in the mud. You think I'm going to be successful, fine. Then you have to be willing to pay the price. Don't expect me to come home and have dinner with you every night."

Miriam had grown up poor. She was a practical girl, and she believed that he was going to do well financially. Although he was far from romantic, he could give her a secure life, in which she would never want. If she did not get sufficient love from him, hopefully their children could fill that void. However, they ended up having only one child, Rebecca, who was born ten months after their marriage. After Scott saw how much the new baby disrupted their sexual life, he told Miriam that she now had her baby to love, and one was enough. "Don't expect more kids from me," he told her. "I need peace and quiet at home, and not a lot of distractions. Remember, it's my job to make money, not populate the next generation."

While Miriam had never hoped for a particularly warm and close relationship with her husband, she underestimated how cold and inaccessible he would become. He was completely consumed by his work. He would rise at five in the morning, to be at the workplace at six. He would explain that he had to arrive an hour before his workers, so they would know that he was not a slacker and that he expected similar devotion from them. Scott's

NEVER FORGET MY SOUL

conviction in the inherent laziness of workers grew in intensity as the years passed. He would say, "If you are not constantly watching the workers, they are either goofing off or stealing, and usually both." His conviction in the laziness of workers was actually rooted in a general conviction that humanity was lazy. He relentlessly complained about how little Miriam accomplished.

When Rebecca was one year of age, she was already walking and she waddled around, pulling books off shelves and food off tables and spreading her toys throughout the apartment. One night around that time, Scott came home, without saying a word to Miriam, a grim impenetrable expression on his face. Miriam did not react to the expression, for she had grown used to it. Scott poured himself a scotch and tonic. He settled into the lounge chair and started reading the newspaper. After a few minutes, he turned to Miriam and said, "What did you do today?" Some questions are requests for information; some are accusations. The tone of Scott's voice indicated that his intent was the latter. Miriam, who was always trying to minimize conflict with her sullen husband, tried to provide a simple answer, patiently explaining the mundane activities of her day, the shopping, the cooking, the extra care to changing the baby and putting on ointment, as she was suffering a bad diaper rash. She concluded by saying, "What can I tell you? I've been busy with this and that."

"Bullsh**," said Scott.

"Excuse me?" asked Miriam.

"You heard me! If you had been busy enough, this place would not look like a pigsty!"

Miriam had had it with her husband's complaints. Her voice raised in pitch and volume and she said, "Look, Mr. Know-it-all, you stay at home and take care of all this for a day, and then you can lecture me on how to do it!"

During the war, Scott had learned the value of decisiveness, in thought and in action. At crucial times, as a fighter, indecisiveness meant certain death — one did not question oneself, one did not look back. One simply intuited the next necessary step and acted without delay. This attitude had created a pattern of action in Scott that some might have called impulsive. But Scott did not see it that way at all. Sure, he appeared to lose his temper at times, sure, he would yell. But it was always yelling for a purpose, to get control of the situation. His wife had just demeaned him, and that was unacceptable. He needed peace and order at home, not challenges and complaint. He was not going to let squabbles interfere with his goals and work. So he intuited what needed to be done and he acted. He calmly arose and walked over to the dining room table, which had already been set for dinner. With a swiftness and fluidity that allowed for no anticipation, he grabbed the edge of the table and flipped it over, sending plates, glasses, silverware and a large glass vase flying against the wall. Rebecca, who had been on the other side of the room at the time, began to cry, and Miriam ran to comfort her.

Scott strode over to Miriam, who was crouching on the floor, holding Rebecca. He looked contemptuously down at her and said between clenched teeth. "Here's your lecture: When you have slept on the ground in the dead of the Polish winter; when you have marched for three days without stopping; when you have worked from dawn to dusk, day after day, as you are being systematically starved; when you have had to dig a home in the ground, in subzero temperatures, only to abandon that home the next day and march for days until you can build another; when you have lived on onions and moldy potatoes; when you have removed bullets from your flesh with a kitchen knife and a bottle of vodka; then you can tell me how hard your work is. In the meantime, when I come home tomorrow, this mess will be cleaned, as will the rest of the apartment. It will be shining. Otherwise, you and the girl will go, and you will never come back."

Scott then put on his shoes and coat and left the apartment.

NEVER FORGET MY SOUL

Deep within the recesses of Rebecca's mind, a preverbal memory was being formed — the anger in her mother's eyes; the coldness in her father's; her father's explosive, unpredictable behavior, and the violence and the odd detachment with which he acted; her father appearing to grow larger, after he had upset the table and spoken to her mother; her mother's shrinkage; and her mother's collapsing on the floor, sobbing, after Rebecca's father left. Rebecca walked up to her mother and began to cry as well. Her mother picked her up, held her, and they cried together.

Miriam could have decided to leave Scott that night. She could have returned to her parents with Rebecca, gotten divorced and started a new life. But going home to her parents meant defeat. It meant admitting that she had made a wrong choice and then listening to her mother's constant complaints that she always thought Scott was a bad pick. Her mother would tell her that she had been too headstrong in getting married, and that Miriam should have listened to her mother's warnings. Miriam decided to stay. After a quarter hour of crying, she pulled herself together, put Rebecca to sleep and started sweeping up the broken dishes and glasses.

As the years progressed, Miriam's sense of independence and individuality became increasingly submerged. She had made her choice to stay, and she was not willing to question it again. As Scott became more successful, she became even more reluctant to leave him, because she became accustomed to the comfort of their lifestyle. As his control over her became more absolute, she experienced a deepening depression. She was able to maintain an external sense of functioning, but there was a deadness in her eyes. Rebecca grew up witnessing this deadness. As is natural for children, she blamed her mother's depression on herself, thinking that she had done something to displease her mother. As a child, Rebecca sought out a variety of ways to cheer up her mother, or at least obtain her mother's attention, and take some of the deadness out of her mother's eyes. But nothing worked. After a while, Rebecca just gave up and started to avoid her mother. Her best refuge was reading. Rebecca learned to read in kindergarten and thereafter was constantly with a book in her hands.

The night that Scott threw over the table was burned into Rebecca's mind as a prototype of her parents' functioning. Her father was powerful, dominating and strong. Her mother was weak and compliant. While Rebecca was afraid of her father, she also gravitated towards him, because he *did not* have dead eyes. They were not warm eyes, but there was life in them — one could elicit a response from him. Eliciting that response was both dangerous and thrilling to Rebecca. Scott respected intelligence, which he felt was associated with power, and Rebecca had intelligence in abundance. She would constantly ask Scott questions, such as "Why is it cold in the winter?" and "Who made the first blacksmith mallet?" and "What makes magnets work?" Her reading supplied her with many of these questions, and answers as well. But she pretended to not know the answers. She wanted her father to be impressed by the questions and to be engaged in answering. Scott, who was pleased by his daughter's inquisitive mind, always tried to give her an adequate answer. But obtaining an answer was only the beginning of Rebecca's game, because answering the question by itself did not draw her father into engagement with her. The engagement resulted from the follow-up question, which indicated that she was considering the question in a sophisticated manner. For example, if her father told her that the first blacksmith mallet was made by the first blacksmith, she followed up with the question, "But what mallet did he use to make it?" At this point, her father would either smile or frown, depending on how artfully she had asked the question. The question had to be delivered in a sense of sweet innocence and perplexity that did not indicate any degree of challenge. If she was successful in her delivery, he would smile, wag his finger at her and say, "You smart little one, that's a good question." He would then scratch his head for a moment and try to provide an answer. However, if he took the question as her implying that *he* did not know what he was talking about, then he would simply frown, mutter to himself and walk away from her. As Rebecca grew into her teen years, the complexity of the follow-up question had to increase, to keep her father's attention. As her learning increased, the potential for discussions to appear as a challenge to him increased. On some occasions, she became frustrated with him, raised her voice and was slapped in the face for her "insolence." One day, when she was sixteen years old, she decided that she had had enough of trying to curry the favor of her sullen father. She turned her attention to dating, with the hope that the young men who courted her would have more appreciation for her talents.

Rebecca's father never spoke to her about the war. Occasionally her mother would allude to it, saying that her father was a great war hero. Miriam would tell Rebecca that they had to be understanding of Scott, because he had suffered greatly during the war and had bravely fought against the Germans. Scott's silence about the war increased the proportions of his heroism in Rebecca's mind. In her imagination, she saw an amalgam of the power he projected at home and war adventures about which she had read. While Rebecca had a fear of her father's anger and hatred of his domination, she paradoxically admired his strength.

When she was eighteen years old, Rebecca attended university, and following university, she was enrolled in law school. When she told her father that she had been accepted to law school, he had replied, "Good, you're certainly bright enough to do that. No daughter of mine is going to turn into some lazy soap-opera-watching house-wife." Rebecca felt a tinge of pain as she realized that this was an insult to her mother, who was a regular watcher of the "soaps." In law school, she met Matthew Barnes. Matthew came from a Christian family. While he was not religious himself, he attended church regularly, so his family "would stay off his back about it."

From the moment she met Matthew, there was something that drew her to him. He was handsome, charming, romantic, confident and strikingly smart. He obtained straight A's, and he hardly ever studied. The night after their first date and their first kiss, she dreamily walked up to her apartment and thought how nice it was to be with a WASP, who did not carry the burden and intensity of the war and the past. Being Jewish always had expectations attached to it. Her father had suffered because of his Jewishness, and now she was expected to make her mark on the world to somehow prove that his survival mattered. She was so tired of inherited guilt. She fell deeper and deeper in love with Matthew, this attentive man who wrote her love poetry and composed songs for her.

In her last year of law school, she announced to her parents that she was getting married. Her father asked in a bland voice, "What is the boy's name?"

Rebecca held her breath for a moment and then answered, "Matthew Barnes."

As was usually the case when her parents were together, Scott did the speaking. It seemed like an eternity before he finally responded. "Matthew," he finally said. "Matthew — he's not Jewish."

"No, he is not," responded Rebecca, her heart starting to race.

After another eternity: "This is not a marriage that will have our blessing," her father said. "And we will not be attending the *wedding and festivities.*" He drew out the words "wedding and festivities" in a contemptuous manner, as if he were smelling a disgusting stench.

"He is a good man, father," Rebecca insisted.

"He is not one of us," he replied. "He cannot be good for you."

Rebecca had suspected such a reaction from her father, although she had tried to hold onto an irrational hope that her father would be supportive or pleased. His reaction maddened her, because it seemed so nonsensical. Here was her father, who had shown no interest in his religion throughout her life, now telling her that she should be marrying a Jew. What did being Jewish matter, if Matthew was a good man who would treat her well? Rebecca envisioned her father turning his back on her, disowning her, never speaking to her again. As much as she feared and hated him, she also dreaded the thought of losing him. She desperately sought some support or understanding.

"Father, I don't know what it means to be Jewish," said Rebecca. "Do you? We never went to synagogue. I never saw you open a Bible or prayer book. What does religion matter? I thought you always wanted me to find a good and strong man, and I have found one. Please, Father."

"Being Jewish means that they killed most of us, except the few of us who were able to fight back. Being Jewish means I know who belongs with me and who is a stranger. This man is a stranger. He cannot be family. *I will not speak of this anymore.*"

Rebecca turned to her mother in a last, futile attempt for support. "Mother, Mother, do you understand?" said Rebecca, beginning to cry.

Her mother simply lowered her head and shook it, not daring to add anything to this conversation.

When men and women are drawn together, the true nature of their attraction is often submerged in their subconscious mind. Consciously, Rebecca was drawn to Matthew's intelligence, confidence and romantic flare, but subconsciously, she was drawn to additional traits that were more central to his personality. These traits gradually revealed themselves after their marriage. To Rebecca's consternation and dismay, the traits were an all-too-familiar echo of her father's personality. Matthew was proud and dominating and insisted on being in control. He would angrily attack anyone who challenged him, which after their marriage included Rebecca.

Rebecca would have left him, if it had not been that their first child, Joe, was already born when Matthew's true nature started to emerge. Rather than leaving Matthew, Rebecca decided to simply increase her already well-developed work ethic, in order to spend less time with Matthew. At work, she was treated well and respectfully and no one yelled at her. So she spent longer and longer hours there.

When Matthew saw that Rebecca had found a refuge from his domination, he turned his attention to dominating Joe. While Rebecca subsequently had two daughters, they were relatively compliant and not a worthy adversary for Matthew. Joe, on the other hand, seemed to be born without fear. He was a very active, loud and precocious child, who craved stimulation and novelty. His father reacted in anger to Joe's restless jumping, singing, running about and rough play. Matthew's expectations for table manners were strict and way beyond the abilities of someone with young Joe's level of activity. **"ELBOWS OFF THE TABLE," "SIT UP, DON'T SLOUCH," "STOP HUMMING," "WIPE YOUR FACE! DON'T BE A PIG!"** His father would yell at him, but the yelling only impacted Joe's behavior for a few moments. Joe rapidly became habituated to the yelling, so that he hardly noticed it any more. It did not take Joe long to become used to the physical punishment as well.

Rebecca would plead with Matthew to not be so harsh with Joe. "He's just a child," she said on one occasion. "Please don't be so hard on him."

Matthew angrily responded, "If you don't teach a child to control himself, then he'll grow up to be a wild beast! This is the way that my parents disciplined me! It worked good enough on me and it's going to work on him!"

Rebecca wanted to respond, but she was just so tired after working a ten-hour day. Anyway, she did not know of any better way to control Joe, who, she had to admit, was too loud, too wild and too physically dominating of his sisters.

By the time he was twelve, Joe openly argued with his father. On one occasion, his father told him to clean up his room and he responded, "Why do I have to? It's my room; that's how I like it. If you don't like it that way, you clean it up."

His father slapped him for this insolence, and then shouted, **"YOU'RE NOT A WILD BEAST! YOU LIVE IN A HOUSE, NOT A CAVE, AND YOU WILL CLEAN UP AFTER YOURSELF LIKE OTHER HUMANS DO!"**

As his father yelled at him, an odd change came over Joe's face. At first his face was serious and intense, but then it relaxed and he smirked at his father. "I'm the beast? You can't even control your *f***ing filthy* slapping hands." Joe knew the response that his words would elicit from his father, and he was prepared to take action. Matthew lunged at Joe's throat and Joe ducked, stepped to the side, evading his father's grasp. He hurdled the couch, knocking over a lamp with a crash, and dashed out of the house. This was the first, but not the last time, he ran away from home. His parents found him sleeping in a local park, two days later. He was grounded for a month because of his behavior. But the grounding was not properly enforced and had little effect on him. On three or four afternoons a week, he would sneak out of his window and play basketball with friends for a couple of hours, before returning home.

After Joe had absconded from his home for the first time and was found, Rebecca was flooded with emotion. The first emotion she felt was relief, as she no longer felt the agitated anxiety about the wellbeing of her missing son. But soon this relief gave way to a mix of guilt and new anxiety. As much as Rebecca did not know how to handle this boy, Matthew did not know how to either. She worried about how Joe would develop in his teenage years, driven by his rage and defiance. Without some sense of limits and duty, would he simply pursue a path of self-gratification and self-destruction? She felt guilty for not having been more involved in his life. Should she spend more time with him? She could, but Joe seemed uninterested in this, and she suspected her new show of parental interest would be met by only cold indifference or hostility. Where to turn? Suddenly, the thought came to her that at least he should know that he is a Jew. She did not know much about Judaism, but she did know that Judaism was an ancient system that taught about responsibility and self-control. Perhaps if she could get him to connect to a rabbi and a Jewish community, someone might get through to him, someone could provide an understanding that was beyond what Matthew and she could give.

Joe sneered and laughed at his mother when she suggested that they attend a local Conservative synagogue the following Saturday. "I can think of ten things I would rather do," he said.

As a lawyer, Rebecca had learned that one must come to every negotiation prepared. "How do you know you won't like it? Why don't you give it a try?" she asked.

He was obviously unimpressed, which she had anticipated, so she moved quickly to her bargaining chip. "I'll give you ten dollars if you go."

Without batting an eyelid, he responded, "Ten is not enough for such boredom. But I'll do it for twenty."

"Deal," she answered.

The next Saturday, Joe and his mother entered the large prayer hall. Joe looked stiff and uncomfortable in his best suit. He kept pulling at his collar, as if it were choking him. He sat beside his mother, jiggling his foot and fidgeting in his seat. His mother thrust a prayer book in his hand and picked one up herself. On a raised platform in the center of the room, a man stood chanting some incomprehensible words. The rest of the community was muttering other incomprehensible words. Rebecca had no idea where to turn in the prayer book, but another thing she had learned as a lawyer is to always look like you know what you are doing. So, she confidently turned to a random page. She saw that pages alternated between Hebrew and the English translation. Having no knowledge of Hebrew, she proceeded to mumble the English to herself. Joe was uncharacteristically humbled by being in such an unfamiliar place. Thus, he did not lay down his prayer book. He kept it open in his lap, to maintain a pretence that he knew what he was doing and was following along. But his eyes did not focus on the book. He just aimlessly looked around the room, wishing that the service was over.

After what seemed like an eternity, the service did end. After the service, Rebecca took Joe by the hand and went to introduce herself to the rabbi. The rabbi, who had a round face and wore glasses, appeared to be in his thirties. He had black hair and dark brown eyes. After engaging in a few minutes of small talk, the rabbi, whose last name was Pearlman, turned to Joe and asked, "How old are you, Joe?"

"I'm twelve," answered Joe.

"So, you studying for your bar mitzvah?" asked Rabbi Pearlman.

"No," said Joe looking down at the floor. "We don't really do that."

Rebecca gave a nervous laugh and said, "We never have been active synagogue-goers ... and we have not pursued a Jewish education for Joe."

"Oh, I see," said Rabbi Pearlman, stroking his curly black beard and looking thoughtful. "Well, Jewish learning you may not have, but a Jewish soul you do and every Jewish soul thirsts for our teachings." He smiled at Rebecca and said, "I'd be happy to teach the boy, send him to me for an hour a week and I'll prepare him for his bar mitzvah. We'll work out the details after the Sabbath."

Rebecca was filled with a mix of excitement and trepidation — excitement about the rabbi reaching out to Joe and offering to take him under his wing and trepidation about Joe's likely unwilling attitude.

Joe responded as she expected, "Sorry, but I'm not interested."

"I'll talk with him," Rebecca said hastily, in as reassured and confident a tone of voice as she could muster. "We'll get back to you about it."

The negotiations between Rebecca and Joe ensued in the following week. Finally, a contract was drawn up: Joe agreed to attend classes with Rabbi Pearlman and participate in the bar mitzvah ceremony. Rebecca promised him, in return, that he could attend an expensive summer sports camp, as well as receive a five hundred dollar bonus. They both knew that Matthew would adamantly oppose such "spoiling of the boy," so they kept the deal secret from him. Rebecca managed to obtain Matthew's approval for the camp with the argument that development of sports skills might lead to more of a sense of team spirit and responsibility for others. She was luckily aided by the fact that Matthew had been avidly involved in sports when he was younger and associated many positive formative experiences with this involvement.

Joe's attitude during the meetings with Rabbi Pearlman was mixed. On the one hand, given his animosity towards all authority figures, Joe wanted to maintain a sense of boredom and disengagement. On the other hand, Joe hated anyone to take him for a fool. He quickly learned and retained the Hebrew language skills and other concepts that the rabbi was teaching him, and demonstrated this understanding to the rabbi. Rabbi Pearlman began the course of instruction by teaching Joe the Hebrew alphabet. After two sessions with the rabbi, Joe was starting to read Hebrew. When the rabbi asked Joe if he had been practicing, Joe just shook his head. "This is an uncommonly bright boy," the rabbi thought to himself. As the rabbi continued to work with Joe, he came to realize how true his observation was. Joe seemed to retain everything that he heard, and one hearing was sufficient. When the rabbi repeated something from a previous week, Joe would interrupt the rabbi,

NEVER FORGET MY SOUL

tell him that the rabbi had said this before and, if asked, accurately repeat the substance of the prior lesson.

After Rabbi Pearlman had assisted Joe in learning to chant his assigned Torah portion and reading from the Prophets, the rabbi began to discuss with Joe possibilities for his speech. It was the custom of the synagogue for the bar mitzvah boy to make a short speech relating to the week's Torah reading known as the *parsha*. Rabbi Pearlman told Joe various homiletic stories relating to the *parsha*. Seeking to inspire some independent thought and enthusiasm in the boy, the rabbi would often ask him to say if he liked any of these stories and if he would like to discuss them at his bar mitzvah. Invariably, the rabbi's question would receive only a shrug and blank-eyed indifference. The rabbi found himself becoming irritated with the attitude of this brilliant boy who was unwilling to show enthusiasm for any of their work.

"Look, everyone makes a speech, and you have to as well!" he scolded the boy, with a note of irritation and frustration in his voice.

Again the blank stare – or was there something else behind that stare…veiled hatred? The look was disconcerting, and the rabbi quickly continued. "If you're not going to choose, then I will, and that's just what we're going to do." He took a deep breath to calm himself and let the breath out with a sigh. He rubbed his forehead for a few moments. He deliberately changed the harsh expression on his face to one of inviting warmth, and then he said, "Joe, I want to tell you a story. It's a good story and we will use this as the basis for your bar mitzvah speech.

"This week's Torah reading is about the noble qualities of the founding father of our religion, Abraham. One of the most notable qualities of this great man was his love for all people. This week's *parsha* begins at a time which is three days after Abraham has been circumcised. He is ninety-nine years old, recovering from an operation and in great pain. In appreciation of his faithfulness and in order to support him in his time of pain, God Himself visits Abraham. At that very moment, when God is visiting with Abraham, Abraham notices three wayfarers passing by his tent. Abraham's whole life mission was to show kindness to other people. You or I might have ignored the passing strangers because of a belief that it is more important to communicate with God, when one has a chance to, than to be distracted by passersby. Not so Abraham. Despite the pain of his operation, he springs out of his seat, away from the presence of God and towards the three strangers. He implores them to come rest, eat and refresh themselves. He rushes around his camp to ensure that the most royal feast possible is made for them. It is only then that they reveal that they are angels who have come to bring him news about a number of things. One of those pieces of news is that, at the ripe old age of one hundred, Abraham will become the father of the first and only child that he has with his wife, Sarah. Although the visitors were angels, Abraham did not treat them so royally because he knew of their special status. They appeared to him in human form and that was what he took them to be. He treated them with such honor because he had great love for all human beings. Perhaps the fact that they turn out to be angels teaches us that every man is holy and every man is God's messenger. But we can only see people this way if we try to see each man with love.

"The parsha goes even further in demonstrating the extent of Abraham's love for people. After the angels depart from Abraham, they travel towards a second mission, to destroy the city of Sodom. Why did God want to destroy Sodom? Sodom was a rich and fertile region, which attracted many people who wanted to increase their fortune. It was a city devoted to greed, so much so that it was illegal for any man to do charity for another. One of the most hateful things to God is coldness and indifference to the plight of another. This extreme lack of care for others was so hateful to God that He intended to destroy the city. And yet, God pauses, and asks Himself this question, what would the man who has devoted his whole life to love and charity say? Would Abraham agree with God and endorse the destruction of Sodom? God announces His plans to Abraham. And what does Abraham say? He starts to argue on behalf of the righteous minority that may still be in Sodom. He challenges God. Abraham suggests that perhaps there are fifty righteous people who remain in Sodom, and he questions the justice of killing the righteous along with the wicked. In addition, he argues that if a core group of good people can be found, then perhaps there is still hope that those who are doing evil can be brought around to good. God accepts Abraham's arguments and states that He will not destroy the city if fifty righteous people can be found. But then, Abraham has a worry. Did he bid too high, perhaps the fifty might lack five? How terrible for the city to be destroyed if forty-five righteous people still remained. Abraham again petitions God to be willing to save the city for the sake of forty-five righteous individuals. God agrees. Now, please understand that this is not an easy thing that Abraham is doing. He is debating with the most powerful force in the universe, God Himself, who can wipe out Abraham in an instant. Abraham is presuming to question the One who made everything and knows everything. It seems crazy. But that is what Abraham is doing. And what is even more amazing is that God allows the debate. And the debate does not stop there. Abraham bargains lower — forty people. Again God agrees to the lower number and proceeds to agree to Abraham's arguments of thirty, then twenty, then ten. Abraham is successively pushing the number down, because even if there are just a handful of righteous people, he longs for a chance for all the people of the city to be spared. Abraham looked for the good in each person and loved each human being so much that he strenuously argued with God for the salvation of a city of sinners.

"OK, Joe, these are the ideas I want you to work with. Next time I want to see the first draft of a speech based on these ideas."

The rabbi paused to see if Joe would give a response. The rabbi knew that he had spoken with Joe on an adult level, but assumed that, given Joe's intelligence, Joe would be able to comprehend what had been said.

Joe stared back at the rabbi with cold eyes for a few moments and then said, "I got a question for you. OK, so this Abraham is a great loving guy. But what about God? He doesn't seem so loving to me. Seems to me that He wants to smash everybody at the first chance He gets. So what's the point of your story? Is it just that Abraham is kind or that God is cruel?"

Rabbi Pearlman was suddenly angered by the question. "This isn't a real question," he thought. "He's just debating with me to show how clever he is. I've had it with this boy's attitude." Nonetheless, the rabbi tried to calm himself and answer the question. He stroked his beard for a long time and finally said, "We don't know the mysteries of God's ways. But we know one thing — that He is not cruel. All of his actions are motivated by love."

"That's not an explanation...That's nothing," responded Joe, exasperated.

The rabbi then assumed a note of authority in his voice, "You can't have answers to everything, boy. Next time, I expect you to bring in that first draft of your speech. Now run along, our time is over." He brusquely dismissed Joe. Joe looked at him again with a blank and hateful stare and then turned to depart.

On their next meeting, Rabbi Pearlman followed up by asking Joe, "Have you written the first draft of your speech, as I told you?"

"No," came the indifferent reply.

"I thought I made it clear, Joe, that you needed to do so for today."

"I don't need to, Rabbi."

"What do you mean?"

"I know my speech. I don't need to write it out."

"You mean you are prepared to present it to me in full now," said the Rabbi.

"Sure," said Joe, unperturbed.

"OK, go ahead," said the Rabbi, hoping that the boy would stutter, get lost, shame himself, and thus, learn a lesson for next time.

Joe began speaking and the rabbi got ready to jump in and tell the boy how the speech was inadequate and how preparation is much more important than overconfidence and thinking oneself smart. The rabbi was prepared to tell Joe that there is a difference between being smart and wise, in that the wise know their limitations. But Rabbi Pearlman never got the chance to offer these insights. Joe reiterated all of the rabbi's teachings that were offered the week before. He repeated the stories, including all the important details, and ended with the uplifting moral that men like Abraham knew how to love with a love so deeply that they inspire us to love deeply and show kindness and understanding to those around us. Joe spoke in an unhurried pace. He was confident and eloquent. There was absolutely nothing to criticize.

When Joe was finished, the rabbi congratulated him on having obviously worked so hard in preparing such an excellent speech. What the rabbi did not know is that Joe's work had been minimal; instead Joe simply had excellent memory. The rabbi then tested Joe on his Hebrew readings for the bar mitzvah, which were once again executed without flaw. The rabbi congratulated Joe for all he had accomplished and told him that he was indeed ready for the bar mitzvah, which was to take place in three weeks. Joe's eyes did not meet the rabbi's eyes, as he spoke.

"Well, goodbye, Joe," Rabbi Pearlman said, offering a handshake to Joe. "You have done well. You can take the next few weeks off. Just remember to practice your Torah and *Haftorah* readings."

Joe did not take his hand. Still looking at the floor, he said, "Yeah, see you in a few weeks, Rabbi." With these words, he looked up at the rabbi and grinned, a malicious grin, perhaps. The rabbi was not sure, but there was something in the boy's manner that made him uncomfortable. Joe then grabbed a jacket and ran out of the rabbi's house, closing the door loudly behind him.

Joe's mother, grandmother and two sisters attended his bar mitzvah. Scott had responded to Rebecca's invitation over the phone that he "is not interested in Jewish rituals." He added, "I'm not interested in asking God to do for me; I'll just do for myself." Matthew had told Rebecca that he figured he did not belong in a synagogue and that he much preferred a quiet morning at home. As Rabbi Pearlman expected, Joe did well in his Torah and *Haftorah* readings. But then came the time for Joe to make his speech and something happened that the rabbi entirely did not expect.

Rabbi Pearlman had heard many bar mitzvah speeches. They were characteristically presented in a mumbling and rushed half-tone that listeners had to strain to hear. Joe's manner was much different. He walked up to the raised lectern, with slow confidence, and delivered his speech in the same manner. The confidence of Joe's manner before a large audience, approximately two hundred and fifty listeners, was surprising to the rabbi. But what was *shocking* was what Joe said.

"In this week's *parsha,*" Joe began speaking, "we read about a very troubling event. Abraham, the founder of our religion, has suffered through many years, unable to have a child with his beloved wife Sarah. Then, finally, at the age of one hundred years, Abraham is blessed to have a child with Sarah, a son. They name him Yitzchak, meaning laughter, because his joyous coming has filled their hearts with laughter. Then, out of the blue, for no apparent reason, God gives Abraham an absurd command. He tells Abraham to take his son, whom he loves, travel with him to a faraway mountain, slaughter him, and offer him as a sacrifice, a burnt offering, to God. This is troubling enough, but it gets worse. Does

Abraham protest, does he argue? No. Why should he? It's only his son, the one he *loves*." He drew out the word "love" with sarcastic emphasis. "Abraham gets up early in the morning, saddles his donkey, takes the boy and off they go on their adventure to murder Yitzchak. Finally, they see the destination for the terrible deed, a place called Mount Moriah. As they climb the mountain, Yitzchak asks his father, in worried bewilderment, 'I see the materials to make fire and the wood, but where is the lamb for the offering?' Abraham avoids telling the truth. He merely hints by saying, 'God will seek out for Himself the lamb for the offering, my son.' And with these two words, 'my son,' Yitzchak gets the hint, that the offering is himself. What does the boy do? Does he protest? Does he rebel? Does he say, 'But father, how can you, the man who devoted his life to kindness, kill his own son?' No, he says nothing. He just goes along with Dad. So they come to their destination. Abraham builds an altar, arranges the wood, and ties up his son to prepare him for the slaughter. Abraham raises the knife to follow God's orders. At that moment, an angel appears. 'Do not kill the boy,' the angel cries, 'for now I know you will not withhold the boy from me.'

"I have learned two things from this story. One is that the moment that we blindly obey others, terrible things can happen. Look what Abraham was about to do to his son. But the second thing that I learned is even more important. You see, when you are God, you hold all the cards, you can tell others to do whatever you please, no matter how absurd it is. I think He was just playing with Abraham, having a little fun, torturing him because God was tired of causing hurricanes or destroying cities. But if His so-called servants want to be the self-proclaimed faithful, they have to march to the absurd commands. This has taught me that in life it is better to have power than to not have power, because then I can give the commands and not have to worry about what others are demanding of me. Now, the job of God is taken, but I intend to at least seek as much human power as I can. I intend to be rich, have lots of influence, serve my own needs and *I will answer to no one.* I intend to devote my life to serving my own pleasure. And, God, if you intend to call me for any special missions... Shop's closed. So in closing, I wish to thank my parents who, by their wonderful example, have made me into the man that I am becoming today."

When Joe had finished speaking, the community sat in stunned silence. Rabbi Pearlman sat wondering why he had not intervened to stop this hateful speech earlier. Somehow, it seemed to have all happened so fast. The speech had started out somewhat irreverent, but only in its conclusion did it lash into hateful condemnations. By the time the rabbi had resolved to stop the speech it was over. What astounded Rabbi Pearlman most of all was how such chilling cynicism could exist in the mind and heart of one so young. It was only later, when the stinging embarrassment about Joe's behavior wore off, that the rabbi found himself wishing that he could talk with the boy one more time. (Such an opportunity did not arise because neither the boy nor his mother returned to Rabbi Pearlman's synagogue.) Joe had, on his own, at his young age, developed questions that had troubled some of the greatest rabbinic minds in history. Of course, his irreverence was quite different from the rabbinic sources. But the questions were good ones, and there *were* good answers to give Joe from these rabbinic sources, answers that respected the difficulty of the questions. The truth was, however, that, at this point in his life, Joe would not have been interested in answers. He was only interested in defiance.

After finishing his speech, Joe looked at the audience for a few more moments, as if he were staring it down. Then he stepped down from the lectern and walked down the aisle and out of the building, leaving his mother mortified and fuming. At least the community members were so uncomfortable about the whole affair that they did not pester her with the question of why her son had spoken as he did and walked out on his own bar mitzvah. As Miriam, the boy's grandmother, saw the boy striding out of the synagogue, she was beset with one unshakable and chilling thought: Joe's rage and defiance brought her husband to mind. "How can he know the soul of his grandfather so well?" she wondered. And with that thought, she began to weep quietly to herself.

Joe bound out of the synagogue into a clear, blue-skied day. He found a place to change, tore off his suit and quickly replaced it with the sneakers, shorts and T-shirt that he had been carrying in a bag. He knew that his behavior would probably result in his mother withdrawing the promised rewards. He didn't care. He had come to hate the feeling of being controlled by her payoffs, and he had come to hate the rabbi even more for his nonsensical assurances of the good within God and man, in a world where Joe saw only selfishness and cruelty. He spent the rest of the day playing basketball with his friends, throwing himself into the heat and excitement of the game and happy to forget everything else.

───────◦◦◦────────

As Joe grew into his mid-teens, he developed an ever-deepening contempt for adult values and expectations. He saw the adult world as filled with hypocrites. His mother was always telling him how dear he was to her and how he should try to do well at school and make her proud. But it was clear to Joe that she neither cared about him, nor cared to know anything about him. The only thing she loved was her work. She was Mrs. Big-shot Lawyer, who was dreaming of one day obtaining a judgeship, so she could even be more Mrs. Big-shot. As far back as he could remember, he felt like his mother simply could not hear him. When he was young, he would tell her of a problem he was having at school or with a friend or with his father, and she would absentmindedly reply, "Yes, dear, we have to talk about that some more. I'm sure we'll find a solution." Joe learned to translate her response into, "Leave me alone. I'm way too overwhelmed with my own problems and troubles to deal with yours." His father's hypocrisy took a different form. Matthew would tirelessly preach about how he was disciplining Joe for his own good, so Joe would learn self-control. But Joe concluded that his father only cared about two things — not being bothered by his children and avoiding the negative opinions of outsiders. When Joe was younger and Matthew took him to church, it mortified Matthew that Joe could not sit still and was always fiddling with something. Matthew would pinch, punch and shove Joe under the pew and nervously look around, as if he feared the reprimand of others telling him that he could not control his own son. Everywhere Joe looked there was hypocrisy — the minister who preached that the greatest privilege of his work was to help mold young minds and who would then scowl at the young children who played too loudly and disrupted his service; the schoolteacher who angrily silenced Joe, when he pointed out a contradiction in what she had been teaching; the police who arrested people for smoking pot and then went home to get blasted on booze. Joe learned to screen out whatever adults told him, because he was certain that it was all a lie.

Every human soul needs a goal, even those who reject deferred gratification as a value. Joe looked around him and saw adults chasing after money, fame, and the accolades or approval of others. These pursuits reminded him of his parents and eventually disgusted him. Many of his peers were talking about different goals — love, peace, enlightenment, brotherhood — but he was just as cynical about these things, which just all seemed so empty. Since he did not believe in seeking material success, social approval, or world improvement, he was only left with one possible goal to seek — pleasure, and he sought this goal with wild abandon.

By the time he was fifteen, he was deeply immersed in the drug world. "You name it, I've tried it," he would say — pot, coke, mushrooms, LSD — whatever he could obtain. He would frequently not come home at night and the harangues of his father began to make his appearances at home even less frequent. He was well-liked by the girls and went from sex partner to sex partner, often sneaking into the rooms of teenage girls to indulge himself, amid stifled giggles of "my parents better not find out." Sometimes, the parents found out and threatened him or ordered him never to return. This was of little concern to Joe, and he would either find alternate locations for these activities or simply move on to another partner. He formed no emotional attachment with any of these girls.

Joe relentlessly sought stimulation. He would shoplift for the thrill and when that became boring, he transitioned into burglary. He would steal cars for fun and then would race them with friends. Even the most daring of his friends were a little afraid of Joe because *nothing* seemed to intimidate him. When challenged by others, he would merely stare at them with an unflinching eye and a smirk that made the boldest turn aside. Joe was not to be defied and it was best to stay on his good side.

Although Joe gave minimal attention to his schoolwork, he was able to pass courses without difficulty. His parents put him in inpatient and outpatient treatment, but Joe quickly learned to mouth the necessary words, in order for his therapists to say that he was making progress. None of those therapists had any impact on him. He graduated from high school and attended university. Matthew and Rebecca were just happy to get him out of the house and paid for his living expenses and tuition.

One night, in his sophomore year, Joe and a female companion took LSD and then had sex behind a bush. Afterwards, they climbed up the fire escape of a twelve-story apartment building. Under the influence of the drug, Joe envisioned himself as a blue bull, with a grotesque face and sharp metal horns. His teeth were razors and his eyes were burning flames. He saw naked, emaciated, human forms marching in a circle on the roof and wailing. He wildly ran around, spearing them with his horns, tearing them up with his teeth, so that their oppressive wailing would stop and their horrid forms would disappear. Each time he tore one up, it would vanish. He jumped around on the roof, shouting, "I am death, I am death." The girl was terrified by his behavior, and ran off the side of the building, shrieking. When she fell, he did not realize what had happened to her. After he finally came down from the trip, he descended the fire escape, to find the girl crushed, bleeding and dead on the pavement. Joe felt nothing when he saw her — neither sadness nor regret. But a question did rise to the surface of his mind, a detached question, as if he were asking it about someone on the other side of the world: "If I keep going the way I'm going, how much longer until that's going to be me on the pavement?"

On that day, Joe decided he had to make a choice. There was nothing wrong with seeking pleasure, but he was out of control. He needed to put himself in a situation that would create structure in his life, so that he would not self-destruct. He decided that medical school would serve that purpose. At university, he had maintained good grades, not because he particularly cared about them, just because it was so effortless for him. He was easily accepted into a medical school program.

At the age of twenty-two, he entered medical school and was exposed to a type of structure and demand that he had never experienced in his life before. There were no angry condemnations, no threats of punishment, no enraged pronouncements that he was a lazy good-for-nothing who better shape up. The attitude of the medical school was eloquently summed up by the dean who made a speech to the entering class.

The dean opened up the speech saying, "In one year, half of you will not be here. That is not a threat; that is not intended to scare you. It is merely a statistic and a fact. We do not beg anyone to stay here; that's up to you. What we do expect is, if you want to try to stay here, you realize that one does not become a medical doctor on a lark. It is not easy. It takes work and devotion — more work than you have ever done in your life. When — that is, if — you graduate, you will command the respect of others and likely make good money. And you will have those benefits because you will have completed what few can. No one will be looking over your shoulder here to make you work. We are all adults here. So if you really want to stay here, I suggest you familiarize yourself with our expectations and get started on fulfilling them..."

The coolness and detachment with which this speech was delivered gave Joe nothing to rebel against. He also realized that remaining in medical school was essential in preventing his own self-destruction. So for the first time in his life, Joe worked for a long-term goal.

Four years later, his parents, sisters and grandfather, Scott, attended Joe's graduation. Scott had doggedly avoided any interaction with Matthew through the years, but Scott had seen Joe on a number of occasions, and Scott found himself responding with a natural, inexplicable liking for the boy. There was something about the way the boy looked him directly in the eye that reminded Scott of himself, when he was a proud, defiant partisan during the war years.

After Matthew had congratulated Joe and walked away from him, with an understanding that he and Scott could not occupy the same space, Scott approached Joe. Rebecca, who had also been talking with Joe, stepped back as her father approached, instinctively repelled from whatever "words of wisdom" Scott wanted to share with Joe. Scott now was a bent, graying old man, but there was still a sense of pride in his glance and stride. He furrowed his eyebrows, gazing at Joe, and extended his hand. Joe took it.

"So, Joe," Scott said, "you're finally a man."

"I guess you could say that," Joe responded.

"No, Joe," said Scott, "there are plenty of people in this world who *know* things. If you're just guessing, then they won't give a crap about what you have to say. If you are a man, then just say so, and get out there and do something with your life. Don't listen to detractors or doubters or people who want to stand in your way. And don't waste your time on goofing off, like when you were a kid. That's the one-way express ticket to nowhere. No one lifted you out of your mess but yourself, and you've made something of yourself. Now don't expect anyone to save you if you slip off again. The only one a man can rely on is himself. Don't look back, don't think of the past, don't let anyone distract you from your goal and you will be successful."

Joe did not take kindly to lectures from anyone, but in a strange way, he could accept it from Scott, because Scott seemed to be merely dictating Joe's own musings back to him. The difference between Scott's warnings and the prior warnings of his father was that Joe did not feel that Scott was ashamed of him. In a way, Scott's attitude was similar to the attitude of Joe's medical school professors. Scott had no desperate need for Joe to succeed. He was merely giving Joe a piece of advice on how to do so, and then Scott was willing to leave the rest to Joe.

"You're right, Grandpa," said Joe. "I am a man. You'll see, by the time I'm forty, I'll be making a million a year."

Scott smiled broadly, "Now that's talking, my boy. Maybe you have Grandpa's Midas touch." He put his hand on Joe's shoulder. "Remember, Joe. Most people in this world are cowards, lazy or both. If you don't stay in charge, then others will be happy to be in charge of you."

Scott gave Joe one more meaningful stare, turned and walked away. As Joe saw his grandfather merge into the crowd, he had a flashback of his LSD trip on the apartment roof. The form of his grandfather melded with the naked, emaciated figures that he had seen during the trip, and then the whole crowd of people in front of him became those figures. Joe shuddered, closed his eyes, opened them again, and the vision was gone.

CHAPTER NINE

D avid sat in his home study, at midnight, hunched over a book entitled "The Holocaust Legacy: Experiences of Children of Survivors." An overhead desk lamp traced a circle of light around his work space, intensifying the haunting darkness from a nearby window. Scattered over his desk were other books on a variety of related topics. To his right lay a pile of history books with titles such as "A Complete History of the Second World War," "The Final Solution: Hitler's Systematic Plan of Genocide," and "Hitler's Willing Executioners." These books were his reference section, to provide a backdrop for a world that he realized he knew too little about. The books to his left were more spread out. Many of them were open. These books contained titles such as, "Multigenerational Legacies of Trauma," "Interventions for Trauma Reactions," "Bearing Shattered Worlds: The Therapist and Vicarious Traumatization." A number of scholarly articles were scattered beside these books, all relating to trauma and many relating specifically to the Holocaust. Directly in front of David, on the far side of the book that he was reading, were three other books, piled one on top of each other. One of the books in this pile was entitled "Stories from Hell: First-Hand Accounts of Holocaust Survivors." The second was "Diary of Anne Frank," and the third was entitled "In the Shadow of Destruction." This third book was one woman's poignant account of her experiences growing up with parents who were Holocaust survivors. These three books were the first he had turned to in his attempt to understand Adam's and Joe's past. He kept them directly in front of himself, as a reminder that there was something infinitely more precious than any academic theory or tome — and that was the direct experience of those who had suffered and were willing to share their story. He did not want all his reading of psychological theories and techniques to obscure the reality of these sufferers.

Every night for the past week, he had stayed up past midnight, intensely studying these resources that he had collected the day after the last group session. He had had a free morning the day after that session. He usually made use of that time to catch up on reading, phone calls and various errands. But, instead of engaging in such tasks, he had gone to a local university library, at eight o'clock that morning, as the doors were being unlocked, to start his research. He spent three hours at the library, and when he finished, he collected so many books that he needed to make two trips to his car with all of them. He also left with a pile of articles that he had copied.

David had not been aware, prior to the last group session, that Joe's grandfather had been a survivor of the concentration camps. Joe had told David most of the important details about his background in prior individual sessions, but this one fact had been omitted. Upon hearing this revelation, David's eyes widened and a feeling of excitement gripped him — perhaps the mystery of Joe's and Adam's struggle was beginning to unravel.

David was sure that the objective observer would say that David had become obsessed. He paused from his reading and imagined some unidentified person leaning over his shoulder, saying, "David, enough. You're not going to get a Ph.D. in Holocaust Studies in one week. This is way beyond conscientious study to improve your clinical knowledge. You're losing perspective." The voice is right and wrong, mused David. Sure, this went way beyond improving his clinical treatment skills, and maybe the war era was growing to such proportions in his mind that he was losing sight of everything else. But he did not think that he was really losing perspective. He was merely throwing himself into a particular world view in order to gain a new perspective. One thing that he had learned about Holocaust survivors and their children was that the wartime experience remains in the mind like a thick cloud, threatening to darken or even blot out future experience. To those with the Holocaust legacy, experiences and events were frequently viewed through the lens of the war. And it was that perspective that David was trying to understand. Something had moved him about the intensity of Joe and Adam's struggle, and he felt compelled to understand it.

David then heard a new voice echo in his imagination — it was the voice of Dr. Owens. "David, never fool yourself that a particular case stimulates your interest for only intellectual reasons. There is *always* a story behind what stimulates our interest. Something from our experiences, something from our past makes that case particularly resonant for us. Connect with *your own experience,* as it relates to the case. Otherwise, you will be walking into your treatment blind and you will end up letting the patient treat you, rather than vice versa."

Dr. Owens had drilled this concept into David so often that a strong reaction to a case automatically elicited Dr. Owens' warnings in David's mind. "So how are Adam and Joe particularly relevant to me? " David wondered. His life had been relatively easy, certainly far from traumatic. He had grown up with his mother and stepfather — good, nurturing and reliable people, who had raised David with a healthy sense of self-esteem. He had had good friendships in school, met and dated Margaret in college, shared a wonderful marriage with her and been blessed with beautiful children. Of course, there had been the death of his father when David was five. David was now fifty years old and it was difficult to recall any memories of his father. He had vague recollections of a quiet, loving man who gently held David and rocked him to sleep. David remembered his mother telling him that his father had gone to heaven, the tears in his mother's eyes, and David instinctively reaching out to his mother, more to soothe her than to soothe himself, because he did not yet have a real understanding of what death meant. Now as an adult, he could not say that he missed his father, but the memories of his father were intermingled with the tremendous sense of loss his mother had suffered.

David let his eyes drift over his desk, until they came to rest upon a book entitled "Inherited Memories." Inherited memories — Joe and Adam were burdened and driven by memories that they had never directly experienced, oppressed by a life they themselves had never actually lived. Of course that was a simplification. Joe and Adam were driven not only by their parents' suffering, but also by the way their parents behaved towards them. Adam's parents had been emotionally broken people, lacking the accessibility and emotional aliveness that children yearn for, and, in the case of his father, with a quick and sometimes violent temper. David was unsure about Joe's story, but suspected that it was similar. From David's reading, there was something to this idea of inherited memories. Children of survivors were often very intuitive and seemed to sense their parent's Holocaust experiences, even without the parent ever discussing them in front of their children. He thought of one case history of a woman who suffered from low sexual desire for ten years. Whenever her husband would approach her sexually, she would seek a reason to argue, in an unconscious attempt to be protected from physical intimacy with him. She worked for years with therapists on this problem, and the therapists used a great variety of techniques, but made absolutely no progress with the problem. The breakthrough came when her mother told her that she had been raped in a concentration camp, and had never been able to trust men sexually after that. When the daughter connected with the inherited memory of the rape, she then had a context in which to work and was finally able to overcome her sexual difficulties with her husband.

As David continued to consider the words "inherited memory," an image came to his mind. It was a picture of his father in military uniform, which had been in the family photo album when he grew up. The face had been proud, young and strong. His father had fought in the Second World War. Once, his mother had wistfully pointed out that picture to David and said, "Your father was a brave man. He sacrificed his life so others could be free. He was injured badly in the war. He was never able to work after he returned. He became weaker and weaker over the years, and then his body just ran out of strength to live." That was the extent of what his mother had told him about his father's wartime experience. But that memory started David wondering. What wartime action *had* his father seen? Was his father's history somehow more intimately intertwined with Adam and Joe than simply sharing their forebear's war? Had David's father been involved in the liberation of the camps? David did not know, and at this point it was all speculation. His mother had been dead for ten years.

David put aside the book that he had been reading and reached for a book entitled "A Pictorial History of the Holocaust." As he leafed through the pages he saw pictures of crowded Jewish ghettos; marching lines of Jewish prisoners, flanked by German soldiers; shaven-headed, emaciated concentration camp prisoners; and piles of naked corpses. Suddenly he stopped, transfixed on one picture. It was a photograph of a United States soldier, standing beside a just recently liberated concentration camp prisoner, who was seated on a bench. The former prisoner was painfully thin, with sunken eyes. He had an expression of dull emptiness and disbelief in his eyes. The American soldier appeared tall, well-fed and strong. But there was something haunting in the soldier's face. David's eye widened with a realization. He arose and went down to the basement, where he stood on a chair and removed a box from a shelf. He searched through the box until he found an old, brown, imitation-leather-covered photo album. He brought the album upstairs to his desk and turned the pages until he came to a photograph of his father after the war. There it was! The look — the same haunting look that was on the face of the soldier in the Holocaust book. It was a mixture of world-weariness and dis-belief. Disbelief — that was the commonality between the three people — the former prisoner and soldier in the book and David's own father in the album. The disbelief, thought David, is about the magnitude of horror that man can inflict on man. And the dis-belief was double for the former prisoner — disbelief about the extent of the horror to which he had been exposed and disbelief that it had finally come to an end.

"It's all my own imagination and supposition," David warned himself. He did not know whether his father had liberated a camp. He did not even know if he was accurately reading the expressions of his father or the American soldier. Perhaps David had so im-mersed himself in the Holocaust era, over the past week, that he was really seeing his own reactions, reading them into the faces of those soldiers. But David *did* know the following: his father had fought in a terrible war and had suffered near-fatal wounds. The war had forever changed his father's life and had eventually robbed David of his father. So what David did know was that Hitler's mad hatred had brought destruction into David's ancestral past, just as it had to Joe and Adam. What had his mother said? David's father had "sacrificed his life so that others could be free."

"Maybe that's what draws me so much into this subject,"

David thought. "I'm continuing the work that my father did. He exposed his body to the war's destructiveness in order to fight and overcome evil. If he was willing to do that, the least I can do is expose my mind to this evil, to help the suffering next generation find liberation. That's my inherited memory. I'm still fighting my father's war."

He was about to begin reading again, when he felt two gentle hands on his shoulders. It was his wife, Margaret. He turned around to see that familiar face, which had never lost its beauty to him. Her mouth smiled, but her eyes had a worried look.

"David," she said, "you've been working so hard. I know you said this is important to you. But you need your rest. You won't be able to function if you keep on going like this."

David took her hand and led her to a couch in the next room.

"Please sit with me for a few minutes," he said.

"Gladly," she replied.

They sat on the couch and he put his arm around her. As she cuddled close to him, he felt the warmth of her body.

"I'm afraid, Margaret," he said.

"What of, honey?" she replied.

"I'm afraid that I'll take the easy way out and try to dominate a group, so I don't have to feel their suffering," he replied. Margaret had learned how to deal with such statements made out of context and without explanation. She knew and accepted that he would not discuss details about his groups. She also realized that the details were not so important. He was not looking for a solution; he only wanted her understanding.

Margaret was quiet and pensive for what seemed to be a long time. She finally responded, "Even if it happens, you'll notice it and correct it. You're a good, wise and courageous man, David. You'll do good by them. I have no doubts about that."

In David's experience, when a group had a particularly emotionally evocative session on a prior week, there were two characteristic ways that they generally responded. The first type of response was to pick up where the group had left off and engage in further reflection and discussion of the issues that had been raised in the prior group. The second type of response was to act as if the prior event had never happened. It turned out that in the next group session, Joe and Adam tried to take the second course of action. Joe had revealed his Holocaust past at the very end of the last session, and there had been no time to hear people's reactions. David had no doubt that Adam had many reactions, if he would only have the courage to talk about them. However, it was Terry who at least initially spared Joe and Adam from reconnecting with last week's discussion.

Terry opened up the group session. After sitting down heavily in her seat, she said, "I need to talk about something today. My sister stopped by two days ago. She was going on and on about this beautiful handmade jewelry that she had seen at a craft show. She reminded me about when I made craft jewelry, as a teen, and she said that I had a real talent for it. She said I should start doing it again. It would be something to keep me busy, and I could make a little income. You know what my first thought about this was? I'm not a jewelry maker! I'm a full professor and biomedical researcher! So I guess I was short with her, and she got offended by it. I really didn't mean to hurt her. I'm just getting so frustrated and angry. Is this why I worked my butt off for all those years, to make silly little jewelry!? It's gotten so I resent almost everything I do during the day — fighting with insurance companies, doctor's appointments, watching TV, eating, sleeping — everything I do is so meaningless, because I'm not doing what I was meant to do — to be at the university, researching, discussing new concepts with colleagues — that was living to me. Now, I'm just existing. The future is uncertain, and now my doctors tell me that

NEVER FORGET MY SOUL

they don't think it's likely that my health is going to improve. One doctor said to me I should be happy that I seem to have stabilized; I'm not presently getting worse. He said that's what I should regard as progress, not getting worse. It's all so hopeless. I feel my life's work slipping away from me, and I wonder who I am and what I am without it.

"I just can't win. If I take my pain medication, it absolutely knocks me out. I take it at night so I can sleep, and as hard as I try, I just can't get out of bed until eleven in the morning. And I don't go to sleep late. The medication just knocks me out — makes me sleep eleven or twelve hours. So when I finally get out of bed, half the day is gone. I end up feeling like I haven't accomplished anything that day — maybe a few phone calls, maybe I get out to run one errand — and that's it, the day is over. Not only that, but my medications keep me perpetually in a mental fog. I'm just not as sharp as I used to be and it really disturbs me, like I've lost part of myself. When I don't take the medication, the mental fog clears up, but then the pain is unbearable — unremitting and unbearable. I end up aching all over and all there is, is the pain, so I can't focus or accomplish anything. And that's my normal health. Then there are the infections. My illness makes me prone to infections — cold, flu, skin infections. So, when I have a flare-up in those things, I'm feeling even more lousy and out of it.

"I was so proud when I was named a full professor, and I knew it sent my mother over the moon. She shrieked like a little girl when I told her, bursting with pride at what I had accomplished. 'My daughter,' she said. 'Some day you'll be on the cover of Time magazine: *The Woman Who Found the Cure for Cancer.*' Now there are no cures and there are no answers. I feel robbed and cheated, and I don't even know who to be angry at."

As Terry spoke, Marcia's brow started to wrinkle in concern. When Terry had finished speaking, Marcia said, "You poor dear, I feel so bad for you. Are sure you're getting proper treatment? I mean, maybe you need a second opinion?"

Terry shrugged. "I've gotten second and third opinions. They tell me it's mysterious, it could be this, it could be that. We'll just have to wait and see. In the meantime, all they can do is manage my pain."

Marcia looked pensive for a few moments and then responded, "Are these all regular MDs you go to?"

"What do you mean?" asked Terry.

"I mean, have you tried alternative medicine?" responded Marcia. "I have quite a library on the subject at home. Like mind over matter. There are people who believe that illness and healing start in the mind and with the right attitude you can actually overcome physical illnesses. There are people who say they have healed themselves from many conditions, even cancer, by mental imagery of their body fighting and overcoming the disease. And then there are a lot of other options — herbal cures, dietary changes, acupuncture, homeopathy. There's so much out there that regular physicians don't even consider. If you'd like, I can give you the name of some alternative medicine practitioners."

Terry gave a slight smile and shook her head. "Marcia," she responded, "I want to put this the nicest way I know how. I really appreciate the care that prompts your suggestions. But the way I see it, if I get into all that stuff, it would just be grasping at straws. There is so little science behind any of it. It's just built on the hopes and fears of the desperate. And truth be told, when my health started to deteriorate and I was getting desperate, I read some of that stuff about the mind's role in healing. I tried it — meditation, deep breathing, yoga, mental images of healing. I've been through all that and nothing helped. And one day, I just looked in the mirror and said, 'Who am I kidding?' I'm just like the doctors who treat me. We have no idea of what's going on and we try a little this and a little that to make me feel better, but there is no real cure and there is no real hope. If I go further into the alternative medicine world, I'll just be spending more time running away from my harsh reality. I'm tired of pretending. This is my life, and things are going to stay this way, unless a *real* doctor can figure out what's going on and give me proper treatment for it."

The expression on Marcia's face had become less warm, but she forced a smile. "Well, I don't think alternative medicine practitioners are quacks. They helped me. Three years ago, I had these terrible pains in my chest. My doctors checked me out and said I had almost complete blockage in one of my coronary arteries and that I would need bypass surgery. So you know what I told them? I'm not going under your knife. All they do is cut and sew, but they don't really cure. There are plenty of people who get bypasses and have to come back a few years later with blockages in the bypass artery. So I went to this alternative medicine practitioner and he put me on a strict vegetarian diet, got me exercising and doing yoga, and I joined a support group, where we spoke about ways that we were afraid to trust and love others. After two months the pain went away, and I felt so good and healthy. I never went back to get my arteries checked out. I don't think conventional doctors have anything useful to offer me."

"I'm happy that you feel well," said Terry, "but as a friendly word of advice, it might be good to measure the blood flow to your heart now — just to make sure everything is OK. I mean, perhaps the blood flow in that artery did improve, but that doesn't mean that you're out of the danger zone. When there is limited space, all it takes is a little clot and you could have a heart attack."

Marcia now responded with an edge to her voice, "Maybe that's the difference between you and me, Terry. You need everything scientifically proven. I go by what I feel. I have no doubt that I'm out of the "danger zone," as you call it. I feel so much better now. My head is clear, and I have so much more energy than before."

"But what can it hurt to confirm your feeling?" asked Terry.

"I'm not interested in tests because conventional medicine has nothing to offer me. Let's say they do find a "serious occlusion," what then? Am I going to let them slice me up or poison me with their potions? No, I'd just continue to follow the teachings of Dr. Jennings, the alternative doctor I saw, who told me that if I wanted to be healthy, I should live healthy, rather than looking for treatment only during times of illness. Maybe you just can't understand, Terry. You're part of the establishment — a biomedical researcher. When I criticize doctors, and conventional medicine, you probably feel it's an attack on you."

"One correction," answered Terry, "I *was* a biomedical researcher. Now I'm just a sick lady, killing time."

Marcia's face softened with concern again. "I'm sorry," she said. "Maybe I came on too strong. I didn't mean to attack you. You see, I just have strong feelings about these things. I was just trying to help. I do feel so sorry for you."

"Don't worry. It was *nothing*, really," responded Terry, with a note of sarcasm.

The room was filled with an uncomfortable silence, until David finally broke it.

"I was listening closely to the interchange between Terry and Marcia. I think we should be careful not to be distracted by the 'medical debate,' if we can call it that. I felt that other, more fundamental things are at stake in their discussion — like hope versus despair and control versus helplessness. I wonder if the group has any thoughts about what I've said or about Marcia and Terry's discussion."

"I have a thought," responded Tyrone. "Look, Terry, first I want to say that your situation sounds really sad, and I hope your doctors do figure this thing out for you. But second, and this comment is for you, Marcia, I was really feeling there was something missing from you. This is not about you. No one is attacking you and telling you not to go to your doctors. You turned the discussion into a debate about who is right. Terry didn't open up so we would give her a medical consultation. She wants support and understanding. She doesn't need us pretending that everything can be fixed. Not everything can be. Some things you just have to accept and live with."

"I have to agree with Tyrone," said Grace. "The worst way to suffer is to suffer alone. I've experienced that plenty in my life, being alone and suffering, that is. It's horrible. She needs us to have some empathy for her, and not get selfish or petty. And you know what I was thinking, Terry? As you were talking I was thinking about the difference between losing something and lacking something all your life. Take me, for example, I never felt good enough about myself to even try to accomplish what you have. I was raised to think I was not capable of much, and so I set my sights low. Now, sure it's painful to me that my lack of confidence makes me withdrawn, lazy and bored. But you know what? I'm used to all that. I know my baggage. Although I might not like my baggage, at least I've developed some ways to deal with it. You, on the other hand, you were on the top of the world. Your fall was so sudden and so far, that you must be having a hell of a time dealing with all that. In some ways we're similar — you're bored, I'm bored. But in a more important way, we're different. You've lost everything, and you don't know how to get it back, while me, I never had anything, so it doesn't feel so bad."

"It's funny," said Terry, furrowing her brow, "I got such a sense of warmth from what you just said, Grace — like you really understood me. You hit the nail on the head. For once in my life I am faced with a situation, and I have no idea what to do about it. It used to be the answer to any obstacle was just to be more creative and work harder. Now there is nothing to work at; there is nothing I can do to improve things. If I can't work, then who am I, what value do I have?"

Terry's words stimulated Adam's memory of his studies in

Israel. Adam called to mind Rabbi Goldberg's bright eyes, as he was lecturing to the students about work. "There is a word in Hebrew," Rabbi Goldberg had said, "*avodah*. Some people translate it as "work," but the traditional translation of that word is "service," service of God. It's no coincidence that this word has two different meanings. People get confused about what their real *work* is. When you go to a party and someone asks you '*what do you do*,' what is your answer? You might say, 'I'm a lawyer or a doctor or a plumber.' But I don't know which thing I understand less — the question or the answer. What do they mean, what do you do? I'm sure you do many things — eat, sleep, pray, take care of your children, read, study, visit relatives, exercise, give to charity, garden, listen to music — the list goes on and on. So what sort of 'doing' is that person at the party asking about? And what about the answer — that assumption that what we *do* is our job. Such an assumption is not the Jewish way. In Judaism, we have one simple answer to the question of "what do you do," it is an answer that applies, or should apply, to all people. The answer is, 'I am a servant of God.' Why is it so important to answer the question in this way? Because, if you make work define all of your doing, you will end up making work define yourself. And if you make work define yourself, you will lose your connection with your true self. You will simply become a cog in the industrial machine, without any human feeling. Anything that takes you away from work will be a bothersome nuisance. Your wife calls and says the kids are sick and she needs help, so you'll come and help. Of course, you will, if you can. But still there will be that tinge of resentment towards your wife: Why is she taking you away from your work, your real meaning in life? That resentment will fester and show itself indirectly. Your wife will sense it and take revenge. You take revenge back, and things get worse and worse. Overemphasis on work has ruined the best of marriages.

"But if you say you are a servant of God, then the goal no

longer becomes to work as much as possible or to make as much money as possible. The goal is simply this: to serve God's will as closely as you can in any given moment. If this is the goal, then being away from work does not take you away from your life's purpose. If you help your wife with the children, you are serving God, because He wants you to tend to your children and ease your wife's burden. If you listen to music, you're serving God, because He wants you to be happy. After all, He created this world for your happiness. When you exercise, you're serving God, because He wants you to be healthy, so that you will have more energy to do good deeds, or *Mitzvahs*, as we call them. When you learn the Torah, His teachings, or pray to Him, you're serving His will, because He wants you to make yourself closer to Him. And when you work at your job, you also serve Him, because He wants man to have the material means to sustain Himself, and, in addition, jobs generally involve helping other people in some way. You see, a job becomes one of many ways that you serve God.

"Think of older people who retire from their jobs. Their answer to *what do you do* makes all the difference in the world. Many people die soon after their retirement, and I think it is because they have lost the meaning in their lives. But if their answer to the question has always been, I am a servant of God, then the essentials do not change when they retire. Even if their health deteriorates and they are unable to move around freely or care for themselves, their answer does not change. They can still give of their wisdom to the next generation — that's serving God — and they can pray, learn the Torah, enjoy music, share a smile with another person — these are all acts of service to God. And you really have to ask yourself — whose work, whose *avodah*, whose service is more profound in this world — the workaholic businessman making a million dollars a year, or the loving grandmother whose words of encouragement ease the burden of her grandchild?"

Adam looked at Terry. Her shoulders were slumped, as if

she carried a heavy burden and her face looked weary. His compassion for her and her despair overwhelmed his shyness and he spoke, using a hypothetical example that Rabbi Goldberg had shared with him years ago.

"I have a question for you, Terry," Adam said.

"Yes?" responded Terry.

"Who do you love most in the world?" he asked.

Terry's eyes turned sideways, as she considered the question. Finally, she said, "My mother."

"OK. Now imagine this," Adam said. "Let's say that tomorrow, your mother is in a terrible car accident and ends up in a coma in the hospital. You meet with her doctors and they say that they are not sure if she will come out of the coma, but there is a new therapy that has been developed for coma patients. Let's say research shows that this therapy has to be done by a loved one, such as yourself, for the patient to respond to it. The therapy involves a full day of verbal and physical stimulation. It may take as long as a year of this therapy to show results. Assume that the chances of her coming out of the coma without the therapy would be fifty-fifty and that with the therapy she has about a ninety percent chance of coming out of the coma. If you do undertake this therapy, you will have to quit your job. Your employers are not willing to hold it open for this length of time. Also assume that your mother's long-term care insurance will pay you enough to do this therapy, and that you will be able to live on it, not an extravagant wage, but enough to live on. Finally, let's say there are no other family members available to do this therapy. Would you quit your job and do this for your mother?"

Terry did not even hesitate in her answer. "It's all kind of far-fetched, but if everything you said in the hypothetical situation were true, of course I would, no question about it."

"Now, since you wouldn't have a job, under such circumstances, would you feel that you had no value?" Adam asked.

Terry had to pause and think about her answer. Finally, she said, "No, I would feel that I had a lot of value, because I would be helping my mother."

"Then how can you say that you don't have value if you aren't working now?" Adam continued.

"But I also am not taking care of an ailing mother — she's taking care of me. So what's the point of all this?" Terry responded, beginning to sound irritated.

"The point is that it's not your work that gives you value," said Adam. "It's your choices. If you chose to take care of your mother under such circumstances, you would feel you had tremendous value and importance, because you would be trying to save someone you love. The reason you feel valueless now is not because you are not working. It's because you feel that everything is happening to you and you have no power to choose. But I bet you're overlooking something. Let's say you just disappeared today, would anybody care?"

"Yes, plenty of people would care — my mother, my sister, my cousins, my aunts, my grandparents, my friends," she responded.

"Why would they care?" he asked.

"Because they love me, they like me to be around," she said.

"What do they love about you?" he asked.

"Well, that depends," she said, looking pensive again. "For each of them it's probably a little different. My mother would probably emphasize how devoted I am to her. Before I got sick, I would call her and talk with her, twice a week, and I would write her once a month. And whenever I saw an article that I thought she would be interested in, I would drop it in the mail to her. She would say that I'm always thinking of how to do nice things for her and lift her spirit. My grandparents, my mom's parents, might talk about how funny I can be. I don't know what it is, something about them makes me let loose and we tell funny jokes and stories and laugh for hours. My sister and friends, they'd probably emphasize the advice I give them. They're always calling me with their problems, because they say I can put a fresh perspective on things and give them good advice."

"I think your family and friends would be in great disagreement with you about your lack of value," he said. "Perhaps it's time to reconsider the issue yourself."

"Maybe you're right," Terry responded, smiling briefly at Adam. After the smile faded, she continued, "But this is not easy, Adam. Everything you're saying makes such sense intellectually, and in a way it's helpful, but I feel something is missing from you. You don't understand that it's going to take me time to make peace with my loss and to connect with what my value *is* now. And saying that I am a good daughter or sister or friend isn't enough. I've always enjoyed my intellectual creativity and now I have no outlet for that. I've done so many crossword puzzles recently that I can't stand them anymore. I want an outlet for my mind, but I don't know how much energy I have to pursue anything. I don't know, Adam. I have to say I have mixed feelings about you. Everything is so neat and clear and straightforward for you. You seem to have an answer for everything. In a way, you're trying to fix everything, like Marcia tried to do a few minutes ago. But not everything has a good answer. Sometimes there is just suffering and loss and despair and not knowing how you can go on. Maybe I will come around to your way of thinking, but I find myself resenting that you can't connect with the way I'm feeling."

For a very brief moment, Adam's face registered discouragement and hurt, as Terry criticized him. Then his face settled into a bland, non-expressive position. "I was just trying to help," he responded. "I don't know if I show it or not, but I do care about your predicament and the suggestions I made were my way of showing it."

"Adam," said David, "can you remember what you were feeling, when Terry said that she is wondering what value she has?"

NEVER FORGET MY SOUL

"Well, I found myself thinking about when I studied in religious school in Israel and lessons I learned there about people's value," answered Adam.

"No, Adam," David responded, "I did not ask what you were thinking at that time. I asked what you were feeling."

"Feeling?" asked Adam, looking confused. "I don't know, I don't remember. I just wanted to help her. I just..." His voice trailed off, and he shrugged his shoulders and sat quietly staring in the distance.

David continued, "Earlier in the group, I responded to the interchange between Marcia and Terry by saying that I was thinking about themes of helplessness and control. Maybe the best question for everyone to consider is this: what are we, when we are faced with things that we cannot control? But not only that, there is a second question: How much can any of us control what we feel, and what *are* we when we are overwhelmed by the power of our feelings?"

The group sat for a long time, in quiet contemplation of David's questions. Finally Grace spoke, "I'm not sure I understand all of what you said, David. But something that I *do* feel is that there is nothing more important than us having compassion for one another, in here. Without compassion, I really don't care about anyone's suggestions. I'm not someone's problem to be fixed. I want to know that someone cares about what I'm going through. I had another thought about you, Adam. In some ways, you have spoken up a lot in the group, especially recently. But I just realized that I still know very little about you. You'll debate with Joe, or give advice to other people, but last session was the first time you spoke about yourself. I still know very little about how your life is now and what you struggle with on a day-to-day basis."

Adam shifted in his seat, looking uncomfortable. "It's not easy for me to talk about myself," he replied. "It makes me feel very uncomfortable. I'm just not ready, I'm not ready," he looked down, shaking his head.

Adam started thinking about the time he was eight years old and he made a new friend, a boy in his apartment building. Adam used to play football with the boy, in a small park, near the apartment. One day the boy asked Adam where his parents were from, and Adam responded that they came from Europe, where they had gone through the Second World War. The friend asked if Adam's father had been in the army. Adam replied that both his parents had been in a concentration camp. A few days later there was a chance meeting between Adam's mother and the mother of Adam's new friend. The friend's mother, Mrs. O'Leary, had commented to Adam's mother about how sorry Mrs. O'Leary was that Mrs. Schwartz had suffered so much in a concentration camp. The comment shocked Mrs. Schwartz, who valued her privacy above all else. The ensuing encounter between Adam and his mother was as vivid now as when it occurred, thirty years ago. He recalled how she had laid her hands on both of his shoulders and looked at him with intense eyes that seemed as if they were boring right through him. "You are *never* to tell other people our business, Adam, **NEVER.** I don't need Mrs. O'Leary telling me how sorry she is about my being starved and frozen and beaten by the Germans. I don't believe in her compassion, and I don't need it. It's no one's business that we're Jewish and it's no one's business where we came from. The only thing people will do with information is to use it against you. You are too trusting, Adam. You assume that everyone wants to be your friend. If you had seen what I have seen, you would know different. There is an evil within people, a ferocious hunger to destroy. Do not trust other people. It is the only way to survive. You are just lucky that I am talking to you about this and that it is not your father telling you. If it were him, he would get out the belt. That is why I haven't told him. But don't do it again, Adam, or I will have to tell him. Don't tell other people our business."

As Adam fell silent, David noticed how disengaged Joe appeared. His eyes looked toward the carpet and his face was disinterested. He looked as if he was sitting in the room by himself, beginning to doze in front of a television set.

David decided it was important to draw Joe into this discussion, which was much more relevant to Joe than his present demeanor indicated.

"Joe," said David, "you haven't said anything today. I wonder what your reaction to the group discussion is."

"No reaction," said Joe, lethargically, not even bothering to lift his eyes to meet David's. "I don't see how it's relevant to me."

"Perhaps," responded David, "but I have a question for you. A while back Grace spoke about two types of loss, one is when you lose something precious to you and the other is when you have lacked something important all your life. Which one do you relate to more?"

Joe raised his eyes to David, shook his head and exhaled audibly to express his frustration with David's questioning. "Look, David," he said, "I don't know what all this psychobabble is about. I haven't lost anything. I'm just here because I am frustrated and depressed."

"I didn't say you lost something," answered David. "I was asking if your problem is more like a loss or a lifelong lack."

Joe shook his head again, and responded with mounting irritation in his voice, "I don't understand what the hell you're asking me. Look, I'm depressed, I'm not happy. You know what that means? Do you need a dictionary?"

"So you lack happiness," responded David, not allowing himself to be distracted by Joe's insults and complaints. "How long have you lacked happiness?"

"Crap, I don't know. I didn't mark it in my diary, when it started. Oh, I guess a few years."

"How many years?"

"I don't know how many years."

"Guess."

"What the f*** do you want from me?!"

"Just guess," David said in a gentle, good-humored voice, although David secretly found himself starting to feel irritated with Joe.

"Maybe since I was twenty," said Joe dryly.

"So, you were a happy teen?" David asked.

"You know I wasn't, David, we spoke about that in our individual sessions. What are you pretending?"

"I'm not pretending anything, Joe. I'm just encouraging you to tell the truth. So you were depressed as a teen."

"Yeah," admitted Joe.

"Were you a happy child?" David continued.

"What was there to be happy about?" responded Joe. "A mother who had no interest in me, who lived and breathed her job? I was always in the way, a nuisance to her. And a father whose greatest pleasure in life was bullying me? I don't know why he did. Maybe he was frustrated; maybe my mom didn't give him enough sex. So she ignored me and the attention I got from him was mostly him slapping me around — a lot to be happy about!"

"Seems to me," said David, continuing his very gentle tone of voice, "that you have lacked something all of your life — happiness. Perhaps that's why you have responded so strongly to Grace in the past, because she also said she has lacked something all of her life. Maybe you and Grace understand something very important about each other."

Joe shrugged and did not respond, looking like a sullen adolescent. David decided to not push Joe further, hoping that another group member might keep the momentum going.

Tyrone was the next to speak. "Joe," he said, "your comments about your youth got me thinking. My wife has called me a workaholic. Not that I really see it that way. People pay me a lot of money

NEVER FORGET MY SOUL

to 'get the job done.' They put faith in me and I want to live up to that faith. On the other hand, sometimes I wonder if I am rationalizing. Maybe I overdo it. Maybe I sometimes *use* my work to avoid getting too close to my wife and kids. It's just echoes from the ghetto past — always the doubt as to whom you can trust — that was the ethic of the street. If you let down your guard too much, it could be your last mistake. I built a shell around me. The difference between now and then is that I now have a way to open the shell and let my wife and kids in, but the shell is still there. In fact, I think I draw away from my wife and kids to *prove* to myself that the shell is still there. Somehow it makes me feel strong and safe. Anyway, I had a question for you, Joe. Can you tell me more what it's like to be in a relationship with a workaholic? I'd like to know more about what it's like for those on the receiving end."

Tyrone's question awoke a memory within Joe. It was a memory of when Joe was eight years old and his parents had had a particularly bad fight. Joe had been playing in the basement, when he heard his parents shouting at each other with unusual ferocity. The sound seemed to come from the ground floor, above him. Joe crept up to the uppermost basement step and seated himself there. He peeked into the adjoining room, where his parents were, and listened to their argument.

"*I* don't give anything to this marriage?" boomed his father's voice. "What about you!? You come and go like this is a hotel! Maybe you haven't noticed, but we have *children* here who need to be raised, not just let to run free, like animals. You've worked the last four weekends in a row. I'm not doing this anymore! The place is a mess, and we need to do something with the kids today. You're *not* going anywhere! You're staying here! Your work will wait!"

"What am I, your slave!?" Rebecca responded. "How many weekends have I let you work in the past, so you could 'get ahead?' You didn't take me out once for the first three years that we were married. Remember what you said after Joe was born? You said, 'The baby's your problem, don't come sobbing to me.' You told me you had to work. And I believed you! You didn't *have* to work. You just didn't want to change diapers!"

"So who was going to support us, while you were playing with the baby!?"

"I was *not* playing with the baby! I was raising your son!"

"Raising my son! Well, you've raised him well! He's spoiled. He has no self-control. He thinks everything is coming to him. You weren't raising him! You just sat around on your fat ass, eating chocolate and watching TV!"

"I was going through a rough time! You're such a prick to use that to attack me! Look, after the way *you* behaved, I don't have to listen to your complaints! So I watched TV for a while, but I didn't betray you!"

"Rebecca, we've been through this. It was a one-night thing. She meant nothing to me. I was drunk. I made a mistake. Don't you know what forgiveness is!?"

Rebecca's voice became cold and sarcastic. "Now let me see, what did you call me — oh yes, 'stubborn Jew, no mercy in my heart.' You've always attacked me to avoid looking at yourself. What ever happened to our promise to respect each other's religious views? Anyway, why should I forgive a man who invented the word selfish and isn't willing to do anything about it?"

"Rebecca, we're not going to make this into a religious thing. It's not about that. It's about responsibility. You call *me* selfish! You're the one who is sneaking off for yet another weekend."

Rebecca's manner became controlled and she said through tight lips, "I'm not *sneaking,* Matthew. I'm just going. There comes a time that even the prince of selfishness has some family responsibilities."

Rebecca resolutely picked up her briefcase and walked towards the front door. Matthew quickly strode in front of her and

NEVER FORGET MY SOUL

stood in the doorway, blocking her way.

"No, you are *not* going," said Matthew, his voice almost sounding like a growl.

She lunged for the door, and he grabbed her shoulders and pushed her back. She resisted and tried to swing her body around him towards the door. He grabbed her shoulders again, shook her and pushed her with such force that she fell backwards onto the carpet. She sat up on the floor but did not rise further. She appeared as if she were stunned.

He spoke in a hard voice, without compassion. "*I've* just decided that *I* have work today. You stay with the kids." He grabbed his coat and hat hanging by the door and left the house. Rebecca did not resist.

Joe, who was still seated on the top basement step, hesitated, wondering if he should go to his mother to check if she was all right. But when he saw her rise to her feet, he opted for going back downstairs to play again and ignoring the whole incident.

As Joe, the adult, recalled these events, another memory came into his awareness. It was a memory of one of his mother's diaries that he had found after her death, three years ago. In that diary, he found his mother's account of an altercation, which Joe believed was the same one he had just recalled. After describing what had happened, his mother had written, "It's Daddy all over again. I've been such an idiot! How could I believe that I was marrying someone different? The same pride, the same obsession with control. No one can touch them — Matthew or Daddy. Either you cooperate or they try to crush you. Matthew is never going to touch me like that again. If he does, we're through! I'm going to tell him that. It's just like Daddy used to smack me when I disagreed, but this time I am not going to take the smack. I don't have to. What makes a man into such a twisted thing — no compassion, no one else matters. If they say something, it has to be true, no one dare disagree. I think Matthew and Daddy are weak people inside

— scared and weak people. They can't stand being challenged. I don't know what made Matthew that way. He won't talk about it because he thinks what he does is normal, so there is nothing to explain. There is something haunting about his parents — too perfect, too pleasant, too tense. I think of Matthew's father and I imagine him beating Matthew for some childish prank. I imagine pleasure in his father's eyes, as he beats Matthew — the pleasure of power, the pleasure of revenge, something like the sadistic pleasure that Daddy took in crushing Mommy. Mommy, why didn't you ever fight back? Why did you put up with that? You didn't just let yourself be crushed, you crushed me. You gave me no example of how to resist. I'm trying to figure all this out by myself! I don't know what to do! And Daddy, what happened to you? There's a lot of good in you, I was always looking for it. Sometimes I found it. But you would only let me in so far and you would never give up control. Did the loss of your parents do it to you? Was it the freezing winters? Was it the camp? Mommy told me so little and you told me nothing. You protected yourself and robbed me of understanding. All I saw was your strength, but I needed your tears. It would have helped me to understand, it would have helped me learn how to give myself permission to be human. Daddy, where were you all those years — staring blank-eyed as we had dinner together, and I was too afraid to ask you what terrible things you remembered. So you stared and I wondered, but I never broke the rule, I never asked. And I still don't ask. Not that I could. After I married Matthew, it was as if I stabbed you. You were remote before, now you are simply not there at all for me. Where are you Daddy? Where do we come from? How can you hate me for rejecting a past that you never shared with me? How can I know what being a Jew means to you? But the world is not a safe place, is it, Daddy? Is that what you learned? After all you lost, did you learn that there is no place for weakness in this world? So you hid it away, hid yourself away, froze us in the same winters that froze you. I'm cold, Daddy, who will hold me?"

Joe looked not at Tyrone, but through him. Slowly, Joe's awareness returned to Tyrone's dark brown eyes and the curious expression on his face. Tyrone appeared truly interested in Joe's perspective and this drew Joe back to the present and to the question that Tyrone had asked.

"I guess when I was young it bothered me that my mother wasn't around, but I got used to it," said Joe. "I think people can adjust to almost anything. This world is basically what you make of it. Sure life was pretty sh*tty when I was a child, so it's great that I'm not a child any more and I can make my own decisions. I don't like to think about when I was young. It just pulls me down."

"Look," said Tyrone, "I hear that you don't like to think about those times, but I hope you don't mind if I just ask you a little more. What did you think about yourself, when your mother spent so much time away and left you to be with your father?"

"I thought she was nuts and he was a psychopath," Joe said flippantly. He then paused and added in a more serious tone of voice, "No, that's not exactly true. That's what I thought, when I was nine or ten and after. You don't think such things when you are a young kid. When I was young, I thought that she didn't want to be around because she thought that I was a bad kid, who she couldn't handle. I remember promising myself that I would do better, so that she would be around more and protect me from my father. But I never felt like I was as good as I thought she wanted me to be. I guess I *did* blame myself for a while. Funny... I haven't thought about such things for a very long time..." his voice trailed off.

"Thanks for that, Joe," Tyrone responded. "It gave me something to think about. I don't want to give that message to my kids."

Disconcerted agitation suddenly arose deep within the recesses of Joe's subconscious mind. He had softened for a moment; he had shown too much. This was not acceptable. The breach had to be closed.

"Don't live for your kids, Tyrone," he said, in a cold voice. "The time will come when they have to go their own way and they'll blame you for everything. If you make things easy for them, they'll blame you for not showing them how true life is. If you make things too hard, they'll say you were cruel. So this is the way I relate to my children: I do with them what gives *me* pleasure. Maybe they'll learn to live the same way. I don't know. But at least *I* won't go though life as some scared and miserable wretch, always worrying that I'm not doing good enough. If working gives you pleasure, then work. If kids give you pleasure, then be with them. If you are with them less, then they'll just rely on friendships more. And that's not so bad. Every experience can be used for one's benefit. If you spend your life worrying about being the right type of person, then there is no life ...."

As Joe spoke, Adam started to shake his head, tighten his lips and furrow his brow. His irritation with Joe mounted by the moment, until he could contain himself no longer.

"Everything is so easy for you, Joe," said Adam. "You can take it or leave it. You act like children are on the same level as adults, and if you tire with each other, you can all just go find other playmates. Children are dependent on us, Joe. They can't just go and do everything for themselves. They rely on us to clothe them and feed them and most of all to teach them, to make sense of this world. Forty years ago, my parents made choices about how they would raise my sister and me, and those choices are still with me, they affect my every waking day. Well, I don't know if it was really *choices*. They were so scarred by the war that they thought there was no other way to live. But anyway, what they did to us had important, far-reaching effects. It's worth thinking about, worth coming to a place like this group and trying to understand how I could do things better for *my* kids. Do you have any idea what it's like to be raised by parents who shuddered with fear every time I stumbled, who filled my mind with fears about how treacherous people are, who reacted to every potential risk as if it were life-threatening? Our life was divided between 'in here' and 'out there.' 'In here' was our home — the only safe place — and 'out there' was the rest of the world, where people would betray or attack you at the first opportunity. Is it any wonder that I'm so anxious whenever I talk to people outside my home? Anxiety and guilt — that's my life, anxiety for the danger and guilt for how I hurt my parents by leaving them. Guilt, it was always there in our home. My mother had this overwhelming sense of guilt for having survived her family, who had been murdered in the war. And here I am, guilty for having grown beyond her world. These are the lessons my parents taught me. If parents don't think about what they are doing, they'll end up twisting up somebody's soul. Every step away from the world of my parents is tortured. I can't even pray to God, because He was not part of their world. Sure, I mouth the prayers, but my mind can never stay with them. I just rush on to the next worry, the next problem that has to be solved. But it's not just about prayer. It's about every relationship. I can't stay focused on anyone I'm with, even my wife and children. I can't trust any situation enough to stop worrying. These are the things I inherited from my parents. I don't want to pass them on."

Across the course of the group, Joe had been developing, if not greater respect, at least less contempt for Adam. Now, his tone of voice in responding was matter-of-fact, rather than dismissive.

"Adam, I hear that growing up was not fun for you and you wish things were different. But you admitted yourself that your parents were put together a certain way because of their life experiences and you are doubtful whether they could have done things different in raising you. So what makes you so sure that you are going to change things in raising *your* children? My philosophy is that each of us is affected by our genetic make-up and our life experiences and that's the way we are. There's not much that we can do about it. Might as well be yourself, rather than trying to be the perfect father or husband or whatever."

"That's fatalism, Joe," said Tyrone, "and I don't buy it. You once complimented me for working so hard and rising above the streets. How can you say that people cannot grow beyond where they come from?"

"I'm not saying they don't grow beyond where they come from," Joe responded. "I'm saying that they don't grow beyond what they *are*. Adam is anxious and guilty, and he feels anxious and guilty about being anxious and guilty. It's a trap that endlessly folds in on itself. He'd do a lot better to accept that he's an anxious person and get on with his life."

Marcia had been sulking from Terry's rebuff earlier in the group. But the group discussion stimulated her to participate again. "Then, what's the reason for being here, Joe?" she asked. "If you can't change anything about yourself, what's the point of this group?"

"Well, I want to be less depressed," Joe answered. "So maybe I *do* think feelings can be improved. But I'm not really talking about feelings; I'm talking about the way a person is. I'm a seeker of pleasure and excitement — that's what's always motivated me and nothing that anyone will say or do in here will change that. It's useless for me to even try to be a different type of person."

"There's some sense in that," Tyrone broke in. "I dominated in the streets and I dominate in court — same *modus operandi*, just different setting."

"But have you noticed that you don't dominate in here?" asked David.

"Yes, I guess you're right," responded Tyrone, mentally noting that he was much less overbearing in the group than he generally was in other settings.

"Have you ever wondered why that might be?" David pressed further.

Tyrone studied David's face for a few moments and then

NEVER FORGET MY SOUL

responded: "This group is a special place. Part of it is you, David. You create an atmosphere where everyone is encouraged to be honest, where you don't let us hide or point fingers at each other, without looking at ourselves. And part of it is the group. I've told my story here. I feel I'm understood here. This is one of the few places in my life where I have found that honesty and care are more important than power. I think I have learned in here that I can be me without being exploited or attacked. This group is helping me start to let go of a lot of the anger. It's helping me to mourn what I need to mourn. And something is working — I'm not losing my temper with my wife as much."

"Sounds to me like you *are* changing, Tyrone, profoundly," answered David.

"You're right," said Tyrone, with a smile, his face registering a level of gratitude that he had not shown since Eva had been alive.

Grace entered the discussion at this point. She seemed to have more energy in her manner than usual. She sat erect in her seat and her eyes held an unusual intensity, as her gaze shifted to each of the group members, in turn. "I feel torn between Joe's view and David's view," she said, "but I have to believe in what David is saying. I have to believe that I can make myself different, very different. I can't stand myself the way I am. How can I accept feeling like a blob and sleeping the weekend away and hiding from the world? If I can't make those things better, then I'm useless and there's no hope. My father treated me like garbage. So what am I to do? Just accept that I'm garbage? There's got to be more to life than that."

"But I think you're missing the point, Grace," Terry said. "Joe's not saying that no change is possible. He's just saying you have to know the type of person you are and try to work with it, not against it."

Joe was becoming irritated about the strength of the group's reaction to his statements. He was not sure what he meant himself about the possibility for change. He was also bewildered by the fact that he was being interpreted by others and by the way that they were digging so deeply to understand his meaning. He felt it strange that everyone was looking to him to define an important truth. Usually he took a very different position in social settings. He was the devil's advocate, the counterpoint who stood for nothing and questioned everything. Why was everyone making such a big deal about his philosophy of change?

He broke into what Terry was saying, in an attempt to dispel his discomfort. "Look, everybody come up with whatever you want to believe. I'm not standing for any philosophy here. You're talking about me like I'm some dead philosopher that you read about in a Philosophy 101 textbook. I've told you what I think. Now you go ahead and figure out what *you* think." The annoyance in Joe's voice caused the group discussion to pause.

David had been observing the group's reactions in the latest discussion. He had taken special notice of Joe's extended silence when Tyrone had asked him to describe his recollections of being the child of a workaholic mother. Joe's manner had changed since that time. He was no longer disengaged. He was sitting forward in his seat, eyes scanning the room, looking at each person as they spoke. David suspected that Joe had connected with something important, which had caused him to have a much higher level of engagement with the group. Joe was not the only one who was stimulated by the discussion. The group members had started to engage in a free flow of commentary and reaction that can make a group session particularly exciting and productive. David noticed not only what had been said, but the strong reactions on the listeners' faces. In addition, many members appeared as if they were trying to voice their views at the same time. David was aware that there was limited time left in this group session and Joe was still avoiding something… or, more accurately, someone — Adam. David was convinced that the advice that Joe had tried to dispense to Adam about the futility of trying to change oneself

NEVER FORGET MY SOUL

was primarily a provocation, designed to distance himself from the discomfort Joe felt in listening to Adam's story. Although Joe would not admit it, David believed that *both* Joe and Adam were tormented by memories of a childhood, where they felt trapped and misunderstood. These memories operated on mostly a subconscious level for Joe and a conscious one for Adam. However, David knew that the only consequence of such a distinction was that Joe's memories likely had an even more powerful effect on Joe than on Adam. David considered how he could bring Joe emotionally back to Adam in the group. As usual, David relied on his intuition to lead the way.

David spoke and all eyes turned to him. "I have a question for the group," he said. "A few minutes ago, Grace said that she felt torn between my view and Joe's view. But this present discussion did not begin as a disagreement between *me* and Joe. Can anyone remember how we began all this?"

"It was a disagreement between *Adam* and Joe," responded Tyrone. "Adam told us about how bad things were, growing up in his family, and he said he was going to do his best to make things different for his children. Then Joe said that people are the way they are and they don't change. By the way, Adam, I don't know if anyone else noticed what you did, but I really have to hand it to you. You told us earlier during this group that it's hard to talk about yourself and then you come out and say all these things about your youth, things that must have not been easy to say. I think you showed a lot of guts."

"I agree with you heartily," said David. "Adam showed *a lot* of courage. But I have a question for Adam and Joe. What have you been fighting against during this session?"

"What do you mean?" asked Joe, truly confused about what David was asking of him.

"I mean," replied David calmly, "if you have been resisting something or someone in this session, what would that be?"

Adam understood the question almost immediately. Life was a constant fight for him — fighting his fears, fighting his guilt, fighting to keep himself safe from harm. He was very aware of what he resisted. And yet, there were some battles that he was very uncomfortable to fully admit, even to himself. One of these battles was with the depth of his hopelessness. His religious education had given him an abundance of positive maxims and stories, designed to instill a sense of hope. He had sought refuge within these stories, hoping that a simple faith in a loving God would eventually help him conquer his fears. But he could never shake his haunting doubts: Were these all just pretty stories, which contained reassurance but not truth? Such thoughts disturbed him, because they threatened to shake the foundation of what gave him strength — his religious conviction. So he tried to avoid admitting to such thoughts and to feelings of hopelessness in general, because they were so connected to his religious doubts. However, David's statement that Adam had been courageous had a strange effect on Adam. He told himself that if he could be courageous enough to open up about his youth, then he could be courageous enough to admit to his doubts as well. He was driven forward by an odd defiance against Joe. Who was Joe to tell him that he could not change his fearful and cautious self? Adam would just honestly respond to David's question, a further step on the path of courage.

"I've been fighting a lot of feelings in this session," replied Adam. "One is a feeling of hopelessness, the feeling that the darkness in my own soul is so vast that it will swallow me up, and I will be eternally lost in my fears. I've been fighting the feeling that maybe Joe is right, that maybe people can't change, and that maybe I'm wasting my time here. I've been fighting the destructiveness of the Holocaust and its evil, which consumed my parents and which is trying to pull me down."

"Funny," Joe said, "and I was fighting Adam's conviction that he would be able to change things the way he wanted to. He was

NEVER FORGET MY SOUL

so sure and self-righteous about making things better. I wanted to give him, to give everyone, a dose of reality."

"So Adam was fighting against determinism and Joe was fighting for it," David responded, stroking his beard thoughtfully. Then he continued: "No, I think it was different from that. I think you both are fighting the same thing, hopelessness, or perhaps I should say that you're both trying to *protect* yourself from the pain of hopelessness. The only difference is that, Adam, you protect yourself from hopelessness by denying it, while Joe, you protect yourself from hopelessness by embracing it, by becoming its chief protagonist."

"David," sighed Joe, "you've lost me again."

"I know what he means," said Grace. "I've done it myself. When you become disappointed too many times and you just can't bear to care anymore, then you just give into the hopelessness, accept that life is crap and that it is never going to get better. Then it doesn't hurt anymore. And the deeper the depression, the less the hurt, so you just become numb. I end up telling myself there is nothing I can do about anything and then all the pain and struggle are at an end. Then hopelessness doesn't hurt, it starts to feel like what's natural."

David nodded in approval to this explanation. He paused, wondering if he should continue probing, or if he should let the group members take it from there. David's awareness that Joe was one of the most well-defended men he knew prompted David to take one more step forward.

"Joe," said David, "at the end of the last group session, you denied that the Holocaust had an important impact on your grandfather and said that you were fundamentally different from Adam, in that the war had a much greater impact on his family and him than on you. Has anything happened in today's group that caused you to question these beliefs?"

Now it was Joe's turn to wonder about how honest he would

let himself be. He immediately knew the answer to David's question, as he thought about his mother's diary entry and her tortured longing to understand her father's past. As a matter of pride, he would not let himself take the easy way out and answer in the negative to David's question. He would not let himself be more cowardly than Adam. On the other hand, he was not willing to describe these recollections to the group. That was a level of emotional vulnerability that was presently incomprehensible to Joe.

"I think you're right, David," responded Joe. "Maybe the old man, my grandfather, was more affected by the war than he admitted. Maybe it affected my mother and, through her, affected me. But just because I realize what has affected me, doesn't mean I am able to make big changes in myself. I still think that what I said is true. People are what they are. We may be able to make slight changes, but who we basically are remains the same."

David knew two things, when Joe finished speaking. The first was that it had been difficult for Joe to admit the little that he did. The second was that Joe would not reveal more at this time.

CHAPTER TEN

Marcia opened the next group session. Her usual animated demeanor was somewhat subdued as she spoke.

"I've been dating this guy for two months," she said. "He's really a special guy — nice, considerate, attentive, and fun. We've had such a good time together. There's just one problem. He's always late — sometimes ten minutes, sometimes twenty. I pride myself on being on time. I regard it as a simple matter of respect. When I agree on a meeting time with someone, I'm committing to be ready for them. If I'm not ready, I'm indirectly saying to them that I don't care about wasting their time *and* that I don't care about them. So I make sure that I'm not late — I usually arrive five to ten minutes early, just to make sure. I've told him how I feel about his lateness, in no uncertain terms. He nods, says he's taking it seriously, but nothing changes. Last week we had a fight — well, not really a fight. I just told him I've had enough; I can't be seeing a man who I can't rely on. He pleaded with me to forgive him, to give him another chance. I showed him the door.

I was very self-righteous about it, not a moment's hesitation. But now I'm very conflicted. I mean, I'm still angry with him, but should I have told him that we're through? And then I realized something. It's not really about being on time. It's about keeping promises. Like the promise that my husband made in our wedding vows: 'To have and to hold, for richer or for poorer, for better or for worse, 'til death do us part.' That promise included that he would be faithful to me and not go running after any floozy who caught his eye. You know what he said to me after I caught him running around with another woman yet again and I told him I'd had enough of it? Mind you, this was after ten years of marriage. He said, 'There's just no chemistry between us anymore.' That was his explanation. He said he wanted to stay for the sake of the children, but he was no longer attracted to me. So what did he expect me to do, let him use my house as a place to crash, while he ran around town and gratified his pleasure? I refused to be humiliated like that. I guess I feel that every man who lets me down, even a little, is going to end up abandoning me, like he did. Everyone has his faults, so I end up not being able to trust any man ... I have a question for the men in this group. Can anyone tell me what the phrase means — 'there's no chemistry between us?' What is that supposed to mean in a marriage? I mean, I thought marriage was supposed to be a relationship, not a fifteen-dollar kid's chemistry set. What is that — 'no chemistry?' When the fizz goes out, there's no love? What sort of cheap love is that?"

Tyrone's eyes were fixed on Marcia as she spoke. "I'll try to answer your question, Marcia," he said. "I struggled with some of these things after I was married about five years. It was a year after my wife had her first baby. She was tired from sleepless nights and all the stresses of dealing with a new baby. She didn't take care of herself the way she used to, didn't dress nice or take care of her hair. I'm not proud to say it, but her disregard for her appearance started to turn me off and started to make me resent her. I was also

NEVER FORGET MY SOUL

frustrated about how much time and attention the baby needed and how little was left for me, especially in regard to my wife's interest in sex, or lack thereof. She was stressed, tired and irritable. When I had a free evening, she was more interested in getting extra sleep than in sex. I think I was feeling abandoned by her, feeling that she was like all the other people in my life who abandoned me. Truth is, though, I only developed insight into my feelings at a later time. When I was going through all this, I think I *did* call it chemistry. 'She's just not attractive to me anymore,' I would tell myself. I became less interested in sex with her than she was in sex with me. She would come to me, on occasion, and cuddle up with me, and I would tell her that I was working long hours and I was tired. So I would turn away from her and watch TV. And since I was convinced that we no longer had chemistry, my eye started to wander. I assumed that I had 'fallen out of love' with my wife, so the only way I could get sexual satisfaction again was to find someone with whom I did have chemistry. I came within a hairsbreadth of cheating…Well, I guess it depends on how you define cheating. There was never any extramarital sex, but there was kissing and hugging and more than I would want my wife to know about. I felt both justified and guilty about this behavior. Justified, because a man needs female attention, and my wife no longer attracted me; guilty, because I felt that what I was doing just wasn't right. To deal with these feelings of conflict, I first spoke with my friends. Opinion was mixed. Some friends said that if you don't feel it for a woman, there's nothing you can do about it. They said that when the fire's gone, it's gone. It's biological, they told me. A man needs variety — it's something about encouraging propagation of the species. Others told me that they had been in sexually satisfying relationships for many years — with ups and downs, to be sure, but on the whole, these relationships were satisfying and they would not seriously consider trading their relationship for greater freedom. I was confused and teetering for a long time, until I had some sessions with David. He helped me see that it was all about abandonment, and after I realized how afraid I was of losing my wife's affection, suddenly, without explanation, my passion for her returned and has been fine since."

Tyrone's body relaxed after he finished speaking. He allowed himself to sink into his chair and waited for others to talk next.

Marcia's brow was furrowed as she stared to respond to Tyrone. "Tyrone, what you've said has been helpful, but also makes me worried. I think I have a better understanding of how 'chemistry' could be lost. But what worries me is — it seems too easy to lose the 'chemistry,' and I fear that most men will not have the same wisdom that you had to seek help, when it was lost… Well, Tyrone has weighed in. Anyone else?" Marcia looked at Joe. She intuited that such a discussion was too emotionally challenging for Adam and that he would sidestep it. But Joe, well, wasn't he the one who really should be answering her question? He probably could have a lot to say about chemistry and cheating.

Marcia's attention to Joe was not lost on him. "If there's anyone who doesn't feel chemistry, it's my wife," Joe answered. "There's nothing I can do to make her respond. Sure, she'll let me go through the act. But I always feel like she's waiting for it to be over. She tells me that sex is just not her thing. That's not the way it was when we were dating. If it had been otherwise, I wouldn't have married her. But something happened. I just can't excite her. I still think she's an attractive woman. I'd still like a hot sex life with her. I've tried all sorts of things with her — sexy videos, S and M, fantasy, public places — anything to increase her excitement, but it all falls flat. I don't know what else I could do."

"Have you tried talking with her?" Grace broke in. There was irritation in her voice and anger in her eyes.

Joe was surprised by the comment and by the fact the Grace had made it. He turned to her and said, "I've tried talking to her. We've talked plenty. All she wants to do is talk. But now I just get annoyed when talking with her. When we talk we usually fight and it doesn't lead to anything. Anyway, talk is fine, but what's wrong with some sex?"

"Do you listen to her?" Grace persisted, with a note of defiance.

"As much as I can before I get pissed off at her. Then, when I've had enough, I get in the car and go to my girlfriend, who knows how to appreciate me."

"I don't think you listen to your wife much at all," Grace responded. "I think that's probably the cause of your sexual problems with her."

"Why do you say that?" came Joe's irritated but curious reply.

"Because you usually don't listen to people in here," she answered. "And even when you do, it always comes back to you. Everything's about you. You want to talk about a *turn off*? That's number one, a real biggie."

Joe's face and demeanor went through a variety of stages, in response to this last comment. The first reaction was anger, a reaction that was quickly replaced by an odd sense of superiority. Finally, Joe's face settled into an expression of weariness and indifference, and he sighed. "Grace, you and I have gotten into this before," he said. "I don't want to do this again. I'm not your choice, as a man. Fine, let's just leave it at that. I'm not here to make you happy."

In surveying the group, David noticed, to his surprise, that Adam was trying to speak, apparently to weigh in on the subject at hand. This surprised David, because he believed that Adam could not bear such a level of emotional vulnerability as to talk about such sensitive sexual feelings and doubts. David did not want to break the flow of the group, but he hoped that Adam would find a way in. David kept his eyes on Adam, in tacit encouragement for Adam to find his space in the group.

Terry started to say something, but Adam raised his voice over her and said, "I'm sorry, but I've wanted to say something for a while, and I fear that if I'm silent now I might not get back to it. I want to give an answer to Marcia's question about fidelity. And I realize that I'm getting really nervous even thinking about saying what I'm going to say. My heart is really racing." He sighed and placed his hand on his chest, as if to reassure his heart that it would be all right. "I have thoughts about other women, more than I'd like to admit. This is something that I've never spoken to my wife about. And it makes me feel terribly guilty, like there's something wrong with me. It's not like there is anything wrong about my relationship with my wife. She's a wonderful woman — warm and understanding, satisfying in every way, as much as I can be satisfied, with all my anxiety. But I find myself wondering what it would be like with another woman and sometimes I find myself staring at someone I see in public, and my mind goes to some sexual fantasy with the person that I see. These fantasies scare me, make me wonder if I'll ever just lose control of myself, and do something that I'll regret. Anyway, that's what I wanted to say."

David felt it important that Adam not just leave it there and that he consider the connection between the feelings he had just described and other memories.

David said, "Leaving your parents was a frightening and guilt-ridden experience, but also very exciting, wasn't it, Adam?"

"Sure, it was exciting," said Adam, feeling confused by the abrupt change of subject, but doing his best to answer David's question. "My first step away from my parents was when I went to college. My second step away was when I visited Israel. Both times opened up a whole new world for me, with new experiences, new people. It was a world that put some distance between me and the despair of the past. But what does that have to do with what I was talking about? I don't understand."

David deflected this question by saying, "Can any of the group members help Adam with his question?"

Adam was irked by this response. "I asked *you* a question,

David," Adam said, "about a comment that *you* made. Why can't you answer my question?"

"Because there comes a time for every boy to leave home," David replied, cryptically.

"I still don't understand," said Adam.

David did not respond and the group members were unsure where to go next.

Finally, Grace spoke. "I think I understand. If a person has confused feelings about the home of their youth, then they'll probably be confused about their adult home as well. As a child, being at home meant suffocation for you, Adam. Now, as an adult, you fear that your present home, as good as it is, will also suffocate you. So you fantasize about leaving it. You just use your sexual drive as an excuse to express your fear of getting too close to anyone, because you think that if you get close to someone they'll take away your freedom. I'm a lot like you, Adam. Not with the sexual stuff, but with something more important — that fear of getting close, that fear of being suffocated and crushed by the demands of another person."

"You're on a roll, sister," said Tyrone to Grace, a broad smile on his face. "You're right on target today, first with Joe, then with Adam. I think David and you should switch chairs."

David gave a subtle smile in response to this comment, because he had been thinking the same thing.

"Thanks, Tyrone," Grace said, with an appreciative smile.

"I don't know, Grace," said Adam. "You might be right in what you said. I'll have to think about it."

"Marcia," said Tyrone, "I know you started this discussion by having a question for the guys in the group. I don't know if there was more you wanted to say about all this or if you were done. I don't want to break off into a new direction if you aren't done, but there *is* something that I'd like to discuss today, if you are finished."

"It's OK," Marcia responded. "I'm not sure if I'm looking for one answer or any further discussion. I'll just have to keep on mulling this thing over. You go ahead, Tyrone."

"Thanks, Marcia," said Tyrone. "Well, it has to do with medication. I saw my doctor recently, as a follow-up about pains I've been having in my chest. He said my heart looks OK but my cholesterol is too high and I should find ways to limit my stress. That got us talking about my anger problem. The doctor said that there are medications out there that have helped people control their anger. He said that he thought my anger problem is caused by a chemical imbalance, which can be corrected with appropriate medication. Part of me thinks, sure, why not, maybe medication might help me. But another part of me is really bothered by this, especially about calling my condition a 'chemical imbalance.' How am I supposed to understand that? What happens to my personal responsibility to understand myself and control myself, if it's just a matter of unbalanced chemicals? I fear that if I start taking medications, I'm going to lose something essential in myself. I don't know what to call it … My feelings, my real feelings, my spirit. And what happens if these medications make me happy? How will my wife know if I am happy with her or if I'm just high on the medications? It's like some people I knew back in my drug days. If I was high and they were high, we were both floating and everything was fine. But if they were high and I was not, then their good sprits just seemed like meaningless to me. They weren't happy to see me — I don't think they really saw me at all — they were just getting off on the drug. Man, I tell you, there's nothing more lonely in the world than being with someone who's high when you're not … So I'm wondering what I should do. Do some of you guys take medication?"

"I do," answered Grace. "Here's my experience. If I weren't taking antidepressants, I would not be sitting here. I'd be unable to move. Now, would I *really* be unable to move? I don't know, but it would sure *feel* like that and I'm sure that I would stay put.

Before I started on medications, my depression was so severe that I felt myself physically shutting down, lacking any energy, unable to focus or think. Taking medications does not erase my feelings. They're still there. It just takes the edge off things, keeps me from being paralyzed by my depression."

"I'm glad it works for you, Grace," Terry said. "I had a different experience. In my early twenties I went through some emotional stuff. I think it was related to my parents' divorce. I started getting anxiety attacks. The doctors gave me various medications to overcome the attacks. I guess they found the right medication. The anxiety attacks went away, but my worrying didn't. I felt so pressured and overwhelmed by things that I was constantly worrying. And there was another problem — I just didn't feel like myself on the medication. I felt fake, disconnected. I finally got tired of feeling that way and stopped taking the medication. The anxiety attacks came back. That's when I started jogging, every day. The jogging was my form of meditation. It was a time for me to connect with myself, to listen to what I needed and to keep perspective. I realized that my education was important, but I was overdoing it and not saving any time for what made me happy, like my friendships or painting. I realized the reason for my emotional problems — I had lost touch with a part of myself. The medication did not solve that problem, it just buried it. It's only when I took responsibility for the problem that I got better."

Terry's statement about taking responsibility gave rise to a number of thoughts within David. David himself had long been troubled by the phrase "chemical imbalance." David's studies of the mind and the brain had led him to conclude that both were much more intricately and purposefully structured than was commonly assumed. By "purposefully," he meant that a person's own mind may maintain certain dysfunctional emotional states and behaviors as a deliberate attempt to cope with life circumstances. Thus, "chemical imbalances" in the brain were not just an illness that was an accident of nature; rather, they often arose to provide a protective function. Terry's prior anxiety was an example of this process. David was aware of Terry's past from prior private psychotherapy sessions. After Terry's mother had divorced, she drilled into Terry, over many years, the message that a woman has to be self-reliant and outstanding in order to survive in the world. Self-reliance for Terry's mother, and eventually for Terry, was not just a matter of practicality; it became an issue of emotional survival. After Terry's mother had been devastated by her divorce and the prior reliance she had placed on her husband, she became determined to never need a man in the same way again. She passed these perspectives on to Terry. Thus, when Terry felt she never could stop worrying about her schoolwork and other stresses, it was because her mother had taught her that Terry always had to be in control. Her brain chemicals were doing exactly what she told them to do, subconsciously, to keep her on constant alert, so she could maintain control and self-reliance. That was why the worrying continued even when she was on the medications. In David's experience, the brain was a very stubborn mechanism. Because worrying served an important function for Terry, she was able to maintain her worrying pattern despite the medication. The change for Terry came when she accepted that her problem was not really one about chemical imbalances and did not primarily have a physical cause. Of course, the exercise helped her to decrease the physical anxiety that she was feeling, but it also served as an important message that she was giving to herself. The message was that her survival in the world did not only depend on achievement; it also depended on nurturing her spirit. David had seen how profound insights could change lives, especially in conditions that were the most resistant to being helped by medications.

This was not to say that David dismissed the value of medications. He recognized that there were some conditions in which a life without medications would be one of constant suffering and self-destruction. He had worked with such patients and had seen the difference that medication had made in their lives. It was not medication use itself that troubled David; rather, it was the "physicalization" of psychology, as he called it. In the popular press and parlance, the term "chemical imbalance" was used as a way to define a host of deficiencies in human character and morality. Those who had no self-discipline and wanted to maintain a lifelong childhood could now blame their condition on brain chemicals. Domestic abusers, substance abusers, compulsive spenders, selfish spouses and entitled and destructive juvenile delinquents could all portray themselves as victims of raging chemicals within. With all the talk about how this chemical soup determined behavior, was anyone asking what effect *behavior* had on the chemical soup?

In essence, thought David, this discussion was very much about the same topic that was discussed in the last group session — that is, how much freedom does any person have? David was a proponent of freedom, freedom that arose from the courage to face oneself, to be honest and to develop insight. With his view, he felt himself flying in the face of the modern belief that what we are is determined by our physical makeup. He thought it might be helpful to bring Joe into this discussion, because it was an opportunity for Joe to further explore his views about his own freedom.

The group remained silent after Terry made her comments, so David used that pause as an opportunity to ask, "Joe, do you have any thoughts about Tyrone's question?"

"I've taken medications before," said Joe, "and I've taken drugs before. The drugs were good while they lasted. How *connected* I felt to other people, while I was on them, didn't really matter to me. They just felt good — uppers to give me a rise, downers to calm me down, pot to make me have a good laugh – in fact, I still enjoy a joint now and then – and acid if I was bored and wanted to experience something totally new. The problem with drugs is they don't last. At some point, I would always have to come down and back to the world and when that happened, the depression was there again. When I tried medications, I guess I was less depressed, but I couldn't stand them. They made me feel like I was floating, like nothing was real. Which gets me back to what I said last time — I don't think a person really can change themselves. Sure, you can drug yourself, but that isn't really changing anything, it just makes you ignore a part of yourself. My advice for you, Tyrone, is to just accept that you're an angry guy. It got you to where you are today, so don't try to change it, just accept it."

"Maybe I can accept it, but I doubt my wife will, and I don't want to lose her," Tyrone responded.

"If you live your life for someone else," retorted Joe, "you'll end up living a lie *and* losing yourself. I think all this stuff about changing yourself is useless."

David was getting annoyed with Joe. Joe's comments about change were flying in the face of David's beliefs and his commitment to the process of therapy. David never let go of the vision that he was enriching the lives of others by helping them to know themselves better and thereby understand their ability to choose better lives. He saw it as a battle between dark and light. The darkness would choose isolation and destruction in order to maintain self-protection; the light implored, "Come, open the door, there are friends and life out here." David was continuing his father's war, fighting for the souls of the six clients in this room, who yearned to emerge from the oppression that rose out of hatred and fear. Joe was a casualty of the same war in which David's father fought. Why could he not see that? How could he so smugly deny his suffering and the way that his growth had been stunted? How could he bear the isolation and emptiness of his life without crying out for more, in anguish? These thoughts played through David's mind and caused him to ask the next question. It was not a good time to ask the question. The question had already been asked last week.

Asking it again would only be perceived as a push and a challenge. But David only realized this in silent reflection, at a later time. In the present moment, he let his anger cloud his thinking and he asked the question with an edge to his voice, which made Joe receive the question especially poorly.

"But that gets us back to the same question that Marcia asked you last session," said David. "So why are you in this group?"

Joe looked at David with a defiant glimmer in his eye, "Good question, David," Joe responded, with a combination of self-assurance and indifference. "I'm not going to change myself; you're not going to change me either. This is bullsh**. It's time for me to leave the group."

Joe proceeded to rise from his chair and walk angrily out of the room, shutting the door loudly behind him.

Joe's actions shocked everyone, most of all David. David's first reaction was an urge to race out of the room and beg Joe to stay. But he knew this would be both ineffective and counterproductive. So David did what he had been trained to do, at moments of greatest tension in a group, that is, to do nothing.

Grace was the first to break the shocked silence. "That's just like Joe," she said dryly, "to make a dramatic exit and call all the attention to himself. I think we shouldn't let his self-centeredness disrupt our discussion. Tyrone, you were asking for input on medications. Have we been helpful to you?"

Tyrone hesitated, still affected by Joe's exit and wondering if the group should talk about it. He decided to take Grace's lead and continue the discussion that he had opened. "Yes, what you and Terry said was helpful," he responded. "I'm wondering if anyone else has any thoughts about medications... and about the ability to change oneself."

Adam was strangely disturbed by Joe's exit. Joe's departure, thought Adam, should be a relief to him. After all, Adam always felt either angry or uncomfortable in Joe's presence. Adam shared

Grace's anger towards Joe, and Adam believed Joe had chosen the way to leave that would most disturb the other group members and be most disruptive to the group process. Adam thought it was Joe's way of saying, "So I have come to mean something to all of you. More fool, you — this is what you get for making me important. I told you not to rely on me." Out of his anger towards Joe, Adam forced himself to consider the question that Tyrone was asking so he could return his focus to the remaining group members. The ability to change oneself — that question immediately brought his thoughts to Rabbi Goldberg. Rabbi Goldberg had once walked with him along the streets of Jerusalem, on a cool, dark, clear night. The rabbi had called Adam's attention to the stars twinkling overhead and said, "Look at the stars, Adam. How vast the universe is! How wondrous is creation — each star and planet up there faithfully following the laws of motion and gravitation and energy that were set down from the beginning of the universe. You point to a star and an astronomer will be able to tell you where it will be in a million years, because each star so faithfully follows the laws that were set down for it. The laws of creation are everywhere — they govern the weather cycle, the growth of trees, the way animals raise their young. The laws are understood so well by scientists that we might be deluded into believing that all there is, is those laws, that those laws govern even us, in everything we do, every choice we make. But that, Adam, would be an error, a very grave error. The moment that men forsake their ability to make free choices, then horror is unleashed upon the world. This is because when man abandons his sense of moral responsibility, he will end up only destroying and devouring others. Read about it in history, you will see it happening time and time again. Within every man there are two voices — one prompting us to do good, the other prompting us to do evil. And the true purpose of man in this world is to engage in the struggle between those two voices and choose the good. Ultimately, that is the only thing that matters. The great Rabbi Miamonides spoke about this when he explained the Torah's statement that God made man in His image. Miamonides said that just as God is free to choose, unconstrained by external forces, so are we. Man and God are the only entities in the universe that do not have all of their actions determined by scientific laws. Every drop of water in the ocean follows the laws of motion. But the way that we go is determined by this — our choice. Every day, God calls out to us: 'Today, I put before you a choice — life and death, good and evil, choose good that you may live.'"

While Adam had been recalling Rabbi Goldberg's words, Marcia had been speaking. He missed much of what she had said, but the gist had been that she did not believe in medication and had sufficient help with psychotherapy and holistic drug-free therapies.

Adam's recollections prompted him to weigh in on the group discussion.

"I've been taking medications for a number of years," said Adam. "I have mixed feelings about them. They do help me to function in social situations. But there are side effects, including sexual side effects, lack of sexual drive. I certainly would like to get off of the medications, but I don't think I'm anywhere near being able to make such a step. I'll just say that medications can help with coping, but there is plenty in me that still needs to be changed, regardless of whether I'm taking medication. That's why I come here to try to face the things that I'm afraid of. But there's something else that I wanted to say. It has to do with the ability to change. Tyrone, sometimes I find myself feeling in awe of you and what you have done to turn your life around. I do not believe that you are the same person who dealt drugs and intimidated others on the streets. Maybe there is more growth that you need to do, but the fact that you learned how to respect your mind and how to love another person *was change,* fundamental change, and you should never forget that. If medications will make things easier for you to make the changes you need, then fine, but *never* give up on the faith that you can change things for the better."

"Adam," said David, "when you implore Tyrone to keep faith in the ability to change, I think you're talking not just to Tyrone, but also to yourself."

Adam turned his head towards David, smiled and said, "You're right, David. That faith is the most important thing in my life. Without it, I would be completely lost."

CHAPTER ELEVEN

Ann, Joe's mistress, lay on her back, late on a Sunday afternoon, after an ardent sexual encounter. Joe lay at her side, breathing deeply in his sleep, oblivious to everything. She was motionless, watching the light of day begin to fade, and noticing an oppressive silence in the room. She felt a heavy weight in the middle of her chest and restless unhappiness. She had been lying there for an hour wondering what to do, what to say. She could not take this waiting any longer.

"Joe," she said, shaking his shoulder, "I need to talk to you … JOE!" She shook him more vigorously. His eyes started open and he squinted at her, groggily.

"Ann, please let me sleep. I don't have to leave until seven."

"No, Joe, I have to talk with you," she insisted. "It just can't wait. I'm going to explode!"

Joe wearily propped himself up on one elbow and forced his eyes to open all the way. He blinked until everything came into full focus.

"OK, Ann," he sighed. "What is it?"

"This is not a life," she said.

"What do you mean?"

"I mean, you coming and going like this, squeezing in sex, whenever my husband is away…my disgust for him, my longing for you, but only stolen moments that we can share. *It's not a life, Joe!*"

"Please, Ann," he responded, with a note of irritation in his voice, "I never promised you 'a life.' You remember, we agreed from the beginning — no strings attached. We have fun together, we please each other, we enjoy each other. But it *is* what it *is*. I can't give you more than that."

"But do you love me, Joe?" she pressed insistently.

"Sure, I do," Joe answered too quickly. He smiled, nestled up to her and added, "You're my hot lady."

She drew back. "Stop it, Joe, I want to be serious. Not everything can be solved with a f***."

She got out of the bed and grabbed a robe that was lying on a chair close by. She quickly put on the robe and returned to Joe. She sat on the side of the bed next to him. Joe was now lying on his back. She leaned over, placed her hands on his cheeks and gazed in his eyes. "Look," she said, "if you love me, then marry me. Give us a life, not just stolen moments. Do you know what it's like for me to live with the horrible boredom and emptiness, wondering when we can be together again? Have some guts, Joe! Life is passing us by."

Her gaze and the earnestness of her manner irritated Joe greatly. "Wait, wait, wait, Ann," he responded. "We've always been in this for fun and excitement, remember. Now you're making demands. What the hell is marriage, anyway? It's just an attempt to legislate love, a love guarantee. Like now I have to love someone, because I married them. What crap is that? Anyway, if you're so unhappy about sneaking around your husband, then divorce the guy. Problem solved."

"Problem not solved!" Ann answered angrily. "It's not just

that I don't want him! I want *you*. I want us to live together, share a life, be there for each other."

"We share plenty, Ann, and if you would get your husband out of the picture, we could get together more often."

"Get together! Yeah, get together! I know what you mean when you say that. You mean more sex. Joe, I know that I have your body. But I need more. I want all of you to be there with me. I want to share your soul."

"Look, Ann, you've been reading too many romantic novels. Why don't we just smoke a joint and it will help you to calm down?"

At this last comment, Ann reared up out of the bead, grabbed a glass that was on the nightstand and threw it against the wall. "**I DON'T WANT A F***ING JOINT, I WANT TO FEEL LIKE I MATTER TO YOU!!!**" she screamed.

Joe got up out of bed and started to dress. "Fine, whatever," he replied. "I've had it with this. Have your little fit. This is not what I come here for. I'm going."

She strode to him as he was buttoning his shirt, and placed her face close to his, so they were almost nose-to-nose. "So what do you come here for? An easy f***? A romp in the sack? And moving right along? That's all it is!?"

Joe put his hands on her shoulders and, in a very controlled manner, pushed her back. He said in a quiet, cold voice, "Yeah, that's what I come for. If it's not enough for you, go see what you can get out of your drunk of a husband who can't get a hard on. I'm done with this crap."

Upon hearing these words, she sunk back into the bed, buried her face in her hands and began to cry.

He refused to look in her direction. He simply finished dressing and angrily strode out of the house, slamming the door. As he walked out to his car, he muttered to himself, "That's it! I'm through with her! She's trying to own me."

Strangely, though, as the days passed, Joe found himself

becoming increasingly troubled about his resolve to end their re-lationship. Such feelings were strange to Joe, because he had never had trouble extracting himself from a relationship with a mistress before. When things became too complicated or the woman be-came too possessive, he would give her the it's-been-fun speech and move on. Ann had somehow gotten deeper into him, some-thing he had never wanted. He thought of her scent and the way her body curved so effortlessly into his. He mused about how well she knew his likes and dislikes — how she would create the most delicious meal or how she could turn her face into an iron-ic expression that made laughter irresistible. It was her ability to make him laugh, to pull him out of his most somber and detached moods that was her chief asset for him. When he contemplated a future without her, he felt the stirrings of fear, which was also an unfamiliar feeling to him. He tried to fight this feeling, but the more he fought it, the stronger it would become, and he was con-sumed with an oppressive longing for her.

The next Sunday, he finally gave in and picked up the phone to call her. No answer, just a machine. Hoping that she might have emailed him, he logged onto his email to check. Sure enough, there was the familiar address. He eagerly opened the email. It read as follows:

Dear Joe:

I bear you no grudge. I know you are being yourself, as you have always been. I have had much time to think since we last saw each other. I think I was grasping onto you as a way of trying to grasp hope. I have lived a lie for too long. There is a pain that eats away at me constantly, deep in my chest, and I can't stand it anymore. I just want it to stop. I'll do anything to make it stop. Please don't be mad at me or think me a coward. I hope you find a better life than I have found. Goodbye, Joe.

Ann

NEVER FORGET MY SOUL

As he read the words, Joe felt a rising sense of discomfort. He reread the email, as if he were looking for a hidden message. When he finished reading it a second time, he quickly grabbed his cell phone and tried to call her, only to hear her husband's droning voice on the answering machine. He was suddenly gripped with the undeniable feeling that something was wrong, terribly wrong. He leapt up from his chair, knocking it to the floor and ran out to his car. His children saw him racing out of the house and reported his abrupt behavior to their mother. He had not stopped to say goodbye to anyone or to make an excuse about where he was going. All he could think about was that he needed to get to her house as soon as possible. He raced in his car along the road, taking turns too fast, making U-turns on side streets to avoid red lights, going one hundred miles per hour on the highway. Everything blurred around him, and all that was left was Ann and the maddening miles that separated them. Finally, he pulled into her driveway with a screech and ran towards the house. When he reached the door, he paused for what seemed like an eternity, fearing what he would find inside. This timeless moment passed, and he tried the door. It swung open and he entered. "Ann?" he called out tentatively. No reply. He searched the living room, the kitchen. Nothing. He mounted the stairs to the bedroom. The bedroom door was closed. He turned the knob and swung it open.

There she was — legs bent sideways, torso facing upwards, arms outstretched ... eyes towards the ceiling, but seeing nothing. A pool of blood surrounded her. A gun lay at her side. He staggered forward and grabbed her wrist. No heartbeat. He began CPR, wildly pumping at her chest, trying to breathe life into her lungs. He had no idea how much time passed in these vain efforts. He finally arose and raised his voice into a combination of a scream and a wail. "**WHY?! WHY?!**" he yelled, turning his face upward. He slumped down on the floor in defeat and began to sob. When the sobs subsided, he picked up the bedroom phone and called

911. With a hoarse voice he told the dispatcher, "There's been a suicide here," and proceeded to give all the requested information. After completing the call, Joe went downstairs and began to pace in agitated distraction. His mind reeled in a tumble of anguish, rage and disbelief. Occasionally he would let out a sob, but then he would sternly silence himself, saying, "Joe, stop it! You have to think, you have to *think!*" But thought was exceedingly difficult. He was only able to scrape together some very simple conclusions, while trying to ward off the tumult that threatened to envelop him. His first thought was to make a hasty exit, so as to avoid detection and all the complications that staying might involve. On the other hand, he realized that if he left the house now, he would be exposing himself to great legal peril. His hasty departure might be taken as suggestion of foul play. He decided to stay, and he was not sure if it was for practical reasons, or because of a desire to linger there with Ann, even if that only meant staying in this house, which contained her lifeless body. After arriving at his decision, he continued to pace and frequently look out the window, wondering how long the police would take to arrive. He felt intensely weary, and when he could walk no more, he sunk to the floor. He leaned against a wall, with his knees drawn up to his chest and began to whimper.

After the police arrived and examined the body, they began to question Joe.

"What was your relationship to the lady?" asked the policeman.

Joe stammered for an answer. What could he say, when he did not know the answer himself? Eventually, he heard his voice saying, "We met about once a week, when her husband was away, hung out together, had sex..."

"So," said the policeman dryly, as he made notes in his pad. "You're a paramour.""Paramour" — for some reason, the word sickened Joe.

When the police finished interviewing Joe, they told him

he was free to leave, but not to leave town. Joe went out to his car and grabbed a set of surgical scrubs from the back seat. He hid behind a bush, removed his bloodstained clothing and changed into the scrubs.

He arrived home half an hour later. Luckily for him, when he entered the bedroom, Lisa lay on her side, sleeping. There were no questions, so there would be no need to construct new lies. He lowered himself to their bed, seeking the oblivion of sleep. Feverish thoughts and images formed and reformed in his mind. His weariness cloaked these thoughts and images in a cloud of sleep and drove his anguish into tortured dreams.

The days moved forward, separating Joe from the horrible events. Somehow, he was able to conceal all that had happened from Lisa. He occasionally wondered if Ann's former husband would appear some day and demand an explanation, but he never did. Life went on as normal. At times, Joe's sexual urges would get the better of him and he sought relief in the arms of prostitutes. He found himself experiencing increased depression and agitated boredom with everything in his life. As he would rise in the morning, he felt a sense of heaviness and weariness that was new to him. He had no idea how to shake these feelings.

Notwithstanding his prior comments about leaving the group, Joe decided to stay. He would have been unable to articulate why, beyond the feeling that the group was somehow a lifeline for him and that without it, he would totally succumb to despair. He had been away from the group for two weeks. He called David about continuing and David had gladly consented. David had been very troubled about Joe's abrupt departure, especially because David blamed himself for losing his composure, letting his anger cloud his thinking and pressuring Joe too much. After Joe's departure, David had called him to discuss his intentions regarding the group, but Joe did not return the calls until the day of the next group that he attended. Joe did not provide an explanation to David about the reasons for his change of heart, nor did he explain it to the group. In the group, he did not speak of Ann's death. His interaction with the group members decreased, dramatically, compared to the time before his departure. Many group members noticed and commented on the change. In response, Joe simply shrugged his shoulders indifferently and said, "I just don't feel like talking."

One day, in the group, Terry began talking about her irritation with her mother, who, Terry believed, simply did not understand her.

"She gives me what *she* thinks I need. She's uninterested in what I need. I tell her that I need her to just listen to me when I'm depressed and hear my frustration. She just launches into her reassurances that I've got the best doctors and they're going to find a cure. I don't need her optimistic lies. Maybe they will find a cure, but she has no way of knowing that. She tells me to cheer up, but not because of me. I'm tired of being brave; I need to just let myself cry. But that's not OK for her. *She* can't stand me being down. So who's supporting whom? *I'm* the one who sick — why do I have to keep *her* happy?"

Her words prompted a response from Adam, who discussed the strangling way in which his parents' anxieties and longings preempted any awareness of his emotional discomfort. He felt he was "crushed under the weight" of his parents' problems. Grace then began to discuss how she was required to be the peacemaker in her home, at a young age, helping her mother catch up on chores, in order to avoid a tirade by her father. She added, very quietly, that her father's abuse of her was another example of how his longings preempted and crushed any of her needs.

David's bearded chin rested on his hand as he listened to these comments and looked across the room thoughtfully. He had been feeling concerned about Joe's withdrawal in the group. David wondered if Joe's extended silence in group signaled that

NEVER FORGET MY SOUL

he was contemplating departure again. David intuited that Joe needed the group now more than ever. Thus, David decided to make a slightly provocative comment, in order to draw Joe into the discussion. David said, "Yes, there are many ways that parents can sacrifice their children. Don't you think, Joe?"

Joe sighed in irritation, shaking his head. "Look, David, I don't know what you want from me. I told you. I don't feel like talking." Then, he appeared to have a new thought and said, "Actually, there is something I want to say about sacrifices. It's a question for you, Adam. I figure if anyone could answer this question, it would be you." His voice had a cold and quiet harshness in it, as if he did not expect Adam to be able to give a satisfactory answer. "You know the story in the Bible about when God asks Abraham to sacrifice his son? What's that about? What kind of twisted sadist is God that He tells a father to kill his son and only later says, 'Sorry, I was just kidding?' Does God spend all day thinking of ways to make us suffer? How can you follow a book that tells such a story? How can you believe in such a God?"

Adam paused, considering the question, and then began to speak. "This is not a new question to me, Joe. I remember asking a related question to a very wise rabbi in Israel years ago. He was a survivor of the concentration camps, and a believer in God — now that in itself is amazing. I asked him this question: If God is in control of everything, how could He allow the Holocaust to occur? His answer was that the first step to understanding this question is to make yourself aware of the infinite blessings you receive every day of your life. When I arise from my bed in the morning and place my feet on the floor, do you have any idea of the wondrous structure of the universe that supports such a mundane event? Think of the sun that streams through your window and warms the earth. If the electromagnetic force in the universe were four percent weaker, then there would be no hydrogen and no normal stars. And if the earth were shifted slightly further away from or closer to the sun, the temperature would be too cold or too hot to support life. I'm not going on with this physics lesson, but there are numerous examples of the happy 'coincidences' in the universe that allow life to exist. Then think about the miracle of your own body. You're a doctor, Joe. You should know this. Look at the miraculous design of your body and all the things that have to go right for you to be able to get up in the morning. If one little vessel is closed up, that's it, we're finished. Blood chemistry slightly altered and we could be dead in a few minutes. These things that I describe are more than amazing. They are miracles, based on God's loving desire for us to exist. If you meditate for long enough on these gifts, you can find a sense of awe and gratitude for all that God gives you. That's step one. Now here's the harder part. Could *we* design such a world? Do we have even a remote understanding of the true basic mechanics of how it all works? Every day scientists are finding out new things and debating the meaning of it. If it is true that all the positive aspects of God's designs are too far beyond our true comprehension, then shouldn't this be all the more so true about what appears to be bad? As human beings, our choice is this: Do we drown ourselves in despair, seeking answers for the bad, or do we appreciate the good and trust that God, our Father, has good reasons that are beyond our comprehension?"

As Adam spoke, Joe remembered the impatient countenance of Rabbi Pearlman in response to Joe's challenging and probing questions, over twenty-five years ago. Joe felt the same defiant spirit of his youth filling him. Adam appeared as if he had more to say, but Joe interrupted and said, "Great sermon, Adam, but all you've done is sidestep the question. I asked about Abraham and the sacrifice. You give me generalities. *Why did God need to torture Abraham like that?*"

Adam felt uncommonly confident and undisturbed by Joe's interruption. Adam paused and then proceeded to answer:

NEVER FORGET MY SOUL

"They're not generalities, Joe. I just wanted to explain why these types of questions are so hard to answer. But, truth is, there is a great deal of material written about this very question. I'll give you one explanation. God wanted to test Abraham. Not that God needs anything proven to Himself (He knows everything anyway), but *Abraham* needed the test. You see, in Judaism, potential is not enough — it's *action* that matters. Abraham needed to experience a new aspect of himself, in order to raise to a higher level in his service to God. Abraham had devoted his whole life to love of his fellowman, but the open question, at that time, was whether Abraham demonstrated such love because that was his personality or because God wanted him to act in that way. If Abraham had only acted out of his innate kindness, then Judaism could not last for more than a few generations. That is because Abraham and his descendants would have been kind as long as they *felt like it,* and only until new generations arose that felt like being cruel. The only way to make kindness an eternal value was to tie it to more than a personal inclination, that is, to tie it to the fact that God *expects it of us.* So God was testing Abraham to see if he would faithfully perform *anything* that God told him to do. How does God do this with a man who devoted his life to kindness, who is repulsed by cruelty? The answer is self-evident. Command that he be cruel, and not just to anyone, but to his own son, the circumstance where his heart is most likely to rebel against God. If he passed the test, then Abraham could experience himself as the one who can face death itself and still cleave to his God. Only such a man can establish an eternal mission of doing good in the world."

Adam was silent and Joe considered the answer. It was a good one, one that was better than he had ever thought possible, when he considered the story as an adolescent. But then, Joe had a new thought and he furrowed his brow. "I've just got one problem with all this, Adam. You talk great; it makes sense. But tell me this: why does it not make enough sense *for you?* You've told us about how you feel your prayers are empty and you feel so distant from God. If you really believed all that you were saying, then why are you so anxious? If you really trusted in God, couldn't you relax with the knowledge that whatever happens, He's taking care of you? I can't believe all your pretty words, Adam, if they are just words."

"I know the things that I say are true," answered Adam. "I just have trouble *feeling* their truth."

"If you don't *feel* their truth, then you don't really believe them," said Joe, dismissing Adam.

⸺∘◦∘∘⸺

Joe wandered aimlessly along the city sidewalk, his surroundings only vaguely registering on his awareness. It was early evening on a Sunday, time that he would be spending with Ann if… He avoided finishing that thought. All too frequently, gruesome memories of how he found her lifeless body two months ago would thrust themselves into his awareness. These memories so troubled him that he made increasing efforts to suppress them, but usually with little success.

Last night he had had a dream that he was chained to Adam's corpse. In the dream, he received a panicked telephone call from Ann, saying that she was about to be attacked. Joe tried with much difficulty to drag Adam along as he attempted to get into his car and drive to Ann's house. The journey was very difficult because the road was made of dirt and filled with potholes and bumps. As Joe drove, Adam would moan, even though Joe knew that Adam was dead. In slow motion, Joe drove up Ann's driveway, just in time to see a large monstrous figure, cloaked in shadows, hoist Ann from the roof and hurl her towards the ground. She screamed as she fell and hit the ground with a sickening thud. Joe then awaked and sat forward in startled panic, bathed in sweat, with his heart beating wildly.

Joe's visits to prostitutes had become increasingly unsatisfying. Now a mix of empty heaviness and agitation would return to him even before he would have a chance to leave the room of his sexual encounter. There was nothing that he could do and no place that he could go that would bring him pleasure any more. He dreaded going to sleep because of the nightmares, but he also dreaded having to wake up to a new day that was as oppressing as the day before. Lisa was just pushy and demanding, trying to get his attention, but still uninterested in sex. And now there was the added dimension that he was tightly holding onto a very painful secret. Such a secret can only be held through distance, so Joe had increased his coldness to Lisa. He had also emotionally distanced himself from his children for the same reason. He used work as an excuse to avoid contact with them. He had developed a habit of avoiding eye contact when at home, just to decrease the opportunity for interaction. He also began to dread work. The sight of blood had taken on an added significance for him. The anxiety of his patients irritated him, causing him to be cold and dismissive about their concerns. "I can't stand living like this," he would often repeat to himself. And then, one day, a second thought followed this refrain — "You don't have to go on living like this. You don't have to go on living. Just end it all. Jump off a building, and you can end the pain." At first, the thought disturbed him, but it returned frequently and hardly disturbed him any more. Perhaps it was good advice.

As he walked along the street on that Sunday evening, his eyes drifted upwards to rooftops, surveying possibilities where he could end his life. Then, a thought hit him — he knew of a building close by with access to an open roof. He turned left at the next intersection and headed for the building.

As he walked towards the building, he found his mind drifting, for no explicable reason, to Rabbi Pearlman. He then thought of the story of Abraham and the sacrifice of Yitzchak and Adam's explanation of the events. He felt a rising anger against Adam, the same anger that Joe had felt towards Rabbi Pearlman, all those years ago. "All those pretty words," he thought to himself. "It's all just an attempt to avoid the cold reality of the world. There's no force out there that understands and cares. We are born alone and die alone. We seek pleasure, if we can, or suffer, or choose to end the suffering. That's all there is." Adam was disgustingly ironic, spouting his religious faith, while his guts were wracked with fear. Adam's anxiety, Joe believed, arose from a fear of facing these harsh realities about life. But then Joe stopped walking, because he was struck with another thought. Adam aside, the real reason Joe had been so angry with Rabbi Pearlman all those years ago was that Joe wanted him to be right about the goodness of God and man and, at the same time, hated the rabbi for reawakening this innocent longing that Joe had buried within himself years prior. Suddenly, Joe found himself acting on an impulse that he did not understand. He picked up his cell phone and checked if there was a listing for "Rabbi Eliezer Pearlman."

Rabbi Pearlman was studying the book of Job. He read, in Hebrew, sentences that translate into English as "As for me, I will not muzzle my mouth; I will speak in the anguish of my spirit; I will express myself in the bitterness of my soul." He looked up from the book. He sat at his desk, facing a window that showed little more than the darkness of night. A small lamp sent a circle of light upon the desk surface. The house was quiet and the only sounds he heard were the ticking of the grandfather clock in his study and the occasional passing of a car. As he stared towards the darkness, his thoughts drifted to Rose, his wife of forty years, who had died two years ago. She used to bring him coffee and cake in the evening, as he worked in his study. Not wishing to disturb him while he was working, she would gently kiss him on the top of his head and quietly leave the room. That ritual said so much about her. She was a patient and giving woman, who did not need to draw attention to herself. From their first date, when she listened to his dreams with such warmth and enthusiasm, with a glimmer in her eye, he felt his own soul warmed and soothed. After their first few dates, he told his father about this lovely woman, and his father responded, smiling, "This sounds like a keeper, son."

Adjusting to her loss had been very painful for Rabbi Pearlman. Of course, his community had been supportive, offering to make meals, visiting with him and helping in numerous other ways. At least one of his three children visited him almost daily, and he enjoyed these visits greatly. Plus, he had his work. He was a rabbi to a large congregation with countless needs and concerns — there were always those who were looking for inspiration and guidance, and the rabbi had an open-door policy for those needs. In addition, he had other official duties, such as his weekly sermon and preparing for religious classes that he taught at various times in the week. Still, in losing Rose, he lost part of himself. The pain had turned into a dull ache and then into a sense of wistfulness, which would come and go, unpredictably.

A year after the loss of his wife, he had added the book of Job to his daily studies. With his own loss, he had developed a heightened awareness of suffering in the world. Job told the story of man's struggle for understanding in the face of suffering. While the text was challenging and confusing, Rabbi Pearlman sensed profound wisdom in its pages, wisdom that could be used to help himself and others.

He was aroused from these thoughts by a knocking on the door. The knock had a loud insistence to it. Who would be knocking at this hour? It was nine o'clock and, by this hour, visitors would call to ask if they could come. He arose from the desk, picked up his cane and walked slowly towards the door.

When he opened the door, he was met by a face that was unknown to him. The man had intense dark eyes and a serious expression that made the rabbi uncomfortable. The man wore a grey tracksuit and his hair looked somewhat disheveled.

"Yes?" said the rabbi, tentatively.

"Are you Eliezer Pearlman, the rabbi?" asked the man.

"Yes," the rabbi answered.

"I'm Joe Barns, do you remember me?" said the man.

The rabbi's face went through a range of reactions, all within the space of a few moments — first confusion, then recognition, then surprise.

"Joe Barns? It must be more than twenty-five years! What brings you here, and at this hour!?"

"I need to talk with you, Rabbi."

The rabbi sighed and responded, "Joe, I'd be happy to talk with you, but at a more reasonable time. It's late."

"I know, Rabbi," said Joe. "And I know I am probably being unreasonable. But please hear me out for a moment. This evening, I was seriously considering killing myself. Now before you tell me to go to the hospital or some crap like that, please listen. Psychologists and psychiatrists have nothing to offer me. All they can do is tell me that I should live, and they'll either force me to not kill myself or give me some sort of drugs or advice to try to make life more tolerable. But they cannot tell me *why* I should live. They don't teach such things in medical school. I figured that you, as a rabbi, might have an answer to such a question. So that's why I'm here. If you care enough to share your answer, please let me in. If not, I'll just go back to the only solution I know."

Rabbi Pearlman's first thought was, "He has not changed at all — he's just as self-centered as when he was a teen." But that thought was followed in quick succession with a second thought — "How can I turn him away and maybe never see him again and wonder if I could have made a difference? What if he actually does end his life tonight?" The rabbi then smiled and reached out to place his hand on Joe's shoulder. "Come in, Joe," he said, in a fatherly fashion. "Let's sit down, relax and talk."

The rabbi led Joe down a dimly lit hallway, towards the study. When they reached the study, the rabbi turned on a floor lamp, which bathed the room in a warm glow. The rabbi offered Joe a soft leather couch in which to sit. As Joe allowed himself to collapse into the cushions, he had the strange, but comforting, feeling of being held. At the back of his mind, as if through mist, a question surfaced: "How long has it been since I actually had the sensation of being held?"

"Would you care for something to eat or drink?" asked the rabbi.

"I could use some coffee," said Joe, and then added, in a hesitant afterthought, "Th-thanks."

As the rabbi went to prepare the coffee, Joe had a few minutes to survey the room. The rabbi's study was filled with books, from the ceiling to the floor. Almost all of the spines of the books had Hebrew writing on them. The shelves were packed to capacity with these books, as horizontally placed books topped the vertically arranged ones and filled the space between one shelf and the next. Many of the books had a worn look, indicating years of use and study. Across the room from Joe was the rabbi's desk. Two piles of books lay on the desk and in the front midsection of the desk, a few books lay open. Next to these open books was a writing pad, with a pen laying on it. To Joe's left was a fireplace. On the mantle piece stood some framed pictures. One frame contained a black and white photograph of a bride and groom. Other frames displayed color photos — a man and woman with five children, standing in front of a mountain range and blue sky; three children splashing at a beach; a young adolescent boy dressed in a prayer shawl and phylacteries, standing beside a proud-looking man; and Rabbi Pearlman, in what seemed to be a recent photograph, with a bright-eyed toddler girl in his lap. Above the mantle piece was a painting of an elderly, bearded man reading from a Torah scroll, as other men stood beside him and peered intently at the scroll. The rabbi returned, precariously balancing a coffee cup and saucer in one hand, as he supported himself with his cane in the other hand. Joe looked up and realized the navigation challenges that the rabbi faced. Joe quickly rose and took the saucer and cup from the rabbi, then thanked him. The rabbi asked if Joe needed milk or sugar, but Joe declined, not so much out of compassion for the rabbi's limited mobility, but more out of impatience to begin their conversation. The rabbi pulled up a chair, close to Joe, and sat down, with a sigh.

"So, Joe," the rabbi began, "it's been twenty-five years, what's been going on?"

When Joe looked back on this evening, he wondered how Rabbi Pearlman was able, with this simple question, to prompt Joe to talk about his life with such openness. Somehow the rabbi accessed an overwhelming desire in Joe to speak, and the contents of his tormented soul flowed out for an hour and a half. Joe did most of the speaking. When Joe's monologue would lapse, the rabbi would ask a question, and the flow would begin again. Joe found himself talking about his overbearing father, his distant mother, his gnawing unhappiness that he had attempted to drown with drugs, his frustrating and unfulfilling relationship with his wife, his succession of affairs, Ann's suicide and Joe's resulting breakdown. He described his work with David and the group therapy, Joe's discussions with Adam and Joe's growing awareness that the Holocaust may have affected Joe more than he had previously realized. Throughout Joe's account, the rabbi's dark brown eyes attended patiently to Joe's story, his head often nodding in understanding, and his brow furrowing as some particularly painful events were described.

After an hour and a half of this interaction, the rabbi asked,

NEVER FORGET MY SOUL

"Joe, have you told anyone else about what happened to Ann?"

Joe appeared irritated by the question. "I told the police. I didn't want to get implicated in a murder. Who else do I need to tell?"

"I'm not saying that you need to tell anyone," replied the rabbi. "It's just such a heavy secret to carry all alone."

"Excuse me, rabbi," said Joe, "but I've heard that 'carrying pain alone' crap before, and I think its bullsh**. Telling other people about what happened is not going to make me feel better, it's not going to bring Ann back, and it's not going to take away the nightmares and all the questions I have about what I could have done to prevent her death. 'Sharing my secret' means relying on other people, which is something that I never wanted to do. That's the mistake I made with Ann — I got too emotionally involved. I don't need anyone's pity. I rely on myself and I try not to need anyone. It's always worked for me before."

Joe was surprised to find that the rabbi did not respond to these comments. The two men's eyes met, and Joe stared at the rabbi with the same defiant gaze the rabbi remembered from Joe's youth. The rabbi's eyes shifted away from Joe and became distant. The two men sat in an extended silence. Joe began jiggling his leg in agitation. Joe finally become impatient with the silence and said, "Well, I guess I'll be going now. Thanks for the therapy, Rabbi, but it didn't help."

"Wait, Joe, wait," urged the rabbi. "Nothing gets solved in a rush. Every difficult problem requires patience... I have a question for you. Can you, by any chance, tell me what the *parsha*, the Torah portion, was for your bar mitzvah?"

"How should I remember what it was called?" said Joe impatiently.

"Can you remember anything that it was about?"

"Sure. It was about Abraham and the angels and the destruction of Sodom — "

"The destruction of Sodom," repeated the rabbi. "Yes, that's right, just as I thought." He then smiled, looking pleased, and continued, "It's nice, Joe, that this old mind can still remember a few things. I have an answer for you, Joe."

"An answer to what — To why I shouldn't kill myself?"

"Well, yes, but I'm not really getting to that yet. I was actually thinking about a question you asked me a long time before today."

"I don't remember any question."

"That's a pity, Joe, because you asked good questions. In fact, I think some of your questions were better than I was equipped to answer all those years ago. But you did ask me a particularly good question, and I just dismissed it and told you that you can't have answers to everything. You asked me why it was *Abraham* that had to have mercy on Sodom and bargain with God that He not destroy its inhabitants. Why did not God himself initially have that mercy on them and be willing the spare the city for the sake of the righteous minority, even without Abraham's intercession? Here is my answer to that question," the rabbi paused and took a deep breath, as he considered how he could best communicate a concept to Joe that might be difficult for him to absorb. Then the rabbi continued, "The root of all human goodness and happiness is the awareness that we are not alone in this world, and the root of all evil and despair is the belief that we are alone. Abraham's life was infused with the awareness that he was not alone. He was the founder of monotheism, so some might say that Abraham's awareness that God was always near to him kept Abraham aware that he was not alone. But I think this is not the most important reason why Abraham did not feel alone. Even more than his relationship with God, Abraham is remembered for his relationship with his fellow man. The real reason that Abraham knew that he was not alone is because he felt that all people were his brothers and sisters and he believed that he had a responsibility to promote the wellbeing of any person whom he could influence. In considering what to do about Sodom, God carefully arranged the circumstances so that Abraham could play a role in the decision that God made. God did this for two reasons. The first reason is that the interaction between Abraham and God serves as a model for how deeply we all should yearn for and work for the wellbeing of others. If Abraham was willing to question God Himself, the most powerful force in the universe, to save a city of ninety-nine percent sinners, then certainly we can put forward our best efforts to fight for the wellbeing of others. Those others might be your wife and children, members of your community or those who are suffering on the other side of the world. Of course, your primary responsibility is to those who are closer to you, but to the extent that we can, that responsibility extends to all of humanity. Now, Joe, there is only one way that a person can have that level of commitment to the wellbeing of others. *You have to perceive that other people are real and that other people are part of you.* If my neighbor is hungry, then, in a sense, I am hungry. If a little girl in Asia is raped or tortured, then it's happening to me. Abraham felt this as a reality, and that fueled his passion for the wellbeing of others.

"I told you there were two reasons why God acted the way he did. The second reason is simply this: God was giving Abraham an opportunity. The opportunity was to strengthen Abraham's awareness of his connectedness to others. It is one thing to *say* that you love humanity, but it's just words and not deeply felt until one actually puts this love into action. God did not initially withhold mercy from Sodom to be cruel to Sodom. Rather, He did so to show kindness to Abraham. What was the nature of this kindness? This kindness was giving Abraham the greatest gift that a man can have — the profound awareness of the importance of others and one's connectedness to them. God loved Abraham, so He gave him many opportunities to experience this highest of all gifts — the opportunity to demonstrate love of others in our actions. The action that was required of Abraham in the story of Sodom was to stand his ground with God himself and bargain for the possibility that Sodom be spared. The truth is that God loves all of us. He gives us all countless opportunities to access this highest of all gifts. The real challenge is to notice that this gift is being offered."

The rabbi stopped speaking. Joe looked back at him with attentive, but hopeless, eyes. "I see no gifts, Rabbi," he responded, "only a cold world, where the strong survive and the weak are crushed. I see death and destruction. Love and justice are only for dreamers. I have never known how to dream."

The rabbi look intently back at Joe, struck by how profoundly untouchable Joe appeared. Then the rabbi's eyes brightened, as he was struck by an idea. Into his mind came these words that he had read, years ago, in a book about counseling: "To treat the darkness, you have to bear your own entry into the darkness."

Then the rabbi said, "Joe, are you familiar with the story of Job?"

Joe shook his head.

"Then bear with me," the rabbi continued, "I want to tell you a story. Once, long ago, there lived a man, and his name was Job. He was a good man, who avoided all evil. When God Himself scrutinized Job's ways, God could find no trace of sin in Job. Job had ten children, and he was very wealthy and prosperous. Then, one day, God took it all away. His livestock were taken or destroyed, his servants were killed, and his children died when a great wind caused their house to collapse upon them. But that was not all. Job was then afflicted by a terrible illness. He was covered with agonizing boils, from the sole of his foot to the top of his skull. His skin began to peel off and he had to scratch himself with a pottery shard to try to have some temporary relief. But the only true relief he could envision was death, and he sat on the ground longing and waiting for it. Three close friends came to him, while he was in this state, and started to talk to him. His friends were all of one opinion: God rules the world with justice. Good men are rewarded for their good deeds and evil men are punished. Thus, they told Job, Job was afflicted due to some sin that he had previously committed and for which he had not repented. All he needed to do was repent from this sin and God would remove his afflictions. Job resisted this interpretation. He insisted that he was a righteous man. He could identify no sin for which he needed to repent. He asserted that there was no justice in the suffering that he was given. His friends responded that Job was presumptuous, and God was all-good and all-knowing. They insisted that Job had a hidden sin for which he had not yet searched deeply enough. As these discussions proceeded, Job became increasingly angry. He felt his friends were giving him empty arguments, mere platitudes about one's need to have faith in God, without sincerely trying to understand Job's situation. He replied to his friends that if he had some subtle, hidden sins, then they likely did, too. Why was he afflicted and they not? He expressed increasing anger towards God, with whom he wanted to debate. He was tired of just talking about God. He wanted to talk *with* God. He wanted to present his case to God, insist on his innocence, prove that he did not deserve the suffering that he was given. In his suffering, he felt that God had abandoned him. His soul yearned to approach God and come to understand the reason behind his suffering. Job and his friends argued for hours. Job could not understand his friends, nor could his friends understand him. His friends offered intellectual and theological arguments, and Job howled out in increasing anguish and pain, feeling that no one could hear the depth of his suffering. Finally the friends fell silent, realizing that they were unable to have any impact on Job.

"It was then that an observer to this debate spoke out. His name was Elihu. He was younger than the three friends, and, in deference to their age and wisdom, he had, up to now, remained silent. But throughout the debate, he had been experiencing increasingly conflicting emotions and his anger had been growing.

He saw Job — destitute and suffering … and abandoned — abandoned by his three friends, who spoke *at him* but not *with him*, who were unwilling to *take in* the depth of Job's suffering. They preached to Job, they condemned him as a sinner, but did not cry with him. Elihu became furious with their callousness. At the same time, he was angry with Job. Elihu had full faith in the goodness of God. He knew that Job's anger with and defiance of God was distancing Job from the only source that could give him true consolation. Elihu is the heart of this story — a youthful heart who can feel the suffering of another, who is willing to embrace Job's despair on its own terms without cold philosophizing. Elihu spoke out of compassion. First and foremost, he told Job that he was not there to silence Job. Elihu had listened intently to Job. If there was more that Job had to say, Elihu invited him to speak. But then Elihu went on to say that there was something that he needed to tell Job. Elihu added something for Job to consider, something that his friends had neglected to say. Elihu told Job that God's actions appear like injustice only because His ways are so much greater than our understanding and are thus so hidden. In trying to comprehend God's ways, we are as ants, trying to comprehend the expanse of the ocean. But, Elihu maintained, if we were truly able to encounter God on his own terms, all we would see is compassion and love. Everything that God gives us is given to teach us something or to make us improve our character. Elihu had been moved by Job's despair. Out of love for his fellow man, for Job, Elihu reminded Job that his God loves him, has always loved him, and even in the depth of his suffering, anguish and anger, has not abandoned Job.

"When Elihu finished speaking, God began to speak directly to Job. Elihu's compassion and empathy had created a doorway for Job, had opened him up, so Job could encounter God directly. But God gave Job no answers. He only asked Job a series of questions, questions that are unanswerable to man. Questions like: Where were you when I designed the earth? Where did light and darkness, snow and thunder originate? Who created the wisdom that resides within our body and allows it to sustain itself? Who gave the rooster the instinct to crow at dawn? God described the complexity and wonder of his creations and made clear to Job how inherently unable he was to comprehend God's explanations. When God finally fell silent, Job stated that he realized it was pointless to question God and Job would cease from doing so. Job repented from his former adversarial position.

"God then spoke to Job's friends. He told them that he was angry with them, because they had not spoken properly about God. They had presumed to have all the answers and to be able to speak on behalf of a power that is completely beyond their understanding. But strangely enough, God does *not* say that he is angry with Job. Why should this be? It seems that Job did much worse than his friends did. All the friends did was presume to explain that which they truly could not understand. Job went further and wanted to argue with and defy God. Why did God not say that he was angry with Job? The best answer that I have heard to this question is something that is written in the Talmud, to the effect that man is not punished for what he says when he is troubled. Job's statements were an outpouring of emotion, arising out of a severed relationship. Before his calamity, he had trust and faith in God. When his faith was ruptured, he cried out in anger and despair, as is normal in such circumstances. We are not made of stone. God understands this and will not punish us for statements made under the influence of such suffering. In fact, one might say that the honest acceptance and expression of that anger is an essential step to coming back to God. If we do not let ourselves yell or cry, then we are not offering these feelings to Him to be healed.

"Why do I tell you this story?" asked the rabbi, as Joe felt like the rabbi was reading his thoughts. "I tell you this story, so you can know about Elihu. Elihu was willing to take on the burden of feeling Job's pain. He suffers with Job and tries to draw him near with words of compassion. Those words open up Job to hear God and heal his relationship with God. There is no answer to suffering, Joe. It lays in wait for each of us at some point in our lives. Suffering is a given in life. But there is something else that is not a given, that lays in our hands to uphold or dismiss. That something is love, that something is having the courage to believe that we are not alone, that others matter, and that a life in which we do not extend ourselves for others and feel ourselves as part of others is not a life.

"Joe, I believe that you loved Ann, and you only discovered that when it was too late. I think you have been driven to despair, because you have lost one of the only people who has ever really mattered to you." The rabbi, paused, looked at the floor and sighed, "Joe, I lost my wife two years ago. We were married for forty years. I loved her as a second soul. I feel for your loss." The rabbi paused. His voice choked and tears welled in his eyes. He briefly composed himself and then continued, "A loss of a loved one is irreplaceable. But, thank God, I am not alone. I have my children; I have my community and people who come to me for counsel. It is upon these things that I sustain my soul. You're not alone either, Joe. I suspect from how you describe Lisa, that she wants you more than you realize. Reach out to her. See what happens. And your children, they need you, you know that. These are the things that can sustain you; these will save you from self-destruction.

"My answer to you, Joe, is that no words will be able to convince you of the worth of life, but love can. If you are willing to love and be loved, then you will find the strength to live."

The rabbi was silent, wanting to say more, but unsure what to say. His eyes drifted upwards to the black and white wedding photo on the mantle piece, a picture of his own wedding. Joe observed the rabbi's gaze, suspected that the rabbi was looking at his wife, and a thought struck Joe that the rabbi had suffered a

NEVER FORGET MY SOUL

greater loss than Joe, but had not given up on life. In fact, thought Joe, the rabbi valued life so much that he devoted two hours late at night to retrieve Joe himself from the abyss. Joe did not understand why, but he now knew that suicide was absurd and he had a lot of work to do.

"I need some rest," said Joe. "I've been thinking crazy. I don't want to die. I just need some peace."

<hr />

Joe arrived home at midnight that evening. He found Lisa in their bed sleeping. He wearily undressed and climbed under the covers. He felt the warmth of her body and drew himself close to her. She sighed in an unconscious acknowledgement of his presence and molded her body to his. Her warmth covered and surrounded him and led him into the peaceful darkness of sleep.

Joe rose at eight o'clock the next morning. He lay in bed, gazing through the window at the morning sky, which was luminous with renewal. A shaft of light flowed into the room and illuminated the wall beside him. He reviewed, in his mind, the events of the last evening. He needed some time to let everything sink in … and he needed to talk with Lisa. There was nothing essential occurring at work today. He reached for the phone and called in sick.

Joe entered the kitchen and found Lisa cleaning the counters. Upon hearing his footfall, she turned to him and smiled.

"Hi, Joe," she said.

He returned both the greeting and the smile. However, his smile had a note of weariness to it, like a soldier who had brushed too close to the jaws of death.

There was a boyish neediness in his expression, and she instinctively reached out to soothe him. She approached him and wrapped her arms around him. They held each other for what felt to Joe like a timeless span.

As they held each other, she spoke quietly, with her mouth close to his ear. "You cuddled up with me last night," she said. "... It was nice."

"Yeah, it was," he responded, "I'd like to do that more often."

"Sit, Joe, I'll make you some breakfast," she said. "Do you want some eggs?"

He nodded and said, "Yes, thanks."

When the eggs were ready, he ate them in silence, staring beyond the wall, which he faced, deep in thought. Lisa had often seen him being distant, but there was something different in his manner today. It seemed to her that, in his previous distant manner, Joe was not only distant from others but also distant from himself. Today, there was a quietness to his manner that reassured her that he was present, not restless, discontented, or irritated; rather, just listening within and (dare she think it?) invoking his soul. She patiently went about various tasks in the kitchen, hoping that when he was ready, he would speak.

After he finished eating, he walked up to Lisa and took her hand.

"Lisa," he said, "I need to talk to you." She was struck by the earnestness on his face. Joe had the sort of look that a man has when he is about to make an irreversible step.

"What about?" she asked, starting to feel apprehensive.

"Just please come with me," he answered, leading her towards the living room. They sat together on the couch. Joe glanced at Lisa, turned his eyes to the floor, and then began to speak.

"Lisa, I've been cheating on you for a long time," Joe began. "It's not something that I'm proud about, and I fully understand if you're furious with me. But I know one thing. I've been living a lie and it's hurt you, me and the kids." Joe proceed to tell Lisa about his five-year involvement with Ann, Ann's pressure for Joe to marry her, her ensuing suicide, Joe's deepening depression after her death, his visits to prostitutes, his own near suicide and his meeting with Rabbi Pearlman the night before. Joe concluded his confessions by saying, "Lisa, I understand that after hearing all this you may want to leave me. I would not be surprised, nor would I blame you. You've been good to me, Lisa, and patient. You've tried a lot more in this marriage than I have. This morning, I decided that you deserve the truth. Look, this is my mess that I got myself into it. I guess I'll just have to get myself out alone."

"But you're *not* alone, Joe." She reached out and took his hand, and after she did so, he looked at her face. He only had looked at her face in fleeting glances, when he had just spoken. This was the first time he had *really* looked at it. If he had looked at it closer earlier, he would have seen an intricate play of emotions as he spoke. When he first mentioned his infidelity, she responded with a mix of shock and recognition. She was not shocked by the revelation of infidelity — she had long suspected it. But she *was* shocked that Joe had dared to bring it into the open. Lisa's face did not register shock for long; soon, her face molded itself into the furrowed brow and penetrating gaze of a listener who is fully engaged in understanding the world of another. What was compelling to Lisa was not the infidelity, but where Joe was going with all this. As he spoke, she wondered what had changed in him so fundamentally that he was willing to be so open, and what the implications were for their marriage. She was surprised with herself — while other spouses might listen to such a story and either be angered or sink into despair, Lisa felt renewed hope, the hope that comes from looking into dark, decaying and forbidden places, cleaning them out, and starting anew.

Although Joe did not perceive all of these emotions on her face, he now noticed what was most essential. It was a look of compassion … and of love.

"Joe," she said in a sweet, warm voice, like a caretaker speaking to a seriously ill patient, "I've known about your cheating for a long time. No, I didn't know names and dates and places. But things have changed between us so completely in the bedroom and there were just things about your routine, things that didn't make sense, things that made *too* much sense, and little hints I would sometimes find in the car and on your clothing. I don't want to get into all that. I just knew. Not that I was always willing to face it. I kept on telling myself that I did not know for sure, but that was because I was unwilling to deal with it. You've given me a gift. The gift is that now I have to deal with it. But at the moment, what I feel most of all is sad for you — sad that you went through such a horrible death of someone you loved and sad that for the past months you had to walk around here pretending that everything was normal, when you were dying inside. Joe, this is not the way life should be," she said with a pleading look in her eyes. "We don't have to go through life with our guts torn up and bleeding, pretending that we don't need anything, turning away from those who are closest to us. I believe you turned to Ann and those other women because we lost touch with each other a long time ago. I'm not looking to blame anyone. We just lost touch, developed separate worlds. Joe, you're hurting. Let me help you. Let's put all the pain behind. I'm willing to let all the blame go, if you will promise me one thing — that you will continue to be honest to me, like you were today. If you promise me that, then we'll have something in our marriage that I think we've never had. And with that honesty, I think we'll be OK."

Tears welled in Joe's eyes as Lisa spoke — tears arising from her kindness, from his years of repressed pain — uncried tears from a lifetime of living with the belief that tears can only weaken and destroy. For perhaps the first time in his life, Joe's soul relaxed, and the endless tears flowed out. He laid his head on her lap and she stroked his hair patiently.

Finally, when the tears subsided, he sat up and said, "Lisa, I promise, I will never do it again — "

"Shhh," she said, putting her finger to his lips. "Wait before you make that promise, think it through. I want it to mean some-thing. It *has* to mean something. I won't continue this marriage, if we go back to the old way of doing things, if you have to sneak around looking for the love that you are afraid to ask me for." Her manner was not harsh and did not feel, to Joe, like a reprimand. In that moment Lisa appeared strong and indescribably beauti-ful, and was simply stating a nonnegotiable requirement for their relationship. (When Joe finally did make his promise of fidelity to Lisa, weeks later, it felt solid, earnest and real to Lisa, and Joe was surprised that he was so confident in making the promise.)

He drew her close to him, and she willingly laid her head on his chest. "I'm so tired, Lisa. I need to rest."

"Rest, rest, Joe, you've been on the go for years. Now rest. There will be time enough to fix things. Let's just enjoy being to-gether." They sat together for a long time, in silence. It seemed to Joe as if she were melting together with him, as the gnawing dis-content in his chest and stomach dissipated. The war was over, finally over.

CHAPTER TWELVE

J oe sat in the therapy room at the beginning of the group session, surveying the faces that were familiar to him, but that
today were strangely new. He looked across at Grace, who recently was carrying herself with more confidence. He thought
about how far she had come, and of how much her father had hurt,
betrayed and confused her. He also thought about the strength
of personality and insight that she had been demonstrating in recent groups. He glanced at Tyrone, who was seated next to Grace.
Tyrone was a proud and confident warrior, someone who would
always rise above his circumstances. Joe noted Tyrone's erect
and confident bearing and the intensity of his dark eyes. But as
Joe continued to look at Tyrone, he noticed an additional qual-
ity, which was hard to describe. Finally, the words "brave enough
to be soft" came to mind. Tyrone had a pleasant, even-tempered
and undefended demeanor that was truly surprising for someone with his background. There was something soothing and reassuring about his presence. To Joe's right, he saw Terry slumped
in her chair, looking as if a great weight was bearing down on her.

Joe suddenly felt a worry gripping at him: What if Terry's disease was more serious than anyone realized? He had grown used to her complaints about exhaustion and lethargy. But what if it was more than complaints? What if her life were slowly draining out of her? He had come to like her levelheaded, unsentimental manner. She was always on time to the group sessions, and in her stability, he envisioned her as an anchor in the group, someone who did not need to talk, but was constantly present, listening. To Joe's left sat Adam, Marcia and David. Marcia wore a turquoise dress with a simple white belt. The dress emphasized her figure and Joe acknowledged to himself that she was truly an attractive woman. He thought of her anger, of how her husband had undermined her ability to trust, of the ways that she was continually at odds with herself — drawing in others' attention, but making sure no one would come too close. He appreciated her vivacity and drive, and he even, or perhaps, *especially*, appreciated the ways that she had challenged him, making him consider the effects of his prior infidelity. Joe then looked with new eyes at Adam. Gone were Joe's animosity and his desire to challenge and dismiss Adam's religious convictions. Gone were the disdain and the vague sense of discomfort that Joe had experienced whenever he heard Adam speak or even looked at him. In the place of those prior reactions were respect, gratitude and pity — respect for what Adam had taught Joe and the courage with which Adam had overcome his shyness, so that he could challenge Joe; gratitude for the fact that Adam had reminded Joe that he was a Jew, taught him what that meant, and indirectly prompted Joe to remember Rabbi Pearlman, who had drawn Joe back from the precipice; and pity for the unremitting fear which burdened Adam and tormented his life and relationships. Joe gazed at Adam and perceived both strength and frailty in this troubled man. "My brother," thought Joe, "we know the same horror. We just took different paths to escape it. It is you, Adam, that I can know the best." Next, Joe's eyes came to

NEVER FORGET MY SOUL

rest on David. During Joe's musings, none of the group members whom he had been considering had met his eyes, because they were either speaking or listening to the group discussion. But it did happen now that David's eyes met Joe's. In David's eyes, Joe sensed the gaze of a father who patiently guides, teaches and sees the uniqueness of each of his children.

When David's eyes met Joe's, David sensed receptivity and openness. David's first thought was, "This man is a different man... he wants to hear and be heard, he is looking for a friend."

Joe waited for a lull in the conversation and then spoke. He told the group members that he had been withholding important information from them, that his life had undergone fundamental changes and he had been avoiding discussing them for months. He then proceeded to tell his story — all the way from the circumstances surrounding Ann's death to the unburdening of his soul that he had experienced with Lisa. The group took in his revelations with rapt attention, moved by his story and astounded that Joe could speak with such sincerity and openness of heart.

After Joe finished describing the chain of events that led up to his talk with Lisa, he said, "David once asked me if the Holocaust has affected me. When he did I answered in the affirmative, but there was so much that I could have said that I held back. My mother died three years ago, and shortly after her death, I was going though her stuff and I discovered her diary, from years ago, when I was a young kid. It was all there, the whole answer to what made me the way I am. She wrote about the way her father froze out the whole world because he was unwilling to risk being hurt again, after he had suffered the losses and anguish of the Holocaust. She wrote about her weak, spineless mother, who never gave her a model for how to stand up to a man; of the way both her father and her husband insisted on control of everything and would not tolerate any questioning; of her own feelings of restlessness, agitation and emptiness; and of how alone in the world she felt. Now that I think of her words, I can imagine myself, as a child, long-ing to break though her wall of unhappiness and agitated distance, only to face repeated disappointment, and eventually developing my own shield of anger and defiance. And I think the thing that I was defying most of all was fear — the fear that trapped my grand-father in his proud, cold, inaccessible world and the fear that made my mother deal with her relationship problems by using work to hide from my father, my sisters and me. So I thrust myself into high-risk, high-stimulation activities — drugs, lots of sex, pet-ty crime, car racing on the streets at midnight. It was my way to spit in the face of fear. It was also my way to say that life was not about work for me, it was about play. When I thought of my par-ents working, I imagined them as being stressed and joyless, sink-ing under the weight of an ever-increasing burden. I also read in my mother's diary about how my grandfather was a workaholic. I think I was instinctively rebelling against this family legacy, the motto that said 'Don't feel, work'. *I* was not going to live that way, I told myself. I was going to do what felt good and do what I want, and who cares about the opinion of others…Only now do I real-ize that I had developed not a new motto, just a new twist on the old one. It was, 'Don't feel, play.' I only allowed myself to experi-ence surface emotions; no depth was allowed. I would have fun, have sex, but I would not truly need someone and I would not love. The true family legacy was to protect oneself and that I fol-lowed with devoted loyalty."

Joe had thus far been addressing the whole group. Now he turned to Adam, with a look of gentleness, warmth and compas-sion. The depth of Joe's compassion surprised Joe himself.

"Adam," said Joe, "I now see what David has often hinted at. There is much that unites you and me. Your soul and mine have known of the deepest horrors of this world, and neither of us has seen those horrors directly. But we still know those horrors very well. Our parents taught us about them, you explicitly, me implicitly. But, that's not an important difference, because we both learned the lesson that our parents were trying to teach — that evil predominates in this world and that trust is not an option. Now I see that in an important way, I built a life that was similar to yours. The similarity is that our worlds are small, well, maybe I can say *was* for myself, I think my world is starting to expand. But what my life was like was … well, *only me*. I was the only one who mattered; I could not feel the reality of another person. Each person was just an experience to me; they were only what they could give me, nothing more. You're not as selfish as me, but the similarity is that you also make your world very small. You are constantly defended, obsessed with your control of other people's impressions of you, so obsessed with it that if someone liked you or even loved you, you could not really see it. Your worries and your fears would just drown it out. But Adam, a friendly word of advice, from someone who knows: your attempts to protect yourself are not protecting you … They're strangling you."

As Joe spoke, Adam felt like he was in a dream. This was not real. Joe was the man who was filled with distain; Joe had no compassion; Joe could not love. These were the initial observations and, subsequently, firmly held convictions that Adam had developed about Joe over their tenure in the group. "But this *is* real," Adam told himself. "Remember, people can change. Isn't that what you insisted to everyone here?"

"Joe," Adam said, "I must say that I'm astounded to hear the way that you are speaking today. It's like you're a different man. And I understand what you are telling me about making my world small. I've said all the same things to myself countless times. But that doesn't change anything. My mind knows what the truth is. It knows what I should do. But the fear and the constriction are in my body. They control me, cloud my thinking, emotions and reactions, so I just can't change. I sit with my wife at night, trying to be attentive to her, but obsessed with my own fears and worries and then obsessed that she will reject me because I am so distant. I pray in the synagogue and I feel nothing, nor can I keep my mind on my prayers. I cannot break out of my little world."

Joe was suddenly struck by a memory. He saw himself reading the Bible alone in his room, during the period that he was studying for his bar mitzvah. Within his twelve-year-old mind, many thoughts played out. He thought of a secret longing that he had experienced over the last few months, a longing which he hardly dared to admit to himself. It was the longing of a child who intensely feels a lack of parental love and both hurts for the lack of that love and stubbornly denies the need for it. It was a longing to know a parent who is above all parents — God — who sees and understands all, who, as Rabbi Pearlman had told him, loved Joe more than he ever could imagine. This was the God for whom Joe had secretly begun to harbor a hope. That very afternoon, Joe had come home humming a tune from the Jewish liturgy, which he particularly liked. He walked up to his mother in the kitchen and was about to tell her what he was learning with Rabbi Pearlman (a first for Joe), when his father, who was watching a game of football, bellowed, "Shut up, Joe! I'm trying to watch here!" Joe turned to the living room to see his father's enraged face, and he turned back to his mother and saw only empty indifference. Joe's eyes stated an unspoken question: Are you going to let him talk to me that way, for nothing? Joe's mother shrugged. Joe shrugged in response — a shrug to his father, to his mother and to her stupid religion. Nonetheless, when he got up to his room, a few moments later, he picked up the Bible on impulse and began to read his bar mitzvah portion in English. When he finished reading it, he felt anger rising within him against God, who was so cruel and heartless as to tell a man to slaughter his beloved son. He thought of parents' cruelty towards children. He thought of the blindness of parents who utterly miss their children's good intentions and strictly reprimand them, and who repeatedly ignore

　　　　　　　　NEVER FORGET MY SOUL

their children's yearning hunger for attention. He thought of what Rabbi Pearlman had taught him about the history and suffering of the Jewish people. He thought of the wars, murders, torture, and callous indifference within the world. And Joe's heart rebelled — he would not accept such a God, a God who would let all these things happen — and Joe began to hate anyone who would try to make him accept such a God in his life. This hatred was the origin of Joe's cynical speech that shocked the synagogue.

And Joe, the forty-year-old man, sitting in his group therapy, realized something: He no longer hated God. Not only that, but he had a vague but undeniable sense that all of the events of his life had been guided by a force which sought only good for Joe. And Joe felt an emotion that he had not felt for almost all of his life, which he last felt when Lisa had responded to him with such warmth and understanding; it was gratitude.

Then Joe spoke to Adam. Joe was not sure why he said what he said, but before he could deliberate further the words were forming in his mouth: "Adam, I want to tell you something that Rabbi Pearlman told me, on the night that I was thinking of killing myself. He told me the story of Job. Are you familiar with the story?"

Adam nodded.

Joe continued, "Well, the strange part of the story is why Job, who is angry with God and wants to argue with him, is not censured by God, while Job's three friends, who defended God, are rebuked by Him. Rabbi Pearlman told me that the friends were only interested in defending their precious philosophy about God, but had no interest in showing compassion to Job. And, as for Job, the reason why God does not condemn him for his words is that God does not hold us accountable for words we say that arise out of our pain. I'll tell you what I think that means. God did not make us to be machines — we feel, we get hurt, we cry out in pain, we may say angry words towards people, even towards God. And anger towards God is not a sin. There is something much worse than anger towards God, which is making Him irrelevant, not seeking a relationship with Him. And it's no better to defend Him so incessantly that you never look inside and ask yourself what you really feel and what your true relationship with Him is. What *is* your relationship with God, Adam — not the God you talk *about*, not the God that you defend before all of us; I mean the God you talk to, or who you wish you could talk to, honestly, but who you have to keep running away from because you fear His rebuke. Or maybe it's not fear at all, maybe it's just anger, the anger about how He could let His chosen people go through the gates of hell, alone and friendless, how He could let us be tortured, slaughtered and mutilated, until we lost the will to live, anger at the horror that gets passed from generation to generation, anger against a God that forced you to carry six million corpses on your back."

Adam began to sob. Tears streamed down his face and the sobs grew in intensity. He covered his face in his hands, as his body convulsed with years of pent-up anguish. He doubled over almost all the way to his lap. He looked very young and frail. He felt his body melting into his tears, and he was overwhelmed by a force that was immeasurably bigger than he. Through his tears, he muttered to himself in a hoarse voice, "Why, why?" It was a question without an answer, the question of the forsaken, the question of those who have been brought beyond the limit of hope and understanding.

David patiently waited as Adam cried. His crying finally subsided, but Adam continued to rest his face in his hands.

"Look around you, Adam," said David, in a very gentle voice.

Adam slowly sat up and surveyed the faces of the group members. The first person he looked at was Joe, and Adam was struck by the tenderness of his expression. Adam had the undeniable feeling that Joe understood him more profoundly than perhaps anyone had in his life. Adam proceeded to look at the other group members. Where he had expected to find harshness, rejection and condemnation, he found patience, attentiveness and care. David was smiling, as if he was proud of Adam. Grace's face was creased with lines of concern. Tyrone had a look of admiration, and Adam suspected it was admiration for a man who would not shy away from difficult and dark places. As Adam looked at the faces of the group members, he was surprised to notice that his feelings of discomfort, disconnection and anxiety, which he generally felt in the presence of others, had vanished.

After a protracted silence, Adam finally said, "Joe is right. I am afraid of getting too close to God, because the intensity of my anger scares me. And I'm afraid of getting too close to other people for the same reason. If I trust them, then they might hurt me and then I'd have to deal with anger or pain or hate. I just don't know how to handle those feelings."

"You handle them by not trying to control them," said David. "You just let them be. When you try to crush them, you yourself are crushed. There is much life buried underneath all of that anger."

"This is hard. I don't know if I can learn to do this," Adam responded.

"You just *did* it," responded David, smiling, "and we'll give you plenty more opportunities to practice."

EPILOGUE

One year later, Adam drove home from a scientific conference where he had just given a presentation. He found his thoughts drifting to his group therapy. Much had happened over the course of the past year. Shortly after Adam's emotional outpouring in group, Grace announced that she had followed Joe's advice and Adam's example. She had gone on a date and just had decided that she was going to accept herself and not worry about what anyone thought of her. "It was surprisingly easy," she reported, "and I had a blast — best time I can ever remember having. We spent the whole evening talking and laughing with each other, and then we went dancing. I was having such a good time that I didn't think of myself as fat for the whole evening." Six months later, she announced that she was getting married. The group members beamed with pleasure upon hearing this news. Marcia had not been so fortunate. She still could not overcome her distrust of men, and she was looking more depressed now than Adam had ever seen. He wanted to help her, to give her some words of encouragement, but he was unsure how to help. Tyrone had sold his law practice and opened a special education school for emotionally disturbed inner-city youths. He reported that "I have never had more satisfaction with my work before." His work hours had drastically decreased, and he was grateful to be able to spend more time with his wife and children. He still fought with his wife, from time to time, but the intensity and frequency was much reduced.

Terry's health had worsened, which caused her to be hospitalized frequently and miss many of the group sessions. Last month, Adam had organized a visit for the group members to see Terry in the hospital. Their visit was unannounced and they came bearing handfuls of flowers, balloons and candy. When Terry saw all of them enter the room, her face brightened and she sat up in her bed. "We decided to have the group session here tonight," Tyrone announced jokingly. The group sat together in the hospital room, chatting with Terry, filling her in on group news and listening to her complaints about hospital food.

Adam's thoughts turned to Joe. The past year had been one of considerable emotional struggle for Joe. Notwithstanding the profound changes that he had experienced a year ago, he was beset with a myriad of temptations. He was plagued with an irrational urge for a vice. He found his eye wandering to other women again and at times he succumbed to the urge to flirt with them. He confided in the group about these encounters and related that he had somehow been able to hold himself back from going further. He had asked the group's advice as to whether he should tell Lisa about these encounters. David had responded to this question: "Joe, there is no Mommy to grab you and pull your hand away from the stove top. Don't try to make Lisa into your mother. You will only hate her and end up resisting her if you do." Joe had been angered by this comment and had abruptly walked out of the group. But he was back the next week with the admission that David had been right and that Joe needed to take responsibility

NEVER FORGET MY SOUL

for his actions. On some occasions over the past year, the urge to "misbehave" had been so strong that Joe had turned to cocaine on two occasions, which he had not used for close to twenty years. During the second occasion of cocaine use, he was dissatisfied with the result and went in search of something better. On his way to do so, he was in a car accident, which he took as a sign that he needed to get himself back in control. He had not used drugs since. Accompanying his urge for a vice was a sullen irritability that would arise unexpectedly in Lisa's presence. At times, Joe would provoke Lisa over something petty for no reason other than that he wanted to fight. Lisa was aware that she had too often acquiesced in her dealings with Joe and that their relationship would continue to suffer if she avoided expressing her anger to him. So they fought with intensity, but the fights did not last for long and Joe and Lisa usually made up quickly. Even with all of this conflict, Joe felt a powerful connection to Lisa. Two months ago, Joe had informed the group that his wife was pregnant. After hearing the news of his wife's pregnancy, Joe's restless temptation for a vice dissipated and he experienced a new harmony with Lisa. He said that he and his wife were overjoyed about the pregnancy and that they were sharing a depth of love that was entirely new to them. "If it's a boy," he had said, "we want to name him Raphael — it means 'God's healer.'" For the past six months, Joe had attended two Judaism classes a week and attended synagogue with his family weekly. Last month, Joe had terminated the group therapy. Upon leaving, Joe had thanked all of the group members for being his "teachers" and for putting up with him, even though he had sometimes been, in Joe's words, "the biggest asshole in the history of mankind." Joe hugged the group members at the end of his last group. With Adam and David, the hugs had lingered longer than with the other group members. While hugging Adam, Joe had whispered, "Be brave." While hugging David, Joe had whispered, "Thank you."

In the midst of these musings and recollections Adam was struck by a new thought: Here he was, letting his mind wander, not obsessed by the events of this present day. That was very new for him. In the past, he would berate himself for all of his shortcomings after completing a professional presentation. Now he had not even been thinking about it. The presentation had, by no means, been easy. Adam was nervous before and during the presentation, still fearful of the harsh criticism or scorn of others. But these feelings had transformed themselves from near panic to milder anxiety that dissipated shortly after the presentation. In general, Adam was less on edge in the presence of others. To be sure, there were some days in which, for reasons unknown to Adam, the same old intense anxiety and tension returned. But those days passed, like a disturbing memory that dissipates over time, and he returned to his improved state.

One thing that had changed profoundly for Adam was his ability to pray. He was not sure when and how it happened, but gradually his obsessions and worries during his prayers simply vanished. After his cathartic group session, Adam started to pray to God in a different way. He told God that he was angry, that he did not understand how God could allow his forebears to suffer in the way they had, that he wanted to believe in God's compassion and His care for His creations, but could not do so, and even that he found himself doubting God's existence. "Please, God," he would implore, "I want to believe in you. I just feel so far away from you. Show me a light in this darkness. Help me to live. Help me to breathe. Help me to believe in the good. I'm so alone." Tears were his frequent companions during his prayers. Over time, the tears grew less and Adam was infused with a new feeling during prayer. It was a gentle quiet that descended upon him, a stillness and new calm. He grew to understand that true prayer occurred in the same way that he had learned to cope with his anger. True prayer was not about controlling something or making something happen;

NEVER FORGET MY SOUL

it was simply being oneself in the presence of God, and speaking one's deepest longings. In prior times, he had carried the weight of the world during his prayers. Now, he let himself be carried.

Adam pulled into his driveway and saw Devorah, gardening on the front lawn with his daughters, while his sons were tossing a football to each other nearby. Upon seeing the car, his daughters dropped their gardening tools and ran towards Adam to embrace him. He scooped them up, one in each hand, and comically pretended to stagger under their weight. At the last moment, when he was pretending that he was about to fall, he suddenly straightened up and swung his body in a circle, to the delighted squeals of his daughters. He then put them down and motioned to his eldest son to throw him the ball. The ball came down toward Adam a little too high and he leaped into the air to try to catch it. He managed to grasp it in the tips of his fingers and threw the ball back to his younger son. By this time, Devorah was standing at his side.

"Hi, darling," she said, putting her hand on his shoulder. "Got any hugs for me?"

"More than you can count," said Adam smiling.

They hugged for at least half a minute and Adam felt the tension of the day drain out of his body, as he rested in the loving arms of his wife. After hugging her, he took a step back and looked in her face, while grasping her hands. Her dark brown eyes were smiling, shimmering with joy and gratitude. He wanted to hug her again, and began to, when he heard the voice of Shoshi, his six-year-old.

"Daddy," she said.

"What?" he said, in a somewhat irritated tone of voice, not wanting his time with Devorah interrupted. "I want you to see me," she called back in squealing delight.

Adam looked up to see his daughter, riding a bicycle, on a path in front of their house. It was the first time Adam had seen his daughter ride a bicycle unassisted. For the last few weeks, he had been gradually teaching her how to ride a two-wheeler. She had been very anxious and was too reliant on him supporting her as she rode. Adam had told Devorah that Shoshi never would learn to ride on her own this way. "She just wants me to hold her up all the time," he had said.

Upon seeing Shoshi ride now, Adam let out an excited cheer. He jumped in the air and started applauding his daughter.

"Great job, Shoshi!" he said, "You're amazing!!!"

"She told me today that she had decided that she was going to be brave and ride the bike herself. She figured it out all by herself. I told her I didn't have time to help her do it today. She fell off a few times. There were a few scraped knees, a few tears. But she did not give up. And look at her! Look how proud she is. She's riding!!! *We're riding*, if you know what I mean, Adam. Things are so much better than they were. Thank you, Adam, and give my thanks to David."

"I do give my thanks to him," said Adam, turning to his wife, and adding the word, "often."

Suddenly, Adam heard the sound of Shoshi and her bike scraping against the ground. He looked up to see Shoshi struggling to free herself from her bike, which had fallen upon her. He ran forward towards her and lifted her. Her arm had a nasty scrape from the fall. Shoshi was sobbing. Adam calmly took her into the house, washed off the scrape and held her until her tears subsided. He knew there would be other scrapes, other tears, other wounds to clean and reassuring parental hugs. These things were lessons for Shoshi, about the pain and exhilaration of living, and about the sources of comfort and healing. What Adam had struggled so hard to find, she was being given as a gift. And it was a gift that Adam felt very blessed and privileged to be able to provide.

The End

CPSIA information can be obtained at www.ICGtesting.com
Printed in the USA
BVOW022245110912

300197BV00004B/37/P

9 780615 554891